D1624951

10/87

THE

THE BEAST TAKES POSSESSION

INDWELLING

Books by
Tim LaHaye and Jerry B. Jenkins

The Left Behind series
Left Behind
Tribulation Force
Nicolae
Soul Harvest
Apollyon
Assassins
The Indwelling
The Mark—available fall 2000

Left Behind: The Kids
#1: The Vanishings
#2: Second Chance
#3: Through the Flames
#4: Facing the Future
#5: Nicolae High
#6: The Underground
#7: Busted!
#8: Death Strike
#9: The Search
#10: On the Run

Books by Tim LaHaye
Are We Living in the End Times?
How to Be Happy Though Married
Spirit-Controlled Temperament
Transformed Temperaments
Why You Act the Way You Do

Books by Jerry B. Jenkins
And Then Came You
As You Leave Home
Still the One

THE

THE BEAST TAKES POSSESSION

INDWELLING

TIM LAHAYE
JERRY B. JENKINS

Bookspan Large Print Edition

Tyndale House Publishers, Inc.
WHEATON, ILLINOIS

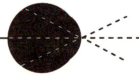

**This Large Print Book carries the
Seal of Approval of N.A.V.H.**

chief; in love with David Hassid; New Babylon

Leah Rose, late thirties; former head nurse, Arthur Young Memorial Hospital, Palatine, Illinois; on assignment in Brussels from safe house

Tyrola ("T") Mark Delanty, late thirties; owner/director, Palwaukee Airport, Wheeling, Illinois

Mr. and Mrs. Lukas ("Laslos") Miklos, mid-fifties; lignite mining magnates; Greece

Abdullah Smith, early thirties; former Jordanian fighter pilot; first officer, Phoenix 216; New Babylon

The Enemies

Nicolae Jetty Carpathia, mid-thirties; former president of Romania; former secretary-general, United Nations; self-appointed Global Community potentate; assassinated in Jerusalem; lying in state at GC palace complex, New Babylon

Leon Fortunato, early fifties; Carpathia's right hand and assumed succes-

sor; GC supreme commander; New
Babylon

The Undecided

Hattie Durham, early thirties; former
Pan-Continental flight attendant; former
personal assistant to Carpathia; imprisoned in Belgium

Dr. Chaim Rosenzweig, late sixties; Israeli botanist and statesman; discoverer
of a formula that made Israeli deserts
bloom; former *Global Weekly* Man of
the Year; apparent stroke victim; Jerusalem

*To our agent, Rick Christian,
who recognized the value of the idea and
the potential of the partnership
and introduced us to each other*

FORTY-TWO MONTHS
INTO THE TRIBULATION

The Believers

Rayford Steele, mid-forties; former 747 captain for Pan-Continental; lost wife and son in the Rapture; former pilot for Global Community Potentate Nicolae Carpathia; original member of the Tribulation Force; an international fugitive in exile; fleeing Israel, site of the assassination of Carpathia

Cameron ("Buck") Williams, early thirties; former senior writer for *Global Weekly*; former publisher of *Global Community Weekly* for Carpathia; original member of the Trib Force; editor of cybermagazine

The Truth; fugitive in exile on assignment in Israel

Chloe Steele Williams, early twenties; former student, Stanford University; lost mother and brother in the Rapture; daughter of Rayford; wife of Buck; mother of fourteen-month-old Kenny Bruce; CEO of the International Commodity Co-op, an underground network of believers; original Trib Force member; fugitive in exile, safe house, Mount Prospect, Illinois

Tsion Ben-Judah, late forties; former rabbinical scholar and Israeli statesman; revealed belief in Jesus as the Messiah on international TV—wife and two teenagers subsequently murdered; escaped to U.S.; spiritual leader and teacher of Trib Force; cyberaudience of more than a billion daily; fugitive in exile at safe house

Mac McCullum, late fifties; pilot for Carpathia; New Babylon

David Hassid, mid-twenties; high-level director for the GC; New Babylon

Annie Christopher, early twenties; Global Community corporal, Phoenix 216 cargo

PROLOGUE

From *Assassins*

Buck had ducked under a scaffold at the sound of the gun. A tidal wave of humanity swept past him on both sides, and he saw glee on some faces. Converts from the Wailing Wall who had seen Carpathia murder their heroes?

By the time Buck looked to the stage, the potentates were leaping off, the drapery was flying into the distance, and Chaim appeared catatonic, his head rigid.

Carpathia lay on the platform, blood running from his eyes, nose, and mouth, and—it appeared to Buck—from the top of his head. His lapel mike was still hot, and because Buck was directly under a speaker tower, he heard Nicolae's liquid, guttural murmur, "But I thought . . . I thought . . . I did everything you asked."

Fortunato draped his stocky body over Carpathia's chest, reached beneath him, and cradled him. Sitting on the stage, he rocked his potentate, wailing.

"Don't die, Excellency!" Fortunato bawled. "We need you! The world needs you! *I* need you!"

Security forces surrounded them, brandishing Uzis. Buck had experienced enough trauma for one day. He stood transfixed, with a clear view of the back of Carpathia's blood-matted skull.

The wound was unmistakably fatal. And from where Buck stood, it was obvious what had caused it.

"I did not expect a gunshot," Tsion said, staring at the television as GC Security cleared the stage and whisked Carpathia away.

Two hours later GC CNN confirmed the death and played over and over the grieving pronouncement of Supreme Commander Leon Fortunato. "We shall carry on in the courageous spirit of our founder and moral anchor, Potentate Nicolae Carpathia. The cause of death will remain confidential until the investigation is complete. But you may rest assured the guilty party will be brought to justice."

The news media reported that the slain potentate's body would lie in state in the New Babylon palace before entombment there on Sunday.

"Don't leave the TV, Chloe," Tsion said. "You have to assume the resurrection will be caught on camera."

But when Friday became Saturday in Mount Prospect and Saturday night approached, even Tsion began to wonder. The Scriptures had not foretold of death by projectile. Antichrist was to die from a specific wound to the head and then come back to life. Carpathia still lay in state.

By dawn Sunday, as Tsion gloomily watched mourners pass the glass bier in the sun-drenched courtyard of the GC palace, he had begun to doubt himself.

Had he been wrong all along?

Two hours before the burial, David Hassid was called in to Leon Fortunato's office.

Leon and his directors of Intelligence and Security huddled before a TV monitor. Leon's face revealed abject grief and the promise of vengeance. "Once His Excellency is in the tomb," he said, his voice thick, "the world can approach closure. Prosecuting his murderer can only help. Watch with us, David. The primary angles were blocked, but look at this collateral view. Tell me if you see what we see."

David watched.

Oh, no! he thought. *It couldn't be!*

"Well?" Leon said, peering at him. "Is there any doubt?"

David stalled, but that only made the other two glance at him.

"The camera doesn't lie," Leon said. "We have our assassin, don't we?"

Much as he wanted to come up with some other explanation for what was clear, David would jeopardize his position if he proved illogical. He nodded. "We sure do."

"The second woe is past. Behold, the third woe is coming quickly."

Revelation 11:14

Monday of Gala Week

Leah Rose prided herself on thinking under pressure. She'd been chief administrative nurse in a large hospital for a decade and had also been one of few believers there the last three and a half years. She had survived by her wits and eluded Global Community Peacekeeping Forces until finally having to flee and join the Tribulation Force.

But on the Monday of the week that would see the assassinations of the two witnesses and the Antichrist, Leah had no clue what to do. In disguise and under her alias, Donna Clendenon, she believed she had fooled authorities at the Belgium Facility for Female Rehabilitation (BFFR, or Buffer). She had passed herself off as Hattie Durham's aunt.

A squinting guard, whose nameplate read CROIX and whose accent was unmistakably French, asked, "And what makes you think your niece is incarcerated here?"

"You think I'd come all the way from California if I had any doubt?" Leah said. "Everybody knows Hattie is here, and I know her alias: Mae Willie."

The guard cocked his head. "And your message can be delivered only in person?"

"A death in the family."

"I'm sorry."

Leah pursed her lips, aware of her artificially protruding teeth. *I'll bet,* she thought.

Croix stood and riffled through pages on his clipboard. "Buffer is a maximum security facility without standard visiting privileges. Ms. Durham has been separated from the prison population. I would have to get clearance for you to see her. I could give her the message myself."

"All I want is five minutes," Leah said.

"You can imagine how short staffed we are."

Leah didn't respond. Millions had disappeared in the Rapture. Half the remaining population had died since. Everybody was short staffed. Merely existing anymore was a full-time job. Croix asked her to wait in a holding area, but he did not tell her she would see no personnel, no inmates, or even any other visitors for more than two hours. A glass cubicle, where it appeared a clerical person had once sat, was empty. No one was there whom Leah could ask how long this might take, and when she rose to look for someone else, she found she was locked in. Were they onto her? Was she now a prisoner too?

Just before Leah resorted to banging on the door and screaming for help, Croix returned. Without apology, and—she noticed—avoiding eye contact, he said, "My superiors are considering your request and will call your hotel tomorrow."

Leah fought a smile. *As if I want you to know where I'm staying.*

"How about I call you?" Leah said.

"Suit yourself," Croix said with a shrug. *"Merci."* Then, as if catching himself: "Thank you."

Relieved to be outside, Leah drove

around to be sure she wasn't being followed. With puzzling instructions from Rayford not to call him until Friday, she phoned Buck and brought him up to date. "I don't know whether to bolt or play it out," she said.

That night in her hotel room, Leah felt a loneliness only slightly less acute than when she had first been left behind. She thanked God for the Tribulation Force and how they had welcomed her. All but Rayford, of course. She couldn't figure him. Here was a brilliant, accomplished man with clear leadership skills, someone she had admired until the day she moved into the safe house. They hadn't clicked, but everyone else seemed frustrated with him too.

In the morning Leah showered and dressed and found something to eat, planning to see Hattie as soon as she had permission. She was going to call Buffer from her untraceable cell phone, but she got caught up watching on television as Carpathia taunted Moishe and Eli before the eyes of the world.

She sat, mouth agape, as Carpathia murdered the two witnesses with a powerful handgun. Leah remembered when TV cameras would have been averted in the face of such violence. Then came the earthquake that left a tenth of Jerusalem in rubble.

The GC global network showed quake scenes interspersed with footage of the silent witnesses badgered by the smirking Carpathia before their ignominious ends. The slow-motion pictures were broadcast over and over, and repulsed as she was, Leah could not turn away.

She had known this was coming; they all had—any students of Tsion Ben-Judah. But to see it played out shocked and saddened her, and Leah's eyes swam. She knew how it was to turn out, too, that they would be resurrected and that Carpathia would get his. Leah prayed for her new friends, some of whom were in Jerusalem. But she didn't want to sit there blubbering when she had work to do too. Things would get a lot worse than this, and Leah needed the training of performing under pressure to prepare herself and to convince herself she was up to it.

The phone at Buffer rang and rang, and Leah was at least warmed to know that the world government suffered just like the rank and file with the loss of half the population. Finally a woman picked up, but Leah couldn't get her even to acknowledge an employee named Croix.

"A French guard?" Leah tried.

"Ah, I know who you mean. Hold on."

Finally a man picked up. "Who are you holding for, please?" he said, in a hurry.

"Guard Croix," she said, "about six feet—"

"Croix!" the man hollered. "Phone!"

But he never came to the phone. Leah finally hung up and drove to the prison, leaving her phone in the car for safety.

At long last Croix ushered her into yet another private room. This one had a large window that Leah thought might be a two-way mirror. Again she feared her cover might have already been blown.

"I thought you were going to call," the guard said, pointing to a chair, ubiquitous clipboard in hand.

"I tried," she said. "This place is poorly run."

"Understaffed," he said.

"Can we get on with it?" Leah said. "I need to see my niece."

"No."

"No?"

Croix stared at her, apparently unwilling to repeat himself.

"I'm listening," she said.

"I'm not at liberty to—"

"Don't give me that," Leah said. "If I can't see her, I can't see her, but I have the right to know she's healthy, that she's alive."

"She is both."

"Then why can't I see her?"

Croix pressed his lips together. "She's been transferred, ma'am."

"Since yesterday?"

"I'm not at liberty to—"

"How long has she been gone? Where is she?"

He shook his head. "I'm telling you what I was told. If you'd like to get a message to—"

"I want to see her. I want to know she's all right."

"To the best of my knowledge, she's fi—"

"The best of your knowledge! Have you an inkling how limited your knowledge is?"

"Insulting me will not—"

"I don't mean to insult you, sir! I'm merely asking to see my niece and—"

"That's enough, Officer Croix," came a female voice from behind the glass. "You may go."

Croix left without a word or a look. Leah detected an Asian accent in the woman. She stood and stepped to the mirror. "So, what's next, ma'am? Am I to leave too, or will I get some word about my niece?"

Silence.

"Have I now become a prisoner too? Guilt by relation?"

Leah felt conspicuous and wondered whether anyone was behind the glass after all. Finally she marched to the door but was not surprised to find herself locked in again. "Terrific," she said, heading back toward the mirror. "What are the magic words that get me out of here? C'mon, lady! I know you're back there!"

"You will be free to go when we say you are free to go."

The same woman. Leah pictured her older, matronly, and clearly Asian. She raised her palms in surrender and plopped into a chair. She started and looked up when she heard a buzz in the door latch. "You may go."

Leah shot a double take at the mirror. "I may?"

"She who hesitates . . ."

"Oh, I'm going," she said, rising. "Could I at least see *you* on my way out? Please? I just want to know—"

"You're trying my patience, Mrs. Clendenon. You have received all the information you will get here."

Leah stopped with her hand on the doorknob, shaking her head, hoping to weasel something from the disembodied voice.

"Go, ma'am!" the woman said. "While you have the option."

Leah had given her best. She wasn't willing to go to prison for this caper. For another effort, maybe, another assignment. She would sacrifice her freedom for Dr. Ben-Judah. But for Hattie? Hattie's own doctor had died treating her, and she seemed barely grateful.

Leah moved briskly through the echoing corridors. She heard a door behind her and, hoping to catch a glimpse of the woman, turned quickly. A small, trim, pale, dark-haired woman in uniform turned and headed the other way. Could that have been her?

Leah headed for the main entrance but turned at the last instant and stepped behind a bank of phones. At least it looked like a bank of phones. She wanted to pretend to be talking on one while anyone who might follow her rushed out the door, but every phone was in shambles, wires hanging.

She was about to abandon her plan when she heard quick footsteps and saw a young Asian woman hurry out the front door, car keys jangling. Leah was convinced this was the same woman who had ducked away when she turned around. Now Leah was following *her.*

She hesitated inside the glass doors, watching as the woman trotted to the visitor parking lot and scanned the area. Apparently frustrated, she turned and walked slowly back toward the entrance. Leah nonchalantly exited, hoping to get a straight-on look at the woman. If she could get her to speak, she would know whether she had been the one behind the glass.

An employee of the GC and she's worse at this than I am, Leah thought, as the woman noticed her, appeared startled, then fought to act normal. As they neared one another, Leah asked where a washroom was, but the woman tugged her tiny uniform cap tighter onto her head and turned away to cough as she passed, not hearing or pretending not to.

Leah pulled out of the unattended lot and waited at a stop sign a quarter mile away, where she could see the prison entrance in her rearview mirror. The woman hurried out and hopped into a compact four-door. Determined to lose her, Leah raced off and got lost trying to find her hotel via side streets.

She called Rayford again and again. No way this could wait until Friday. When he didn't answer she worried that his phone might have fallen into the wrong hands. She left a cryptic message: "Our bird has flown the cage. Now what?"

She drove into the country, convinced no one was following her, and found her way back to the hotel at dusk. She had been in her room less than half an hour when the phone rang.

"This is Donna," she said.

"You have a visitor," the clerk said. "May I send her back?"

"No! Who is it?"

" 'A friend' is all she'll say."

"I'll come there," Leah said.

She stuffed her belongings into a bag and slipped out to her car. She tried to peer into the lobby through the plate glass, but she couldn't see who was there. As she started the car, someone drove behind her and stopped. Leah was pinned in. She locked her doors as the driver emerged from the other vehicle.

As Leah's eyes adjusted to the light, she could see it was the same car the woman had driven from the prison. A knock made her jump. The woman, still in uniform, signaled her to lower her window. Leah lowered it an inch, her heart thudding.

"I need to make a show of this," the woman whispered. "Play your part."

My part? "What do you want?" Leah said.

"Come with me."

"Not on your life! Unless you want your car in pieces, get it out of my way."

The woman leaned forward. "Excellent. Now step out and let me cuff you and—"

"Are you out of your mind? I have no intention of—"

"Perhaps you cannot see my forehead in the darkness," the woman said. "But trust me—"

"Why should I—?"

And then Leah saw it. The woman had the mark. She was a believer.

The woman pointed to the lock as she removed handcuffs from a holster on her belt. Leah unlocked the door. "How did you find me?" she said.

"Checked your alias at several hotels. Didn't take long."

"Alias?" Leah said as she alighted and turned so the woman could cuff her.

"I'm Ming Toy," she said, leading Leah to the backseat of her car. "A believer comes all the way to Brussels to see Hattie Durham and uses her own name? I don't think so."

"I'm supposed to be her aunt," Leah said as Ming pulled out of the parking lot.

"Well, that worked on everybody else," she said. "But they didn't see what I saw. So, who are you and what are you doing here?"

"Would you mind if I double-checked your mark, Miss Toy?"

"*Mrs.* I'm a widow."

"Me too."

"But call me Ming."

"I'll tell you what you can call me as soon as I can check your mark."

"In a minute."

Ming pulled into a GC Peacekeeping station. "I need an interrogation room," she barked at the man behind the desk, still holding tight to Leah's left biceps.

"Commander," the man said with a nod, sliding a key across the counter. "Last door on the left."

"Private, no viewing, no bugs."

"That's the secure one, ma'am."

Ming locked the door, angled the lamp shade toward them, and released Leah from her cuffs. "Check me out," she said, sitting and cocking her head.

Leah gently held the back of Ming's head, knowing already that anyone who would let her do that had to be genuine. She licked her thumb and ran it firmly across the mark on Ming's forehead. Leah slumped into a chair across from Ming and reached for both her hands. "I can't wait to get to know you," she said.

"Likewise," Ming said. "Let's pray first."

Leah couldn't keep from welling up as this brand-new friend thanked God for their propitious meeting and asked that he allow them to somehow work together.

"First I'll tell you where Hattie Durham is," Ming said. "Then we'll trade stories, and I'll take you back to your hotel, tell my associates that you check out as Hattie's aunt, and let them think that you believe Hattie was transferred but that you don't know where."

"She wasn't transferred?"

Ming shook her head.

"Is she alive?"

"Temporarily."

"Healthy?"

"Healthier than when we got her. In fact, she's in quite good shape. Strong enough to assassinate a potentate."

Leah furrowed her brow and shook her head. "I'm not following you."

"They let her go."

"Why?"

"All she talked about was killing Carpathia. Finally they told her that as it was clear she had lost his baby, she was no longer a threat and was free to go, with a tidy settlement for her trouble. Roughly one hundred thousand Nicks in cash."

Leah shook her head. "They don't consider her a threat? She wants to kill him for real."

"They know that," Ming said. "In my opinion, they think she's dumber than she looks."

"Sometimes she is," Leah said.

"But not dumb enough to lead them straight to the rest of the Tribulation Force," Ming said. "The simplistic plan is that they follow her to the Gala in Jerusalem and to some sort of a rendezvous with one of you Judah-ites."

"I love that title. I'm a believer first, but also proudly a Judah-ite."

"Me too," Ming said. "And I'll bet you know Ben-Judah personally."

"I do."

"Wow."

"But, Ming, the GC is wrong about Hattie. She's crazy enough to go and try to kill Nicolae, but she has no interest in contacting any of us."

"You might be surprised."

"How so?"

"She didn't go to Jerusalem like they hoped. We've tracked her to North America. I think she's onto the GC and wants to get back to safety as soon as she can."

"That's worse!" Leah said. "She'll lead them to the safe house."

"Maybe that's why God sent you here," Ming said. "I didn't know what I was going to do to protect you people. Whom was I supposed to tell? You're the answer to my prayer."

"But what can I do? I'll never be able to catch her before she gets there."

"You can at least warn them, right?"

Leah nodded. "My phone's in my bag in my car."

"And my phones are all traceable."

They traded stories on the way back. Ming was twenty-two years old, a native of China. Her husband of two months had been killed a few minutes after the disappearances when the commuter train he was on crashed when the brakeman and several controllers vanished. She had joined the GC in a paroxysm of patriotism shortly after the treaty was signed between the United Nations and Israel. She had

been assigned to the reconstruction administration in what used to be the Philippines,
but there she had become a believer
through the letters of her brother at home,
now seventeen. "Chang's friends had led
him to faith," she said. "He has not yet told
my parents, who are very old school and
very pro-Carpathia, especially my father. I
worry about Chang."

Ming had applied for work in the peacekeeping forces, hoping for just this sort of
opportunity to aid fellow believers. "I don't
know how much longer I can remain inside
undercover."

"How did you get to a position of authority over so many guards?"

"It's not so big a deal as it sounds. The
population decimation didn't hurt."

"C'mon! You're in management."

"Well, in all humility, a stratospheric IQ
doesn't hurt. That and wrestling," she
added, seeming to fight a smile. "Two out
of three falls."

"You're not serious."

"They know Greco-Roman. I know mar-
tial arts." Ming pulled into the hotel parking
lot. "Call your friends right away," she said.

"And stay away from Buffer. I'll cover for you."

"Thank God for you, Ming," Leah said, again overcome. They traded phone numbers. "The day will come when you need a safe place too. Keep in touch." They embraced, and Leah hurried to get her bag and get back into her room.

There was no answer at the safe house, and Leah worried it had already been compromised. Had it already been overrun? And what of her new friends? She tried Rayford's number, then the safe house, again and again.

Unable to reach anyone, Leah knew she had a better chance of helping the Trib Force in North America than from a Brussels hotel room. She found a flight and headed home that very night. All the way back she tried the safe house phone, to no avail.

ONE

Buck braced himself with his elbow crooked around a scaffolding pole. Thousands of panicked people fleeing the scene had, like him, started and involuntarily turned away from the deafening gunshot. It had come from perhaps a hundred feet to Buck's right and was so loud he would not have been surprised if even those at the back of the throng of some two million had heard it plainly.

He was no expert, but to Buck it had sounded like a high-powered rifle. The only weapon smaller that had emitted such a report was the ugly handgun Carpathia had used to destroy the skulls of Moishe and Eli three days before. Actually, the sounds were eerily similar. Had Carpathia's own weapon been fired? Might someone on his own staff have targeted him?

The lectern had shattered loudly as well, like a tree branch split by lightning. And that gigantic backdrop sailing into the distance . . .

Buck wanted to bolt with the rest of the crowd, but he worried about Chaim. Had he been hit? And where was Jacov? Just ten minutes before, Jacov had waited below stage left where Buck could see him. No way Chaim's friend and aide would abandon him during a crisis.

As people stampeded by, some went under the scaffold, most went around it, and some jostled both Buck and the support poles, making the structure sway. Buck held tight and looked to where giant speakers three stories up leaned this way and that, threatening their flimsy plywood supports.

Buck could choose his poison: step into the surging crowd and risk being trampled or step up a few feet on the angled crossbar. He stepped up and immediately felt the fluidity of the structure. It bounced and seemed to want to spin as Buck looked toward the platform over the tops of a thousand streaking heads. He had heard Carpathia's lament and Fortunato's keening, but suddenly the sound—at least in the speakers above him—went dead.

Buck glanced up just in time to see a ten-foot-square speaker box tumble from the top. "Look out!" he shrieked to the crowd, but no one heard or noticed. He looked up again to be sure he was out of the way. The box snapped its umbilicals like string, which redirected its path some fifteen feet away from the tower. Buck watched in horror as a woman was crushed beneath it and several other men and women were staggered. A man tried to drag the victim from beneath the speaker, but the crowd behind him never slowed. Suddenly the running mass became a cauldron of humanity, trampling each other in their desperation to get free of the carnage.

Buck could not help. The entire scaffolding was pivoting, and he felt himself swing left. He hung on, not daring to drop into the torrent of screaming bodies. He caught sight of Jacov at last, trying to make his way up the side steps to the platform where Carpathia's security detail brandished Uzis.

A helicopter attempted to land near the stage but had to wait until the crowd cleared. Chaim sat motionless in his chair, facing to Buck's right, away from Carpathia and Fortunato. He appeared stiff, his head cocked and rigid, as if unable to move. If he had not been shot, Buck wondered if he'd had another stroke, or worse, a heart attack. He knew if Jacov could get to him, he would protect Chaim and get him somewhere safe.

Buck tried to keep an eye on Jacov while Fortunato waved at the helicopters, pleading with one to land and get Carpathia out of there. Jacov finally broke free and sprinted up the steps, only to be dealt a blow from the butt end of an Uzi that knocked him off his feet and into the crowd.

The impact snapped Jacov's head back so violently that Buck was certain he was unconscious and unable to protect himself from trampling. Buck leaped off the scaffold and into the fray, fighting his way toward Jacov. He moved around the fallen speaker box and felt the sticky blood underfoot.

As Buck neared where he thought Jacov should be he took one more look at the platform before the angle would obscure his view. Chaim's chair was moving! He was headed full speed toward the back of the platform. Had he leaned against the joystick? Was he out of control? If he didn't stop or turn, he would pitch twelve feet to the pavement and certain death. His head was still cocked, his body stiff.

Buck reached Jacov, who lay splayed, his head awkwardly flopped to one side, eyes staring, limbs limp. A sob worked its way to Buck's throat as he elbowed stragglers out of the way and knelt to put a thumb and forefinger to Jacov's throat. No pulse.

Buck wanted to drag the body from the scene but feared he would be recognized despite his extensive facial scars. There was nothing he could do for Jacov. But what about Chaim?

Buck sprinted left around the platform and skidded to a stop at the back corner, from where he could see Chaim's wheelchair crumpled on the ground, backstage center. The heavy batteries had broken open and lay twenty feet from the chair, which had one wheel bent almost in half, seat pad missing, and a footrest broken off. Was Buck about to find another friend dead?

He loped to the mangled chair and searched the area, including under the platform. Besides splinters from what he was sure had been the lectern, he found nothing. How could Chaim have survived this? Many of the world rulers had scrambled off the back of the stage, certainly having to turn and hang from the edge first to avoid serious injury. Even then, many would have had to have suffered sprained or broken ankles. But an elderly stroke victim riding in a metal chair twelve feet to concrete? Buck feared Chaim could not have survived. But who would have carried him off?

A chopper landed on the other side of the platform, and medical personnel rushed the stage. The security detail fanned out and began descending the stairs to clear the area.

Four emergency medical technicians crowded around Carpathia and Fortunato while others attended the trampled and the crushed, including the woman beneath the speaker box. Jacov was lifted into a body bag. Buck nearly wept at having to leave his brother that way, yet he knew Jacov was in heaven. He ran to catch up with the crowd now spilling into the streets.

Buck knew Jacov was dead. From the wound at the back of Carpathia's head, he assumed Nicolae was dead or soon would be. And he had to assume Chaim was dead too.

Buck longed for the end of all this and the glorious appearing of Christ. But that was still another three and a half years off.

Rayford felt a fool, running with the crowd, the hem of his robe in his hands to keep from tripping. He had dropped the Saber and its box and wanted to use his arms for more speed. But he had to run like a woman in a long skirt. Adrenaline carried him, because he felt fast as ever, regardless. Rayford really wanted to shed the robe and turban, but the last thing he needed just then was to look like a Westerner.

Had he murdered Carpathia? He had

tried to, intended to, but couldn't pull the trigger. Then, when he was bumped and the gun went off, he couldn't imagine he'd been lucky enough to find his target. Could the bullet have ricocheted off the lectern and into Carpathia? Could it also have passed through him and taken out the backdrop? It didn't seem possible.

If he had killed the potentate, there was certainly no satisfaction in it, no relief or sense of accomplishment. As he hurried along, the screams and moans of Carpathia's faithful all around him, Rayford felt he was running from a prison of his own making.

He was sucking wind by the time the crowd thinned and began to disperse, and when he stopped to bend at the waist, hands on his hips, to catch his breath, a couple hurrying past said, "Isn't it awful? They think he's dead!"

"It's awful," Rayford gasped, not looking at them.

Assuming TV cameras had caught everything, especially him with the gun raised, it wouldn't be long before he would be sought. As soon as he was away from the busy streets, he shed the garb and stuffed it in a trash barrel. He found his car, eager to get to Tel Aviv and out of Israel before it became impossible.

Mac stood near the back of the throng, far enough from the gun that the report didn't reach his ears until after the massive crowd began to move. While others near him shrieked and gasped and pleaded to know what was going on, he kept his eyes on the stage, relief washing over him. So, he would not have to sacrifice himself and Abdullah to be sure Carpathia was dead. From the commotion down front and from his view of the platform via jumbo screens nearby, it was clear to Mac that Nicolae had suffered the massive head wound believers knew was coming.

Ever the professional, Mac knew what would be expected of him. He slid his cell phone from his jacket and dialed the Tel Aviv tower. "You got a jockey certified to shuttle the 216 to Jerusalem?"

"Already looking, sir. This is a tragedy."

"Yeah."

Mac dialed Abdullah. From the limited noise in the background, he could tell his first officer was not at the Gala. "You hear, Ab?"

"I heard. Shall I go get the Phoenix?"

"Hang loose; they're trying to get it here. I saw you leave the hotel. Where are you?"

"Doctor Pita's. I suppose I'll look suspicious finishing my meal when the big boss is dying and everyone else has run into the streets looking for a TV."

"Stick it in your pocket, and if you don't hear from me, meet me at Jerusalem Airport in an hour."

Mac made his way to the front of the plaza as the place emptied in a frenzy. He flashed his ID when necessary, and by the time he reached the platform, it was clear Carpathia was in the final throes of life. His wrists were drawn up under his chin, eyes shut tight and bleeding, blood trickling also from his ears and mouth, and his legs shook violently, toes pointed, knees locked.

"Oh, he's gone! He's gone!" Leon wailed. "Someone do something."

The four emergency medical technicians, portable monitors beeping, knelt over Carpathia. They cleared his mouth so they could administer oxygen, studied a blood pressure gauge, pumped his chest, cradled his head, and tried to stanch the flow from a wound that left them kneeling in more blood than it seemed a body could hold.

Mac peeked past the panicky Fortunato to see Carpathia's normally tanned hands and face already pale. No one could survive this, and Mac wondered if the bodily movements were merely posthumous reflexes.

"There is a hospital nearby, Commander," one of the EMTs said, which threw Fortunato into a rage. He had just made eye contact with Mac and seemed about to say something when he turned on the EMT.

"Are you crazy? These—these *people* are not qualified! We must get him to New Babylon."

He turned to Mac. "Is the 216 ready?"

"On its way from Tel Aviv. Should be able to lift off in an hour."

"An hour?! Should we helicopter him straight to Tel Aviv?"

"Jerusalem Airport will be faster," Mac said.

"There's no room to stabilize him in a chopper, sir," the EMT said.

"We have no choice!" Fortunato said. "An ambulance would be too slow."

"But an ambulance has equipment that might—"

"Just get him into the chopper!" Fortunato said.

But as the EMT turned away looking disgusted, a female colleague looked up at him. Carpathia was still. "No vitals," she said. "He's flat lined."

"No!" Leon bellowed, bullying his way between them and kneeling in Nicolae's blood. Again he leaned over the body, but rather than holding Carpathia to him, he buried his face in the lifeless chest and sobbed aloud.

Security Chief Walter Moon dismissed the EMTs with a nod, and as they gathered up their equipment and went for the gurney, he gently pulled Leon away from Carpathia. "Don't drape the body," he said. "Let's load 'im up now. Say nothing about his condition until we're back home."

"Who did this, Walter?" Fortunato whined. "Did we catch him?"

Moon shrugged and shook his head.

*   *   *

Buck ran toward the hostel. He dialed Chaim's number again, as he had all along the way. Still busy. The people in Chaim's house—Stefan the valet, Jacov's wife, Hannelore, and Hannelore's mother—had to have been watching on TV and were likely calling anyone they knew for news of their loved ones.

Finally, Hannelore answered. "Jacov!" she shouted.

"No, Hannelore, this is Greg North."

"Buck!" she wailed. "What happened? Where—"

"Hannelore!" Buck said. "Your phone is not secure!"

"I don't care anymore, Buck! If we die, we die! Where is Jacov? What happened to Chaim?"

"I need to meet you somewhere, Hannelore. If Chaim shows up there—"

"Chaim is all right?"

"I don't know. I didn't see him after—"

"Did you see Jacov?"

"Meet me, Hannelore. Call me from another phone and—"

"Buck, you tell me right now! Did you see him?"

"I saw him."

"Is he alive?"

"Hannelore—"

"Buck, is he dead?"

"I'm sorry. Yes."

She began to wail, and in the background Buck heard a scream. Hannelore's mother? Had she deduced the news?

"Buck, they're here!"

"What? Who?"

He heard a door smashing, a yell, another scream.

"GC!" she whispered fiercely. And the phone went dead.

Onboard the Phoenix 216, Nicolae Carpathia's personal physician examined him and pronounced him dead.

"Where were you?" Leon demanded. "You could have done something."

"Where I was supposed to be, Commander," the doctor said, "in the auxiliary trailer a hundred yards behind the platform. Security would not let me out, fearing more gunfire."

As the 216 taxied toward the runway, Leon came to the cockpit and told Abdullah, "Patch me through to Director Hassid at the palace, secure line."

Abdullah nodded and glanced at Mac as Fortunato backed out. The first officer made the connection and informed Leon over the intercom. With creative switch flipping, Abdullah allowed Mac to listen in, while muting the input button to keep out noise from the cockpit.

"You're aware of the awful news, David?" Leon said.

"I heard, yes, sir," David said. "How is the potentate?"

"He's dead, David . . ."

"Oh."

". . . but this is top secret by order of Chief Moon until further notice."

"I understand."

"Oh, David, what will we do?"

"We'll look to you, sir."

"Well, thank you for those kind words at such a time, but I need something from you."

"Yes, sir."

"Scramble the satellites to make it impossible for those who did this to communicate with each other by phone. Can you do that?"

A long pause. "Scrambling the satellites" was not the exact terminology, but David could produce Fortunato's desired result. "Yes," he said slowly. "It's possible, of course. You realize the ramifications . . ."

Mac whispered to Abdullah. "Call Buck, call Rayford, call the safe house. Leon's going to shut down communications. If they need to talk to each other, it has to be now."

"Tell me," Leon said.

"We're all served by the same system," David said. "It's the reason we've never been able to shut down the Judah-ites' Internet transmissions."

"So if they're shut down, we're shut down?"

"Exactly."

"Do it anyway. The landlines in New Babylon would still be operable, would they not?"

"They would, and this would not affect television transmission, but your long distance is all satellite dependent."

"So those of us in New Babylon would be able to communicate only with each other."

"Right."

"We'll get by. I'll let you know when to unscramble."

Two minutes later Leon called David again. "How long does this take?" he said. "I should not be able to reach you!"

"Three minutes," David said.

"I'll check back in four."

"You'll not reach me, sir."

"I should hope not!"

But four minutes later Leon was preoccupied with the doctor. "I want an autopsy," he said, "but zero leaks about cause of death." Through the reverse intercom bug, Mac heard Leon's voice catch. "And I want this man prepared for viewing and for burial by the finest mortuary technician in the world. Is that understood?"

"Of course, Commander. As you wish."

"I don't want the staff butcher in the palace, so whom would you suggest?"

"One who could use the business, frankly."

"How crass! This would be a service to the Global Community!"

"But surely you're prepared to reimburse—"

"Of course, but not if money is the primary concern. . . ."

"It's not, Commander. I simply know that Dr. Eikenberry's mortuary has been decimated. She's lost more than half her staff and has had to reorganize her business."

"And she's local?"

"Baghdad."

"I do not want Nicolae shipped to Baghdad. Can she come to the palace morgue?"

"I'm sure she'd be more than happy . . ."

"Happy?"

"Willing, sir."

"I hope she can work miracles."

"Fortunately his face was not affected."

"Still," Leon said, his voice husky again, "how do you hide the, the . . . awful injury?"

"I'm sure it can be done."

"He must look perfect, dignified. The whole world will mourn him."

"I'll call her now."

"Yes, please try. I'd like to know whether you're able to get through."

But he was not able. Global telephone communications were off the air. And Abdullah too had failed to reach anyone.

Mac was about to shut off the intercom bug when he heard Leon take a huge breath and let it out. "Doctor?" he said. "Can your mortician, ah—"

"Dr. Eikenberry."

"Right. Can she do a cast of the potentate's body?"

"A cast?"

"You know, some sort of plaster or plastic or something that would preserve his exact dimensions and features?"

The doctor hesitated. "Well," he said finally, "death masks are nothing new. A whole corpse would be quite an undertaking, pardon the expression."

"But it could be done?"

Another pause. "I should think the body would have to be dipped. The palace morgue has a large enough tank."

"It could be done then?"

"Anything can be done, Excellency. I'm sorry, I mean Commander."

Fortunato cleared his throat. "Yes, please, Doctor. Don't call me Excellency. At least not yet. And do arrange for a cast of the potentate's body."

TWO

Beside the desk in her hangar office, David stood facing Annie and holding both her hands.

"You're trembling," she said.

"I thought *you* were," he said. "You're not as scared as I am?"

"At least," she said. "What's going on?"

He sighed. "I just got a call from a mortician in Baghdad. Says she was told to go through me for large purchases. She wants several liters of some sort of a plastic amalgam delivered to the palace morgue as soon as possible."

"For?"

"I can only imagine. This stuff is used to make casts of faces, body parts, tire tracks, that kind of thing. But she wants enough to fill a tub the size of a whirlpool bath."

"She's going to make a cast of Carpathia's whole body?"

He shrugged. "That's my guess."

"Whatever for?"

"She didn't sound too sure herself. She kept asking how much water would have to be added to how much solution and if that would fill the stainless steel container. She also wanted to know how long I thought it would take that much solution to harden, how long it would remain pliable before drying, all that."

Annie slipped her hands around David's waist and laid her head on his chest. "Someone's put her up to it. Maybe to make a replica of the body so they can make him look better lying in state?"

He pondered that. "I just wonder if they've heard about the prophecy of his resurrecting and want to keep the real body somewhere convenient, just in case."

"They don't believe the prophecies, do they?"

"How could anyone not by this time?"

She looked up at him and shook her head. "What's going to happen around here when, you know . . ."

"It happens?"

"Yeah."

"It's not going to be pretty. I can't wait to see what Dr. Ben-Judah has to say about you-know-who when he's no longer really himself."

"You think there'll be any of the man left of him?"

David cocked his head. "His body, sure. Maybe he'll sound like himself and have the same mannerisms, but he's supposed to be indwelt, and indwelt means indwelt. When I was promoted, I moved into the quarters of that director who was reassigned to Australia, remember?"

"Yeah."

"It's the same place. Same walls, same bed, same lav, everything. It looks the same, but it's not. I'm the new dweller."

She held him tighter. "I don't want to know the new dweller of the potentate."

"Well, it'll be no more Mr. Nice Guy."

"Not funny," she said.

"They should be here any minute, babe."

"I know. My ears are tuned to the '16. I know how long it takes to get the hangar doors open and to position the forklift and winch. I hope security keeps its distance. Did you see all of 'em out there? Have you heard all the rules?"

"Have I! You'd think you were off-loading the body of the king of the world."

She snorted. "Tell you the truth, I'd like to drop the box and run over the whole thing with the forklift. Let's see *that* come back to life."

David tugged her toward the door. "What if he comes back to life while you're transporting the body?"

She stopped and closed her eyes. "Like I wasn't freaked out enough. You'd have to find me in heaven." A hum vibrated the office window. "You'd better go. They're about three minutes away."

Rayford could not believe his luck at Tel Aviv. He hurried past the busy counters and out a side exit toward the small-craft hangars. The Gulfstream sat gleaming in Hangar 3.

An armed guard doing double duty as manifest coordinator checked Marv Berry off his list and said, "Wait a minute, there's something else I'm s'posed to ask. Ah, yeah, flight plan reported to tower?"

"You bet," Rayford said, "but they weren't happy with how slow the small craft were being cleared, so I'd better keep you out of trouble by getting out of here quick."

"I 'preciate that," the guard said, clearly more comfortable with a gun than a pen. "They expect lots of passengers on the big birds tonight and want to get the little ones out of the way."

"Understandable," Rayford said. "I'll do my part."

"Wish I'd a been in Jerusalem tonight," the guard said as Rayford circled the Gulfstream, doing a quick preflight.

"Yeah?"

"I'd a killed somebody, guilty or not."

"That so?"

"Dang straight. Somebody'd pay for that. Who'd wanna go and kill our only hope?"

"I can't imagine."

"You're American, right, Mr. Berry?"

"You could tell?"

"Sure, me too."

"You don't say."

"Colorado," the young man said. "Fort Collins. You?"

"What're you doing here?"

"Wanted Gala duty. This is as close as I got. Hoped for potentate bodyguard, but I guess that's all political."

"Like everything else," Rayford said, pulling open the Gulfstream's door and steps.

"Need some help there, Mr. Berry?"

"Got it, thanks."

"Where'd you say you were from?"

I didn't, Rayford thought. "Kalamazoo," he said, mounting the steps and tossing in his bag.

"That's what, Midwest?"

Rayford hated the small talk, not to mention the delay, only slightly less than the prospect of being detained and put to death. "Michigan!" he called out, pulling the door.

"Hang on a second, sir," the guard said. "Squawk box is for me."

"I gotta go," Rayford said. "Nice talking to you."

"Just a minute, please," the young man said with a smile. "Another minute won't kill you, will it?"

It just might. "I've really got to go, son."

"Wyatt."

"Why?"

"Wyatt. That's my name."

"Well, thanks, Wyatt, and good-bye."

"Mr. Berry!"

"Yes, Wyatt."

"I'm not gonna be able to hear the box here if you fire up. Can't you give me a second?"

From the radio on Wyatt's makeshift desk in the middle of the hangar: "Officer 423, do you copy? Initiate code red screening effective immediately."

"This is Wyatt. You mean those thorough checks on everybody, even small craft?"

"Where are you, 423?"

"Small-craft Hangar 3, sir."

"Then that is what I mean, yes!"

Rayford quickly closed the door, but before he could settle into the cockpit, Wyatt came running. "Mr. Berry, sir! I'm going to have to ask you to step out of the craft!"

Rayford initiated the starting sequence, which only caused Wyatt to rush in front of the Gulfstream, waving, rifle dangling. He didn't appear alarmed or even suspicious. It was clear he simply thought Rayford couldn't hear him.

He motioned for Rayford to open the door. Rayford considered simply starting up as soon as Wyatt was clear of the front, hoping the GC was thin staffed enough and busy enough that they would ignore him. But he couldn't risk an air pursuit or gung ho Wyatt from Fort Collins shooting at him on the runway.

He moved to the door and opened it three inches. "What is it, Wyatt?"

"I've been instructed, sir, to do a thorough check and search of even small craft before departure tonight, due to what happened in Jerusalem."

"Even me, Wyatt? A small-town guy like you? An American?"

"Got to, sir. Sorry."

"Wyatt, you know the Gulfstream, don't you?"

"The Gulfstream, sir?"

"This aircraft."

"No sir, I don't. I'm not an aviation man. I'm a soldier."

Rayford peeked through the slivered opening. "If you knew this plane, Wyatt, you'd know that if the door opens all the way, I have to start the whole ignition sequence over."

"You do?"

"Yeah, some kind of a safety mechanism that keeps the engines from starting until the door is closed."

"Well, I'm sorry, but I have to—"

"I'm sorry, too, Wyatt, because the tower guys were complaining about you, and I was trying to keep you out of trouble, make you look good, by getting away quickly."

"But my commanding officer just told me—"

"Wyatt! Listen to me! You think I shot Carpathia?"

" 'Course not. I—"

"I'd need you to teach me about weapons, for one thing."

"I could sure teach you, but—"

"I'll bet you could. And I could teach you to fly—"

"I have to—"

"Wyatt, I just heard on the radio that two wide-bodies are in landing sequence right now, with another waiting to take off. Now my perimeter flange is going to overheat if I don't get going, and you don't want a fire in here. Tell your boss I was already on my way out when you got the order, then we're both covered. You look quick, you avoid a fire, and you're still following orders."

Rayford kept a careful eye on Wyatt's hands and flinched when the young man moved his right. If he leveled that rifle at him, Rayford would have to comply. But Wyatt saluted and pointed at Rayford. "Good thinkin', sir. Carry on."

Rayford fired up the engines and maneuvered onto the tarmac. He couldn't wait to tell Mac about this one. He heard about other planes on a radio that wasn't on yet? Perimeter flange? Fire? Tsion taught that part of the population decimation might be God's way of removing his most incorrigible enemies in anticipation of the coming epic battle. Wyatt was living proof that the inept had survived. Rayford knew he wouldn't always enjoy such fortune.

"Ben Gurion Tower to Gulfstream!"

Rayford leaned forward and looked as far as he could in both directions, both on the runway and in the sky.

"Gurion Tower to Gulfstream, do you copy?"

He was clear.

"Gulfstream, you are not cleared! Remain stationary."

"Gulfstream to Tower," Rayford said. "Proceeding, thank you."

"Repeat, Gulfstream, you are *not* cleared!"

"Cleared by Officer 423, Tower."

"Repeat?"

". . . been . . . leared . . . two-three . . . wer."

"You're breaking up, Gulfstream! You are not cleared for takeoff. Repeat, not cleared!"

". . . nection . . . wer, thank y—"

"Do we have your flight plan, Gulfstream?"

". . . o copy, tow—"

"Flight plan?"

". . . icer fo—, two, thr—"

"If you can hear any of this, Gulfstream, be aware that satellite coordinates have been scrambled and there is only manual positioning. Copy?"

Rayford depressed and released the talk button rapidly, then held it halfway down, creating static on the other end. *No satellite capability?* For once he would be glad for that. He needn't worry about pursuit. If he was flying blind, so would the GC. Did that mean the phones were out too? He tried the safe house, then Laslos. Nothing. He only hoped he could connect with the Greek believers before he put down there. It made no sense to try to make it back to America. If Leah's message meant what he thought and Hattie was no longer in Belgium, she could have long since led the GC to the safe house. He only hoped his message had gotten to David's computer before the satellites went down.

Buck had been angry with his father-in-law before, but never like this. No contact? Nothing? What was he supposed to do, collect Leah from Brussels, and it was every man for himself? Now the phones didn't seem to be working.

Did he dare try to make it to Chaim's house and see what was going on? Why would the GC storm the place and force their way in? Were they too looking for Chaim? And why? Buck knew somebody already had to have the old man. Someone had spirited him, or his body, from the Gala site. No way a wheelchair-bound stroke victim could have made his own way out of that place with his contrivance in pieces on the ground.

Buck took a cab to the small place he had once used as an Israeli safe house. No one he recognized was living there. He walked several miles in the darkness through rubble, never far from the cacophony of sirens and the flashing light shows of emergency vehicles. When he finally arrived at Chaim's, the place was deserted and dark. Had everyone been taken away? Emergency personnel were stretched, of course, but if they expected Chaim, wouldn't someone be left to guard the place?

Buck crept to the back, suddenly aware of his fatigue. Grief and trauma did that to a person, he told himself. He had not gotten to know Jacov well, but how he had thrilled to the young man's coming to belief in Christ! They had kept up some, not as much as either had liked, due to the risk of discovery. And though he knew he would see Jacov at the Glorious Appearing—if not before—he dreaded having to break the news to Jacov's friend and coworker, Stefan.

Buck had the advantage of knowing, really knowing, this house. He feared he might be walking into a trap. He didn't think the GC knew he was in Israel, but one could never be sure. Maybe they lay in wait for Chaim or even Jacov. It was possible Jacov's death had not made the GC databases yet, though that was unlikely. But where was everyone else?

Buck found the back door unlocked, and he slipped in. A rechargeable flashlight was usually plugged into a socket near the floor, behind the food preparers' table. Buck felt for it and found it, but he didn't want to test it until he was confident no one was waiting to ambush him. He took it into the pantry and waited until he shut the door to turn it on. Then he felt foolish, reckless. He'd never been comfortable with the role he had been thrust into, still part journalist but also freedom fighter, raconteur. What kind of a swashbuckling Trib Force veteran backs himself into a closet with nothing more to defend himself with than a cheap flashlight?

He tried the light switch on the pantry wall. Nothing. So the power had been cut. Buck flipped the flashlight on, then off quickly. Something in his peripheral vision froze him. Did he dare shine the light that way? He let out a quavery breath. Who would lie in wait in a pantry?

Buck aimed the light that direction and turned it on. Just an unusual arrangement of boxes and cans. He doused the light and moved quietly to the door. Creeping through the kitchen into the dining room, the parlor, and then the front room, Buck held the flashlight in front of him as if it were on, but it served more like a blind man's cane. As his eyes began adjusting to the darkness, he became aware of pinpoints of light from the street, and he still heard sirens in the distance.

Later Buck would wonder whether he had smelled the blood before he heard it. Yes, heard it. He knew something was wrong as soon as he reached the front room. It was in the air. Heat? A presence? Someone. He stopped and tried to make out shapes. He felt his own heart, but something reached his ears more insistently even than that thumping. Dripping. *Drip, drip,* pause, *drip-drip, drip.* From two sources? Part of him didn't want to know, to see. He turned his back to windows at the front, pointed the flashlight toward the sounds, and braced himself, ready to defend himself with bare hands and the flashlight, if necessary.

He turned on the light but immediately shut his eyes to the horror. He dropped to his knees, the wind gushing from him. "Oh, God," he prayed. "No! Please!" Was there no end to the carnage? He would rather die than find his friends, his comrades (someday his own family?) like this. In the split second he had allowed himself to take in the scene, it became clear that two victims sat side by side in wood chairs, Hannelore on the left, her mother on the right. They were bound and gagged, heads tilted back, blood dripping into pools on the floor.

Buck did not want to reveal himself to anyone outside. Plainly, this scene was created to "welcome" someone home; certainly the perpetrators had no idea *he* would stumble upon it. Buck knelt before the chairs, repulsed by the sound of the drips. He knew if either of the women had survived, their respiration would have been noisy with their heads in that position. Still, he had to make sure. He lodged the flashlight between his knees, angled it toward the women, and turned it on. As he reached to check for Hannelore's pulse, the flashlight slipped and illumined her ankles, tied securely to the front legs of the chair. As he angled the light up again and tightened his knees to support it, he noticed her wrists tied behind her. A smallish woman, Hannelore's torso was stretched to allow her hands to go around the back of the chair. Great gushes of air rushed past Buck's gritted teeth.

He grabbed the flashlight and moved behind the chair to feel her wrist, but that put his arm in line with the blood dripping from her head. And though her wrist was warm, as he feared, there was no pulse.

Hannelore's mother, less than a foot away, was bound in the same position. A squat, heavy woman, her arms had been yanked into contorted positions to allow her wrists to be tied. She too was dead.

Who could have done this? And wouldn't Stefan, his Middle East maleness coming to the fore, have fought to the death to prevent it? Where could he be? Buck wanted to pan the light back and forth along the floor toward the front, but that might have been suicidal, he would be so obvious from the street. It was all he could do to keep from calling Stefan's name.

Chaim had not been home when Buck had talked with Hannelore on the phone. Did this massacre mean Chaim had arrived, or that he hadn't? Had Chaim himself been forced to witness this? Buck's first task was to locate Stefan, his second to check the entirety of the huge house for Chaim. If Chaim had not returned and this was all meant as a warning for him, could the place be staked out, surrounded? Perhaps it was.

Buck feared he would find not just Stefan's body, but also Chaim's. But how would Chaim have gotten there? Who might have caught him, rescued him, or helped him off that platform? And what was the purpose of murdering these innocents? Had they been tortured for information and eliminated once they provided it, or because they had not? Or was this simply vengeance? Chaim had been vitriolic in his revulsion of GC Peacekeepers, of the breaking of the covenant between the GC and Israel. Though he had never been a religious Jew, he expressed horror over the intrusion of the world government into the very affairs of the temple. First the Jews had been allowed to rebuild; then they were not allowed to conduct themselves the way they wished in the new temple.

But do you extinguish the household of a statesman, a national treasure, for such an offense? And what of the man himself? Buck's head throbbed, his chest felt tight, and he was short of breath. He was desperate to be with Chloe and Kenny and felt as if he could hold them tight for three and a half years. He knew the odds. Each had only a one in four chance of surviving until the Glorious Appearing. But even if he, or they, had to go to heaven before that, he didn't want it to be this way. No one deserved this. No one but Carpathia.

It had been a long time since David had suffered such carping. On the way to his office from the palace hangar, past a full-dress color guard of pallbearers and a heavily armed ring of security personnel, his beeper had signaled a top-level emergency message. The call could have originated only locally, of course, but this sort of a code was reserved for life-and-death situations. He did not recognize the call-back number but knew it was located in the palace proper.

Normally he would have called back immediately, fearing danger to Annie or himself, but he took a moment to trace the number against the personnel list and found that the call came from the Arts and Sciences wing. He had been there only once, knew virtually no one there, and had been so repulsed by what was considered artistic that he recalled rushing back to his quarters feeling soiled.

Wanting at least one more clue before replying, David called his own voice mail, only to be met by the foul, nasty rantings of a sassy *artiste.* David had not heard such profanity and gutter language since high school. The gist of the message: "Where are you? Where could you be at a time like this? It's the middle of the night! Do you even know of the murder? Call me! It's an emergency!"

David's beeper vibrated again—same number. He waited ninety seconds and called his voice mail again. "Do you know who I am? Guy Blod?!" The man pronounced *Guy* as *Gee* with a hard *G,* the

French way, and *Blod* to rhyme with *cod,* as if Scandinavian. David had seen him scurrying around a few times but had never spoken with him. His reputation preceded him. He was the temperamental but lauded painter and sculptor, Carpathia's own choice for minister of the creative arts. Not only had he painted several of the so-called masterpieces that graced the great hall and the palace, but he had also sculpted many of the statues of world heroes in the courtyard and supervised the decorating of all GC buildings in New Babylon. He was considered a genius, but David—though admittedly no expert—considered his work laughably gaudy and decidedly profane. "The more shocking and anti-God the better" had to have been Blod's premise.

Part of David wanted Guy Blod to have to wait for a callback, but this was the wrong time to start puffing his anti-GC chest. He would take no guff from Guy Blod, but he had to remain above suspicion and ingratiated to Fortunato. He dialed Blod as he settled behind his computer and began to program it to record directly from the morgue on a sound-activated basis.

As Blod answered, David noticed a list of messages on his computer. "This is Guy," he announced, "and you had better be David Hassid." He put the emphasis on the first syllable.

"It's *hah-SEED,*" David said.

"That should be easy enough to remember, Mr. Hayseed. Now where have you been?"

"Excuse me?"

"I've been trying to call you!"

"That's why I called you, sir."

"Don't get smart with me. Don't you know what's happened?"

"Nobody tells me anything, Mr. Blod." David chuckled. "Of course I know what's happened. Did it occur to you that that might have been why I was difficult to reach?"

"Well, I need stuff and I need it right now!"

"What do you need, sir?"

"Can you get it for me?"

"Depends on what it is, Blod."

"That's Mr. Blod to you, sweetie. I was told you could get anything."

"Well, almost."

"I have nowhere else to turn."

"I'll do my best."

"You'd better. Now come to my office."

"Excuse me?"

"Is this a bad connection? I said, come . . . to . . . my . . ."

"I heard you, sir, but I have many things on my plate tonight, as you can imagine, and I can't just—"

"You can do as you're told. Now get your tail over here, and I mean right now." *Click.*

David hung up and checked his messages. Most alarming was one from Rayford: "Our botanist reports the bird has flown. May need new real estate soonest. Signed, Geo. Logic"

David squinted at the screen for several seconds, wishing he could call someone at the safe house, or Rayford. He was tempted to put the satellites back in operation just long enough to do it, but he knew someone would discover that and he would have to answer for it. So Hattie was gone and the safe house was in jeopardy. He deleted the message and hacked his way into the mainframe database of abandoned, condemned, destroyed, and/or radioactive buildings in the Midwest. He looked at his watch when the phone rang. Six minutes had passed.

"What are you doing?"

"I'm sorry?"

"Is this David Hayseed?"

"This is Director Hassid, yes."

"Do you know who this is?"

"Yes! It sounds like Minister Blood. Haven't talked to you in ages. Good to hear from you again—"

"That's Blod, and did I or did I not tell you to get over here?"

"Is this multiple choice? I believe you did."

"Then why are you not here?"

"Let me guess. Because I'm here?"

"Agh! Listen here, you! Get over here this instant or—"

"Or what? You're going to tell my mom? I don't recall being subordinate to you, sir. Now if you have something you need me to procure for you, and you have clearance from the Supreme Commander—"

"A purchasing agent is not subordinate to a cabinet minister? Are you from Mars?"

"Actually Israel, sir."

"Would you stop calling me *sir?*"

"I thought *you* called *me,* sir."

"I mean quit calling me that!"

"What? *Sir?* I'm sorry, I thought you were male."

"You stay right where you are, Director. I'll be right over."

"That wasn't so hard, was it, Guy? I mean, it's you who wants to talk with me, not the other way 'round."

Click.

THREE

Rocketing over the Mediterranean in the middle of the night, Rayford had about a two-hour flight to Greece. For the first fifteen minutes he monitored the radio to be sure he was not being pursued or triangulated. But the radio was full of merely repetitious requests for more aircraft to help evacuate Jerusalem in light of the earthquake and the assassination. There were also countless calls for planes available to cart the mourning faithful to New Babylon for what was expected to become the largest viewing and funeral in history.

When the Gulfstream was far enough

out over the water, local tower radio signals faded without satellite aid. Rayford tested that by trying to call his compatriots, to no avail. He switched off phone and radio, which left him in virtual silence at thirty-one thousand feet in a smooth-as-silk jet, most of the noise of the craft behind him.

Rayford suddenly felt the weight of life. Had it really been a mere three and a half years ago that he had enjoyed the prestige, the ease, and the material comfort of the life of a 747 captain for a major airline? He'd been no prize, he knew, as a husband and father, but the cliché was true: You never know what you've got till it's gone.

Life since the Rapture, or what most of the world called the disappearances, had been different as night and day from before—and not just spiritually. Rayford likened it to a death in the family. Not a day passed when he didn't awaken under the burden of the present, facing the cold fact that though he had now made his peace with God, he had been left behind.

It was as if the whole nation, indeed the whole world, lived in suspended mourning and grief. Everyone had lost someone, and not a second could pass when one was able to forget that. It was the fear of missing the school bus, losing your homework, forgetting your gym clothes, knowing you'd been caught cheating on a test, being called to the principal's office, being fired, going bankrupt, cheating on your wife—all rolled into one.

There had been snatches of joy, sure. Rayford lived for his daughter and was pleased with her choice of a husband. Having a grandchild, sobering though it was at this most awful time of history, fulfilled him in a way he hadn't known was possible. But even thinking about Chloe and Buck and little Kenny forced reality into Rayford's consciousness, and it stabbed.

With the Gulfstream on autopilot nearly six miles above the earth, Rayford stared into the cosmos. For an instant he felt disembodied, disconnected from the myriad events of the past forty-two months. Was it possible he'd, in essence, lived half a lifetime in that short span? He had experienced more emotion, fear, anger, frustration, and grief that day alone than in a year of his previous life. He wondered how much a man could take; literally, how much could a human body and mind endure?

How he longed to talk with Tsion! No one else had his trust and respect like the rabbi, only a few years older than he. Rayford couldn't confide in Chloe or Buck. He felt a kinship with T Delanty at the Palwaukee Airport, and they might become true friends. T was the kind of a man Rayford would listen to, even when T felt the need to rebuke him. But Tsion was the man of God. Tsion was one who loved and admired and respected Rayford unconditionally. Or did he? What would Tsion think if he knew what Rayford had done, starting with abandoning both Leah and Buck, but worse, wanting, intending, trying to murder the Antichrist, then perhaps doing so by accident?

Something about the altitude, the coolness he allowed in the cockpit, the tension he could postpone until overflying Greece, the comfort of the seat, and the artificial respite he enjoyed from his role as international fugitive, somehow conspired to awaken Rayford to what had become of him.

At first he resisted the intrusion of reality. Whatever comfort he had found in the buffering quality of life on the edge was stripped away when he allowed raw truth to invade. He told himself to stay with the program, to keep himself as well as his plane on autopilot, to let his emotions rule. What had happened to the scientific, logical Rayford, the one who had been left behind primarily due to that inability to accede to his intuitive side?

When he heard himself speaking aloud, he knew it was time to face the old Rayford—not the pre-Rapture man, but the new believer. He had wondered more than once during the past few months whether he was insane. Now talking to himself in the middle of the night in the middle of nowhere? Much as he hated the prospect, introspection was called for. How long had it been since he had indulged, at least honestly? He had questioned his sanity the past few months, but he seldom dwelt on it long enough to come to any conclusions. He had been driven by rage, by vengeance. He had grown irresponsible, unlike himself.

As Rayford allowed that to rattle in his

brain, he realized that if he pursued this, turned it over in his mind like the marshmallows he had tried browning evenly as a child, it would not be himself he would face in the end. It would be God.

Rayford wasn't sure he wanted the blinding light of God in his mental mirror. In fact, he was fairly certain he didn't. But the hound of heaven was pursuing him, and Rayford would have to be thoroughly deluded or dishonest to turn and run now. He could cover his ears and hum as he did as a child when his mother tried to scold him. Or he could turn on the radio, pretending to see if the satellites had been realigned, or try the phone to test the global system. Maybe he could take the plane off autopilot and busy himself navigating the craft through trackless skies.

Down deep he could never live with himself if he resorted to those evasive tactics, so Rayford endured a shudder of fear. He was going to face this, to square his shoulders to God and take the heat. "All right," he said aloud. "What?"

Buck straightened to relieve the aching in his joints from kneeling to check the lifeless women. Standing in the darkness of his old friend's sepulchral home, he knew he had never been cut out to be a hero. Brave he was not. This horror had brought a sob to his throat he could not subdue. Rayford was the hero; he was the one who had first come to the truth, then led the way for the rest of them. He was the one who had been rocked only temporarily by the loss of their first spiritual mentor but stood strong to lead.

What might Rayford have done in this same situation? Buck had no idea. He was still upset with the man, still puzzled over his mysterious self-assigned task that had left Buck and Leah on their own. Buck believed it would all be explained one day, that there would be some sort of rationale. It shouldn't have been so surprising that Rayford had grown testy and self-absorbed. Look what he had lost. Buck stubbornly left him on the pedestal of his mind as the leader of the Tribulation Force and as one who would act honorably in this situation.

And what would that entail? Finding Stefan, of course. Then challenging whoever was watching this house of death, fighting them, subduing them, or at least eluding them. Eluding didn't sound so heroic, but that was all Buck was inclined to do. Meanwhile, the most heroic he would get would be to finish the task inside—finding Stefan and Chaim, if they were there—and then running for his life.

The running part was the rub. It would be just like the GC—even decimated by population reduction, busy with the Gala, pressed into extraordinary service by the earthquake, and left in a shambles by the assassination—to dedicate an inordinate number of troops to this very house. It would not have surprised Buck an iota if the place was surrounded and they had all seen him enter, watched him find what he found, and now waited to capture him upon his departure.

On the other hand, perhaps they had come and pillaged and slaughtered and left the place a memorial husk.

Feeling ashamed, as if his wife and son could see him feeling his way in the dark, fighting a whimper like a little boy rather than tramping shoulders-wide through the place, Buck stepped on flesh. He half expected the victim to yelp or recoil. Buck knelt and felt a lifeless arm, tight and muscular. Was it possible the GC had suffered a casualty? They would not likely have left one of their own behind, not even a dead one.

Buck turned his back to the windows and switched on the flashlight again. The mess the enemy had left of Stefan made Buck's old nature surge to the fore. It was all he could do to keep from screaming obscenities at the GC and hoping any one of them was within earshot. Revolting as it was, Buck had to look one more time to believe what he saw. Stefan lay there, his face a mask of tranquility, eyes and mouth closed as if he were asleep. His arms and legs were in place, hands at his sides, but all four limbs had been severed, the legs at the hips, the arms at the shoulders. Clearly this had been done after he was dead, for there was no sign of struggle.

Buck dropped the light, and it rolled to a stop, luckily pointing away from the windows. His knees banged painfully on the floor, and when he threw his palms before him to break his fall, they splashed in thick, sticky blood. He knelt there on hands and knees, gasping, his belly tightening and releasing with his sobs and gasps. What kind of a weapon would it have taken and how long must the enemy have worked to saw through the tissue of a dead man until he was dismembered? And why? What was the message in that?

How would he ever tell Chaim? Or would his dear old friend be his next discovery?

At four o'clock in the afternoon Friday in Illinois, Tsion sat near the TV, trying to sort his emotions. He was still able to enjoy, if that was an appropriate word anymore, the ceaseless curiosity and antics of a one-year-old boy. Kenny cooed and talked and made noises as he explored, climbing, grabbing, touching, looking to his mother and to "Unca Zone" to see if he would get a smile or a no, depending on what he was doing.

But Kenny was Chloe's responsibility, and Tsion didn't want to miss a second of the constant coverage of the assassination. He expected news of Carpathia's resurrection and allowed himself only brief absences from the screen. He had moved his laptop to the living room, and his phone was close by. But his main interest was in Israel and New Babylon. It would not have surprised him if Carpathia was loaded onto his plane dead in Jerusalem and worshiped as he walked off under his own power in New Babylon.

Tsion was most upset at hearing nothing from other members of the Trib Force, and he and Chloe traded off trying to raise them, each of them, by phone. The last word they had heard from overseas was that Leah had not seen Hattie in Brussels, that she had told Buck Hattie was gone, and that she had not been able to communicate with Rayford. Since then, nothing.

Worried about the ramifications, Tsion and Chloe left most of the lights off, and they double-checked the phony chest freezer that actually served as an entrance to the underground shelter. Tsion normally left strategy and intrigue to the others and concentrated on his expertise, but he had an opinion on the security of the safe house. Maybe he was naïve, he told Chloe, but he believed that if Hattie were to give them away, it would be by accident. "She'll more likely be followed to us than send someone for us."

"Like she did with Ernie and Bo."

Tsion nodded.

"And who knows whom *they* might have told before they died?"

He shrugged. "If she was to give us up just by telling someone, she would have done it before she was imprisoned."

"If she *was* imprisoned," Chloe said. And suddenly she was fighting tears.

"What is it, Chloe?" Tsion asked. "Worried about Cameron, of course?"

She nodded, then shook her head. "Not only that," she said. "Tsion, can I talk with you?"

"Need you ask?"

"But, I mean, I know you don't want to miss anything on TV."

"I won't. Talk to me."

Tsion was alarmed at how much it took for Chloe to articulate her thoughts. They had always been able to talk, but she had never been extremely self-revelatory. "You know I will keep your confidences," he said. "Consider it clergy-parishioner privilege."

Even that did not elicit a smile. But she managed to shock him. "Maybe I've been watching too much TV," she said.

"Such as?"

"Those staged rallies, where everyone worships Carpathia."

"I know. They're disgusting. They refer to him as 'Your Worship' and the like."

"It's worse than that, Tsion," she said. "Have you seen the clips where the children are brought to him? I mean, we all know there's not a child among them older than three and a half, but they're paraded before him in their little GC outfits, saluting over their hearts with every step, singing praise songs to him. It's awful!"

Tsion agreed. Day care workers and parents dressed the kids alike, and cute little boys and girls brought flowers and were taught to bow and wave and salute and sing to Carpathia. "Did you see the worst of it?" he asked.

Chloe nodded miserably. "The prayer, you mean?"

"That's what I mean. I was afraid of lightning."

Tsion shuddered, remembering the knockoff of the Lord's Prayer taught to groups of children barely old enough to speak. It had begun, "Our Father in New Babylon, Carpathia be your name. Your kingdom come, your will be done. . . ." Tsion had been so disgusted that he turned it off. Chloe, apparently, had watched the whole debacle.

"I've been studying," she said.

"Good," Tsion said. "I hope so. We can never know enough—"

"Not the way you think," she said. "I've been studying death."

Tsion narrowed his eyes. "I'm listening."

"I will not allow myself or my baby to fall into the hands of the enemy."

"What are you saying?"

"I'm saying just what you're afraid I'm saying, Tsion."

"Have you told Cameron?"

"You promised you would keep my confidence!"

"And I will. I'm asking, have *you* told him your plans?"

"I have no plans. I'm just studying."

"But you will soon have a plan, because it is clear you have made up your mind. You said, 'I will not . . . ,' and that evidences a course of action. You're saying that if we should be found out, if the GC should capture us—"

"I will not allow Kenny or me to fall into their hands."

"And how will you ensure this?"

"I would rather we were dead."

"You would kill yourself."

"I would. And I would commit infanticide."

She said this with such chilling conviction that Tsion hesitated, praying silently for wisdom. "Is this a sign of faith, or lack of faith?" he said finally.

"I don't know, but I can't imagine God would want me or my baby in that situation."

"You think he wants you in *this* situation? He is not willing that any should perish. He would that you would have been ready to go the first time. He—"

"I know, Tsion. I know, all right? I'm just saying—"

"Forgive me for interrupting, but I know what you're saying. I just don't believe you are being honest with yourself."

"I couldn't be *more* honest! I would kill myself and commit inf—"

"There you go again."

"What?"

"Buffering your conviction with easy

words. You're no better than the abortion-
ists who refer to their unborn babies as
embryos or fetuses or pregnancies so they
can 'eliminate' them or 'terminate' them
rather than kill them."

"What? I said I would com—"

"Yes, that's what you said. You didn't
say what you mean. Tell me."

"I told you, Tsion! Why are you doing
this?"

"Tell me, Chloe. Tell me what you are
going to do to—" He hesitated, not wanting
to alert Kenny they were talking about him.
"Tell me what you're going to do to this little one, because obviously, you have to do
it to him first if it's going to get done. Because if you kill yourself, none of the rest
of us will do this job for you."

"I told you what I would do to him."

"Say it in plain words."

"That I will kill him before I let the GC
have him? I will."

"Will what?"

"Kill him."

"Put it in a sentence."

"I will. I will . . . kill . . . my own baby."

"Baby!" Kenny exulted, running to her.
She reached for him, sobbing.

Quietly, Tsion said, "How will you do this?"

"That's what I'm studying," she managed over Kenny's shoulders. He hugged her tight and scampered away.

"And then you will kill yourself, why?"

"Because I cannot live without him."

"Then it follows that Cameron would be justified in killing himself."

She bit her lip and shook her head. "The world needs him."

"The world needs you, Chloe. Think of the co-op, the international—"

"I can't think anymore," she said. "I want done with this! I want it over! I don't know what we were thinking, bringing a child into this world. . . ."

"That child has brought so much joy to this house—" Tsion began.

"—that I could not do him the disservice of letting him fall into GC hands."

Tsion sat back, glancing at the TV. "So the GC comes, you kill the baby, kill yourself, Cameron and your father kill themselves . . . when does it end?"

"They wouldn't. They couldn't."

"You can't. And you won't."

"I thought I could talk to you, Tsion."

"You expected what, that I would condone this?"

"That you would be sympathetic, at least."

"I am that, at the very least," he said. "Neither do I want to live without you and the little one. You know what comes next."

"Oh, Tsion, you would not deprive your global church of yourself."

He sat back and put his hands on his knees. "Yet you would deprive *me* of *yourself*. You must not care for me as much as I care for you, or as much as I thought you did."

Chloe sighed and looked to the ceiling. "You're not helping," she said in mock exasperation.

"I'm trying," he said.

"I know. And I appreciate it."

Tsion asked her to pray with him for their loved ones. She knelt on the floor next to the couch, holding his hand, and soon after they began, Tsion peeked at a sound and saw Kenny kneeling next to his mother, hands folded, fingers entwined, eyes closed.

*   *   *

David found Guy Blod more outrageous and flamboyant in person. He showed up with a small entourage of similarly huffy and put-out men in their late thirties. Despite their differences in nationality, they could have been quints from the way they dressed and acted. David offered only Guy a chair across from his desk.

"This is what you call hospitality?" Guy said. "There are six of us, hello."

"My apologies," David said. "I was under the impression it was the responsibility of the *guest* to inform the *host* when uninvited people were coming."

Guy waved him off, and his sycophants glumly stood behind him with arms crossed. "The Supreme Commander has commissioned me to do a sort of bronzy iron thingie of Nicolae. And I have to do it fast, so can you get me the materials?"

They were interrupted by an urgent knock on the door. A woman in her late sixties, blue-haired, short, and stocky, poked her head in. "Miss Ivins," David said. "May I help you?"

"Excuse me," Guy said, "but we're in conference here."

David stood. "It's all right, Miss Ivins. You know Guy."

"Of course," she said, nodding sadly.

"And Guy, you know Vivian is—"

"Yes, the potentate's only living relative. I'm sorry for your loss, ma'am, but we—"

"How may I help you, ma'am?" David said.

"I'm looking for crowd control volunteers," she said. "The masses are already showing up from all over the world, and—"

"It's after midnight!" Guy said. "Don't they know the funeral isn't for at least two days? What are we supposed to do with them all?"

"Commander Fortunato is asking for any personnel below director level to—"

"That leaves me out, Vivian!" Guy said. "And Hayseed here too, unfortunately."

"How about your assistants, Guy?" David suggested.

"I need every last one of them for this project! Viv, surely you don't expect—"

"I'm aware of your assignment, Guy," Viv Ivins said, but she pronounced his name in the Western style, and he quickly corrected her. She ignored him. "I'm on assignment too. If either of you gentlemen could spread the word among your people, the administration would be grateful."

David returned to his seat and tapped out the notice to be broadcast to his workers' E-mail addresses as Miss Ivins backed out and shut the door.

"Aren't we efficient?" Guy said.

"We try," David said.

"I know what her assignment is," Guy said. "Have you heard?"

"I have enough trouble keeping up with my own."

David had acted uninterested enough that Guy turned to his own people and whispered, "That regional numbering thing." David was dying of curiosity but unwilling to admit it. Guy spun in his chair to face David. "Now, where were we?"

"I was about to check my catalog file for bronze and iron thingie suppliers, and you were going to be a bit more specific."

"OK, I'm gonna need a computer program that allows me to figure out how to do this. I'm going to be supplied by the coroner with a life-size cast of Carpathia's body—how ghastly—and I need to quadruple that in size. That means four times."

"Yeah, I recall arithmetic, Guy."

"I'm just trying to help. Truce?"

"Truce?"

"Start over, no hassles?"

"Whatever, Guy."

"Be nice."

"I'm trying."

"Anyhoo, I wanna make this like twenty-four-foot replica of Carpathia out of pretty much bronze, I think, but I want it to come out in a sort of ebony finish with a texture of iron. Ebony is black."

"I remember crayons too, Guy."

"Sor-*ry,* David! You don't want *any* help!"

"I'm going to need it if I'm to find you this material quickly. What do you think you need and how fast do you need it?"

Guy leaned forward. "Now we're getting somewhere. I want the thing to be hollow with about a quarter-inch to three-eighths-inch shell, but it has to be strong enough and balanced enough to stand straight without support, just like Nicolae would if he were that tall."

David shrugged. "So you make him to scale and cheat on the shoes if you have to, since an inanimate object won't make the unconscious balancing maneuvers to stay standing."

"Shoes!?"

"What, your statue will be barefoot?"

Guy giggled and shared the mirth with his clones. "Oh, David," he said, lifting his feet and spinning in his chair. "My statue will be *au naturel.*"

David made a face. "Please tell me you're joking!"

"Not on your life. Did you think the mortician was going to make a body cast of him in his suit?"

"Why not?"

Guy fluttered the air with his fingers and said, "Forget it, forget it, you wouldn't understand. You obviously have some hangup about the human form and can't appreciate the beauty. You just—"

"Guy, I'm assuming this statue is to maintain a prominent place within the palace—"

"Within the palace? Dear boy! This will be THE *objet d'art* of history, my *pièce de résistance.* It shall stand in the palace courtyard not thirty feet from where the potentate lies in state."

"So the whole world will see it."

"In all its glory."

"And it's *your* masterpiece."

Guy nodded, appearing unable to contain his glee.

"So if I took a picture of something and then traced it, I could be an artist too?"

Guy looked disgusted. "You're about as far from an artist as I am from—"

"But what of this reproduction of a dead man's bare body is your work?"

"Are you just insulting me, or is that a sincere question?"

"Call it sincere. I really want to know."

"The concept! I con*ceived* it, David! I will supervise the construction. I will do the finish work on the face, leaving the eyes hollow. I was asked to create a huge statue to represent the greatest man who ever lived, and this came to me as if from God himself."

"You're on speaking terms with God?"

"It's just an expression, Hayseed. It's from my muse. Who can explain it? It's what I blame my genius on, the one thing that keeps me from unbearable ego. Can you imagine how embarrassing it is to be lauded for everything your hands create? I mean, I'm not complaining, but the attention becomes overwhelming. The muse is my foil. I am as overwhelmed at my gift—

the gift from the muse, you see—as any-one else. I enjoy it as the masses do."

"You do."

"Yes, I do. And I can't wait to get to this one. I'm assuming I would have access to the GC foundry, as we won't have time to have this done off-site."

David shut one eye. "The foundry is on three shifts, seven days a week. We could have this more cheaply done in Asia, where—"

"Help me stay civil here, David, as it is clearly my fault for not clarifying. Supreme Commander Fortunato—who, in case you couldn't figure this out on your own, will likely be the new potentate once Carpathia is entombed—wants this monument in place no later than at dawn Sunday."

Guy stared at David, as if to let that sink in. It almost didn't. David looked at his watch. It was crowding 1:00 A.M. Saturday, Carpathia Standard Time. "I don't see it," he said, "but I don't imagine you can be dissuaded."

"Why, I believe we have begun to con-nect!"

Anything but that, David thought.

"Zhizaki," Guy said, "if you please."

With a flourish, an Asian with two-inch green nails produced a computer-generated schedule. It called for the procuring of materials and determining the manufacturing site by noon Saturday, concurrent with computer design by the artist and cast making by the mortician. By midnight Saturday, the foundry was to create a cast to the artist's specifications, produce the shell, and deliver it to the back of the palace courtyard. There Guy and his staff would do the finish work until the product was ready for positioning in view of the mourners just before dawn Sunday.

"That's more than ambitious, Guy," David said. "It's audacious."

"Audacious," Guy said with a faraway look. "Now there's an epitaph."

"You'll have to work with materials already on hand," David said.

"I assumed that. But we'll need you to override current projects, get this at the top of the list, and let me in there to make sure the consistency and the color are right."

"You'll have to wear protective clothing and a hard hat," David said.

Guy looked at his mates. "I love new clothes."

FOUR

It was to Rayford's advantage that the Global Community had rendered the whole of Greece virtually invisible. In realigning the world into ten regions with sub-potentates—which Tsion Ben-Judah insisted were "kingdoms with kings"—the United Holy Land States had appropriated Greece. Her potentate had lobbied for independence, as most countries' leaders had, then pleaded for membership as one of the United European States.

Carpathia himself had mollified the Greeks with a personal visit and several appearances, during which he took full responsibility for their inclusion in "his" region. Lukas (Laslos) Miklos had once regaled Rayford with a dead-on imitation of the potentate's Eastern-flavored Greek as he flattered the nation into compliance.

"You are a deeply religious people," Carpathia had told them, "with a rich place in the histories of many cherished belief systems. You are nearly as close to the cradle of civilization as you are to the United European States, so I personally argued for your inclusion as a Holy Land state. My own origins are not that far north of you. The line of demarcation that puts both my homeland and my current residence in the same region naturally includes Greece as well. I welcome you to 'my' region and trust you will enjoy the benefits from this area's housing the new world capital."

That had won over the majority of Greeks. One huge benefit to tribulation saints was that Greece seemed above suspicion as a spring of rebellion. The exploding church there went underground immediately, worried that it might otherwise draw the attention of the GC. Dr. Ben-Judah corresponded with nearly a thousand Greek evangelists he had identified as likely part of the prophesied 144,000 witnesses. These were Messianic Jews, many of whom had attended the great conference of witnesses in Israel and had returned to their homeland to win tens of thousands of converts to Christ.

Mr. and Mrs. Miklos's own local body of underground believers had mushroomed so that the original assembly had split many times and now met as more than a hundred "small groups" that weren't really so small. The new corporate church was too large to ever meet together without jeopardizing its clandestine identity. The witness-leaders of each faction met monthly for training and mutual encouragement, and of course the entire body counted itself part of the new worldwide band of believers, with Tsion Ben-Judah as its *de facto* cyberspace pastor-teacher.

The covert nature of the Greek church, while clearly not impeding its evangelistic efforts, served to keep from waving a red flag before the GC. Buck Williams's private investigations for his cybermagazine, *The Truth,* found—with the help of ultimate hacker David Hassid—that Greece was all but ignored by GC counterintelligence, security, and peacekeeping forces. The country was low maintenance. Most of the forces assigned there had been redeployed into Israel for the Gala and New Babylon for its aftermath.

Thus it was not a surprise to Rayford to find that the tiny airport in Ptolemaïs was not only closed and unmanned but also dark. He had neither the light power nor the confidence to land on an unlit runway with a plane as powerful and tricky as the Gulfstream. He overflew the airfield a few times, not wanting to draw attention to himself, then headed south about twenty-five miles to Kozani and its larger airport. It too was closed, but one runway remained lit for emergencies and private cargo carriers. Rayford watched a wide-body international delivery craft put down, waited until it had taxied toward the colossal commercial hangars, then set his instruments for landing.

He didn't know how he would get hold of Laslos or find a ride to Ptolemaïs. Perhaps he would be close enough to use his phone without relying on satellite technology. He hated to bother the Mikloses at this hour, but he'd done it before. They always understood. In fact, it seemed they loved the intrigue of the underground, Mrs. Miklos as much as Lukas.

Rayford was strangely calm as he descended into Kozani. He believed he had made intimate contact with God during the flight, had communicated more directly, and felt more personally connected to heaven than he had in ages. This had come when Rayford finally heeded the Scripture "Be still, and know that I am God." After months of rationalizing, self-defense, and taking matters into his own hands, he had finally given up and sought God.

His first overwhelming emotion was shame. God had entrusted him, a brand-new believer, with a scope of leadership. God had used the gifts he had bestowed on Rayford to direct the little band of believers that had become known as the Tribulation Force.

Smarter people were in the Force, Rayford knew, including his own daughter and son-in-law. And where on earth was a more brilliant mind than that of Tsion Ben-Judah? And yet they all naturally looked to Rayford for leadership. He had not sought it, nor did he hoard it. But he had been willing. And as the Force grew, so did his responsibility. But though his capacity could have expanded with the scope of his charge, the illogical had invaded. The man who had prided himself on his pragmatism found himself living by his emotions.

At first, becoming attuned to his emotions had been revelatory. It had allowed him to care deeply for his daughter, to really grieve over the loss of his wife and son, and to understand how much he had loved them. It had allowed him to see himself for who he was, to understand his need for forgiveness, to come to Christ.

But, understandably, Rayford had found it difficult to balance his emotion and his intellect. No one could argue that he had been through more than his share of loss and trauma in three and a half years. But the emotion necessary to round him out as a new believer somehow overrode the levelheaded temperament that made him a natural leader. Never one for psychobabble, when Rayford opened himself to God that night, in his spirit he saw his failure for what it was: sin.

He had become selfish, angry, vengeful. He had tried to take God's place as defender and protector of the Tribulation Force. In the process, he had left them more vulnerable than ever to danger. As Rayford dared peek at himself in that spiritual mirror, he hated what he saw. Here was a man who had been wholly grateful to God for his forgiveness and love and salvation, now living as a maverick. He still called himself a believer. But what had happened to his dependence upon God, upon the counsel of his friends and relatives and spiritual mentors? What had happened to his love for the Bible and prayer, and for the guidance he had once found there?

As God seemed to shine the light of truth into his soul, Rayford pleaded for forgiveness, for restoration. Had his rage been sin? No, that didn't compute. The Scriptures counseled, "Be angry, and do not sin," so the anger itself was not wrong. What he did as a result of it clearly was. He had become consumed by rage and had allowed it to interfere with his relationship to God and to those he loved.

Rayford had become isolated, living out his private ambitions. He had fought to see through his tears as God showed him his

very self in its rawest state. "I'll understand," he prayed, "if I have disqualified
myself from any role with the Trib Force,"
but God did not seem to confirm that. All
Rayford felt was an overwhelming hunger
and thirst for the Bible and for instruction.
He wanted to pray like this from now on, to
constantly be in touch with God as he had
been when he first became a believer.
What that meant to his role as head of the
Tribulation Force, he didn't know. More important was getting back to the basics, getting back to God.

Rayford found the cargo plane crew
busy with their own work as he taxied a
quarter of a mile north to park the Gulfstream. They barely looked up as he hurried past on foot, his bag slung over his
shoulder as if he were headed somewhere
specific. As soon as he emerged from the
airfield's gated entrance and found a dark
spot between road lamps, he phoned the
Mikloses' home. Mrs. Miklos answered on
the first ring.

"This is your friend from America," he
said, and she immediately switched from
Greek to her very limited English.

"Say code so I know," she said.

Code? He didn't remember any code. Maybe that was something among the local believers. "Jesus is the Christ, the Messiah," he said.

"That not code," she said, "but I know voice. Saw on television."

"You did? Me?"

"Yes. Did you shoot Carpathia?"

Rayford's mouth went dry. So the cameras had caught him. "No!" he said. "At least I don't think so. I didn't mean to. What are they saying?"

"Fingerprints," she said. "On gun."

Rayford shook his head. He had been so certain that if he shot Carpathia he would be immediately captured or killed that he had not even worried about fingerprints. He hadn't considered escaping. Some criminal *he* was! Why didn't he think to wipe the handle on his robe before dropping the weapon?

"Are they showing my face?" he asked.

"Yes."

He told her where he was and asked if Laslos was there.

"No. With our shepherd. Praying for you."

"I don't want to compromise you," he said. "I'll just fly on to America."

"Don't know *compromise*," she said.

"Ah, sorry. Give you away. Get you in trouble. Be seen with you."

"Laslos would not leave you alone," she said. "I tell him. He call you."

Rayford hated the idea of jeopardizing Greek believers, but Laslos's English was better than his wife's, so perhaps Rayford would have an easier time dissuading him from becoming involved. He gave her the number and settled in to wait for the call in the shadows of the shrubbery off the makeshift road that led north out of the airport.

Upstairs in Rosenzweig's massive house, Buck used the flashlight sparingly as he searched for any sign of Chaim. From outside he heard noises in the underbrush that paralyzed him. He held his breath and crept to the window, peering down while desperate to stay out of sight. Someone signaled a few others, and their shapes moved about in the darkness. He couldn't imagine a scenario that would allow him to escape until it played out before his eyes.

Suddenly all GC Peacekeeping Forces were rallied for one purpose—to find a fugitive. And when the multi-language announcement came over rolling bullhorns, it was clear whom they were looking for.

"Attention, citizens and all Global Community personnel!" came the announcements. "Be on the lookout for American Rayford Steele, former GC employee wanted in connection with the conspiracy to assassinate Potentate Nicolae Carpathia. May be in disguise. May be armed. Considered dangerous. Qualified pilot. Any information about his whereabouts . . ."

Rayford? Conspiracy? Now the GC was grasping at straws.

From below, the GC Peacekeepers appeared to be arguing whether one or more should stay. Finally their leader barked at them and waved that they should follow. Buck waited a few minutes, then checked every window, staring into the night and listening for any enemy. He saw and heard nothing, but he knew time was his greatest adversary now.

He saved Chaim's workshop till last. It had no windows, so when he threw open the door, he didn't hesitate to shine the flashlight all about. It was empty, but it also looked different from when last he'd seen it. Chaim had shown him his handiwork, but now there was no evidence of that. The place was spotless. Even the vises had been unfastened from the workbenches and stored. The floor was clean, tools hung, counters spotless. It almost looked the way it would if someone were moving or had another function in mind for the room.

Buck backed out and closed the door. Something niggled at his mind, despite the taste of fear and revulsion in his throat. He tucked the flashlight into his pocket and carefully made his way to the front door. The casing had been shattered. Though he was sure the GC had done this and abandoned the place, Buck felt safer leaving the way he had come. As he moved toward the back door, he wondered who had cleaned Chaim's workshop for him. Had he done it himself before the stroke, or had the staff done it after it became clear he would be unable to engage in his hobby?

Buck felt his way through the sparse landscaping in the back and stopped frequently to listen for footsteps or breathing over the sirens and announcements from blocks away. He stayed out of the light and in the middle of earthquake rubble as much as he could until he found an area where the streetlamps were out.

He had to know for sure about Chaim before he could even think about trying to rendezvous with Rayford or Leah. But where should he start? Not that long ago, Buck would have tried to find him through Jacov, Hannelore, her mother, or Stefan. As he broke into a jog, heading for who knew where, tears dripped from his face.

Late Friday afternoon in Illinois, Chloe had been feeding Kenny in the other room when Rayford's photo—the one from his former GC ID—came on television. Tsion blanched and bolted for the set to turn it down and listen from up close. Tsion had been praying for Rayford, worried about him. When Rayford and Leah and Buck had left, Tsion thought he knew their various assignments and missions, and he feared playing mere shuttle pilot would not be enough for Rayford. He had been in the middle of so much action but was now, even more than the rest, merely a fugitive, having to stay out of sight.

Now what would he do? The news implied he had fired the weapon that may have killed Carpathia. How could one do that in such a crowd and escape? Never had Tsion so wanted to talk to Rayford, and never had he felt such a burden to pray for a man.

That compulsion was nothing new. It struck Tsion that he had spent more time in concerted prayer for Rayford than for any-other individual. It was obvious why Rayford needed prayer now, of course, but when Tsion closed his eyes and covered them with a hand, he felt uncomfortable. He knew he would have to tell Chloe soon that her father was a suspect in the assassination—or the conspiracy, as the TV anchors called it—but that was not what made him fidgety. It seemed he was not in the proper posture to pray, and all he could make of that was that perhaps Rayford needed real intercession.

Tsion had studied the discipline of inter-cession, largely a Protestant tradition from the fundamentalist and the Pentecostal cultures. Those steeped in it went beyond mere praying for someone as an act of interceding for them; they believed true intercession involved deep empathy and that a person thus praying must not enter into the practice unless willing to literally trade places with the needy person.

Tsion mentally examined his own willingness to truly intercede for Rayford. It was mere exercise. He could not trade places with Rayford and become a suspect in the murder of the Antichrist. But he could affect that posture in his mind; he could express his willingness to God to take that burden, literally possible or not.

Yet even that did not assuage Tsion's discomfort. He tried dropping to one knee, bowing his head lower, then slipping to both knees, then turning to lay his arms on the seat of the couch and rest his head on his hands. He worried that Chloe would not understand if she saw him this way, suddenly not watching TV obsessively as he had since the assassination, but in a posture of total contrition—something foreign to his nature. He often prayed this way in private, of course, but Chloe would see this "showing" of humility so aberrational

that she would likely feel obligated to ask if
he was all right.

But these concerns were quickly over-
ridden by Tsion's spiritual longings. He felt
such deep compassion and pity for Rayford that he moaned involuntarily and felt
himself sliding from the couch until his
palms were flat on the floor.

His head now pressing against the front
of the couch, his body facing away from
the near silent TV, he groaned and wept
as he prayed silently for Rayford. Having
not come from a tradition comfortable with
unusual manifestations, Tsion was startled
by a sudden lack of equilibrium. In his
mind's eye his focus had suddenly shifted
from Rayford and his troubles to the majesty of God himself. Tsion at once felt unworthy and ashamed and impure, as if in
the very presence of the Lord.

Tsion knew that praying was figuratively
boldly approaching the throne, but he had
never felt such a physical proximity to the
creator God. Knees sliding back, palms
forward, he lay prostrate, his forehead
pressing into the musty carpet, nose
mashed flat.

But even that did not alleviate his lightheadedness. Tsion felt disembodied, as if the present were giving way. He was only vaguely aware of where he was, of the quiet drone of the television, of Chloe cooing and Kenny giggling as she urged him to eat.

"Tsion?"

He did not respond, not immediately aware he was even conscious. Was this a dream?

"Tsion?"

The voice was feminine.

"Should I try the phone again?"

He opened his eyes, suddenly aware of the smell of the old carpet and the sting of tears.

"Hm?" he managed, throat constricted, voice thick.

Footsteps. "I was wondering, should I try calling—Tsion! Are you all right?"

He slowly pulled himself up. "I'm fine, dear. Very tired all of a sudden."

"You have a right to be! Get some rest. Take a nap. I'll wake you if anything breaks. I won't let you miss anything."

Tsion sat on the edge of the couch, shoulders slumped, hands entwined between his knees. "I would be grateful," he said. He nodded toward the other room. "Is he all right for a minute?"

She nodded.

"You'd better sit down," he said.

Chloe looked stricken. "Was there news? Is Buck all right?"

"Nothing from Buck or Leah," he said, and she seemed to finally exhale. "But you need to know about your father. . . ."

David tried e-mailing Viv Ivins a list of those in his department who might be available for double duty over the next few days, but the message bounced back undeliverable. He would go past her office on the way to the hangar anyway, so he printed out the message and took it with him.

On the way he received a call from the foundry foreman. "You know what you're asking, don't you?" the man said.

"Of course, Hans," David said. "You have to know this didn't originate with me."

"Unless it's from Fortunato himself, I don't see how we can be expected—"

"It is."

"—to comply. I mean, this is way too—it is?"

"It is."

" 'nough said."

David slipped the printout into the slot on Viv Ivins's door, but it was not shut all the way and swung open. The small, dark office immediately brightened as the motion-sensitive light came on. The gossip around the palace was that on occasion, Carpathia's alleged aunt on his mother's side dozed for so long at her desk that her office went dark. If something woke her or caused her to move in her sleep, the lights came back on, and she resumed working as if nothing were awry.

David made sure she wasn't in there dozing, then reached to shut the door. But something on her desk caught his eye. She had laid out a map of the world, boundaries between the ten regions clearly marked. It was nothing he hadn't seen before, except that this was an old map, one drawn when the ten regions were members of the newly expanded United Nations Security Council. When Carpathia had renamed the one-world government the Global Community, he had also slightly renamed the ten regions. For instance, the United States of North America became

the United North American States. Viv
Ivins had not only handwritten these ad-
justments, but she had also added numbers in parentheses after each name.

David felt conspicuous and nosy, but
who knew what significance this might hold
for the Trib Force, the Judah-ites, tribulation saints around the world? He con-
cocted his alibi as he moved toward the
desk. If Viv were to return and catch him
studying her map, he would simply tell the
truth about the door tripping the light and
the map catching his eye. How he would
explain his scribbling the numbers, he did
not know.

With one last look out her office window,
David grabbed a business card from his
wallet and wrote furiously in tiny script as
he bent over Viv's map.

The United Holy Land States* (216)
The United Russian States (72)
The United Indian States (42)
The United Asian States (30)
The United Pacific States (18)
The United North American States (-6)
The United South American States (0)
The United Great Britain States (2)

The United European States (6)
The United African States (7)

David traced the asterisk after "The United Holy Land States" to the bottom of the map, where Viv, or someone, had noted in faint, tiny pencil marks "aka The United Carpathian States."

That was a new one. David had never heard another moniker for the Holy Land States. As he was straightening to leave he saw more pencil writing that appeared to have been erased. He bent close and squinted but needed more light. Dare he turn on Viv's desk lamp?

No. Rather, he held the whole map up to the ceiling light, knowing he would simply have to confess to pathological curiosity, if necessary. He only hoped that Viv, like nearly everyone else in the compound, was watching Carpathia's body being transported from the Phoenix 216 to the morgue. He was glad to miss that, knowing that most would hold hands or hats over their hearts, and he wasn't prepared to do that even as a ruse.

With the overhead light shining brightly through the map, David was barely able to

make out the erasures. It appeared someone had written "Only caveat: H. L. highest, N. A. lowest."

David shook his head as he carefully replaced the map and headed out.

Viv Ivins was coming toward him. "Oh,
David," she said, "I wish you could have
seen the spontaneous outpouring of emotion . . ."

"I'm sure there'll be a lot of that over the
next few days."

"But to see the workers, the soldiers,
everybody . . . ah, it was moving. The sa-
lutes, the tears. Oh! Did I leave my light
on?"

David explained the door tripping the
motion sensor.

"And your list is in the door?"

He nodded and his phone rang, startling
him so that he nearly left his feet.

"Carry on," Viv said.

It was Mac. David talked as he walked.
"Half thought you'd be here to greet us,"
Mac said. "Corporal Christopher waited on
the evidence until the pallbearers got the
body out of here."

"The evidence?"

"I don't think I've ever seen pallbearers

in dress unies carrying a big ol' wood crate like it was a polished mahogany casket. Where were you?"

"On my way, but what'd you say about evidence?"

"Annie's off-loading it now. Couple of huge plastic trash bags full of pieces of the lectern. And another crate with apparently the whole fabric backdrop off the stage. Moon wouldn't let us leave Jerusalem without it. You heard about the weapon, right?"

" 'Course. And our friend."

"Funny thing, though, David."

"Yeah?"

"I'd better save this for in person."

"Rayford here."

"Mr. Steele!" came the easily recognized voice of Lukas Miklos. "Where are you?"

Rayford told him.

"Stay in the shadows but walk three kilometers north. We will pick you up north of the three-kilometer marker. When you see a white four-door slow and leave the road, run to us. If there is any traffic, we may pass and come back, but when we pull off, do not hesitate."

"We?"

"Our undershepherd and me."

"Laslos, I don't want you two to risk—"

"Nonsense! Do you have an alias and appropriate papers?"

"I do."

"Good. How fast can you walk?"

"How's the terrain?"

"Not the best, but don't get near the road until we get there."

"I'm starting now."

"Mr. Steele, we feel just like the prayer-meeting people from the New Testament, praying for Peter while he knocked on their door."

"Yeah," Rayford said. "Only he was coming *from* prison."

Exhausted, Buck sat behind a concrete wall, built decades before to protect Israel from shrapnel and mortar from nearby enemies. He was several blocks from the main drag, but close enough to hear the ever-present sirens and see the emergency lights bouncing off the low-riding clouds in the wee hours.

Think, think, think, he told himself. He didn't want to leave Israel without knowing where Chaim was. Buck knew of no other people Chaim might flee to or with if he had somehow survived. If Chaim had defied the odds, he would be looking for Buck as fervently as Buck was looking for him. They could not meet at the obvious places: Buck's hostel, Chaim's house, Jacov's apartment, Stefan's place. What would make sense to both of them?

Buck had never believed in extrasensory perception, but he sure wished there was something to it now. He wished he could sense whether the old man was all right, and if so, that he was trying to somehow communicate with Buck right then. As a believer, Buck was certain that clairvoyance was hogwash. But he had heard credible stories of people, particularly Christians, who somehow knew things supernaturally. Surely it wasn't beyond God's ability to perform such miracles, especially now.

Buck needed a miracle, but his faith was weak. He knew it shouldn't be. He had seen enough from God in three and a half years that he should never again doubt for an instant. What held him up now was that he was dead sure he didn't deserve a miracle. Weren't there bigger, more important things for God to worry about? People were dying, injured, lost. And there was the great supernatural battle between good and evil that Tsion wrote so much about, the conflict of the ages that had spilled out of heaven and now plagued the earth.

"I'm sorry to even ask," Buck prayed, "but at least calm me down, give me a clear mind just long enough to figure this. If Chaim is alive, let us run into each other or both think of a meeting place that makes sense."

Buck felt foolish, stupid, petty. Finding Chaim was noble, but involving God in such a trivial matter seemed, well, rude. He stood and felt the aches. He clenched his fists and grimaced. *Relax! Get hold of yourself! Think!*

But somehow he knew that was no way to open the mind. He had to really relax, and berating himself for being frantic would have the opposite effect. But how could he calm himself at a time like this, when it was all he could do to catch his breath and will his pulse to decelerate?

Maybe *that* was an appropriate request of God, a miracle enough in itself.

Buck sat back down, confident he was

hidden and alone. He breathed deeply and exhaled slowly, shaking out his hands and stretching his legs. He laid his head back and felt the concrete wall against his hair and scalp. He let his head roll from side to side. His breathing became slower and more even; his pulse began to subside ever so slowly. He tucked his chin to his chest and tried to clear his mind.

The only way to do that was to pray for his comrades one by one, starting with his own wife and son, his father-in-law, and all the rest of the brothers and sisters who came to mind. He thanked God for friends now in heaven, including those whose bodies he had just discovered.

And almost before he knew it, he had calmed as much as a man could in that situation. *Thank you, Lord. Now what location would make sense? Where have Chaim and I been together that we would both think of?*

He pictured them at Teddy Kolleck Stadium, but that was too public, too open. Neither could risk it.

And then it came to him.

FIVE

Chloe fell silent at the news. Tsion might have predicted tears, disbelief, railing against someone other than her father. She just sat, shaking her head.

Difficult as it had been to inform her, Tsion was oddly still reeling from what to him had felt almost like an out-of-body experience while praying. He had heard of those and pooh-poohed them as fabrications or drug-induced hallucinations on deathbeds. But this sensation, so real and dramatic that it had temporarily derailed his empathy and intercession on Rayford's behalf, was something else again. He had long advocated checking experience against Scripture and not the other way around. He would, he realized, have to remind himself of that frequently until the glow—which seemed too positive a word for the disturbing residue of the incident—receded into memory. A verse from the Old Testament teased his consciousness, and his mind wandered from the troubled young woman before him.

As Chloe had not yet responded, Tsion said, "Excuse me a moment, please," and brought his whole Bible text up onto his laptop screen. A few seconds later he clicked on Joel 2. He silently read verses 28 through 32, finding that he had been led to a passage that both illuminated his experience and might provide some balm to her as well.

I will pour out My Spirit on all flesh;
Your sons and your daughters shall prophesy,
Your old men shall dream dreams,
Your young men shall see visions.
And also on My menservants and on My maidservants I will pour out My Spirit in those days.

*And I will show wonders in the heavens
    and in the earth: blood and fire and
    pillars of smoke.
The sun shall be turned into darkness,
And the moon into blood,
Before the coming of the great and
    awesome day of the Lord.
And it shall come to pass
That whoever calls on the name of the
    Lord
Shall be saved.
For in Mount Zion and in Jerusalem
    there shall be deliverance,
As the Lord has said,
Among the remnant whom the Lord
    calls.*

Tsion looked up with a start when Chloe spoke at last. He detected no trauma in her voice, nothing that would have given away that she had just learned that her father was the most wanted fugitive in the world—except for her words themselves. "I should have seen it coming," she said. "He tried to divert me to Hattie, which wasn't hard. She never had any qualms about saying she wanted to kill Carpathia."

Tsion cleared his throat. "Why would he

do it, knowing the death wound is only temporary anyway? Is your father capable of such an act?"

Chloe stood and peeked into the other room, where she was apparently satisfied with whatever Kenny was doing with his food. "I wouldn't have thought so until recently," she said. "He changed so much. Almost as dramatically as the difference in him before and after the Rapture. It was as if he had reverted into something worse than he had been before he became a believer."

Tsion cocked his head and sneaked a glance at the television. Nothing new. "I was aware of tension in the house," he said. "But I missed what you're talking about."

"The rage? You missed the rage?"

Tsion shrugged. "I *share* some of that. I still fight it when I think of my family—" His voice caught.

"I know, Tsion. But you have been a man of the Scriptures your whole life. This is new to Daddy. I can't imagine him actually standing there and doing it, but I'm sure he wanted to. If he did, it sure answers a lot of questions about where he's been and what he's been doing. Oh, Tsion! How will he get away? That they say he's at large makes me wonder if it's not just a lie, a smear campaign to make him and you and us look bad? Maybe he's a scapegoat."

"We can only hope."

She dropped into a chair. "What if he's guilty? What if he's a murderer? There's no exception to God's law if the victim is the Antichrist, is there?"

Tsion shook his head. "None that I know of."

"Then mustn't he turn himself in? Suffer the consequences?"

"Slow down, Chloe. We know too little."

"But if he *is* guilty."

"My answer may surprise you."

"Surprise me."

"Off the top of the head, I believe we are at war. In the heat of battle, killing the enemy has never been considered murder."

"But . . ."

"I told you I might surprise you. I personally would harbor your father from the GC if he shot Carpathia dead, even while urging him to seek God about himself."

"You're right," Chloe said. "You surprised me."

David watched Annie work from the corner of the hangar where Mac and Abdullah met him. "What's that smell?" he said.

"Yeah," Mac said, looking at Abdullah. "What *is* that?"

Abdullah shrugged, then held up an index finger. "Oh, I remember now, Captain," he said. "Your idea."

"I'm listening," Mac said.

Abdullah pulled a pungent pita sandwich from his pocket. "Hungry, anyone?" he said.

"Here's hoping I'll never be that hungry," David said, pointing to a trash barrel twenty feet away. Abdullah hit it with a hook shot, and somehow the thing didn't fly apart in the air.

Mac shook his head. "Next you're going to tell me you were an Olympic basketball player."

"Missed the trials," Abdullah said. "Active duty."

David caught Mac's what'd-I-tell-ya look.

"So, Ab," Mac said, "are you 'pout' because you never finished your dinner?"

Abdullah looked away, as if knowing he was being teased but not catching the whole drift. "If I am pout," he said, "it is because I am exhausted and want to go to bed. Is anyone sleeping around here? It seems everyone is about."

"Go," David said. "Don't make it obvious, but go to bed. I'm going to be good for nothing if I don't crash sometime soon too."

Abdullah slipped away. "You look whipped too, Mac," David said.

Mac nodded for David to follow him to his office, across the hall from Annie's. "They're making a big deal about finding Rayford's fingerprints on a Saber," Mac said as he settled into the chair behind his desk. "But who knows if he was even there?"

"I'll find out by listening in."

"I think I already did. The print trace, at least what they said about it on the plane, sounded legit. Israeli-based Peacekeepers found the weapon, bagged it, and immediately lifted prints and started comparing it against the global database. The only reason it took as long as it did was because they tested it against criminals first and against the former GC employee list last. But the funny thing is that nobody's talking about Rayford as the perpetrator."

David flinched. "When they've got him dead to rights?"

Mac showed both palms. "They must know something we don't know."

"Such as?"

"Well, Neon Leon has a bee in his bonnet for the three disloyal regional potentates. He keeps talking about a conspiracy. I mean, everybody hears a gunshot and heads for the hills. People jump off the stage. Carpathia is down and dying. The suspected weapon is found with a disgruntled former employee's prints all over it, and all Leon can talk about is a conspiracy. What does that tell you?"

David frowned and furrowed his brow. "That the shooter missed?"

Mac expelled a resigned breath through his nose. "That's my theory. If it was so cut-and-dried, why don't they just call Rayford the shooter?"

"In public they do."

"But in private they're still looking. David, something stinks here."

David heard Annie's office door and

looked out through the blinds. She was doing the same, and he invited her over with a wave. She held up a finger and motioned that she had to make a call first. When she finally joined them, they brought her up to date.

"You still planning on listening in to the autopsy?" she said.

David nodded.

"Maybe you ought to patch in to the evidence room too."

"Didn't know we had one."

"We do now. They've cordoned off a section under the amphitheater. Lots of room, lots of light."

"Are you sure? That's next to where they've got Guy Blod fashioning a twenty-four-foot Carpathia statue."

"That's where I delivered the evidence. Two plastic bags, one wood crate. Hickman's got a crew of forensic experts scheduled for ten this morning."

David looked at his watch. "It *is* tomorrow already, isn't it? Well, looks like everything happens then, autopsy and all. Guess both sides need sleep first."

"I heard they're trying to start the viewing

at dawn Sunday," Annie said. "That's to-morrow!"

"Bedtime, kids," David said.

Rayford felt grimy and groggy. Despite his fear and the knowledge that his life as a fugitive had escalated a thousand times over, he was buoyed by his eagerness to pray and to get back into the Bible. Maybe it was naïve to think he could elude the GC for long. His recklessness had proba-bly cost him his hope for surviving until the Glorious Appearing. Even forgiven sin, he had learned, has its consequences. He just hoped he hadn't jeopardized the entire Tribulation Force, or worse, saints world-wide.

As he sat praying in the dust fifty yards off the road, the night air dried the sweat on his head and neck and chilled him. In his fatigue and misery he still felt closer to God than he had for months.

His phone chirped, and Rayford hoped against hope it would be someone from the Trib Force, ideally Chloe or Buck. It was Laslos. "Are you in place?"

"Affirmative."

"And you are . . . ?"

"Marvin Berry," Rayford said.

"Check," Laslos said. "We were at a spot about two kilometers back where we could see the entire stretch of road before us. There appears to be no other traffic. You should hear us inside thirty seconds and see our lights soon. Start moving toward the road as soon as you hear us. We will open the back door as we stop, and as soon as you are in and it is shut, we will turn around quickly and head north again."

"Gotcha."

"Repeat?"

"Um, OK!"

Eager to be in the presence of a friend and fellow believer, Rayford was almost giddy under the circumstances. He slapped his phone shut, then opened it again to try one more time to reach anyone long distance. When it was obvious he still could not, he rang off and realized he heard a vehicle. He began jogging toward the road, but something was wrong. Unless he was turned around, it sounded as if the car was coming from the south. Should he dial Laslos back and see if he had misunderstood? But how could he have? Ptolemaïs was north. The church had to be north. Surely

Laslos had said he would be heading south.

The engine sounded much bigger than a small car's. Rayford skidded to a stop in the loose dirt, realizing he had nowhere to hide if a vehicle came upon him from the south. And it was becoming obvious that one was. It was loud and it was big and it was coming fast, but he saw lights only on the northern horizon. That had to be Laslos.

The bigger vehicle from the south would reach him first. Regardless who it was, they would likely stop to check out a walking stranger. Rayford spun, frantically looking for somewhere to hide. His shirt was light colored and might be detectable in the darkness. As the sound rushed toward him, Rayford dove face first to the ground, pulling his dark bag atop his back as he lay there. With his free hand he popped open his phone to warn Laslos to abort and keep going, but when he hit Redial, he got the long distance attempt again and realized he didn't even have Laslos's cell number.

He prayed Laslos would see the oncoming vehicle in time to keep from slowing and pulling off the road.

Rayford's phone rang.

"Yeah!"

"What is coming from the south with no lights?"

"I don't know, Laslos! I'm on the ground! Keep going, just in case!"

The vehicle flew past, and Rayford felt the rush of wind. He tried to get a look at the car but could determine only that it was Jeep-like. "That could have been GC!" he said into the phone.

"It was," Laslos said. "Stay right where you are! It doesn't appear they saw you. They will be able to see us behind them for miles, so don't move. We will come back when we feel it is safe."

"I'd feel safer back in the foliage," Rayford said.

"Better wait. They might be able to see movement. We will see if other GC vehicles are coming."

"Why are they speeding around without lights?"

"We have no idea," Laslos said.

*   *   *

Buck couldn't remember the name of the place, but it was one spot he and Chaim had been to together where no one would expect to see either of them. It took an hour to find an empty cab, and he was informed that any ride, regardless of distance, would cost one hundred Nicks.

Buck described the place to the driver and told him the general area. The man nodded slowly, as if it was coming to him. "I think I know place, or some like it. All work same when you want get, how do the Westerners say, medicated."

"That's what I want," Buck said. "But I have to find the right place."

"We try," the driver said. "Many closed, but some still open."

They rolled over curbs, around crumbled buildings, through dark traffic lights, and past accident scenes. The cabbie stopped at two bars that seemed to be doing land office business, considering, but Buck recognized neither. "It's about the same size as this one, big neon sign in the window, narrow door. That's all I remember."

"I know place," the man said. "Closed. Want these, or other place?"

"I want the other one. Take me there."

"I know is closed. Closed weeks." He held up both hands as if Buck didn't understand. "Nobody there. Dark. Bye-bye."

"That's where I want to go," Buck said.

"Why you want to go where is closed?"

"I'm meeting someone."

"She won't be at closed place," he said, but he drove off anyway. "See?" he said, slowing at midblock nearby. "Is closed."

Buck paid him and hung around the street until the cab left, the driver shaking his head. He soon realized he was in sheer darkness, trees blotting out the clouds and far enough from the emergency action that no lights were visible. The cab lights had shown that the earthquake had leveled several buildings on the street. It was clear now that the power was out in the area.

Would Chaim have come here? *Could* he have? They had come here looking for Jacov the night he had become a believer, Chaim convinced he would be at his favorite bar, drunk as usual. They had found him there all right, and most assumed he *was* drunk. He was on a tabletop, preaching to his old friends and drinking buddies.

Buck was fast losing faith. If Chaim was

alive, if he had been able to find someone
to cart him around, how long would he
have stayed on a deserted, dark, destroyed street? And was there really any
hope that they might both have thought of
this obscure establishment?

Buck pulled the flashlight from his pocket
and looked around before it occurred to
him that Chaim would not likely be in sight,
at least until he was certain that it was
Buck with the light. And how would Chaim
know that? Buck stood in front of the
closed bar and shined the light on his own
face. Almost immediately he heard a rustle
in the branch of a tree across the street
and the clearing of a throat.

He quickly aimed the beam at the tree,
prepared to retreat. Incongruously hanging
out from under one of the leafy branches
was a pajama leg, completed by a stock-
inged and slippered foot. Buck kept the
faint beam on the bewildering scene, but
as he moved slowly across the street, the
foot lifted out of sight. The lower branch
bent with the weight of the tree dweller,
and suddenly down he came, agile as a
cat. Standing there before Buck in slippers,

socks, pajamas, and robe was a most robust Chaim Rosenzweig.

"Cameron, Cameron," he said, his voice strong and clear. "This is almost enough to make a believer out of me. I knew you'd come."

Another unlit GC vehicle raced past while Rayford lay in the dirt. All he could think of was the Prodigal Son, realizing what he had left and eager to get back to his father.

When the predawn grew quiet again, Rayford forsook caution and dashed for the underbrush. He was filthy and tried to brush himself off. Laslos and his pastor had to have seen the other GC vehicle and were playing it safe. Forty minutes later—which seemed like forever to Rayford—a small white four-door slid to a stop in the gravel. Rayford hesitated. Why had they not called? He looked at his phone. He had shut it off, and apparently the battery was too low to power the wake-up feature.

The back door opened. Laslos called, "Mr. Berry!" and Rayford ran toward the car. As soon as the door was shut, Laslos spun a U-turn and headed south. "I don't know where the GC is going, but I'll go the other way for now. Demetrius has a friend in the country nearby."

"A brother?"

"Of course."

"Demetrius?" Rayford said, extending his hand to the passenger. "Rayford Steele. Call me Ray."

The younger man had a fierce grip and pulled Rayford until he could reach to embrace him. "Demetrius Demeter," he said. "Call me Demetrius or brother."

Tsion was moved and took comfort in the verse that reminded him that during this period of cosmic history, God would pour out his Spirit and that "your sons and your daughters shall prophesy, your old men shall dream dreams, your young men shall see visions." The question was whether he was an old man or a young man. He decided on the former and attributed what he had felt on the floor to his drowsiness. He had apparently lost consciousness while praying and nearly slipped into a dream. If the dream was from God, he prayed he would return to it. If it was merely some sleep-deprived fancy, Tsion prayed he would have the discernment to know that too.

That the passage had gone on to reference the heavenly wonders and blood, fire, and smoke the world had already experienced also warmed Tsion. He had been an eyewitness when the sun had been turned into darkness and the moon into blood. He read the passage to Chloe and reminded her, "This is 'before the coming of the great and awesome day of the Lord.' I believe that refers to the second half of the Tribulation, the Great Tribulation. Which starts now."

Chloe looked at him expectantly. "Uh-huh, but—"

"Oh, dear one, the best is yet to come. I don't believe it was coincidence that the Lord led me to this passage. Think of your father and our compatriots overseas when you hear this: 'And it shall come to pass that whoever calls on the name of the Lord shall be saved. For in Mount Zion and in Jerusalem there shall be deliverance, as the Lord has said, among the remnant whom the Lord calls.' You know who the remnant is, don't you, Chloe?"

"The Jews?"

"Yes! And in Zion, which is Israel, and Jerusalem, where we know some of our own were, if they call upon the Lord, they will be delivered. Chloe, I don't know how many of us or *if* any of us will survive until the Glorious Appearing. But I am claiming the promise of this passage, because God prompted me to find it, that our beloved will all return safely to us this time."

"In spite of everything?"

"In spite of everything."

"Is there anything in there that says when the phones will start working again?"

Leah Rose had landed in Baltimore and pondered her next moves. Finding Hattie Durham in North America was like pawing through the proverbial haystack for a needle someone else had already found. The GC was on Hattie's trail and clearly hoped she would lead them to the lair of the Judahites.

If Leah could get her phone to work, she would call T at Palwaukee and see if that Super J plane she had heard so much about was still at the airport and ready for use. On the other hand, if she could get through to T, she could have gotten through to the safe house and sent them running. Did she dare fly commercially to Illinois and rent a car under her alias?

She had no other choice. Unable to communicate except locally, her only hope was to beat Hattie to Mount Prospect. Finding the woman and persuading her to mislead the GC was just too much to hope for.

"How close can you get me to Gary, Indiana?" Leah asked at the counter, after waiting nearly a half hour for the one airline clerk.

"Hammond is the best I can do. And that would be very late tonight."

Having misled the young man about her destination, she switched gears. "How about Chicago? O'Hare and Meigs still closed?"

"And Midway," the clerk said. "Kankakee any help?"

"Perfect," she said. "When?"

"If we're lucky, you'll be on the ground by midnight."

"If we're lucky," Leah said, "that'll mean the plane landed and didn't crash."

The man did not smile. And Leah remembered: *We don't do luck.*

David lay in bed with his laptop, knowing he would soon nod off, but perusing again the abandoned buildings and areas in northern Illinois that might provide a new safe house for the stateside Trib Force. The whole of downtown Chicago had been cordoned off, mostly bombed out, and evacuated. It was a ghost town, nothing living within forty miles. David rolled up onto his elbows and studied the list. How had that happened? Hadn't the earliest reports said the attack on Illinois had been everything but nuclear?

He searched archives, finally pinpointing the day when the GC ruled the city and surrounding areas uninhabitable. Dozens had died from what looked and acted like radiation poisoning, and the Centers for Disease Control and Prevention in Atlanta had urged the ruling. Bodies lay decaying in the streets as the living cleared out.

Remote probes were dropped into the region to test radiation levels, but their inconclusive reports were attributed to faulty equipment. Soon no one dared go near the place. Some radical journalists, Buck Williams wanna-bes, averred on the Internet that the abandoning of Chicago was the biggest foul-up in history, that the deadly diseases were not a result of nuclear radiation, and that the place was inhabitable. *What if?* David wondered.

He followed the cybertrails until he was studying the radiation probe results. Hundreds had been attempted. Not one had registered radiation. But once the scare snare was set, the hook had sunk deep. Who would risk being wrong on a matter like that?

I might, David thought. *With a little more research.*

He had just studied the skyline of Chicago and become intrigued by the skyscraper that had been built by the late Thomas Strong, who had made his fortune in insurance. The place was a mere five years old, a magnificent eighty-story tower that had housed Strong's entire international headquarters. Pictures of the aftermath of the bombing showed the top twenty-six stories of the structure twisting grotesquely away from the rest of the building. The story-high red letters

STRONG had slid on an angle and were still visible during the daytime, making the place look like a stubborn tree trunk that refused to cave in to the storms that leveled most of the rest of the city.

David was about to hack into the blueprints and other records that might show if any of the rest of the structure had been left with any integrity when his laptop beeped, announcing a news bulletin from Global Community headquarters.

His eyes were dancing as it was, so he bookmarked where he had been and determined to go to sleep after checking the bulletin. It read:

"A spokesman for Global Community Supreme Commander Leon Fortunato in New Babylon has just announced that satellite communications have been restored. He asks that citizens employ restraint so as not to overload the system and to limit themselves to only emergency calls for the next twelve hours.

"The spokesman also has announced the decision, reportedly made by Fortunato alone, to rename the United Holy Land States. The new name of the region shall be the United Carpathian States, in honor of the slain leader. Fortunato has not announced a successor to his own role as potentate of the region, but such a move is expected under the likelihood that the Supreme Commander be drafted into service as the new Global Community potentate."

David wondered why he had been asked to interfere with telephone capability and someone else had been asked to reverse it.

SIX

Rayford fought to stay awake in the warm backseat of Laslos's small car. Pastor Demetrius Demeter pointed the way to the rustic cabin in the woods, some twenty kilometers south of Kozani. Laslos avoided any talk of Rayford's guilt or innocence but took it upon himself to cheerfully bring Rayford up to date on the growth of the underground church in northern Greece.

Rayford apologized when a snore woke him.

"Don't give it another thought, brother," Laslos told him. "You need your rest, regardless of what you decide."

Suddenly the car was off the highway and onto an unpaved road. "You can imagine what a great getaway is this cottage," Demetrius said. "The day will come when we, or it, will be found out, and it will be lost to us."

Rayford had gotten only a brief glimpse of the young man when the car door was open. Thin and willowy, it appeared he might be as tall as Rayford. He would have guessed Pastor Demeter at about thirty, with a thick shock of dark hair, deep olive skin, and shining black eyes. He was articulate in English with a heavy Greek accent.

The cottage was so remote that one either came there on purpose or found it while hopelessly lost. Laslos parked in the back where they also entered, using a key Demetrius pulled from under a board near the door. He grabbed Rayford's bag from the car, over his protests. "There's nothing I need from there until I get back home, thanks," Rayford said.

"You must spend at least one night here, sir," Demetrius said.

"Oh, imposs—"

"You look so tired! And you have to be!"

"But I must get back. The stateside people need the plane, and I need them."

Laslos and Demetrius wore heavy sweaters under thick jackets, but Rayford didn't warm up until Laslos had a fire roaring. Laslos then busied himself in the kitchen, from which Rayford soon smelled strong tea and looked forward to it as he would have a desert spring.

Meanwhile, in a small, woodsy room illuminated only by the fire, Rayford sat in a deep, ancient chair that seemed to envelop him. The young pastor sat across from him, half his face in the dancing light, the other half disappearing into the darkness.

"We were praying for you, Mr. Steele, at the very moment you called Lukas's wife. We thought you might need asylum. Forgive my impudence, sir, as you are clearly my elder—"

"Is it that obvious?"

Demetrius seemed to allow himself only the briefest polite smile. "I would love to have you tell me all about Tsion Ben-Judah, but we don't have time for socializing. You may stay here as long as you wish, but I also want to offer you my services."

"Your services?" Rayford was taken aback, but he couldn't shake the feeling that he and Demetrius had immediately connected.

"At the risk of sounding forward or self-possessed," Demetrius said, intertwining his fingers in his lap, "God has blessed and gifted me. My superiors tell me this is not unusual for those of us who are likely part of the 144,000. I have loved the Scriptures since long before I was aware that Jesus fit all the prophecies of the Coming One. It seemed all my energies were invested in learning the things of God. I had been merely bemused by the idea that the Gentiles, specifically Christians, thought they had a corner on our theology. Then the Rapture occurred, and I was not only forced to study Jesus in a different light, but I was also irresistibly drawn to him."

Pastor Demeter shifted in his chair and turned to gaze at the fire. The fatigue that had racked Rayford, which he now realized would force him to at least nap before trying to return to the States, seemed a nuisance he would deal with later. Demetrius seemed so earnest, so genuine, that Rayford had to hear him out. Laslos came in

with steaming mugs of tea, then returned
to the kitchen to sit with his, though both
men invited him to stay. It was as if he
knew Rayford needed this time alone with
the man of God.

"My primary gift is evangelism," Demetrius said. "I say that without ego, for when
I use the word *gift,* I mean just that. My gift
before becoming a believer was probably
sarcasm or condescension or pride in intellect. I realize now, of course, that the intellect was also a gift, a gift I did not know
how to exercise to its fullest until I had a
reason."

Rayford was grateful he could just sit
and listen for a while, but he was also
amazed he was able to stay awake. The
fire, the chair, the situation, the hour, the
week he had had all conspired to leave
him in a ball of unconsciousness. But unlike in the car, he was not even aware of
the temptation to nod off.

"What we who have been called find fascinating," Demetrius continued, "is that
God has seemed to streamline everything
now. I'm sure you've found this in your
own life. For me the sense of adventure in
learning of God was magnified so that my

every waking moment was happily spent studying his Word. And when I was then thrust into a place of service, giftings that might have taken decades to develop before were now bestowed as if overnight. I had had my nose in the Scriptures and commentaries for so long, there was no way I could have honed the skills the Lord seemed to pour out upon me. And I have found this true of my colleagues as well. None of us dare take an iota of credit, because these are clearly gifts from God. We can do nothing less than gleefully exercise them."

"Such as?" Rayford said.

"Primarily evangelism, as I said. It seems most everyone we talk with personally is persuaded that Jesus is the Christ. And under our preaching, thousands have come to faith. I trust you understand I say this solely to give glory to Jehovah God."

Rayford quickly waved him off. "Of course."

"We have also been given unusual teaching and pastoring skills. It is as if God has given us the Midas touch, and not just us Greeks."

Rayford was lost in thought and nearly

missed the humor. He just wanted to hear more.

"But most fascinating to me, Mr. Steele, is a helpful, useful gift I would not have thought to ask for, let alone imagine was either necessary or available. It is discernment, not to be confused with a gift of knowledge—something I have witnessed in some colleagues but do not have myself. Frankly, I am not envious. The specific things God tells them about the people under their charge would weigh on me and wear me down. But discernment . . . now, that has proven most helpful to me and to those I counsel."

"I'm not sure I follow."

Demetrius leaned forward and set his mug on the floor. He rested elbows on knees and stared into Rayford's face. "I don't want to alarm you or make you think this is some kind of a parlor trick. I am not guessing, and I am not claiming that any of this is a skill I have honed or mastered. God has merely given me the ability to discern the needs of people and the extent of their sincerity in facing up to them."

Rayford felt as if the man could look right through him, and he was tempted to ask questions no one could answer unless God told them. But this was no game.

"I can tell you, without fear of contradiction, that you are a man who at this very moment is broken before God. Despite the news, I have no idea whether you shot Nicolae Carpathia or tried to. I don't know if you were there or had the weapon in question or if the Global Community is framing you because they know your allegiances. But I discern your brokenness, and it is because you have sinned."

Rayford nodded, deeply moved, unable to speak.

"We are all sinners, of course, battling our old natures every day. But yours was a sin of pride and selfishness. It was not a sin of omission but of willful commission. It was not a onetime occurrence but a pattern of behavior, of rebellion. It was an attitude that resulted in actions you regret, actions you acknowledge as sin, practices you have confessed to God and have repented of."

Rayford's jaw was tight, his neck stiff. He could not even nod.

"I am not here to chastise you or to test you to see if what I discern is correct, because in these last days God has poured out his gifts and eliminated the need for patience with us frail humans. In essence, he has forsaken requiring desert experiences for us and simply works through us to do his will.

"I sense a need to tell you that your deep feelings of having returned to him are accurate. He would have you not wallow in regret but rejoice in his forgiveness. He wants you to know and believe beyond doubt that your sins and iniquities he will remember no more. He has separated you from the guilt of your sins as far as the east is from the west. Go and sin no more. Go and do his bidding in the short season left to you."

As if knowing what was coming, Demetrius reached for Rayford's cup, allowing Rayford to leave the comfort of his chair and kneel on the wood floor. Great sobs burst from him, and he sensed he was in the presence of God, as he had been in the plane when it seemed the Lord had finally gotten his attention. But to add this gift of forgiveness, expressed by a chosen agent, was beyond what Rayford could have dreamed for.

Fear melted away. Fatigue was put in abeyance. Unrest about the future, about his role, about what to do—all gone. "Thank you, God" was all he could say, and he said it over and over.

When finally he rose, Rayford turned to embrace a man who an hour before had been a stranger and now seemed a messenger of God. He might never see him again, but he felt a kinship that could only be explained by God.

Lukas still waited in the tiny kitchen as Rayford spilled to Demetrius the whole story of how his anger had blossomed into a murderous rage that took him to the brink of murder and may have even given him a hand in it.

Demetrius nodded and seemed to shift and treat Rayford as a colleague rather than a parishioner. "And what is God telling you to do now?"

"Rest and go," Rayford said, feeling rightly decisive for the first time in months. For once he didn't feel the need to talk himself into decisions and then continue to sell himself on them, carefully avoiding seeking God's will. "I need to sleep until dawn and then get back in the game. As soon as I can get through by phone, I need to be sure Buck and Leah are safe and go get them, if necessary."

Laslos joined them and said, "Give me that information. I will stand watch until dawn, and I can try the phones every half hour while you are sleeping."

Demetrius interrupted Rayford's thanks by pointing him to a thick fabric couch and a scratchy blanket. "It is all we have to offer," he said. "Kick your shoes off and get out of that shirt."

When Rayford sat on the couch in only undershirt and trousers, Demetrius motioned that he should lie down. The pastor covered him with the blanket and prayed, "Father, we need a physical miracle. Give this man a double portion of rest for the hours available, and may this meager bed be transformed into a healing agent."

Without so much as a pillow, Rayford felt himself drifting from consciousness. He was warm, the couch was soft but supportive, the stiff blanket like a downy comforter. As his breathing became rhythmic and deep, his last conscious thought was different from what it had been for so long. Rather than the dread fear that came with life as an international fugitive, he rested in the knowledge that he was a child of the King, a saved, forgiven, precious, beloved son safe in the hollow of his Father's hand.

Buck and Chaim sat in an abandoned, earthquake-ravaged dwelling in the middle of a formerly happening Israeli neighborhood where crowded bars and nightclubs once rocked till dawn. With no power or water or even shelter safe enough for vagrants, the area now hosted only an enterprising journalist and a national hero.

"Please douse that light, Cameron," Chaim said.

"Who will see us?"

"No one, but it's irritating. I've had a long day."

"I imagine you have," Buck said. "But I want to see this walking, breathing miracle. You look healthier than I've ever seen you."

They sat on a crumbling concrete wall with remnants of a shattered beam protruding from it. Buck didn't know how the old man felt, but he himself had to keep moving for a modicum of comfort.

"I am the healthiest I have been in years," Chaim exulted, his accent thick as ever. "I have been working out every day."

"While your house staff feared you were near death."

"If they only knew what I was doing in my workshop before dawn."

"I think I know, Chaim."

"Thinking and knowing are different things. Had you looked deep into the closet, you would have seen the ancient stationary bicycle and the dumbbells that put me in the fighting trim I am in today. I laboriously moved my chair through the house so they could hear the whine of it if they happened to be up that early. Then I locked myself in there for at least ninety minutes. Jumping jacks and push-ups to warm up, the dumbbells for toning, the bike for a hard workout. Then it was back inside the blanket, into the chair, and back to my quarters for a shower. They thought I was remarkably self-reliant for an old man suffering from a debilitating stroke."

Buck was not amused when Chaim stiffened his arm, turned one side of his mouth down, and faked impaired speech with guttural rasping.

"I fooled even you, did I not?"

"Even me," Buck said, looking away.

"Are you offended?"

"Of course I am. Why would you feel the need to do that to your staff and to me?"

"Oh, Cameron, I could not involve you in my scheme."

"I'm involved, Chaim. I saw what killed Carpathia."

"Oh, you did, did you? Well, I didn't. All that commotion, that trauma. I couldn't move. I heard the gunshot, saw the man fall, the lectern shatter, the backdrop sail away. I froze with fear, unable to propel my chair. My back was to the disturbance, and no one was coming to my aid. I shall have to chastise Jacov for his failure to do his duty. I was counting on him to come to me. My other clothes were in the back of the van, and I had a reservation at a small inn under an alias. We can still use it if you can get me there."

"In your pajamas?"

"I have a blanket in the tree. I wrapped it around myself, even my head, as I ran to the taxis. I had not expected to have to do that, Cameron, but I was prepared for all exigencies."

"Not all."

"What are you saying?"

"I'll try to get you to your hotel, Chaim, and I may even have to hide out there with you myself for a while. But I have bad news that I will tell you only when we are there. And only after you tell me everything about what happened on the platform."

Chaim stood and reached for the flash-light, using it to find his way to a man-size hole in the wall. He leaned against the opening and switched off the light.

"I will never tell anyone what happened," he said. "I am in this alone."

"I didn't see it happen, Chaim, but I saw the wound and what caused it. You know I couldn't have been the only one."

Chaim sighed wearily. "The eye is not trustworthy, my young friend. You don't know what you saw. You can't tell me how far away you were or how what you saw fits into the whole picture. The gunshot was a surprise to me. That your comrade was even there was also a shock, and him as a suspect now!"

"I find none of this amusing, Chaim, and soon enough you won't either."

Buck heard the old man settle to the

ground. "I did not expect that much chaos. I hoped, of course. That was my only chance of getting away from there with everyone else. When Jacov did not arrive— because of the panic caused by the gunshot, I assume—I leaned on that control stick and headed for the back of the platform, clutching my blanket like a cape. I rolled out of the chair at the last instant, and it went flying. I wish it had landed on one of the regional potentates, who were by then limping away. I tossed my blanket over the side, then rolled onto my belly and threw my feet over, locking them around the support beam. I shinnied down that structure like a youngster, Cameron, and I won't even try to hide my pride. I have scrapes on my inner thighs that may take some time to heal, but it was worth it."

"Was it?"

"It was, Cameron. It was. Fooling so many, including my own staff. Doctors, nurses, aides. Well, actually, I didn't fool every aide. As Jacov and a young nurse's aide were lifting me into the van after my last visit to the hospital, she stalled, locking my wheels and straightening my blanket while Jacov went to get behind the wheel. Just before she closed the door, she leaned close and whispered, 'I don't know who you are or what your game is, old man. But you might want to remember which side was affected when you came in here.' "

Chaim chuckled, which Buck found astounding under the circumstances. "I just hope she was telling the truth, Cameron, that she didn't know who I was. Celebrity is my curse, but some of the younger ones, they don't pay so much attention. I looked desperately at her as she shut the door, hoping she would wonder if it were she who had forgotten. I stayed in character, but if my face flushed it was from embarrassment and not frustration over my lack of ability to speak or walk. She was right! I had stiffened my right arm and curled my right hand under! What an old fool!"

"You took the words right out of my mouth, Chaim. Get your blanket, and let's find a cab."

Without a word, Chaim switched on the flashlight, hurried to the tree, tossed the light back to Buck, and leaped, grabbing the low branch and pulling himself up far enough to grab the blanket. He wrapped it around his head and over his shoulder, then affected a limp and leaned on Buck, chuckling again.

Buck moved away from him. "Don't start that until you need to," Buck said.

Leah Rose awoke with a start and looked out the window. Cities were rarely illuminated in the night anymore, so she had no idea where she was. She tried looking at her watch, but couldn't focus. Something had awakened her, and suddenly she heard it again. Her phone. Could it be?

The one lone flight attendant and the rest of the dozen or so passengers seemed asleep. Leah dug in her bag for the phone and pressed the caller ID button. She didn't recognize the number, but her comrades had assured her the phone was secure. She would not jeopardize them if she answered, even if her number had fallen into the wrong hands.

Leah opened the phone and tucked her head behind the back of the seat in front of her. She spoke softly but directly. "This is Donna Clendenon."

A brief silence alarmed her. She heard a male inhale. "I'm sorry," he began with a Greek accent. "I am calling on behalf of, ah, Mr. Marvin Berry?"

"Yes! Is this Mr. Miklos?"

"Yes!"

"And are you calling from Greece?"

"I am. And Mr. Steele is here. And what is it that those filled with demons cannot say?"

Leah smiled in spite of herself. "Jesus is the Christ, the Messiah, and he will return in the flesh."

"Amen! Rayford is sleeping but needs to know you are safe and how to find y—"

"I'm sorry, Mr. Miklos, but if the phones are working, I have an emergency call to make. Just tell Rayford that I am nearly home so not to worry about me, but that he needs to locate Buck."

Tsion experimented with five-minute cat-naps every few minutes, fearing he would otherwise sleep through the resurrection of the Antichrist. With Chloe and the baby asleep elsewhere in the safe house, the experiment was not working well. He found himself popping awake every fifteen or twenty minutes, desperate to be sure he had missed nothing. There had been no repeat of his dreamlike state while praying for Rayford, and he began to wonder if it had been more related to praying than sleeping. He also began to wonder how long Carpathia was supposed to remain dead. Was it possible he had been wrong all along? Was someone else the Antichrist, yet to be murdered and resurrected?

Tsion couldn't imagine it. Many sincere believers had questioned his teaching that Antichrist would actually die from a wound to the head. Some said the Scriptures indicated that it would be merely a wound that made him appear dead. He tried to assure them that his best interpretation of the original Greek led him to believe that the man would actually die and then be indwelt by Satan himself upon coming back to life.

Given that, he hoped he had been right about Carpathia. There would be no doubt of the death and resurrection if the body had begun to decay, was autopsied, embalmed, and prepared to lie in state. If Carpathia were dead even close to twenty-four hours, few could charge him with faking his demise. Too many eyewitnesses had seen the man expire, and though the cause of death had not yet been announced, that was forthcoming. The world, including Tsion, had to believe the gunshot provided the kill.

The TV carried yet another airing of an earlier pronouncement of grief and promised vengeance from Leon Fortunato. Tsion found himself nodding and dozing until the phone woke him.

"Leah! It's so good to hear your voice. We have been unable to reach—"

She interrupted and filled him in on Hattie and the danger posed to the safe house. Tsion stood and began pacing as he listened. "We have nowhere else to go, Leah," he said. "But at the very least we had better get underground."

They agreed that she would call if she got near the safe house and was sure no one was casing the place. Otherwise, Leah would keep her distance and try to find Hattie. How, she said, she had no idea.

Despite his weariness, Tsion was suddenly energized. He was responsible for Chloe and Kenny, and though the macho stuff was usually left to Rayford or Buck, he had to act. He trotted up the stairs and grabbed a few clothes from his closet and a stack of books. He returned to the first floor and piled these near the old chest freezer that stood next to the refrigerator.

Tsion added his laptop and the TV to the pile, then outed every light in the place except the single bulb hanging from the ceiling in the hall bath. He carefully pushed open the door to Buck and Chloe's bedroom, knocking softly. He did not hear Chloe stir, and he could not see her in the darkness. He knocked again and whispered her name.

When he heard a quick motion from the crib on the far wall, Tsion fell silent, holding his breath. He had hoped not to wake the baby. Clearly, Kenny was pulling himself up to stand. The crib rocked, and Tsion imagined the little guy with his hands on the railing, rocking, making the crib squeak. "Mowning! Ga'mowning, Mama!"

"It's not morning, Kenny," he whispered.

"Unca Zone!" Kenny squealed, rocking vigorously.

And with that, Chloe awoke with a start.

"It's just me, dear," Tsion said quickly.

Twenty minutes later the three of them

were relocated underground, having lifted aside the rack of smelly, spoiled food in the freezer that led to the stairs. Kenny, beaming from his playpen, had loved seeing his mother and Tsion reappear downstairs every few minutes with more stuff. He was not so happy when they muscled his crib down there and he had to make the switch.

Fortunately the underground was large enough that Tsion could set up the TV in a spot where the light and sound did not reach Chloe and Kenny's sleeping quarters. He monitored the doings from New Babylon, but every time he had need to venture into the other part of the shelter, he heard Chloe groggily trying to talk Kenny into going back to sleep.

He poked his head through the curtain. "How about he watches TV with me until he falls asleep again, hmm?"

"Oh, Tsion, that would be wonderful."

"Unca Zone!"

"TV?" Tsion said as he lifted the boy from the crib.

Kenny kicked and laughed. "TV, Unca Zone! Video!"

"We'll watch my show," Tsion whispered as he carried him to his chair.

"You show!" Kenny said, holding Tsion's face in his hands. Tsion was transported to when his teenagers had been toddlers and sat in his lap as he read or watched television. Kenny was quickly bored with the repetitious news, but he quit asking for a video and concentrated on tracing the contours of Tsion's ears, squeezing his nose, and rubbing his palm back and forth on Tsion's stubble. Eventually he began to blink slowly, tucked a thumb in his mouth, and turned to settle into the crook of Tsion's elbow. When his head lolled over, Tsion gently carried him back to bed.

As he tucked a blanket around Kenny he heard Chloe turn and whisper, "Thank you, Unca Zone."

"Thank you," he said.

"Why didn't you just go straight to the hotel?" Buck asked Chaim as he tried to flag down a cab.

"I was lucky enough the cabbie didn't recognize me. How was I going to fool a desk clerk? I was counting on Jacov to get me in. Now I'm counting on you. Anyway, how would we have found each other?"

"How *did* we find each other?" Buck said.

"I couldn't think of any other place you might look, except at my home, and I didn't expect you to risk that. I don't think anybody is there anyway. I haven't been able to raise anybody."

Buck was struck by that unfortunate choice of words.

"They're there, Chaim."

"You *did* go there? Why don't they answer? Did Jacov make it back? I expected he would call me."

Buck spotted a cab sitting a couple of blocks off a busy thoroughfare. Grateful he didn't have to answer Chaim directly yet, he said, "Wait here, and keep that blanket over your face."

"You workin'?" he asked the cabbie.

"Hundred and fifty Nicks, only in the city."

"A hundred, and my father is contagious."

"No contagious."

"OK, a hundred and fifty. We're only going to the Night Visitors. You know it?"

"I know. You keep old man in back, and don't breathe on me."

Buck signaled to Chaim, who shuffled over, hidden in the blanket. "Don't try to talk, Father," he said, helping him into the backseat. "And don't cough on this nice young man."

As if on cue, Chaim covered his mouth with the blanket and both hands and produced a juicy, wheezing cough that made the driver look quickly into the rearview mirror.

The Night Visitors was dark, not even an outside light on. "Are they closed?" Buck said.

"Only for now," the driver said. "Probably open again at dawn. One-fifty. I gotta go."

"Wait until I see if I can rouse anybody," Buck said, getting out.

"Don't leave him in here! I gotta go. Money now!"

"You'll get your money when we get a room."

The driver slammed the car into Park and turned it off, folding his arms across his chest.

SEVEN

Buck's phone rang as he was trying to peer through the front window of the Night Visitors. "Laslos!" he said, stepping around the corner of the building and into the shadows. The cabbie honked, and Buck signaled him to wait a minute.

"Get this man out of my cab!"

"Five minutes!" Buck said.

"Fifty more Nicks!"

"He's there with you, Lukas?" Buck said. "How am I supposed to—does he know he's wanted here—he does? . . . Is Leah with him? . . . Oh, that's good. We need a way out of here, and there's no way he

can risk coming back. Never mind. I'll handle that. Listen, does he have to see anyone before he takes off? . . . You can't be
sure airport personnel won't be on alert.
His face is on international TV every few
minutes. Do you know anyone who can
give him a new look? . . . He'll need new
papers too. Thanks, Laslos! I have to call
my wife."

Buck dialed Chloe, but her phone rang
and rang.

When he returned to the cab, the driver
was out and screaming. "Now! Go! No
more this man in my car!"

Buck paid him and helped Chaim out,
pushing him into an alley while he banged
on the windows and door and tried to
rouse the manager.

Tsion heard something upstairs and ran to
the utility box to shut down the power. If
the GC searched the place, it would be
clear someone had been living there recently, as food in the refrigerator would still
be fresh and lots of personal belongings
remained. But if they found power meters
still spinning, they would know someone
was still there somewhere.

Tsion held his breath in the darkness. It was a phone! Had Chloe forgotten to bring hers down? He rushed to the stairs, pushed the plywood away from the bottom of the freezer, pushed up the smelly rack, and lifted himself out. He felt his way to Chloe's room and followed the sound to her phone. Just as he reached it, it stopped ringing. The caller ID showed Buck's code. Tsion hit the callback button, but Buck's phone was busy.

While continuing to bang with one hand, Buck speed-dialed David Hassid with the other. He got only David's machine. When he hung up, his call button was illuminated. His caller ID showed he had received a call from Chloe's phone. He was about to call her back when a light came on in the Night Visitors, followed by slamming, stomping, and cursing.

"We have a reservation!" Buck shouted.

"You'll have a bullet if you don't shut up!" came the voice from inside. "We closed at midnight and we open again at six!"

"You're up now, so give us our room!"

"You lost your room when you didn't

show up! Who are you, Tangvald or Gold-man?"

Buck whispered desperately to Chaim, "Who are we?"

"Do I look like a Tangvald?"

"Goldman, and my father is sick. Let us in!"

"We're full!"

"You're lying! You held two rooms till you went to bed and then gave them both away?"

"Leave me alone!"

"I'll knock until you let us in!"

"I'll shoot you if you knock once more!"

The light went out. Buck put his phone in his pocket and banged on the door with both fists.

"You're a dead man!"

"Just open up and give us a room!"

More swearing, then the light, then the door opened an inch. The man stuck his fingers out. "Five hundred Nicks cash."

"Let me see the key."

The man dangled it at the end of a six-inch block of wood. Buck produced the cash, and the key came flying out. "Around back, third floor. If I didn't need the money, I'd have shot you."

"You're welcome," Buck said.

The room was a hole. A single bed, one straight-back chair, and a toilet and sink. Buck pulled out his phone and sat in the chair, pointing Chaim to the bed. As Buck tried Chloe's phone, Chaim kicked off his slippers and stretched out on the bed, atop the ratty spread and under his own blanket.

"Tsion!" Buck said. "No, don't wake her. . . . Underground? That's probably good for now. Just tell her I'm all right. I need to get hold of T. May need him to get Chaim and me out of here. . . ."

"I'm not going anywhere," Chaim mumbled from the bed. "I'm a dead man."

"Yeah," Buck said to Tsion, "just like you and me. . . . Kenny OK? . . . We'll keep in touch."

Buck couldn't get an answer at Palwaukee Airport or on T's cell phone. He put his phone away and took a deep breath, kicking his bag under the chair. "Chaim, we have to talk," he said. But Chaim was asleep.

Rayford awoke with a start just after dawn, feeling refreshed. He grabbed his bag and padded past a dozing Demetrius to the bathroom, smelling breakfast from the kitchen. While in the tiny bathroom, however, he heard tires on the gravel and pulled the curtain back an inch. A small pickup pulled into view.

Rayford leaned out the door and called to Laslos. "Company," he whispered. "You expecting anyone?"

"It's all right," Laslos said, setting a pan of food on the table and wiping his hands on an apron. "Get a shower and join us for breakfast as soon as you can."

Rayford tried to run hot water in the sink. It was lukewarm. Laslos interrupted with a knock. "Don't shave, Mr. Steele."

"Oh, Laslos, I really need to. I've got several days of growth and—"

"I'll explain later. But don't."

Rayford shrugged and squinted at himself in the mirror. He was due for a haircut, more and more gray appearing at his temples and in the back. His beard was salt-and-pepper, which alarmed him. Not that he cared so much about gray in his mid-forties. It was just that it had seemed to happen almost overnight. Until this morning, he had felt every one of his forty-plus years. Now he felt great.

The shower, a trickle from a rusty pipe, was also lukewarm. It made him hurry, but by the time he scrubbed himself dry with a small, thin towel and dressed, he was ravenous. And curious. He emerged eager to get going, but also intrigued by yet another guest at the table, a pudgy man a few years older than he with slick, curly black hair and wire-rimmed glasses.

Rayford leaned past Laslos and Demetrius and shook the man's hand. The mark of the believer was on his forehead, so Rayford used his own name.

The man looked at Laslos and shyly back at Rayford.

"This is Adon, Mr. Steele," Laslos said. "He speaks no English, but as you can see, he is a brother."

As they ate, Laslos told Rayford about Adon. "He is an artist, a skilled craftsman. And he has brought with him contraband items that could get him locked away for the rest of his life."

Adon followed the conversation with blank eyes, except when Laslos or Demetrius broke in to translate. Then he shyly looked away, nodding.

As Laslos cleared the table, Demetrius helped Adon bring in his equipment, which included a computer, printer, laminator, digital camera, dyes, hair clippers, even a cloth backdrop. Rayford was positioned in a chair under the light and near the window, where the early sun shone in. Adon draped a sheet around him and pinned it behind his neck. He said something to Laslos, who translated for Rayford.

"He wants to know if it is OK to make you bald."

"If you all think it's necessary. If we could get by with very short, I'd appreciate it."

Laslos informed Adon, whose shyness and hesitance apparently did not extend to his barbering. In a few swipes, he left Rayford's hair in clumps on the floor, leaving him with a quarter inch of dark residue such as Rayford had not seen since high school. "Mm-hmm," Rayford said.

Then came the dye that made what was left of the hair on his head look like the lightest of the gray in the long stubble on his chin.

Adon spoke to Laslos, who asked Rayford if he wore glasses.

"Contacts," Rayford said.

"Not anymore," Laslos said, and Adon produced a pair that completed the look.

Adon asked for Rayford's documents, shot a few pictures, and got to work on the computer. While he transformed Rayford's papers with the new photograph, Rayford stole away to the bathroom for a peek. The shorter, grayer hair and the gray stubble added ten years. In the glasses, he hardly recognized himself.

The technology allowed Adon to produce old-looking new documents in less than an hour. Rayford was eager to get going. "What do I owe you?" he said, but neither Laslos nor Demetrius would translate that.

"We'll be sure Adon is taken care of," Laslos said. "Now, Pastor is going to ride back to Ptolemaïs with him, and I will drop you at Kozani. I called ahead to have your fuel tanks topped off."

David sat bleary-eyed before his computer in New Babylon, his phone turned off. He had programmed the autopsy to be recorded on his own hard drive and anything from the evidence room to go onto Mac's computer. Meanwhile he continued to study the Chicago skyscraper he felt had potential as a new safe house. If he was right, it could accommodate hundreds of exiles, if necessary.

The Strong Building was a technical marvel, wholly solar powered. Giant reflectors stored enough energy every day to run the tower's power plant for weeks. So even a several-day stretch without bright sunlight never negatively impacted the building.

It was clear to David that neither the foundation nor at least the first thirty-five or so stories had been compromised by the damage above. The building appeared to have suffered a direct hit, but the impact had knocked the top half of the floors away from the rest of the structure rather than sending them crashing through those below. The question was what had happened to the solar panels and whether there was any way people could live in the unaffected portion of the structure without being detected.

It took David more than two hours of hacking through a morass of classified layers of information before he was able to turn his code-breaking software loose on the gateways that led to the mainframe that controlled the Strong Building. Reaching that point gave him a thrill he couldn't describe, though he would try to describe it later to Annie.

David was amazed that satellite phone technology got him as far as it did, and he had to wonder how much untapped energy was still operative in the condemned city. The longer everyone else remained convinced the place was radioactively contaminated, the better for him and the Tribulation Force. At every cybergateway along the path, he planted warnings of high radioactive levels. And while he was at it, he launched a robotic search engine that found all the original probe readouts and changed more than half of them to positive results. Civilian and GC planes were automatically rerouted so they couldn't fly over Chicago, even at more than thirty thousand feet.

David had to feather his way through the Strong Building mainframe by trial and error, seeing if he could remotely control the heating and cooling system, the lights, phones, sanitation system, elevators, and security cameras. The best video game in history would not have been more addictive.

The state-of-the-art monitoring system clearly reflected how much of the building was malfunctioning. More than half the elevators were off-line due to incomplete circuits. David clicked on More Information and found "Undetermined error has broken circuits between floors 40 and 80." He checked two dozen elevators that serviced the first thirty-nine floors and found that most appeared in running order.

By the time he had played with the system for another fortyfive minutes, David had determined which security cameras worked, how to turn on lights on various floors, then the cameras, to show him whether the elevators would run, open, and shut. From nine time zones away, he was running what was left of a skyscraper in a city that had been abandoned for months.

Recording his keystrokes in a secure file, David fired up the camera on the highest floor he could find, the west end of the thirty-ninth. It showed water on the floor, but the mainframe indicated that it was being successfully redirected to keep it from flooding the floors below. He maneuvered the camera to show the ceiling and blinked. There was no ceiling, only a three-sided shell of the building that rose maybe another ten stories and revealed the inky sky, moon shining, stars twinkling.

So the Strong Building had been designed to withstand the worst nature could offer and had largely survived even what man threw at it. David stayed with his search until he found cameras that gave him a good view of what now served as the roof of the tower. By the time he had saved most of the information, he had an idea what the place looked like. In essence, it was a modular tower that appeared mortally wounded but had a lot to offer. Unusual in a modern skyscraper, the blueprints showed an inner core of offices hidden from outside view, surrounding the elevators on every floor. Here was unlimited floor space, water, plumbing, power, light—all undetectable by anyone who dared venture into an area that had been officially condemned and rendered off limits anyway.

The open top appeared large enough to accommodate a helicopter, but David couldn't determine remotely whether the new roof by proxy, which at first appeared to be the ceiling of the thirty-ninth floor, would support significant weight. He found parking underneath the tower, though debris from the top floors blocked two of the main garage entrances. It was a long shot, but David believed that if he could get the stateside Trib Force to the place, they could find ways in and out of that underground carport.

And that gave him another idea. The last rain of bombs to hit Chicago had come with little warning. Employees and residents of tall buildings fled to the streets, but no one would have been allowed below ground with buildings falling. Underground garages would have been automatically sealed off with the city so gridlocked. How many vehicles might still be in that garage? David clicked away until he found the underground security cameras and the emergency lighting system. Once he had the lights on in the lowest level, he panned one of the security cameras until the vehicles came into view. Six levels below the street, he found more than a dozen cars. The problem, of course, was that drivers would have had the keys.

David kept trying cameras at different levels, looking for valet parking. He struck pay dirt near the elevators on the first level below the street. Nearly fifty late-model and mostly expensive cars, at least one of them a Hummer and several others sport-utility vehicles, were parked in the vicinity of a glassed-in shack clearly labeled Valet Parking. David manipulated the closest camera until he could make out a wall next to the cash register, replete with sets of keys. It was as if this place was made for the Trib Force, and he couldn't wait to send someone in to investigate. David wondered how soon he and Annie might be living there.

A call startled him. It was the director of the Global Community Academy of Television Arts and Sciences, an Indonesian named Bakar. "I need your help," the man said.

What else was new?

"Fire away," David said, shutting down his computer with everything saved and hidden.

"Moon is all over me about why we didn't bring back the videodiscs from the Gala. I thought we had. Anyway, we have them secured now, and I had arranged to have them flown here commercially. Walter tells me now that he'll have my job if those discs are out of GC hands for one second."

"Who's got 'em, Bakar?"

"One of our guys."

"Can't he just bring them?"

"Yeah, but he'd have to fly commercially."

"So? He's still not letting the discs out of his sight."

"Commercial flights are full coming here, and Moon doesn't want to wait."

"So you want us to send a plane for one guy?"

"Exactly."

"Do you know the cost of that?"

"That's why I'm begging."

"How did I get so popular all of a sudden?"

"What?"

"Nothing. Be at the hangar by ten this morning."

"Me?"

"Who else?"

"I don't want to go, Director. I want our guy picked up."

"I'm not going to have our sleep-deprived first officer fly a multimillion-dollar, er, Nick, fighter to Israel *and* have to find your guy, Bakar. You're going to ride along so Mr. Smith doesn't have to leave the cockpit. And I won't charge you the thousands for fuel."

"I appreciate it, Director. But couldn't I just have my guy be at a certain place and—"

"Earth to Bakar! This is a seller's, or I should say giver's, market, sir. You make Smith go alone and I'll charge you depreciation on the jet, fuel, *and* his time. And his time is not cheap."

"I'll be there."

"I thought you would."

David called Abdullah.

"I was up anyway," Abdullah said. "I was hoping something would take me away from here today."

"You know how to work a disc-copying machine?"

"I don't know, boss. Is it more complicated than a fighter-bomber? Of course."

"I'm sending one with you. When Bakar finds his guy, you take the discs into the cockpit and tell them regulations say you have to personally log all cargo. Copy them, tag them as logged, and give them back to the TV boys."

"And bring you the copies."

"We're on the same page, Smitty."

David was next to giddy about the Trib Force all being in touch with each other via phone. He would feel better when he knew Buck was out of Israel and that Rayford was also on his way home, but David was unaware he had a message to call Buck.

Rayford shook Laslos's hand with both of his, got his promise to again personally thank Pastor Demeter and Adon, then loped into the airport and to the hangar. His head felt cool with so little insulation, but he didn't want to keep running his hand over it for fear of making it obvious that it was new to him.

A tower official met him at the Gulfstream. "You must be Mr. Berry."

"Yes, sir."

"Here's your fuel bill. Your papers?"

Rayford dug them out and paid his bill in cash.

"Lot of currency to have on your person, Mr. Berry," the man said, shuffling through Rayford's documents.

"A risk I'm willing to take to keep from going bankrupt again."

"Credit cards do you in, did they, sir?"

"Hate 'em."

"Wow, this picture looks like it was taken today."

Rayford froze, then forced himself to breathe. "Yeah?"

"Yes, look here. Karl! Come look at this!"

A mechanic in coveralls wandered over, looking peeved that he had been interrupted.

The official held Rayford's ID photo next to Rayford's face. "Look at this. He got this, let me see here, eight, nine months ago, but his hair's the same length and, if I'm not mistaken, he's wearing the same shirt."

"Sure enough," the mechanic said, leaving as quickly as he had come. Rayford watched to make sure he wasn't going to call someone, but he just moseyed back to the engine he'd been working on.

"Yes, that's something," the man said. "Did you notice that?"

"Nope," Rayford said. "Lemme see that. Well, I'll be dogged. I *had* just got a haircut when this was taken, but 'course the hair doesn't grow much anymore, anyway. And that probably *is* the same shirt. I don't have that many."

"Your own plane and not that many shirts? There's priorities for you."

"My own plane, I wish. I just drive 'em for the company."

"And what company's that, sir?" The man handed back his documents.

"Palwaukee Global," Rayford said.

"What do you transport?"

"Just the plane today. They had too many this side of the ocean."

"That so? You could pick up some business running from Jerusalem to New Babylon this week, you know."

"I heard. Wish I had the time."

"Safe flight."

"Thank you, sir." And thank you, Lord.

At ten in the morning in New Babylon, David strolled past the makeshift evidence room, pretending to be checking progress on the nearby Carpathia statue. He knew if he appeared to be snooping on the evidence, Intelligence Director Jim Hickman would shoo him. But Hickman also liked to impress, and allowing a colleague an inside look seemed to make him feel special.

David slowed as he walked by, hoping to run into Jim. Not seeing him, he knocked at the door. An armed guard opened it, and David spotted Jim across the room with a technician on his knees in the middle of a fifteen-by-one-hundred-foot drapery. "Don't want to bother anybody," David said. "Just want to make sure Director Hickman and his team have everything they need. I'll call him in his office."

"I'm in here, David!" Hickman called.

"Oh! So you are!"

"Let 'im in, Corporal! Come over here, David. Slip your shoes off. I wanna show you something."

"I don't want to intrude."

"Come on!"

"If you insist. This is fascinating."

"You haven't seen anything yet."

But David had. Three techies in the corner were hunched over the remains of the wood lectern. They had magnifying lamps and large tweezers, similar to what the technician had in the middle of the drape. He wore a helmet with a light on it and hand held his magnifier.

"Look at this, David," Hickman said, motioning to him. "Got your shoes off?"

"I can come right out there where you are?"

"If I say you can, and I do! Now come on, time's awastin'."

David got to within about ten feet of Hickman and the techie when Jim said, "Stop and look down. Whoever was shootin' at this thing had to know what he was doin'. Looks like it went right through the middle. I mean, I never even knew Steele was a shooter, but to get a round, one round, to go through that pulpit dealie and then through the center of this curtain, well . . ."

"What am I looking at here, Jim?" David said, staring at a strange configuration about ten feet in diameter.

Hickman rose and limped over, joining David at the edge of the pattern. "Gettin' old," he said, grunting. "Now look here. The bullet coming from a weapon like that creates a mini tornado. If a real Kansas twister had the same relative strength, it would mix Florida and Maine with California and Washington. This one popped an eight-inch hole through the curtain there— you can see it from here."

"Uh-huh."

"But what you see at your feet is the effect it had on fibers this far from the center."

The force of the spinning disk had ripped the individual threads out of place and yanked them uniformly to create the huge twisted image.

"Now, c'mere and look at this."

Hickman led David to the top of the curtain, where brass eyeholes were set six inches apart along the whole one-hundred-foot edge. "Hooks went through these holes to suspend the whole thing from the iron piping."

"Wow," David said, astounded at the damage. The eight holes on either side of the center had been ripped clean, brass casings and all. The next several dozen were split apart, then more on each side had mangled hooks still attached, all the way to the ends, where the eyeholes were intact but the hooks were missing.

"Just ripped this thing away and sent it flying into the distance."

"Director!" the techie called.

Hickman started toward the middle again, but David hung back until Hickman motioned him to follow.

"Bullet residue," the techie said, holding a tiny shard of lead between slender forceps.

"Bag that up. Ten'll get you twenty we can trace it to the Saber we found."

The technician began dropping pieces into a plastic bag. "I hate to say it, sir, but fragments like this will be almost impossible to positively match with—"

"Come on now, Junior. We've got eyewitnesses who say a guy in a raghead getup took the shot. We found the gun, got a match on the prints, and we know who the guy is. We found his disguise in a trash can a few blocks away. The fragments'll match all right, even if the lab work is inconclusive. This guy's definitely part of the conspiracy."

"Conspiracy?" David said, as they

moved to the corner where the lectern pieces lay.

"We think the gunshot was diversionary," Hickman whispered.

"But this Steele guy is being accused—"

"Is a suspect, sure. But we're not sure the bullet even came close to Carpathia."

"What? But—"

"Carpathia didn't die from a gunshot wound, David. At least not solely."

"What then?"

"Autopsy's going on right now. We ought to know soon. But let me tell you somethin' just between you, me, and the whatever: Fortunato's no dummy."

David could have argued. "Yeah?"

"If it turns out the kill wound came from the platform, wouldn't that be highly embarrassing?"

"If one of his—our own did it, you mean."

" 'xactly. But the public doesn't know that. The only video that's been shown so far only shows the victim hittin' the deck. People think he got shot. Leon sees that we blame this on the disgruntled former employee, and then he has us deal with the insurrection privately. And by dealin' with it, well, you get my drift."

The technicians digging through the remains of the lectern produced several bullet fragments, some big as a fingernail.

"This sure is fascinating stuff, Jim."

"Well," Hickman said, slowly running his hand through his hair, "it helps if you're a trained observer."

"You're nothing if not that."

"Right as rain, Hassid."

EIGHT

Leah sat fitfully at what was left of the tiny airport in Kankakee. When her phone rang and Rayford identified himself, she was speechless. "I have so much to talk to you about," he said, "so much to apologize for."

"I'll look forward to that," she said flatly. In truth she was more eager to get to the safe house and see Tsion than she was to talk to Rayford. "Thanks for leaving me stranded, but I guess I can see why. Did you kill Carpathia?"

"I just got a call from David Hassid, who seems pretty sure I didn't. I wanted to. Planned to. But then I couldn't do it."

"So what about the gun with your prints? You weren't the shooter?"

"I was, but it was an accident. I was bumped."

"Be glad I'm not on your jury."

"Leah, where are you?"

She told him and filled him in on her plan to fly to Palwaukee and perhaps get a ride with T to near the safe house, where they would try to determine if anyone was casing it. "Problem is, nothing is going that way tonight, and in the morning it's exorbitant. I may hitchhike."

"See if T will come get you. If it's too far to drive, he can fly."

"I hardly know him, Rayford. When will you be here?"

"I should hit Palwaukee about nine in the morning."

"I'll wait for you then, I guess."

"That would be nice."

Leah sighed. "Don't get pleasant on me all of a sudden. I can't pretend I'm not irritated with you. And getting yourself in even deeper trouble with the GC, what was that all about?"

"I wish I knew," he said. "But I *would* like

the chance to talk to everyone face-to-face."

"Thanks to you, that's looking more and more remote. You know Tsion and Chloe and the baby are underground now?"

"I heard."

"And nobody knows where Hattie is."

"But someone told you she was in the States?"

"It's a big place, Rayford."

"Yeah, but I still can't see her giving us up."

"You have more faith than I."

"I agree we need to be careful."

"Careful? If I do get T to take me to Mount Prospect, or if I wait for you, who knows we're not walking into a trap at the safe house? It's a miracle it wasn't found out long before I joined you."

Rayford ignored that, and Leah felt mean. She meant every word, but why couldn't she cut him some slack?

David checked in with Annie—who said she was headed back to bed—then invited Mac to join him in his office to see what was happening in the morgue. They settled close to the computer, and David started by listening live. Dr. Eikenberry was into a routine of announcing for the record the height and weight of the body and her plans for embalming and repair.

"There was some kind of a hassle right at the start," Mac said. "People say she was yelling, demanding the doctor. Can you go back without messing up the recording you're doing now?"

David pinpointed when the microphones in the morgue first detected sound. The time showed just after eight o'clock in the morning, and the recording began with a key in the door and the door opening. It was clear the mortician had two assistants with her, a man and a woman, and both sounded young. She called the young man Pietr and the young woman Kiersten.

The first spoken words were Dr. Eikenberry's. She was swearing. Then, "What is this? They leave the crate in here? Get someone to get it out of here. I'm going to work on this table and I want room. I'm assuming there are no more bodies in storage?"

"I'm here with you, Doc," Pietr said. "I wouldn't know."

"Check, would you? Kiersten, call some-one to get rid of the crate."

In the background Kiersten could be heard talking tentatively to the palace switchboard operator. In the foreground, Pietr could be heard slamming a door. "You're not gonna be happy, ma'am."

"What?"

"There are *no* bodies in here."

"None?"

"None."

"You're telling me Carpathia is not in there either?"

"None means none, ma'am."

She swore again. "Kiersten! Get some-body in here with a crowbar. They left the body in this crate all night? I'll be surprised if he doesn't stink."

After several minutes of muttering, a male voice: "You asked for a crowbar, ma'am?"

"Yes, and someone who knows how to use it."

"I can do it."

"You're a guard!"

"Crowbars are nothing. You want the box opened?"

"Put your weapon down, soldier. Why do they send *you* to do this?"

"Security. They don't want anybody in here but you and your staff."

"Well, I appreciate that, but . . ."

David and Mac heard the crate being torn open.

"No casket?" the doctor said. "Get him into the fridge."

"In the bag or out?" Pietr said.

"In," she said. "I don't even want to think how much blood he's lost in there. I'm not starting till ten, per instructions, but let's get ready."

Several minutes passed with minimal conversation, much of it related to their finding the plastic amalgam and her instructing her assistants how and where and when to have it ready. "You think this winch can handle a man his size?"

"Never saw a portable one before," Pietr said. "We'll make it work."

David fast-forwarded until he heard conversation and stopped only when it seemed meaningful. Finally he was at the ten o'clock point, and the cooler was opened again. Dr. Eikenberry switched on a recorder and spoke into a microphone

David had seen hanging from the ceiling when he helped deliver her supplies.

"This is Madeline Eikenberry, M.D. and forensic pathologist, here in the morgue at Global Community Palace in New Babylon with assistants Pietr Berger and Kiersten Scholten. They are bringing to the table the body of Nicolae Jetty Carpathia, age thirty-six. We will remove the corpse from the body bag into which it was placed following his death approximately fourteen hours ago in Jerusalem, cause to be determined."

David and Mac heard the transfer of the bag from gurney to examining table. "I don't like the sound of that," Dr. Eikenberry muttered. "It feels as if he may have nearly bled out."

"Yuck," Kiersten said.

"Could you spell that for the transcriptionist, dear?" the doctor said. Then, "Oh, no! Oh, my! Agh! Keep it off the floor! Pietr, make sure it drains through the table. What a botch! OK, transcriptionist, you know what to leave out. Pick up here. The body was not properly prepared for transfer or storage, and several liters of blood have collected in the bag. The body remains dressed in suit and tie and shoes, but a massive wound about the posterior head and neck, which will be examined once the deceased is disrobed, appears to be the exit area for the blood."

It sounded to David as if Carpathia's clothes were being cut off. "No apparent anterior wounds," Dr. Eikenberry said, as the sound of spraying water came through. "Let's turn him over. Oh! Be careful of that!" She swore again and again. "Get his doctor in here now! And I mean now! What in the world is this? I was told nothing of this!"

The footsteps must have been Kiersten's running to the door to have someone look for the doctor, because Pietr could be heard as clearly as the doctor. "I thought you were to look for a bullet entry wound."

"So did I! Is someone trying to kill us?"

More spraying, grumbling, and mumbling. Finally the door opened again. Hurried footsteps. "Doctor," Eikenberry began, "why wasn't I told of this?"

"Well, I, we—"

"Turning over a man with this kind of a weapon still in him is ten times more dangerous than a cop sticking his bare hands in a perp's pocket without checking for needles or blades first!"

"I'm sorry, I—"

"You're *sorry?* You want to help pull this out? Ah, never mind. Just tell me if there's anything else I should have known."

The doctor sounded thoroughly intimidated. "Well, to tell you the truth—"

"Oh, please, at *least* do that. I think it's about time, don't you?"

"Uh-huh, well, you know you're to look for bullet—"

"Damage, wounds, yes. What?"

"The fact is, the EMTs are of the opinion—"

"The same ones who prepared, or I should say left unprepared, a body like this?"

"That wasn't their fault, ma'am. I understand the supreme commander was pushing everyone to get the body out of there."

"Go on."

"The EMTs believe you will find no bullet wounds."

A pregnant silence.

"Frankly, Doctor, I don't care what we find. I'll give you my expert opinion, and if there are also bullet holes, I'll include that.

But can you answer me one thing? Why does everybody think there was a shooter, and why is that former employee pretty much being charged in the media? Because his prints were found on a weapon that *didn't* shoot Carpathia? I don't get it."

"As *you* said, ma'am, if you'll pardon me, it isn't your place to care about the cause of death, but only to assess it."

"Well, I'd say about an, oh, say, fifteen- to eighteen-inch, ah, what would you call this, Doctor, a big knife or a small sword?"

"A handled blade, certainly."

"Certainly. I'd hazard a guess that this whatever-it-is entering about two inches below the nape of the neck and exiting about half an inch through the crown of the skull, that certainly didn't enhance the victim's health, did it?"

"No, ma'am."

"Doctor, do you really not know why I wasn't informed of this major, likely lethal wound?"

"I know we didn't want to prejudice you."

She laughed. "Well, you certainly succeeded there! As for nearly slicing open my assistants and me, what do you say to that?"

"I guess I thought you'd see the, ah, sword."

"Doctor, the man was swimming in his own blood! He was on his back! We transferred him the same way, disrobed him, hosed him down, saw no entry or exit wounds on the anterior and, naturally, flipped him to examine the posterior wounds. What do you think I was expecting? I saw the news. I heard the gunshot and saw the people running and the victim fall. I had heard the scuttlebutt that there may have been a conspiracy, that one of the regional potentates may have had a concealed weapon. But I would have appreciated knowing that the man would look like a cocktail wiener with a sword poking through him."

"I understand."

"Do you see the damage this weapon did to significant tissue?"

"Not entirely."

"Well, unless we find bullets in the brain or somewhere else above the neck, it alone killed him."

Water was spraying again. "I see no bullet holes, do you?"

"No, ma'am."

"Pietr?"

"No."

"Kiersten?"

"Nope."

"Doctor?"

"I said no."

"But this blade, and I'll be able to tell you for sure when I get in there, appears to have gone through vertebrae, perhaps spinal cord, the membrane, the brain stem, the brain itself, the membrane again, and then come out the top of the skull, all none the worse for wear."

"That would be my observation too, ma'am."

"It would?"

"Yes."

"Your expert opinion."

"I'm no patholog—"

"But you know enough about the anatomy to know that I should not be surprised if I have guessed the internal damage fairly accurately?"

"Right."

"But more important, that this weapon appears as lethal now as it must have before it was thrust?"

"I'm afraid so."

"You see what I'm driving at?"

"I think so."

"You think so. One of us unsuspecting pathologists so much as brushes a finger against that blade, and we're sliced."

"I'm sorry—"

"And while the victim may be one of the most respected men in the history of the world, we don't know yet, do we, what might be in his blood? Or what might have been on the hands of the perpetrator. Do we?"

"We don't."

"Do you notice anything unusual about the blade, sir?"

"I don't know. I've never seen one quite like it, if that's what you m—"

"Simpler than that, Doctor. The cutting edge is facing out."

"You're sure there's only one cutting edge?"

"Yes, and do you know how I know? Because I was fortunate enough to catch my finger there when we turned over the body. Look here, at the top of his head. As we turned him, my hand went behind the head, and hidden there in the hair was the half-inch protrusion of the blade. As soon as it came in contact with my gloved index finger, I flinched and pulled away. Had I done that on the other edge, I dare say it would have cut my finger off."

"I see."

"You see. Do you also see our challenge in removing the weapon?"

A pause. "Actually, if it is as strong and sharp as you say, removal should be fairly simple. You just pull it back out the way it entered, and—"

"Doctor, may I remind you that the cutting edge is facing away from the body."

"I know."

"Then unless we are precise to a millimeter, the blade could cut its way out vertically. Cardinal rule of forensic pathology: Do as little damage to the body as possible so it is easier to determine how much trauma was actually inflicted from without."

"Ah, Madeline, if I could have a word."

"Please."

"Privately."

"Excuse us," she said, obviously looking at her assistants. Footsteps.

"Madeline, I apologize for any part I played in this dangerous situation. But we have been friends a long time. I sold the supreme commander on you because I wanted you to have the honor and the income. I resent being berated in front of your subordinates and—"

"Point well taken. I'll say nice things about you when you're gone. And I do appreciate the assignment. I don't know what the benefits are to a mortician asked to evaluate the most famous victim in history, but I do owe you thanks for that."

"You're welcome," he said flatly, and David heard him leave.

Pietr and Kiersten returned. "Wow," Pietr said.

"Wow is right," Dr. Eikenberry said. "That man?"

"Yes."

"That doctor who just left?" she clarified.

"Yes."

"I must tell you, he is a complete idiot."

The mortician told the transcriptionist to please disregard everything since the turning of the body and to pick up at that point. She explained how she had irrigated the entire wound area and found "just the one entry and one exit wound, with weapon still in place. The entry wound is considerably larger than the exit, and nearly all the blood flow came from the neck, though understandably there is evidence of blood exiting through eyes, nose, mouth, and ears as well. That the entry wound is clearly larger, while the blade itself is not that much wider there, indicates that the weapon was dug and twisted aggressively. The skull would have held the top of the weapon in place, but the bottom appears to have been flexible enough to inflict severe trauma."

David looked at Mac and exhaled. "Rayford's in the clear. I mean, he might get busted for shooting *at* Carpathia, but he couldn't have killed him."

Mac shook his head. "Sounds to me like Carpathia was murdered by one of his own people."

"It sure does," David said. "There was talk of one of the potentates with something in his coat, but I want to see the videodiscs."

Buck awoke late morning, stiff and sore. The sun blinded, but Chaim remained asleep. Buck took a closer look at Chaim's ratty blanket. The inside was blood encrusted, and he wondered how the old man could stand it. He also worried that some of the blood might be Chaim's own.

Buck carefully tugged at the blanket to see if any blood stained Chaim's pajamas. But Chaim held tight and turned over, exposing his back. No wounds or stains that Buck could see.

"You awake?" the old man mumbled, still facing away from Buck.

"Yes. We have to talk."

"Later."

"Now."

"Why don't you go find me some clothes? I need to get home, and I can't go like this."

"You don't think the GC is waiting for you there?"

Chaim rolled over to face Buck, squinting against the sunlight. "And why would they be? Where's my phone? I want to call the house, talk to Jacov."

"Don't."

"Why not?"

"Don't, Chaim. I know the truth. I know what happened."

"You saw nothing! No one saw anything!"

"You can't admit to me what I know already? What kind of a friend are you?"

Chaim got up and relieved himself, then returned to sit wearily on the bed. His white hair pointed everywhere. "You should be happy," he said.

"Happy?"

"Of course! What do you care how the deed was done, so long as it was done?"

"I care because *you* did it!"

"You don't know that. And what if I did?"

"You'll die for it, that's what! You think I want that?"

Chaim cocked his head and shrugged. "You're a better friend than I, Cameron."

"I'm beginning to think so."

Chaim chuckled. "I can't cheer you, eh?"

"Tell me how you did it, Chaim."

"The less you know, the less you have to answer for."

"Oh, don't be naïve! You've been around too long for that. I have to answer for everything. I have to be grateful for facial lacerations, because if I had not suffered them, I would have had to change my appearance anyway. Telling me you murdered Carpathia won't add much to my plate. They have enough on me, manufactured and otherwise, to put me away on sight. So, tell me."

"I'm telling no one. This is mine alone."

"But you know you can't go home."

"I can tell my people where I am, that I am all right."

"You must come to the States with me."

"I can't leave my country, my staff."

"Chaim, listen to me. Your staff is dead. They were tortured and massacred last night by the GC, probably trying to get to you."

Chaim looked up slowly, his hair casting wild shadows on the far wall. "Don't talk crazy," he said warily. "That is not amusing."

"I wouldn't joke about that, Chaim. Jacov was killed by a blow to the chin that broke his neck. A guard hit him with the butt end of an Uzi when he tried to rush to you."

Chaim put a hand over his mouth and sucked in a noisy breath. "Don't," he said, his words muffled. "Don't do this to me."

"I didn't do it, Chaim. You did it."

"He's dead? You know for certain he's dead?"

"I checked his pulse myself."

"What have I done?"

"Hannelore and her mother and Stefan are gone too."

Chaim stood and moved toward the door as if wanting to leave but knowing he had nowhere to go. "No!" he wailed. "Why?"

"Someone had to know, Chaim. Someone had to have seen you. Surely you didn't expect to get away with it."

Chaim's knees gave way and he hit the floor hard, a high-pitched cry in his throat. "You checked the pulses at my home too?"

Buck nodded.

"That was not smart. You could have been killed too."

"And *my* death would have been your fault too, Chaim. Look what's happened!"

Chaim turned and leaned over the bed, still kneeling. He buried his face in his hands. "I was willing to die," he managed. "I didn't care about myself. The sword was perfect and fit into the tubing of my chair just so. No one knew. Not even Jacov. Oh, Jacov! Jacov! What have I done to you? Cameron! You must kill me! You must avenge those deaths!" He stood quickly and opened the window. "If I lose my nerve, you must push me! Please, I cannot bear this!"

"Shut the window, Chaim. I'm not going to kill you, and I won't let you kill yourself."

"I'll not turn myself in to those swine. I wouldn't give them the satisfaction! Oh, I *will* kill myself, Cameron. You know I will!"

"You'll have to try without me present. I love you too much, Chaim. I will die before you do to keep you from going to hell."

"Hell? If God would send me to hell for murdering such a monster, I will go happily. But he *should* send me to hell for what I did to my people! Oh, Cameron!" He collapsed onto the bed, rolling into a fetal position and groaning as if about to burst. Suddenly he sat up, seeming eager to relive the deed.

"I was going to leap from my chair at just the right moment, weapon in hand. He is so much taller, I had been practicing my jumping. I was going to leap as high as I could and, with both hands on the handle, drive the blade down through the top of his head. The whole world would see and know.

"There were all those shenanigans on the stage, people standing, sitting, moving, laughing. I joined in, measuring the distance, seeing where I could maneuver the chair. When he came to greet me and lift my hand, I came close to reaching across my body to lift out the sword and plunge it into his heart. But my angle was wrong. I would not have had the leverage to get the blade out, let alone to thrust it where I needed to.

"I was rolling toward him finally as he moved my way. My plan was to turn quickly at the last minute and trip him. Then I would leap from the chair and kill him. But just as he got near me, the gun went off. At first I thought I had been detected and that his security guards had shot me. But he lurched my way, away from the sound of the gun and the shattering lectern.

"I could see that he was about to tumble into my lap, so I quickly withdrew the blade. I didn't have time even to orient it in my hands. I pointed it straight up and held steady as he fell back onto it. I held firm and tried to scrape the brain from his evil head. He jerked, and I let go. He rolled to my feet. It was chaos. People came running. I steered away and, for an instant, I thought I had gotten away with it. The timing! The shot! I could tell it came from the crowd, and as I ran away I wondered if it might be mistaken for a two-person crime.

"I had plotted an unlikely escape just on a lark. And here I am. Who would have believed it?"

Buck sat shaking his head. Chaim rolled back over, moaning. "You're right," he whispered. "It's all on me. I did this to them. Oh, no, no, no . . ."

Buck heard voices below the window. Three vagrants sat sharing a bottle. "Which of you would like a fifty-Nick note?" he called down.

Two waved him off, but a young drunk stood quickly. "What I gotta do?"

"Buy me some clothes and shoes with this twenty, and when you bring 'em back, keep the change and get another fifty."

The other two laughed and tried to sing. The young drunk squinted and let his head fall back. "How do you know I won't run off with your twenty?"

"My risk," Buck said. "Your loss. You want twenty or fifty?"

"Gimme," the man said, reaching. Buck let the bill flutter down, which brought the other two to their feet to compete for it. The younger shoved them away and got it easily. Buck felt better about his chances when the man turned back to him and said, "What size?"

"No deal," Abdullah said on the phone.

"What's the problem?" David said.

"The guy had the fear of God in him. Wouldn't let those discs out of his sight. I didn't even get the machine out of my bag. He said he'd stand there and watch while I logged them in, if I had to."

"I just hope they're not bringing them here to destroy them. They're the only hope of exonerating Rayford."

"Exonerating? What's that mean?"

"Getting him off the hook."

"No, sir," Abdullah said. "He didn't even have to pull the trigger to be guilty. He drew down on Carpathia. What more do they need? He needs to stay as far away from here as he can."

NINE

Seven Hours Later

David hated getting so little time with Annie, but he knew their exile was fast approaching. Then, if they could pull it off, they would be together as much as they wanted—and probably a long, long way from New Babylon.

What an incredibly beautiful city New Babylon would have been under other circumstances. Carpathia had employed the best architects and landscapers and designers and decorators. And except for the absence of any God-honoring works of art, the place looked magnificent, particularly at night. Great colored spotlights accented the massive, crystalline buildings. Only since the recent decimation of another huge percentage of the population and the resulting personnel shortages had the place begun to evidence the lack. It took longer for refuse removal or for lights to be repaired. Yet still the skyline was stunning, a man-made marvel.

As dusk crept over the horizon, David sat listening to Fortunato, Hickman, and Moon through the bug in Carpathia's office. He couldn't tell whether Leon was actually in Nicolae's chair, but it sure sounded like it. They were watching the videos that had been brought back from the Gala. David sat with his head in his hands, using earphones to be sure to catch every detail. He wished he could see the videos, but that was not his call.

They played and replayed and replayed clips that included the gunshot. "See?" Moon said. "He's right down there, stage right, about three or four deep, there! See? Pause!"

"I see it, Walter," Leon said. "Good thing we've got fingerprints. I would not have been able to tell who that was in a million years."

"Good getup," Hickman said. "The gray hair stickin' out of the turban. Nice touch. Robes. I woulda thought he was an Arab."

"Some kinda raghead anyway."

They all chuckled.

"Rayford Steele," Leon said softly. "Who'd have believed that? Wouldn't murder be against his religion?"

Laughter. Silence. Then, "I don't know." It was Hickman. "Maybe he convinces himself it's a holy war. Then I guess everything goes."

"Fact is," Moon said, "he missed."

"You look close," Hickman said, "and he had a better shot earlier. He fires then, he's our guy. But I don't think he even meant to shoot when he did."

"What're you talking about?"

"Look. Slow motion, well, back it up a second first. Look! Right there! Somebody bumps him. A little person. A woman? Can you zoom?"

"I don't know how to run these crazy machines," Leon said. "We oughta get Hassid in here."

"You want me to call him?"

"Maybe. Just a minute. Here, OK. Slow and zoomed. What do you see?"

"There!" Hickman said again. "She trips, loses her balance or somethin'. Ha! Who's that look like? Wally, who's that remind you of?"

"Nah."

"No? Come on! Who am I thinkin' of?"

"I know who you're thinking of, but we've got her eyeballed in North America. Probably trying to get to her sister's funeral. She doesn't know it was a month ago."

They chuckled again, and David picked up the phone. "Rayford," he said, "maybe Hattie's *not* on her way to the safe house yet. GC's tracked her out west, trying to make her sister's funeral."

"That's a relief. Maybe we're OK for a while."

"Don't get overconfident. I uploaded a whole bunch of stuff to Chloe's computer so you can see your new digs, if you need 'em. Where are you?"

"Well, I was about to put down at Palwaukee when I heard from Leah. I'd been having trouble reaching T to see if he could go get her in Kankakee, southeast of here. She never got him either, so I'm on my way to get her. We'll come back here and use Buck's car to see if we can get to the safe house."

"Call Tsion first. Last time I talked to him he said he thought he heard car noises."

"That's not good."

"Tell me about it," David said. "Hey, Leah might need a new alias."

"Yeah? Why?"

"She's been asking around about Hattie using that Clendenon name. They might try to follow her to Hattie."

"They're already onto Hattie. They don't need Leah."

"Whatever you say, Rayford. Just a thought."

"I appreciate it."

"You'd better be careful. They're going to try to pin this on you." David told him of the autopsy and evidence investigation.

"So I missed, just like you thought?"

"Looks pretty sure at this point."

"Then how can they pin it on me?"

"What, they're obligated to the truth? If you didn't do it, someone on the platform did."

"My money's on one of the three insurgent kings," Rayford said. "Probably Litwala."

"Even if you're right, you're a less embarrassing assassin than somebody behind Nicolae. I'll bet you're the scapegoat."

Buck had sat with the morose Chaim Rosenzweig the whole day. The old man had alternately slept and wept, threatening suicide. Buck wanted to go out and find them something to eat, but he didn't dare leave Chaim. The drunk came back to toss a bundle of used clothes up to the window, but he wasn't interested in more money to find food. Once he had his fifty, he was gone.

Buck called the desk. "Anybody down there that could bring us some food for a fee?"

"What, you think we got room service?"

"Just tell me if you know anybody who wants to make a few Nicks."

"Yeah, OK. When the concierge gets off his break, I'll send 'im up. You'll recognize him by his tuxedo."

Amazingly, ten minutes later someone knocked tentatively. Buck wished he had a gun. "Who is it?"

"I'll get you food," a man said. "How much?"

"Ten."

"Deal."

Buck sent him out for local fare. It was all he could do to get Chaim to eat a few bites. Presently, David called.

"Is it true?" he asked. "About Chaim?"

Buck was stunned. "What about him?"

"That he's dead, burned up at his home along with his whole staff?"

"You know that's not true, David. Hasn't anyone told you I'm with him?"

"I'm just telling you what's on television."

"So that's how they're going to spin it? Hero statesman dies in a fire. That keeps him out of the conspiracy?"

"They're convinced one of the three insurgents did it," David said, "but that would be bad for morale. What's Chaim's theory? He was right there."

"We need to talk about this later, David. I need to get him out of here."

"How?"

"I finally got hold of T. He's bringing the Super J. I directed him to a blocked-off road. We have to be there when he puts down so he can be in the air again before anyone's the wiser. We'll have to stop in Greece for fuel, though—wouldn't want to risk it over here."

Tsion was alarmed. Chloe was proposing madness. "Can I trust you with Kenny," she said, "that you won't fall asleep?"

"I would give my life for that child, you know that. But you must not go. This is foolishness."

"Tsion, I can't sit here doing nothing. I have informed everybody in the co-op generally what's going on, but there's little I can do until the buying-selling restrictions are sanctioned. Don't keep me from doing something worthwhile."

"I am not your superior, Chloe. I could not deprive you of anything. I'm just urging you to think this through. Why must you go? And why must it be now? Cameron's car is at the airport. If you take the Suburban, you leave me with no vehicle."

"You have nowhere to go, Tsion. You can't outrun the GC anyway. Your best bet is to stay right here, listen for them, turn the power off if you hear them, and become invisible."

Tsion threw up his arms. "I cannot dissuade you, so do what you are going to do. But don't be long."

"Thank you. And promise me you will do anything but let Kenny fall into GC hands."

"I would die first."

"I want *him* to die first."

"That I will not do."

"You would let them take him."

"Over my body."

"But don't you see, Tsion? That's how it will be! You'll be a martyr, but you will still have lost Kenny to the enemy."

"You're right. You'd better stay here."

"Nice try."

"This is not a smart thing to do in broad daylight."

"I'll be careful."

"Too late. You're already being reckless."

"Good-bye, Tsion."

"What do you make of this?" Hickman was saying as David listened in.

"Ramblings," Leon said. "Hallucinations. Gibberish. Not uncommon in such a situation."

"But first he said that about thinking he

had done all you asked. What was that about?"

"Nicolae was not addressing me! I have never, would never, could never ask him to do anything! Anyway, if he was talking to me, it would indicate that he thought I had attacked him."

"But then what is his obsession with the— what does he call it?"

"The veil? Or the vale? What?"

"Listen. Listen to what he says."

David pressed both earphones close and listened carefully. After Carpathia's first lament, which echoed through the sound system, the PA system appeared to have failed, but his next words were picked up through the videodisc machine mike. "The veil," Carpathia rasped. "Was it rent in twain from the top to the bottom?" Carpathia struggled to make himself understood. "Father," he managed. "Father, forgive them, for they know not what they do."

David shuddered.

The exchange reminded him of something he and Mac had heard from the morgue. He called Mac. "What was it Dr. Eikenberry said about reports of Nicolae's last words?"

"Just that it would have been impossible."

"That's what I thought. Once she got in there and saw the damage, she said he wouldn't have been able to speak, right?"

"Exactly."

David re-cued the recording and found it.

"Well," Dr. Eikenberry said, "this gives the lie to the 'last words' business, doesn't it?"

"It sure does," Pietr said. "Unless he could speak supernaturally."

He and the doctor and Kiersten laughed. "This man could not have said a word," Dr. Eikenberry concluded. "Maybe they want to invent something for posterity, but no one had better ask me if it was possible."

A few minutes after nine in the morning, Central Standard Time, Rayford put the Gulfstream down in Kankakee. He had told Leah to watch for a smallish jet and to be ready to board quickly. But as he taxied by the terminal, he saw her sleeping in a chair by the window.

He left the jet whining on the tarmac, knowing how conspicuous that would look to ground control, and sprinted into the terminal. "Donna!" he said, as he approached. "Donna Clendenon!"

She jumped and squinted at him. "Do I know you?" she said, clearly terrified.

"Marv Berry," he said, grabbing her bag. "We've got to go."

"Hi, Marv," she whispered. "You've got to tell a girl when you get a makeover."

Rayford heard some kind of warning through the PA system, and a couple of orange-vested officials started his way. He ignored them and was airborne quickly, certain that Kankakee had no GC pursuit craft and little interest in a small jet flyer who had boorishly violated their protocols.

He told Leah, "All I get out of Palwaukee is a tower guy who says T is not there and won't be back until tomorrow, and that he's not at liberty to say where he went."

"I got the same. What do you make of it?"

"I don't know. Wish there was someone in his church I could ask. But T and I have never needed to communicate through third parties. He's usually reachable by cell. He's always wanted to be in on the action, and I need someone to go and ferry Buck and Chaim over here. I'm tempted to call Albie and see if he can find someone."

"Now there's a name I haven't heard," Leah said.

"Albie? Long story. Good guy."

"So tell me."

"Not until you and I clear up a few things."

"Until you do, you mean," she said.

Rayford told her what had happened to him in Israel, on the flight to Greece, and in Greece. "I know that sounds a little too convenient," he said, "and I wouldn't blame you if you thought I just made it up to—"

"Made it up?" she said, obviously emotional. "If you made that up, you'd burn in hell."

"So, will you be the first to forgive me?"

"Of course. And I need to apologize too. I—"

"You've done nothing close to what I did," Rayford said. "Forget it."

"Don't brush me off, Rayford. I feel awful about how I've responded to you."

"Fair enough. We're even."

"Don't be flippant."

"I'm not. You can imagine how I feel about—"

"I'm not saying I was as terrible as you," she said wryly.

David responded to an announcement that all GC management personnel from director level and above were to report immediately to the small theater in the education wing. What now?

As dozens crowded into the room, Fortunato stood at the lectern like a professor. "Quickly now, quickly please, find your seats. I've been informed that more than a million people are in New Babylon already with probably at least two million more to come. Our social services are being taxed to their limits, and these people have no outlet for their grief. I want to know if there is any reason we cannot put the body of the potentate in position even this evening and begin the procession past the bier. We're estimating that not half the mourners will stay for the burial, which may have to be postponed as well. Do we have adequate lighting?"

Someone shouted yes.

"And concessions? Stations with water, food, medical services?"

"Could be in place within an hour!" someone said.

"Good. The bier itself and its pedestal?"

"Pedestal is finished and waiting."

"Bier is finished! Per specifications."

"Really?" Fortunato said. "I was told there was some question whether it could be vacuum sealed—"

"Solved, with a little help. Once the body is, ah, placed inside, the air can be quickly removed and the hole secured. The stopper is a hard rubber compound that will be screwed into the Plexiglas—"

"Thank you, we can skip the details. The entire container is transparent?"

"Yes, sir. And on the pedestal it will sit nearly fifteen feet off the ground."

"Yet the mourners will have access . . . ?"

"Via stairs leading up one side and down the other. They will, of course, be unable to touch the glass, as they will be separated from it by approximately five feet with velvet ropes and, um, armed security."

"Thank you," Fortunato said. "Now there are certain details I would like us all to hear, except those of you who need to supervise construction of the restoring stations. You may be excused now, and let's shoot for an 8:00 P.M. start time. Let's get the word out to the people so they can begin assembling. Yes, Mr. Blod."

Guy had been waving and now stood.

"I'm afraid my statue will not be ready until dawn, as originally planned. We're making progress, and I believe it will be stunning, but even the initial goal was nearly impossible."

"No problem. You may go now too, and we'll all look forward to your handiwork."

As Guy rushed from the room, Leon called upon Dr. Eikenberry to come to the microphone. "It has been her difficult duty to prepare for burial the body of our beloved leader. As she is a loyal citizen of the Global Community and was a great admirer of the potentate, you can imagine what an emotional task this was. I have asked her to report on her findings and summarize the challenges she faced to allow the mourners to have one last encounter with His Excellency in as dignified and memorable a manner as possible, under the circumstances."

Dr. Eikenberry had lost the severe look David had seen when he first met her. Her white coat was gone, and she seemed to have applied fresh makeup and had her hairdo softened. He wondered when she had had time for that.

"Thank you, Supreme Commander," she began. "This has indeed been a most difficult and emotional day for me and my assistants, Pietr Berger and Kiersten Scholten. We treated the body of Nicolae Carpathia with utmost reverence and respect. As expected, the cause of death was severe brain trauma caused by a single bullet from a Saber handgun. The projectile entered the potentate's body just below the nape of his neck in the posteri— in the back and exited through the top of the crani—through the top of his head. The particularly devastating power of this type of projectile destroyed two vertebrae, severed the spinal cord, obliterated the brain stem and posterior of the brain, and left residual damage to the carotid artery and much of the soft tissue in the throat.

"Because of the spinning bullet, the back of the neck and head were laid open, causing the greatest challenge for repair and reconstruction. Without getting into the details, the gaping wound has been stapled and stitched, camouflaged with wax and putty and coloring and a minimum of artificial hair. If the result contributes to an appropriate farewell to the greatest leader the world has ever known, I am grateful and consider it a privilege to have served the Global Community this way."

Amid tears and sustained applause, Dr. Eikenberry began to leave, then returned to the podium with an index finger raised. "If I may add one thing," she said. "There is recorded evidence that His Excellency's last words were an expression of forgiveness to the perpetrator of this heinous crime. Forgiveness has long been ascribed to the divine, and as a medical professional, I must tell you why I concur with this assessment. Besides the *sentiment* of those last words, I can tell you that there is no human explanation for the potentate's ability to speak at all, given the physical damage. Truly this was a righteous man. Truly this was the son of god."

At Palwaukee Rayford tried in person to get more information out of the tower fill-in. "I'm sorry, sir," the man said. "But not only am I not at liberty to tell you, I couldn't if I wanted to. He didn't tell me where he was going but only when he expected to return."

"Do you know who I am?"

"No, sir."

"You haven't seen me around here, don't know I'm a friend of T's?"

The man squinted at Rayford, and Leah cleared her throat. "He, ah, may not recognize you."

Rayford couldn't believe his own stupidity. "Listen, son, I have permission to take an associate's vehicle, but he neglected to leave the keys with me. I need to know you won't feel obligated to phone any authorities if I were to hot-wire the car."

The man's look was not as reassuring as his words. "I won't even be looking your direction."

"He doesn't trust you," Leah said as they strode to the Land Rover.

"Why should he? I wouldn't either. See? Even forgiven sin has its consequences."

"Do we have to spiritualize everything?" Leah said, but Rayford could tell she was bemused. Once they were on the road, she said, "We're not going straight to the safe house in broad daylight, are we?"

"Of course not. We have a stop first."

He drove to Des Plaines and the one-pump gas station run by Zeke and Zeke Jr. Zeke emerged quickly but hesitated when he saw Rayford. He looked past him to Leah. "I recognize the vehicle," he said. "But not the occupants."

"It's me, Zeke. And this is Leah."

"That wasn't Z's handiwork, was it?"

"Hers was."

"Humph. Not bad. Yours either. Need auto work?"

"Yup."

Zeke ignored the pump and opened the ancient garage door. Rayford pulled in, and he and Leah got out so Zeke could raise the car on the rack. Then the three of them took a hidden staircase to the basement, where Zeke Jr. looked up expectantly. " 'sup?" he said.

"You know me?" Rayford said.

"Not till you spoke, but I woulda got it. Wha'dya need?"

"New ID for her."

Zeke Jr. stood, rolls of fat jiggling under his black vest and shirt. "Gerri Seaver," he said.

"Excuse me?"

"How's Gerri Seaver sound?"

"How does she look?" Leah said.

Zeke grabbed a file. "Like this."

"You're a genius," she said. The blonde was roughly her age, height, and weight. "I don't know how you do it."

"Lots more to choose from these days," he said shyly. He directed her to a sink and gave her the chemicals necessary to make her a blonde. She and Rayford drove off two hours later with foodstuffs, a full tank, and Leah in a scarf over wet, freshly bleached hair. Her dental appliance had been changed, as had the color of her contacts. In her purse was a wallet with documents to match.

"I'm going to take the northern route," Rayford said. "That'll give us a good look at any other traffic."

"Unless they're hidden."

"Not too many places to do that," he said. "Shall we wait till dark too?"

"You're asking me?"

"We both live or die by the decision," he said.

"That helps."

He phoned the safe house. Tsion answered. "She's where? . . . Tell me she's not! . . . Oh, Tsion! What about the radiation, the—"

Tsion told him what David had told them about the radiation. Rayford pulled over and covered the mouthpiece. "We're waiting till dark," he said, popping a U-turn.

"Where to till then?"

"Chicago, and watch our backs in case you were right about tower boy."

Rayford phoned Chloe and eschewed any pleasantries. "Where are you?" he said.

"Palos area," she said. "I'm guessing, where the Tri-state used to intersect Harlem."

"Ninety-fifth Street?"

"Uh-huh."

"What now? You going the rest of the way on foot?"

"I may have to."

"That'll take hours!"

"What else have I got to do, Dad?"

"At least wait for us. You're more likely to give us away than Hattie is. We've got both vehicles out in the daytime. On foot you'll stick out like a sore thumb. We're as exposed as we've ever been."

"Just tell her what to do, Rayford," Leah said. "You're back in charge, remember?"

"What?" Chloe said.

Rayford covered the phone. "She's a married adult, Leah, not my little girl anymore."

"But she's subordinate to you in the Trib Force. Do what you have to do."

"Chloe?"

"Yes."

"Stay put until we can find you. We're not doing this thing until after dark."

TEN

Buck was having a crisis of conscience. It would have been one thing to be harboring Carpathia's assassin, had it been Rayford or another misguided believer for whom the deed could have at least been rationalized as an act of war. But Chaim?

He professed no faith, no acrimony toward Carpathia from a spiritual standpoint. The man had committed first-degree murder, and regardless of what Buck thought about the victim, it was a crime.

"So, what are you going to do?" Chaim pressed him as they languished at the Night Visitors hotel in Jerusalem. "Turn me in? Abandon me? Your conscience can't take what I did to your worst enemy. I cannot abide what I have done to my dearest friends. They died for me."

"Greater love hath no man . . ."

"You've quoted that before, Cameron, and I know where you want to go with it. But they had no choice. Perhaps they would have died for me voluntarily, but this was my doing. I forced their deaths."

"Would you have done the same for them? Would you have died for them?"

"I'd like to think I would. I should now."

"Stop talking like that."

"You think I am not sincere? The only things standing in the way are you and my cowardice."

"Cowardice? You planned the assassination for months, virtually told me you were going to do it by showing me your blade making—I don't know where my head was—and you pulled it off according to plan. Right or wrong, it was hardly evidence of cowardice."

"Ach!" Chaim waved him off. "I am a fool and a coward, and the blood of my people is on my hands."

Buck paced. "Because the GC are already announcing that you're dead, they can kill you without explanation."

"Let them. I deserve it. I'm a murderer."

Buck turned the chair backward and straddled it. "What happens when your victim comes back to life? Then what is your crime? Attempted murder? What if there is no evidence of the wound you inflicted?"

"You're talking crazy now, Cameron."

"It's going to happen, Chaim."

"I know you say that, and Tsion says that. But come now. The man was in my lap when I thrust the blade into his brain. For all practical purposes, he was dead before he hit the floor. He could not have survived it. You can't really believe he is coming back to life."

"What if he does?"

Chaim waved him off again.

"Don't do that. You're an intellectual, a lifelong student and teacher and scientist. Humor the debate. What if Carpathia comes back to life?"

Chaim rolled on the bed and turned his back to Buck. "Then I guess you'll all be right; I'll be wrong. You'll win."

"You're not pretending that it has actually happened."

"You said yourself I have a thinking man's brain. I find it impossible to consider impossibilities."

"That's why we've never gotten through to you? All our arguing and pleading . . . ?"

"You've gotten through more than you know, Cameron. I have come from atheism to agnosticism and finally to belief in God."

"You believe?"

"In God, yes. I told you that. Too many things have happened that can be explained no other way."

"Then why not Carpathia's resurrection?"

"You can't tell me that you yourself actually believe this," Chaim said.

"Oh, yes, I can. And I do. You forget I was there when Eli and Moishe came back to life after three days in the hot sun."

"You believe what you want to believe."

Buck looked at his watch. "I wish it would get dark. I want out of here."

"You should leave me, young friend. Distance yourself from me. Pretend you never met me."

Buck shook his head, though Chaim was still turned away from him. "Can't do that," he said. "We go back way too far."

"I was merely the subject of an article. We didn't have to become friends."

"But we did. And now I love you and can't let you go. You think you have nothing else to live for—"

"True enough."

"But you do. You do! You know what I fear for you, Chaim?"

"You're afraid I will die in unbelief and go to hell."

"There's something more frightening. What if you wait too long to change your mind and God hardens your heart?"

"Meaning?" Chaim rolled over to face him.

"Meaning that you finally decide it's true and want to give yourself to Christ, but you had already pushed God past where he would allow you to come back."

"Explain to me how that fits with your view of a loving God who is not willing that any should perish."

"I don't understand it myself, Chaim. I'm new at this. But Dr. Ben-Judah teaches that the Bible warns about just that during the end times. Be careful that you don't go too far, that you ignore too many warnings and signs."

"God would do that?"

"I believe so."

"To me?"

"Why not?"

Chaim let his head rest on the mattress, then covered his face with his arms.

"Ready to engage in the debate?" Buck pressed.

"I'm tired, Cameron."

"You slept well."

"I slept. Not well. How could I?"

"I can't imagine. But this is too important for you to brush aside."

"You have pleaded with me before! I have heard every argument from you and from Tsion. I could make your case for you!"

"Then think about what may happen to you. Say I get cold feet and abandon you. Even if you are a coward and unable to take your own life, someone is going to take it for you. Then what?"

"I like to believe death is the end."

"It's not," Buck said.

"Listen to the new believer, full of knowledge. You can't know."

"Chaim. If all this stuff that has amazed you and made you believe God is real, why shouldn't heaven and hell be real? If there's a God, why would he want you to die and disappear into nothingness? It makes no sense."

"You're repeating yourself."

"You're holding out, Chaim. You're like the fainthearted who want one more sign. I just don't want you to wait past the point of no return."

"Ach!"

"Just think about it, will you? What it would mean if the prophecy were fulfilled, Nicolae was the Antichrist, and he resurrected from the dead."

"I don't want to think about it. I want to die."

"You wouldn't if you believed what I believe."

"That, I agree with."

"You do?"

"Of course. Who would want to go to hell?"

"You don't have to, Chaim! God has—"

"I know! All right? I know! Stop talking."

"I will, but just consider—"

"Please!"

"—how you would feel if Nicolae—"

"For the love of—"

"I'll shut up now, Chaim. But—"

Buck's phone rang.

"Maybe there is a God," Chaim said. "The patron saint of phones has saved me."

"This is Buck."

"Buck, is it really you?"

"Hattie!" Buck stood so quickly his chair bounced away. "Where are you?"

"Colorado," she said.

"You're on a secure phone?"

"One thing I absconded with, one of those from your friend on the inside."

"I'm listening."

"The GC think I'm dumber than I am. They released me from prison, gave me money, and then followed me here. I know they were disappointed I didn't go to Israel, but I wanted to see if any of my family was left."

"And?"

Her voice caught. "No. Not for a while. But you know where they hope I'll go now."

"Exactly where I hope you won't go."

"Buck, I have nowhere else to turn."

He ran a hand through his hair. "I'd love to help you, Hattie, but I—"

"I understand. I had my chance."

"That's not it. I—"

"It's all right, Buck. You owe me nothing."

"It has nothing to do with owing you anything, Hattie. I'm in the middle of a situation myself, and until you can shake the GC, I can't advise that you head back to the safe house. Everybody's welfare is at stake."

"I know," she said, and he heard the terror in her voice. "Would you please tell everyone that I never told anyone where they were?"

"Hattie. You as much as put Bo and Ernie on our doorstep."

"They couldn't have found their way back there. Anyway, they're both dead, and if they had told anyone, you'd have been raided by now."

"What will you do, Hattie?"

"I don't know," she said wearily. "Maybe I'll just run these goons on a wild-goose chase until they get tired of me. Heaven knows they gave me enough money."

"They're not going to let you out of their sight. And don't think they couldn't patch in even to this call."

"They're watching my car. They think I'm eating."

"Good time to slip away?"

"Too open. I've got to get them to somewhere more densely populated. Maybe Denver."

"Be careful."

"Thanks for nothing."

"Hattie, I'm sorry. I—"

"I didn't mean that, Buck. I was trying to be funny. Nothing's funny anymore, is it?"

"If you shake them and are sure, try me again. We may not be at the same place, but if we can accommodate you . . ."

"You would, wouldn't you?"

"Of course we would. You know us."

"Yes, I do. You all were better than I deserved. I'd better get off."

"Yeah. I s'pose you've heard they're trying to pin the assassination on Rayford."

"I heard. Has to be a frame-up. He probably wasn't even there."

"He was there, but he didn't do it."

"You don't have to convince me. Rayford kill somebody? Not in a million years. I know him better than that. Listen, just tell everybody I'm safe and so are they and thanks for everything I didn't deserve."

"Hattie, we all love you and are praying for you."

"I know you are, Buck."

David, stunned at the difference between Dr. Eikenberry's public pronouncements and the autopsy, frantically searched his database for a meeting between her and Fortunato prior to the meeting with management. He had to know what approach Leon had used, in case Leon tried the same with him. Via his hard drive, he bounced all over the compound but had no luck. He did, however, come upon a private meeting between Leon and an unidentified male in a conference room near Carpathia's office.

". . . and how long have you been working for us, sir?"

"Almost from the beginning, Mr. For— Supreme Commander."

"And you're from?"

"Greenland."

"You enjoy your work?"

"Until the assassination, yes."

"The shooting?"

"Well, I meant the stabbing. The assassination of those two guys at the Temple

Mount, that was exciting. I mean, to see His Excellency put them in their place . . ."

"But you didn't enjoy your job so much when you saw the potentate himself murdered."

"No, sir. I kept the camera right on him, but it was the hardest thing I've ever done."

"You know the autopsy is finished, and it was the gunshot that killed the potentate."

David could not decipher the response, but it sounded like a snort.

"But there was only one gunshot, Commander—"

"There was only one needed, son. It was a weapon identical to the one His Excellency used on the troublemakers at the Wailing Wall."

"I understand that, but from where I sat, above stage left, I saw the wood speaker's thing—"

"The lectern."

"Yeah, that. I saw that get hit and the curtain go flying. No way that bullet also hit the potentate. He was closer to me."

"Nevertheless, it has been determined that—"

"Excuse me, Commander, but the real

murder happened right below me, and I saw it happen."

"And you have reviewed this?"

"Watched it over and over. Couldn't believe it."

"And you discussed it with whom?"

"Just my boss."

"That would be Mr. Bakar?"

"Yes, sir."

Footsteps. A door opening. More faintly: "Margaret, would you have Mr. Bakar join us, please? Thank you."

The door shut and David heard Leon's chair. "Look into my eyes, son. There, yes. You trust me, do you not?"

"Of course."

"When your superior gets here, I am going to tell you both what you saw and what you will remember."

"Excuse me?"

"I am going to tell you what you saw and what you will remember."

"But, sir, I know what I—"

"You understand that I will soon become the new potentate, don't you?"

"I assumed that, yes, sir."

"You did?"

"I think most people assume that."

"Do they?"

No response.

"Do they?" Leon repeated. "Don't just nod. Tell me."

The young man's voice sounded hollow. "Yes."

"You understand that my new title will be Supreme Potentate and that I must also be addressed as Excellency?"

"Yes, Commander."

"You may try out the new title now."

"Yes, Excellency."

"And you realize that I will not only be worthy of worship, but also that worship of me will be mandatory."

"Yes, Excellency."

"Call me Potentate. Supreme Potentate."

"Yes, Supreme Potentate."

"Would you like to kneel before me?"

Silence. Then a knock and a loud sigh from Leon. The door opening. "Excuse me, Commander, but Mr. Bakar is currently engaged in—"

"Margaret!" Leon hissed fiercely. "Do not interrupt me again!"

"I'm, sorry, sir, I—"

"I don't want apologies and I don't want to hear that my subordinates have more important things to do! The next person through this door had better be Mr. Bakar, and for your sake, it had better be within ninety seconds."

"Right away, sir."

The door. The chair. "Now then, son, where were we?"

"I was worshiping you, Supreme Potentate." Another chair.

"That's it. Yes, kneel before me and kiss my ring."

"I see no ring, sir."

"Kiss my finger where the ring will soon be."

A quick knock and the door opening. Bakar's voice: "Forgive me, Commander, I—what the devil is going on?"

"Sit, Director."

"What's he doing on the floor?"

"He was just about to tell me what was on the videodisc you brought back from Jerusalem."

"You've seen it, haven't you, Supreme Commander?"

"Of course, but it seems there's a discrepancy between what he and I saw and what you apparently saw."

"Oh?"

"Yes," Fortunato said. "Return to your chair and tell your boss what you saw."

"I heard the gunshot and saw the potentate's head snap back."

"I get it," Bakar said. "A joke. Now the gun killed him? We all know that's not true."

"It's true," the cameraman said.

"Yeah, I was born yesterday and went blind today."

"Did you go blind, Bakar?" Leon said soothingly.

"Wha—?"

"Lean across the table here and let me see your eyes."

"My eyes are fine, Le—er, Commander. I—"

"Bakar, are you listening to me?"

"Of course, but—"

"Are you listening?"

"Yes!"

"Are you listening? Really listening?"

Silence.

"I have your attention now, don't I, Bakar?"

"You do, sir."

"Bakar, you understand that I will soon become the new potentate, don't you?"

David could stand to listen no more and clicked away from the feed. He stood, dizzy and sick to his stomach. He called Annie and apologized for waking her.

"What is it, David?" she said.

"I need you," he said. "Meet me soon, before I get called in to see Fortunato."

Rayford and Leah agreed to meet Chloe in a mostly destroyed banquet hall that had been turned into a dimly lit, dingy bar. They were ignored, sitting in a dark corner, huddled against wind that gusted through huge gaps in the wall.

Rayford and Chloe embraced, but he wasted little time chastising her. "This is more dangerous than staying put, even if Hattie leads the GC right to the safe house. There's a chance they won't find the underground."

"We need the new place, Dad," she said. "And I'm tired of doing nothing."

"Granted, but let's not get crazy."

Leah's phone chirped. "This is, um, Gerri Seaver."

"Oh, I'm—I'm sorry, I—" *Click.*

"Oh, no!" Leah said. "That was Ming, I'm sure of it."

"Hit Callback," Rayford said.

*   *   *

Any doubts Buck had about Chaim's physical condition were erased when they finally left the Night Visitors. Chaim knew exactly where they were headed. He had ripped from one clean corner of his blanket a piece large enough to fit under his hat and extend down the back of his neck and both sides of his face. His nondescript shirt and blowsy pants made him look like any other Israeli day laborer, and he had replaced his slippers with boots.

Buck had a tough time keeping up with him. He jogged as Chaim walked quickly, and though the man was a foot shorter and more than thirty years older, he wore Buck out.

"We get to America and what, I'm holed up with Tsion and you? I won't need to kill myself. You'll both talk me to death."

"There's nothing we could say that you haven't heard already," Buck said, gasping and grateful that that comment had made Chaim stop briefly.

"Now there's the truest thing I've heard all day."

"That's not so," Buck said, slow to start moving again when Chaim took off.

"What?" Chaim said, a step and a half ahead.

"The truest thing you heard today was that you are lost!"

Again Chaim stopped and turned. "I'm lost?"

"Yes!"

In the dim light in the middle of the ravaged City of God, Buck saw the pain in his friend's face.

"You don't think I know I'm lost?" Chaim said, incredulously. "If there's one thing I do know, one thing I am certain of, it is that I am lost. Why do you think I would sacrifice myself to murder the greatest enemy my country has ever had? I did not expect to survive! I was ready to go! Why? Because I am lost! Nothing to live for! Nothing! My farewell act was to be of some benefit to Israel. Now the deed is done and I am here and yes, I am lost!"

Buck was desperate that Chaim not give them away with his ranting. But that was only one reason he approached his dear friend, arms outstretched, and embraced him.

"You don't need to be lost, Chaim. You don't need to be."

And the old man sobbed in Buck's arms.

ELEVEN

"Don't hang up. It's Leah." She had moved out to the Land Rover to make the call.

"It sounded like you," came the voice Leah never felt fit the delicate Ming Toy. "But who is Gerri something?"

"We international fugitives have to keep changing identities, Ming. If it weren't for the intrigue, what would be the appeal?"

"I don't know how you keep your sense of humor. This is too dangerous, too frightening for me."

"You handle it well, Ming."

"I called with a question. Your friend, Williams?"

"Buck, yes."

"No, not Buck. Longer name."

"Cameron?"

"Yes! Where's his family?"

"West somewhere, why? I think only his father and brother are still around."

"I don't think they're around either. There was lots of talk at Buffer today about what happened to Dr. Rosenzweig's house and his people. They don't know where he is, but they're making it look like everybody died in the fire."

"Yes?"

"They're saying the same thing will happen to Cameron Williams's people if they don't give him up."

"His relatives don't know where he is!" Leah said. "He's smarter than to give them that kind of information."

"Leah, they may already be dead. This was supposed to happen right away."

"What was?"

"Torture. Dismemberment. They tell or they are killed. Then comes the fire to cover it up."

"I don't know what to do."

"Just have your friend check on them. Maybe he can warn them in time."

"I will, Ming. How are you doing? Ready to come see us? Whoops! Hang on." Leah slid down in the seat as two uniformed GC officers strolled by. They stopped right next to the Rover, chatting and smoking. "Ming," Leah whispered, "can you still hear me?"

"Barely. What's going on?"

"I've got company. If I don't say anything, you'll know why."

"If you need to hang up—"

"I'd rather stay on with you. Let me give you Rayford Steele's number in case I get caught. He'll answer to Marvin Berry."

"Got it."

Leah felt the vehicle rock. "They're leaning against the car," she said. "Luckily all the windows are tinted except the windshield."

"Where are you?"

"Illinois."

"I mean in the car."

"Floor of the front seat. Wish I were daintier. The gearshift is killing me."

"They don't see you?"

"Don't think so. I can hear them plain as day."

"What?"

Leah didn't want to speak louder. The

Peacekeepers were trading wild party stories. She wanted to say, "Yeah, and I'm the Easter bunny," but she lay still.

"This hunk of junk looks like it's been through a war," one said.

"It has, stupid. It's old enough to have been through the war and the earthquake."

"Tough make."

"Not as tough as the Land Cruiser."

"No? Same company?"

"Toyota."

"Really?"

"Expensive."

"More than this?"

"Quite a bit more."

"No kiddin'? This thing's loaded. I think it's got a GPS."

"This rig? Nah."

"Betcha."

"How much?"

"Ten-spot."

"You're on."

"Oh, no," Leah whispered, "they're coming to the front."

"You need me to call Rayford?"

But Leah didn't answer. She tucked the phone between the seats and pretended to sleep.

"See, isn't that the positioning system right there. Hey! She all right?"

"Who? Oh, man! Door's unlocked. Ask her."

A rap on the window. "Hey, lady!"

Leah ignored it, but moved slightly so they wouldn't think she was dead. When one opened the passenger door, she sat up, trying to look groggy. "Hey, what's the deal?" she said. "You want me to call a Peacekeeper?"

"We are Peacekeepers, ma'am."

"There a law against a girl getting some shut-eye?"

"No, but what're you doin' on the floor? Backseat's wide open."

"Trying to stay out of the sun."

She sat up in the seat, desperate to remember her new address and hometown. Zeke Jr. had reminded her more than once to memorize it as soon as possible. She hated being so new at this part of the game.

"This your vehicle?"

"Borrowing it."

"From?"

"Guy named Russell."

"That a first or last name?"

"Russell Staub."

"He know you're borrowing it?"

" 'Course! What're you driving at?"

"Run a check on it," one told the other, who immediately got on his phone. "Where's he from, ma'am?"

"Mount Prospect."

"What're you doing all the way down here?"

She shrugged. "S'posed to meet some friends."

"We're gonna find this Rover registered to a Staub in Mount Prospect, right?"

She nodded. "I don't do his paperwork for him, but that's whose it is and that's where it's from."

"You got any ID, ma'am?"

"Yeah, why?"

"I'd like to see it."

"You've come a long way from wondering if I was all right to accusing me of stealing a car."

"I didn't accuse you of anything, lady. You feeling guilty about something?"

"Should I be?"

"Let me see your ID."

Leah made a show of digging through her purse even after she had located the new documents so she could take a last peek at the new information.

"This your current address, Miss, ah, Seaver?"

"If it says Park Ridge, it is."

"You're a long way from home too."

"Only because there are hardly any roads anymore."

"That's the truth."

"Staub, Mount Prospect," the other officer said. "No outstandings and no reports."

Leah raised her eyebrows, her pulse racing. "Satisfied?"

He handed back her ID. "Don't be out and about without something to do, ma'am. Why don't you get this vehicle back to the owner and get on home."

"Can't I get a drink first, in case my friends show up?"

"Don't be long."

"Thank you." She pushed open the car door and saw Rayford and Chloe on their way out, concern on their faces. "Oh, there they are now! Thanks again, officers!"

Annie had hurried to David's office. They pretended it was a normal superior/subordinate meeting, and he quickly told her what he had heard.

She paled. "That sounds like what Buck Williams went through with Carpathia at the UN."

"But who knew Fortunato could do that?"

"Is *he* the Antichrist?" Annie said.

David shook his head. "I still think it's Carpathia."

"But he's really dead, David. I mean really. How long was he in that bag and in that box? I thought he was supposed to come back to life right away."

"Dr. Ben-Judah thought so too," he said. "What do we know? If we had this stuff figured out, we probably would have figured out the rest and wouldn't have been left behind."

David's secretary buzzed him. "The Supreme Commander would like to see you."

Annie grabbed his hands. "God," she whispered, "protect him on every side."

"Amen," David said.

Buck and Chaim sat shivering in a ditch at the far north end of a deserted and blocked-off road. Only a small stretch remained smooth, and Buck began to wonder whether it was long enough for the Super J. The jet might be able to land and take off without attracting attention, but if T had to circle or take more than one shot at it, who knew?

Worse, the stretch was unlit. T would use his landing lights only as much as he had to, counting on Buck to guide him in by phone. That meant Buck would have to stand at one end of the makeshift runway or the other. He opted for the front end so he could talk T through coming straight over his head, then he could spin and try to keep him straight until he landed. The only danger was T's coming in too low too quickly. Buck would have to leap out of the way. Still, that seemed easier than trying to elude a plane careening toward him at the other end.

"This is a lot of trouble for someone who doesn't want to leave," Chaim said.

"Well, *I* want to leave even if you don't."

Buck's phone rang, and he assumed it was T, though he had not heard the plane yet. It was Rayford.

"We have a situation here," Rayford said, quickly bringing him up to date on

Hattie. "The question is whether now is the time to talk."

"It's not," Buck said. "But in a nutshell, what's up?"

"Wouldn't do that to you, Buck. Call us when you're in the air or in Greece. And greet the brothers for us."

"Will do," Buck said, puzzled at Rayford's new tone. It was as if he were talking to his old father-in-law.

"Chloe sends her love and wants to talk with you when you have time."

"Thanks. Me too."

"I love you, Buck."

"Thanks, Ray. I love you too."

David realized how petrified he was when he nearly blundered by heading straight toward the conference room upon reaching the eighteenth floor. "He in there?" he said, trying to mask his anxiety.

"No," Margaret said, clearly puzzled. "He's with Messrs. Hickman and Moon in his office. They're expecting you."

I will not kneel, David vowed. *I will not worship or kiss his hand. Lord, protect me.*

Leon and the other two directors huddled around a TV monitor. Leon still appeared grief stricken. "Once we get His Excellency into the tomb," he said, his voice thick with emotion, "the world can begin approaching some closure. Prosecuting his murderer can only aid in achieving that. Watch this with us, David. Tell me if you see what we see."

David approached the monitor, certain Fortunato could hear his heartbeat and see the flush of his face. He nearly missed the chair, then settled in awkwardly.

Shot from above, the videodisc was crystal clear. At the sound of the gunshot from Carpathia's left, he had turned and run into the wheelchair as Chaim rolled toward him. Chaim grabbed at the metal back support over his left shoulder and quickly produced what appeared to be a two-foot sword. As Nicolae tumbled atop him, Chaim whipped the weapon in front of him, holding it with both hands, point up, sharp edge facing away from the potentate.

Chaim lifted his forearms as Carpathia's body met the blade, and the sword slipped into his neck and straight through the top of his head as easily as a bayonet would slice a watermelon. Carpathia's hands shot to his chin, but David kept his eyes on Chaim, who violently twisted the handle at the base of Nicolae's neck. He let go as Carpathia dropped, then quickly steered stage left and sat with his back to the dying man.

"Well?" Leon said, peering at him. "Is there any doubt?"

David stalled, but all that served was to make the other two glance at him.

"Cameras don't lie," Leon said. "We have our assassin, don't we?"

Much as he wanted to argue, to come up with some other way to interpret what was clear, David would jeopardize his position if he proved illogical. He nodded. "We sure do."

Leon approached him, and David froze. The supreme commander took David's face in his fleshy hands and looked deep into his eyes. David fought the urge to look away, praying all the while that he would do the right thing and hoping that Annie was continuing to pray too. Like Nicolae, here was a man with clear mind control over unbelievers. He felt his pulse in his ears and wondered if Leon could detect his panic through his fingers.

"Director Hassid," Leon said, eyes boring into his. "Rayford Steele shot dead our beloved potentate."

Rayford? Hadn't they watched the same video?

Leon would be suspicious if David agreed too quickly.

"No," David said, "the disc was clear. Dr. Ro—"

"A stroke victim and a great loyal statesman would be incapable of such an act, would he not?"

"But—"

Fortunato's sweaty palms still cupped his cheeks. "The only killing weapon was the Saber in the hands of Rayford Steele, who shall have to pay for his crime."

"Rayford Steele?" David said, his voice cracking like a junior high schooler.

"The assassin."

"The assassin?"

"Look again, David, and tell me what you see."

David was terrified. He had not noticed anyone switching discs, yet this version indeed showed Rayford firing at the stage. David wondered if he was weaker than Buck had been three and a half years before. Was it possible that Leon *could* make him see something that wasn't there? He stared, unblinking. Time seemed to stand still.

Someone had to have changed the disc while he was distracted in Leon's hands. This was no concoction, no mind game. For while this showed the gunshot, it also showed Nicolae falling into Chaim's lap.

"Slow it down," David said, trying to mimic the flat voices he had heard earlier. He believed his ruse was failing miserably, but he had no choice but to play it out.

"Yes, Walter," Leon said. "Show the fatal shot again and slow it down."

David fought for control, determined to watch the lectern, the curtain, the kings. As soon as the flash of fire and the puff of smoke appeared at the end of the Saber, the lectern split, and the pieces hurtled toward the ten kings. The curtain seemed to twist on itself from the middle and shoot into the distance. Chaim appeared to come from behind the falling potentate and steer toward the center of the stage. The angle was wrong for seeing what he had actually done.

To his disgust, David had to submit a

second time to Leon's hands on his face. "Well?" Leon said, peering at him. "Is there any doubt?"

This time David could not stall. He was suddenly aware of Leon's overbearing cologne. How had he missed that before?

"Cameras don't lie," Leon said. "We have our assassin, don't we?"

David nodded, forcing Leon to loosen his grip. "We sure do," he managed. "Steele must pay."

"I hate this," Leah said as the three sat inside again. "It's nerve-racking. We shouldn't be out during the day. Too many things can go wrong."

"You shouldn't have gone to the car," Chloe said.

Leah cocked her head and gave Chloe a stare. "*I* shouldn't have gone to the car? I'm not the reason we're here, dear."

"I didn't ask you to come," Chloe said.

"Stop," Rayford said. "This gets us nowhere. Now, Chloe, I'm sorry, but this was a monumentally stupid thing to do."

"Dad! We need to get to the new place."

"And we have to check it out, but we're way past where we can get away with being out one second more than necessary, except at night."

"All right! OK! I'm sorry!"

Leah reached for her hand. "Me too," she said, but Chloe pulled away.

"C'mon, don't do that," Leah said. "I shouldn't have said that, and I'm sorry. We have to be able to work together."

"We need to get out of here," Rayford said. "Those guys think we're just friends in here for a drink. We can't stay till dark."

"We should get closer to Chicago," Chloe said.

"That'll look *more* suspicious," Rayford said, "unless we can find a place where we could leave the cars out of sight and still be able to walk into the city."

"Where the L tracks end now?" Chloe suggested.

"They end everywhere," Leah said. "Totally shut down, right?"

"Well," Chloe said, "the tracks are torn up heading in from the south, and then they're OK in the city, but they're closed."

Rayford looked to the ceiling. "So how about we find a place to hide the cars down that way, coming in from separate directions, then follow the tracks into the city."

Leah nodded. "Good idea."

Chloe said, "That's what I thought."

"If you're where I think you are," T said, "it looks impossible."

"You can see the road?" Buck said. "Why can't I hear you?"

"Wind, maybe, but you'll hear me soon. I'm already lower than I want to be, but I sure hope I'm looking at the wrong road."

"There's only one possibility in this area," Buck said. "If you see any stretch of open road, you're looking at us."

"Buck, do you have any idea how long it takes for one of these to stop? An aircraft carrier would be easier."

"Any options?"

"Yeah! I land at Jerusalem Airport or better yet, Tel Aviv, and we hope for the best."

"It would be more efficient for Chaim to commit suicide right here than to risk that, T. They're looking for him."

"I'm willing to try this, Buck, but it sure seems an uninspired way to become a martyr."

"I hear you."

"Thanks."

"I mean I literally hear you. Flash your landing lights. . . . I see you! You're way to my right!"

"Adjusting."

"More. More! More! There! No, a little left now! Hold."

"I see nothing!"

"Use your lights when you need to. That'll help me too."

"I don't like what I'm not seeing." The landing lights came on and stayed on this time. "Now I don't like what I *am* seeing."

"You seem high. I thought you were too low."

"I was lower than I wanted to be with all those emergency lights off to the left down there. Let's hope they're too busy to look up."

"You still seem high."

"I am. But I still don't see you either."

"If you stay up there, I'm safe. You gonna go 'round again?"

"Negative. I have one shot and I'm going to make it work."

"You'd better start dropping."

"Here I come."

Buck put his phone down and waved, though he couldn't imagine T seeing him from that angle. The plane drifted right, and Buck tried to signal T back to center. With his lights still on, T should have been able to see that for himself.

As the Super J screamed past him, Buck grabbed his phone and shouted, "You straight?"

"Straight as I can get! No way this works! Too steep! Too fast!"

"Abort?"

"Too late!"

Buck shut his eyes as the plane dropped and the hot exhaust swept past him. He covered his ears, knowing that would never block the sound of the impact. But what he heard wasn't a plane crash. He thought he detected the screech of tires over the din of the jets, but that may have been wishful thinking. He peeked through the dust and exhaust to see the plane bounce a couple of feet, the red exhaust flame pointing at him.

The next impact resounded like a rifle shot. White smoke billowed from beneath the craft, and the plane began spinning wildly—the red exhaust, then the landing lights, then the exhaust again. Suddenly the lights went off, but the jets continued to burn. The noise abated except for the whine of the engine, but Buck no longer saw anything. The plane had to be facing him. He had not heard the fuselage break up, as he had feared if T couldn't stop.

He ran toward the plane, amazed to see Chaim beside him, keeping pace.

The New Babylon night was warm and dry. Spotlights from a dozen angles bathed the palace courtyard, nearly bright as day. Nothing would compete with the merciless, cloudless, sun-filled daytime sky, but until then, everyone could clearly see all there was to see.

David and Annie were among the hundreds of employees allowed—or in their case assigned—to file past the bier ahead of the pilgrims from around the globe. The couple waited on the steps while ten pall-bearers—four men on each side and one at each end—solemnly carried in the draped Plexiglas box, accompanied by a live orchestra playing a dirge. From behind the barricades an eighth of a mile away, the mourning began. Employees began to wail too. The men gently placed the bier atop the pedestal and carefully positioned it. A technician, with what appeared to be a portable vacuum cleaner tucked under one arm, knelt between one of the end men and a side man and screwed a pressure gauge into the rubber stopper at the foot end. He checked the readout twice, then hooked a hose to the stopper, twisted a dial, and ran the suction machine for two seconds. He checked the pressure once more, removed everything but the stopper, then hurried away.

The eight side men backed smartly away while the two on the ends removed the shroud. Annie seemed to recoil. David was stunned. He had expected Carpathia to appear lifelike. The work of Dr. Eikenberry had been astounding, of course, as there was no evidence of trauma. Yet somehow, even in a dark suit, white shirt, and striped tie, Carpathia appeared more lifeless than any corpse David had ever seen.

The bier itself was shaped like an old-fashioned pine box, the torso area expanding to contain Carpathia's robust physique. The lid was two inches thick and bolted to the sides with huge, stainless steel screws that bit deep into the plastic, pulled the casket gasket tight, and were secured at their undersides by self-locking washers and screws.

The lid was not three inches above Carpathia's face, and as people passed, they could lean over the velvet ropes and see their breath on the top. If this was Carpathia, he would be closer to his people in death than he had ever been in life.

David had listened to the revised autopsy report wherein all references to the sword and its damage were omitted and the bullet trauma was added. At the end of that, Dr. Eikenberry had launched a clinical play-by-play as she secured the eyelids with adhesive and stitched the lips with invisible thread.

David was curious and wanted a closer look. Fortunately, the cluster in front of them paused for more than a minute. David leaned forward and studied the remains, knowing this probably made him look grief stricken. He wondered if this was really Carpathia. The body looked stiff, cold, pale. Could it be a wax figure? Might the resurrection occur in the morgue refrigerator? The vacuum-sealed Plexiglas bier certainly would not be conducive.

Carpathia's hands were more lifelike and convincing. Left was draped over right at the waist, and they looked manicured and only slightly paler than in life. They rested within a quarter inch of the transparent lid. David almost wished the man were worthy of this display.

David was stunned when several ahead of him made religious gestures, from crossing themselves to bowing. A woman nearly toppled as she gave in to tears, and David wondered what the outcry from the public would be like if GC personnel reacted like this.

Three armed guards stood on the other side of the bier. When any mourner touched the glass, the closest guard leaned over and wiped the prints away, polishing, polishing.

Finally the line moved, and David tried to guide Annie for a closer look. She surreptitiously stiffened, and he let her stay outside him as they passed. The man behind David collapsed to his knees upon full view of the body and moaned in a foreign tongue. David turned to see it was Bakar.

Annie left, still looking exhausted, and David moved atop an observation deck that had been fashioned as the second floor of one of the medical tents. He watched as the barricades were pulled away and the crowd slowly began to move toward the bier.

Someone hurrying around the outside of the courtyard distracted David, heading toward where the evidence room had already been dismantled. It was a woman carrying a bulky, paper package. He scampered down and excused himself through the crowd to get to the area from the opposite direction of the woman.

When he arrived he saw her, Dr. Eikenberry, hurrying back the way she had come. Guy Blod stood there with the package. He looked at David and shrugged. "We're going to make dawn," he said. "Thanks to your help."

David didn't want to be pals with Guy. But he did want to know what was in the package. "What've you got there, Minister Blod?"

"Just something she said the Supreme Commander wants in the statue."

"*In* the statue?"

Guy nodded. "Which means it has to go in now, because once we weld this together, the only things that will get inside it will have to be smaller than the eyeballs, nostrils, or mouth. I mean, at four times life-size, they'll be plenty big, but . . ."

"May I?" David said, reaching for the package.

"Whatever," Guy said. "It's going to burn anyway."

"Burn?"

"Or melt. The hollow legs will be an eternal furnace; don't you love it?"

"What's not to love?" David said, peeking through a corner of the paper. In his hands was the real murder weapon.

TWELVE

As Rayford followed Leah and Chloe out of the ersatz bar, one of the GC Peacekeepers was coming in. "You wouldn't be Ken Ritz, would you?"

Rayford fought for composure and noticed Leah stiffen and Chloe shoot the man a double take. With a furtive nudge, Rayford urged Chloe to keep moving and hoped Leah would do the same.

"Who's askin'?" Rayford said.

"Just yes or no, pardner," the guard said.

"Then no," Rayford said, brushing past.

"Hold on a second there, pop." Rayford preferred *pardner.* "Let me see some ID."

"I told you I'm not whoever you're look-ing for."

The guard stood in the doorway with his hand out. Rayford showed his papers.

"So, Mr. Berry, you *know* Ken Ritz?"

"Can't say that I do."

"How about your friends?"

"Guess you'd have to ask them."

"No need to be a smart aleck."

"My apologies, but how would I know about them if I don't know him?"

The guard nodded his dismissal, and as Rayford emerged, he heard him calling out in the bar: "Ken Ritz in here? R-I-T-Z!"

Leah and Chloe waited by the Rover while the other guard had one foot on the bumper of the Suburban. He was on the phone.

Rayford walked nonchalantly to the driver's side of the Rover, and the three climbed in. As he pulled away, Rayford said, "Well, so much for the Suburban."

"Thanks to me," Chloe said. "Go ahead and say it, you two. This is all my fault."

Chaim's bravado had finally cracked. Buck thought it might have been due to exhaus-tion from the running, but for whatever reason, the old man was in a panic. Buck was strangely encouraged. There was little more difficult than rescuing someone who didn't care to be rescued. At least Chaim retained a degree of self-preservation. It was a start.

The Super J sat at a severe angle with a blown tire. The door swung down and T leaned out. "You must be Dr. Rosenzweig," he shouted.

"Yeah, hey, hi, how are ya," Chaim said with a wave. "You know we got people coming, and you've got a flat tire?"

"I was afraid of that," T said. He reached to shake Rosenzweig's hand.

"Save the introductions until the GC shoots us," Chaim said. "We've got to get out of here. Have you taken off in a plane with only one tire?"

"We're not going to outrun anybody on foot. Let's give this a try."

Buck stepped up behind Rosenzweig and tried to guide him up the stairs. He wouldn't be moved. "This is lunacy, Cameron! There's barely enough road here to take off if the plane was healthy."

"You ready to turn yourself in?"

"No!"

"Well, we're leaving. You coming or taking your chances?" Buck pushed past him up the steps. He grabbed the handle and set himself to lift the door. "Last call," he said.

"There's *no* chance on the plane," Rosenzweig whined. "We're all going to die."

"No, Chaim," Buck said. "Our *only* chance is in the air. Have you given up?"

Rosenzweig leaped aboard as T muscled the plane to the end of the road, turned around, and gave it full throttle. Buck and Chaim, listing far to the left, buckled themselves in. Buck prayed. Chaim muttered, "Lunacy, lunacy. No chance. No hope."

With the engines screaming, the plane was suddenly level, though they weren't moving. Buck didn't know how T was doing it, but he used the propulsion and the brake to feather the craft up onto its one good tire. As he released the brake and maneuvered the controls, the Super J teetered crazily as it shot down the road.

At the other end the pavement had been twisted and tossed up onto its side to form a four- or five-foot barrier. As they hurtled straight toward it, Buck knew T had to find the right combination of speed and runway to pull this off. Buck couldn't tear his eyes from the barrier. Chaim sat with his head between his legs, hands clasped behind his head. He moaned, "Oh, God, oh God, oh God," and Buck had the impression it was a sincere prayer.

It seemed there was no way the J would get enough lift to clear the barrier. T seemed to be doing everything he could to keep the plane level, but the imbalance had to be affecting speed too. At the last instant T seemed to abandon balance and put all his efforts into thrust. The jet lifted off the road, then dropped, and the tire chirped on the pavement before lifting yet again.

Buck grimaced and held his breath as they swept toward the barrier. T must have adjusted one flap to avoid a direct hit, because the plane lurched right, and something underneath slammed the barrier. Now they were in no-man's-land.

"God forgive me!" Chaim shouted as the jet was tossed back to the left, then dipped and nearly crashed as T pulled out all the stops. The tail seemed to drag, and Buck couldn't imagine how it stayed airborne.

They headed for a grove of trees, but it was as if T knew he couldn't afford the drag that a turn would require. He seemed to set the jet at the shallowest possible angle to clear the trees and set it at full power. That was their one chance to get airborne, and if successful, the Super J would rocket into the night toward Greece. T would have to worry later about conserving fuel and landing on one tire.

Buck sat with fists clenched, eyes shut, grimacing, fully expecting to hit the trees and crash. He was pressed back against his seat, his head feeling the G forces as the Super J broke into open sky. He allowed his eyes to open, and in his peripheral vision, Chaim remained hunched over, now lamenting in Hebrew.

Buck unstrapped but found himself struggling to step toward the cockpit against the centrifugal force. "You did it, T!"

"Lost what was left of that bad tire, though," T said. "Think we lost the whole wheel assembly. I thought we were going down."

"Me too. That was some takeoff."

"I've got about two hours to decide how

to land. I know one-wheel landings can be done, but I'd almost rather pull up the one good wheel and go in belly first."

"Would this thing take it?"

"Not like a big one would. I'd say we're fifty-fifty for success either way."

"That's all?"

T reached for Buck's hand. "I'll see you in heaven, regardless."

"Don't say that."

"I mean it. If I didn't believe that, I'd have taken my chances with the GC back there."

Buck started when Chaim spoke, and he realized the Israeli was standing right behind him. "You see, Cameron? I was right! I should not have come! Now we have a one-in-two chance of surviving, and you two are just fine, knowing where you're going . . ."

"I wouldn't say I'm fine, Chaim," Buck said. "I'll be leaving a wife and son."

"You've already given up?" T said. "I said we've got a fifty-fifty chance of landing successfully. Even a crash landing doesn't have to be fatal."

"Thanks for that cheery word," Buck said, turning to head back to his seat.

"Pray for me," T called after him.

"I will," Buck said.

"So will I," Chaim said, and Buck shot him a look. He didn't appear to be kidding.

After Rosenzweig was buckled in, Buck leaned over and clapped him on the knee. "You don't have to be afraid of death, you know. I mean dying, yeah, I'm afraid of that too, afraid it'll hurt, that I might burn. I hate leaving my family. But you're right. T and I know where we're going."

Chaim looked terrible, worse than Buck had seen him since the night before. He couldn't make it compute. Chaim had seemed almost giddy after escaping the Gala. Then he was suicidal after hearing about Jacov and his family and Stefan. But now he looked grave. So, he was human after all. Despite all the talk of suicide, he was afraid to die.

Buck knew he had to be as forthright with Chaim as he had ever been. "We may meet God tonight, Chaim," he began, but Rosenzweig immediately made a face and waved him off.

"Don't think I wasn't listening all these years, Cameron. There is nothing more you can tell me."

"Still you refuse?"

"I didn't say that. I just said I don't need to be walked through this."

Buck couldn't believe it. Chaim said that as if he were going to do "this" on his own.

"I do have one question, however, Cameron. I know you don't consider yourself an expert like Dr. Ben-Judah, but what is your best guess about how God feels about motives?"

"Motives?"

Chaim looked frustrated, as if he wished Buck caught his drift without Chaim having to explain. He looked away, then back at Buck. "I know God is real," he said, as if confessing a crime. "There has been too much evidence to deny it. I can't explain away any of the prophecies, because they all come true. The evidences for Jesus as Messiah nearly convinced me, and I had never been a Messiah watcher. But if I were to do what you and Tsion have been pleading with me to do for so long, I confess it would be with the wrong motive."

Except for the likelihood that they might be dead within a couple of hours, Buck wished Tsion was with them right then. He wanted to ask Chaim what his motive was, but he sensed he would lose him if he interrupted.

Chaim pressed his lips together and hung his head. When he looked up again, he seemed to fight tears. He shook his head and looked away. "I need to think some more, Cameron."

"Chaim, I've pleaded with you before to not run out of time. Clearly I'm on solid footing to say so now."

Suddenly Rosenzweig leaned over and grabbed Buck's elbow. "That's the very issue! I'm scared to death. I don't want to die. I thought I did, thought it was the only answer to being a murderer, even if I believed I was just in killing the man. But I did it with forethought, with months of forethought. I planned it, fashioned my own weapon, and saw it through. I have no pity, no sympathy for Nicolae Carpathia. I came to believe, as you do, that he was the devil incarnate."

That wasn't quite accurate, but Buck held his tongue. While believers were convinced Carpathia was the Antichrist and deserved to be killed and stay dead, they knew that he would not literally be Satan incarnate until he came back to life.

Whether he deserved to live again or not, that was what was prophesied.

"It's hard for me to fathom that I might have been in God's plan from the beginning. If it is true that Carpathia is the enemy of God and that he was supposed to die from a sword wound to the head, I feel like Judas."

Judas? A nonreligious Jew knows the New Testament too?

"Don't look so surprised, Cameron. Everyone understands what a Judas is. Someone was to betray Jesus, and it fell to Judas. Someone was to murder Antichrist, and while I cannot say it actually fell to me, I took the job into my own hands. But say it *was* my destiny. Though apparently God *wanted* it done, it certainly was not legal. And look at what it has cost me already! My freedom. My peace of mind, which, I admit, is only a distant memory. My loved ones.

"But Cameron, can God accept me if my motive is selfish?"

Buck squinted and turned to look out the window. The dim, sparse lights of Israel receded fast. "We all come to faith selfish in some ways, Chaim. How could it be otherwise? We want to be forgiven. We want to be accepted, received, included. We want to go to heaven instead of hell. We want to be able to face death knowing what comes next. *I* was selfish. I didn't want to face the Antichrist without the protection of God in my life."

"But Cameron, I am merely afraid to die! I feel like a coward. Here I did this rash thing, which many would say took courage and even strength of character. At first I took pride in it. Now I know, of course, that God could have used anyone to do it. He could have caused something to pierce Carpathia's head during the earthquake. He could have had a political rival or a crazy man do it. Perhaps he did! Part of it was compulsion, especially perfecting the weapon. But I had motives, Cameron. I hated the man. I hated his lies and his broken promises to my homeland. I hated even what he did to the practicing Jews and their new temple, even though I did not count myself among them.

"I am without excuse! I am guilty. I am a sinner. I am lost. I don't want to die. I don't want to go to hell. But I fear he will cast me out because I squandered so many opportunities, because I resisted for so long, because I suffered even many of the judgments and still was cold and hard. Now, if I come whimpering to God as a child, will he see through me? Will he consider me the little boy who cried wolf? Will he know that down deep I am merely a man who once had a wonderful life and enjoyed what I now see were bountiful gifts from God—a creative mind, a wonderful home and family, precious friends—and became a crazy old fool?

"Cameron, I sit here knowing that all you and Tsion and your dear associates have told me is true. I believe that God loves me and cares about me and wants to forgive me and accept me, and yet my own conscience gets in the way."

Buck was praying as he had not prayed in ages. "Chaim, if you told God what you're telling me, you'd find out the depth of his mercy."

"But, Cameron, I would be doing this only because I'm afraid I'm going to die in this plane! That's all. Do you understand?"

Buck nodded. He understood, but did he know the answer to Chaim's question? People through the ages had all kinds of motives for becoming believers, and surely fear was a common one. He'd heard Bruce Barnes say that people sometimes come to Christ for fire insurance—to stay out of hell—only to later realize all the benefits that come with the policy.

"You said yourself that I don't consider myself an expert," Buck said, "but you also said you knew you were a sinner. That's the real reason we need Jesus. If you weren't a sinner, you'd be perfect and you wouldn't need to worry about forgiveness and salvation."

"But I knew I was a sinner before, and I didn't care!"

"You weren't staring death in the face either. You weren't wondering whether you might end up in hell."

Rosenzweig rubbed his palms together. "I was tempted to do this when I was suffering from the locust attack. I knew that was a prophesied biblical event, but I also knew that becoming a believer would not speed my recovery. You told me that yourself. And relief would have been my only motive then, as I fear it is now. What I should do, intellectually, is wait and see if I survive this landing or this crash or what-

ever it is we're going to do. If I am not facing imminent death, I won't be so suspicious of my own intentions."

"In other words," Buck said, " 'get me out
of this and I'll become a believer'?"

Chaim shook his head. "I know better
than to bargain with God. He owes me
nothing; he need not do one more thing to
persuade me. I just want to be honest. If I
would not have come to the same conclusion on the ground or in a plane with two
good tires, then I should not rush into it
now."

Buck cocked his head. "Friend, rushing
into this would be the last way I would describe you. My question is, why do you
feel in any more danger now than you did
on the ground, or than you will feel if we
land safely?"

Chaim raised his chin and shut his eyes.
"I don't. The GC has already announced
my death and is now free to exterminate
me without the nuisance of publicity. That's
why I found myself running to this plane. I
don't need to tell you the dread of living in
exile."

"But whatever motive you have now, you

will also have if we survive. Nothing changes."

"Maybe I'll lose the urgency," Rosenzweig said, "the sense of imminence."

"But you don't know that. They may have to foam the runway, bring out the emergency vehicles, all that. You can't hide under a blanket or claim to be contagious when we leave the plane. And you can't hide in the lav until the coast is clear. You're going to be as exposed and as vulnerable as ever, safe landing or no."

Chaim held up a hand and slowly closed his eyes. "Give me a minute," he said. "I may have more questions, but just leave me alone a moment."

That was the last thing Buck wanted to do just then, but neither did he want to push Chaim away. He settled back, amazed at how smooth was the ride that might lead them to eternity.

Kenny Bruce took long afternoon naps, and Tsion looked forward to that. He loved the boy and had had a lot of fun with him for the last fourteen months, even in cramped quarters. He was a good-natured, though normal, kid, and Tsion loved teasing him and playing with him.

Kenny could be wearying, however, especially for one who had not been around infants for nearly twenty years. Tsion needed a nap himself, though he was still desperate not to miss whatever was going to happen in New Babylon.

"Mama?" Kenny asked for the dozenth time, not troubled but curious. It was unusual for her to be gone.

"Bye-bye," Tsion said. "Home soon. Getting sleepy?"

Kenny shook his head, even as he rubbed his eyes and appeared to be trying to keep them open. He yawned and sat with a toy, soon losing interest. He lay on his back, feet flat on the floor, knees up. Staring at the ceiling, he yawned, turned on his side, and was soon motionless. Tsion carried him to the playpen so he wouldn't fuss if he awoke before Tsion did. There were plenty of things to keep him occupied there.

Tsion settled before the TV again and put his feet up. The underground was cool, so he draped a blanket over himself. He tried to keep his eyes open as the GC

CNN pool camera remained trained on the transparent coffin and the endless line of the mourning faithful from around the world.

Knowing that young David Hassid and his lady friend Annie Christopher were there, along with who knew how many other believers, he began silently walking through his prayer list. When he closed his eyes to pray for his comrades and his cybercongregation (more than a billion now), he felt himself nodding and his brain longing for sleep.

He peeked at the digital clock on the videodisc player atop the TV. He set the machine to record, just in case he fell asleep and was unable to wake up in time for "the" event. As he settled back in to try to pray, knowing full well he would drift off, the clock showed 12:57 in the afternoon.

Tsion began praying for Chloe, Leah, and Rayford, whom he knew were in the state. Then he prayed for T, Rayford's friend, who was presently unaccounted for. Then Cameron, always in the middle of something and who knew where. As his mind drifted to his old friend and professor, Dr. Rosenzweig, Tsion began feeling a tin-

gle, much like when he had tried to intercede for Rayford.

Was it fatigue, a hallucination? So dis-
concerting, so real. He forced his eyes
open. The clock still read 12:57, but he felt
as if he were floating. And when he let his
eyes fall shut again, he could still see plain
as day. The cramped cellar was cool and
musty, the sparse furniture in its place.
Kenny slept unmoving in the playpen, blanket still tucked around him.

Tsion saw this from above now, as if in
the middle of the room. He saw himself
asleep on the couch. He had heard of out-
of-body experiences but had never had
one, or dreamed one. This didn't seem like
a dream, didn't feel like one. He felt
weightless, moving higher, wondering if the
joists from the flooring above would conk
him on the head as he rose and whether
that would hurt a floating, hallucinating,
dreaming, praying, or sleep-deprived man.
He wasn't sure what kind of a man he was
right then, but despite his incredible light-
ness of being, he felt as conscious and
aware as he had ever been. Though he
knew he was unconscious, he had never
been so attuned to his senses. He could

see clearly and feel everything from temperature to the air moving over the hair on his arms as he ascended. He heard every noise in the house, from Kenny's breathing to the refrigerator kicking on as he passed it.

Yes, he had drifted through the first floor, but he could still see Kenny and neither worried nor felt guilty about leaving him. For he saw himself too, still on the couch, knowing that if Kenny needed him, he could return as quickly as he had left.

The fall air was crisp above the house, yet he was glad he was in shirtsleeves. It was not uncomfortable, but he was so aware of everything . . . feeling, seeing, hearing—the wind through the dead-leafed trees. He even smelled the decaying leaves on the ground, though no one burned them anymore. No one did anything anymore that used to be mundane. Life was about surviving now, not about incidentals. If a task did not put food on the table or provide shelter, it was ignored.

In an instant Tsion instinctively shot his arms out for balance and felt as if he had returned almost to his sleeping form in the underground. But the house, the half-destroyed village of Mount Prospect, the northwest suburbs, the twisted ribbons that used to be highways and tollways, the whole Chicago area had become minuscule beneath him.

Would he soon grow colder, lose oxygen? How could it be that he was this far from home, now looking at a blue globe that reminded him of the hauntingly beautiful pictures of earth from the moon? Daylight turned to night, but the earth was still illuminated. He felt as if he were in the deep recesses of space, maybe on the moon. Was he on the moon? He looked about him and saw only stars and galaxies. He reached for the earth, because it seemed to recede too quickly. In a strange way, though he could not see it anymore, he sensed he and Kenny still slept in Mount Prospect at the safe house.

He was soon able to see the planets as he drifted, drifted, farther and farther from all that he knew. How fast could he be going? Such physical questions seemed pedestrian, irrelevant. The question was, where was he and where was he going? How long could this go on?

It was so, so strange and wonderful, and

for the briefest instant, Tsion wondered if he had died. Was he on his way to heaven? He had never believed heaven was on the same physical plane as the universe, somewhere rocket men could go if they had the resources. And at the same time he had never before felt so thoroughly alive. He was not dead. He was somewhere in his mind, he was convinced.

In an instant, as he seemed to hang weightless in space, it seemed he accelerated yet again. He raced through the vast universe itself, with its numberless galaxies and solar systems. The only sound was his own breathing, and to his amazement, it was rhythmic and deep, as if, as if, as if he were asleep.

But he wondered how so puny a mind could dream such a vista. And as if a switch had been pulled, the darkness turned to the brightest light, obliterating the utter darkness of space. Just as the stars disappear in the light of the sun, so everything he had passed on his way to this plateau vanished. He hung motionless in soundless, weightless animation, a sense of expectancy coursing through him.

This light, like a burst of burning magnesium so powerful as to chase even a shadow, came from above and behind him. Despite the sense of wonder and anticipation, he feared turning toward it. If this was the Shekinah glory, would he not die in its presence? If this was the very image of God, could he see it and live?

The light seemed to beckon him, to will him to turn. And so he did.

THIRTEEN

Rayford drove as close as he could to the Chicago city limits, staying on a rebuilt collar road that had ominous warning signs its entire length, prohibiting traffic beyond its northern line. Patrolling GC cars ignored the sparse traffic, so Rayford looked for a turn that would appear to take him into a local area but which might lead him off-road to the city.

He felt as conspicuous and obvious as he had in a long time, bouncing over dusty lots and through closed forest preserves in the middle of the day. But he detected no tail. He parked the Land Rover beneath a crumbling former L station. He and Chloe and Leah sat in the shade, Rayford beginning to feel the fatigue that had preceded his wonderful sleep in Greece.

"This is my fault," Chloe said. "I was impatient and stupid and selfish. No way we can walk into Chicago until tonight. And how far is it? Twenty miles to the Strong Building? It'll take hours."

Leah shifted in her seat. "If you're looking for someone to argue with you, I can't. I'm not trying to be mean, but we're going to sit here until dark. Then we're going to walk at least five hours to what, check out our next safe house?"

Chloe sat shaking her head.

"We're not walking anywhere," Rayford said. "I know this town like the back of my hand. When it's good and dark, we're going to drive to the building with our lights off. The GC aren't keeping people out of here for fun. They really believe it's contaminated. If we have to turn on the lights now and then to keep from getting swallowed up in a hole and some surveillance plane spots us or some heat detector locates us, at worst they'll warn us to get out. They're not coming in after us."

"No, Dad," Chloe said. "The worst that will happen is that they force us out and figure out who you are."

"They would keep their distance and check us for radiation first."

"And finding none, there goes our whole plan."

"There's enough to think negatively about these days," Rayford said. "Let's think positive. Bad enough I have to give Buck the news about his family soon."

"Let me do that, Dad."

"Are you sure?"

"Absolutely. When he calls, let me talk to him."

But when Buck called, it was clear this was still not the time to give him news like that. Rayford watched as Chloe seemed to disintegrate on the phone. "Thank you, sweetheart," she said. "Thanks for telling us. We'll be praying. I love you too, and Kenny loves you. Call me as soon as you can. Promise me."

Chloe rang off and quickly brought Rayford and Leah up to speed.

"So that's where T is," Rayford said. "Good thinking on Buck's part. We need to pray for them right now."

"Especially for Chaim," Chloe said. "He sounds close."

"Landing on one wheel is risky," Rayford said, "but it can be done. I think this is T's first time in a Super J, though."

"What kinds of odds would you give them?" Leah said, then appeared to regret asking, realizing Chloe could lose her husband within the next twenty minutes.

"No, I want to know too," Chloe said. "Really, Dad. What are their chances?"

Rayford stalled but saw little value in getting Chloe's hopes up. "About one in two," he said.

Chaim called for Buck, who had joined T in the cockpit. Buck went back and knelt near Chaim's seat. "One more question," Rosenzweig said. "Dare I test God?"

"How?"

"Tell him I want to believe, offer him what's left of my life, and just see if he'll accept me in spite of my selfish motive."

"I can't speak for God," Buck said. "But it seems to me if we're sincere, he'll do what he promised. You already know that this is about more than mere believing, because you believe now. The Bible says the demons believe and tremble. It's a decision, a commitment, a receiving."

"I know."

"We're about fifteen minutes out, Chaim, give or take circling and getting some tower help. Don't stall."

"But you see?" Chaim said. "That just contributes to my problem. I won't be any more just because my time may be running out. I may be even less."

"Let God decide," Buck said.

Chaim nodded miserably. Buck didn't envy his having to work this out while wondering how long he had to live. Chloe and Kenny were at the forefront of Buck's mind, and knowing he would see them again in three and a half years regardless did nothing to abate his desperation not to leave them.

He headed back to the seat next to T. "I've been in touch with the tower at an airport south of Ptolemaïs called Kozani. They agree I might have a better shot trying a belly landing than trying to put down on one wheel. No telling how strong that one is, or how good a pilot I am. If I'm not perfect, we bounce and that's it. Going in flat will allow me to land at the slowest possible speed and hope for the best."

"You've got to really be smooth, don't you?"

"Tell me about it."

"You gonna fly over low first and see if they can get a look at the wheels?"

T pointed to the fuel gauge, buried on empty. "You tell me."

"Well, that could be good news, couldn't it?"

"How so?" T said.

"If we crash, we don't burn."

"If we crash, Buck, you're going to want to burn. You're going to wish we were vaporized."

Tsion felt such a sense of peace and well-being that he didn't want this to end, dream or not. He knew he should be terrified to turn and face the light, but it was the light itself that drew him.

He did not move as if in water or in a vacuum. He didn't have to move his limbs. All he had to do was will himself to turn, and he turned. At first Tsion believed he was looking into a bottomless crevice, the only dark spot in a wall of bright white. But as he backed away from the image, so real he believed he could touch it, other dark spaces of relief came into view. As his eyes adjusted to the light, he pulled back far enough to make out a face. It was as if he dangled between the nose and cheekbone of some heavenly Mount Rushmore image.

But this was neither carved from stone nor made of flesh and bone. Huge and bright and strong, it was also at once translucent, and Tsion was tempted to will himself to pass through it. But as it should have been frightening and was not, he wanted to see the whole. If a head, then a body? He pulled back to see the face ringed with hair massive as prairie grass. It framed a face kindly and yet not soft, loving and yet confident and firm.

Tsion knew beyond doubt he was imagining this, and at the same time it was *the* most sensory-rich experience of his life. It burned into his mind's eye, and he believed he would never forget it nor experience anything like it again as long as he lived.

His voice nearly failed him, but he managed to croak, "Are you Jesus the Christ?"

A rumble, a chuckle, a terrestrial laugh? "No," came a gentle voice that surrounded him and, coming from a mouth that size, should have blown him into oblivion. "No, son of the earth, I am merely one of his princes."

Tsion pulled back farther to take in the scope of this beautiful heavenly being. "Gabriel?" he whispered.

"Gabriel and I are as brothers, child. He announces. I command the heavenly host."

It came to Tsion at once. The great sword long as the Jordan, the breastplate big as the Sinai. "You are Michael! The prince who shall defend my people, the chosen ones of God."

"You have said it."

"Prince of God, have I died?"

"Your time has yet to come."

"May I inquire more?"

"You may, though I prefer righteous warfare to conversation. Gabriel announces. I engage in battle."

"A selfish question, sir. Will I remain until the Glorious Appearing?"

"It is appointed unto men once to die, and—"

"But will I die before the—"

"That is not for you to know, created one. It has no bearing on your obligation to serve the Most High God."

Tsion wanted to bow to this being and to the truth he spoke. He could not believe he had interrupted Michael the archangel, one of only two named angels in all of Scripture.

"Why am I here if I am not dead?"

"You have much to learn, teacher."

"Will I learn the identity of Antichrist, the enemy of God?"

Michael seemed to grow stony, if that were possible for an angel. It was as if the mere mention of Antichrist had stoked his bloodlust for battle. He spoke again: "Antichrist shall be revealed in the due time."

"But, sir," Tsion said, feeling like a child, "is not now the due time?"

"We measure past, present, and future with different rods than you, son of earth. The due time is the due time, and to the prudent and watchful ones, the revelation will be clear."

"We'll know for sure the identity of the . . . of the enemy?"

"So I have spoken."

"Teach me all I am here to learn, great

prince who stands watch over the sons of Abraham, Isaac, and Jacob."

"Stand silent," the angel said, "observe, and give ear to the truth of the war in heaven. Since the calling up of the righteous dead and alive, the enemy has competed with the hosts of heaven for the remaining souls of men.

"The evil one, that old serpent, has had access to the throne of the Most High since the beginning of time, until now, the appointed time."

What was he saying? That Tsion was there to witness the end of Satan's access to the throne, where for millennia he had exercised his power to accuse the children of God? Tsion wanted to ask how he earned so great a privilege, but Michael put a finger to his lips and beckoned with his other hand for Tsion to look past him to the very throne room. Tsion immediately fell prostrate in what seemed the midair of the extended universe. He saw only one figure, bigger, brighter, and more beautiful than Michael himself.

Tsion covered his eyes. "Is it the Lamb of God who takes away the sin of the world?"

"Silence, son of earth. This is neither Son nor Father, whom you will not see until *your* due time. Before you is the angel of light, the beautiful star, the great deceiver, your adversary, Lucifer."

Tsion shuddered, repulsed, yet unable to look away. "Is this the present?" he asked.

"Eternity past and future are the present here," Michael said. "Listen and learn."

Suddenly Tsion was able to hear the beautiful angel plead his case before the throne, which was beyond Tsion's view.

"Your so-called children are beneath you, ruler of heaven," came the persuasive mellifluous tones of the eternal solicitor. "Abandon them to me, who can fashion them for profit. Even after being called by your name, their natures reek with temporal desires. Allow me to surround myself with these enemies of your cause, and I will marshal them into a force unlike any army you have ever assembled."

From the throne came a voice of such power and authority that volume was irrelevant: "Thou shalt not touch my beloved!"

"But with them I shall ascend to a throne higher than yours!"

"No!"

"They are weak and ineffective in your service!"

"No!"

"I can salvage these hopeless wrecks."

"Thou shalt not."

"I beseech you, ruler of heaven and earth—"

"No."

"Grant me these or I will—"

"No."

"I will—"

"No."

"I will destroy them and defeat you! I shall bear the name above all other names! I shall sit high above the heavens, and there shall be no god like me! In *me* there shall be no change, neither shadow of turning."

Suddenly from Tsion's right he saw the flash in the eyes of Michael the archangel, and he spoke with great emotion. "God, the Father Almighty," he shouted, causing the evil one to look his way in disgust, then anger, "I beseech you allow no more blas-phemy in the courts of heaven! Grant that I destroy this one and cast him out of your presence!"

Yet Michael apparently neither heard nor

sensed the permission of God. Lucifer glared with contempt at Michael, smirking, laughing. He turned back to face the throne.

"Michael, your master shall not assign you an impossible task! He knows I am right about the sons of God. He will eventually concede them to me. You are a fool, weak and unable to face me on your own. You shall lose. I shall win. I shall ascend—"

But as Tsion watched and listened, Lucifer's voice changed. It became high-pitched and whiny, and his persona began to change. As he railed and begged and challenged and blasphemed, the voice from the throne continued to deny him. His bright shining robe lost its luster. His face curled into a hideous mask of scales. His hands and feet disappeared, and his garment fell off, revealing a slimy, writhing, coiling serpent. His eyes sank under deep hoods and his voice became a hiss, then a roar as he seemed to transform himself.

His hands and feet reappeared, but his fingers and toes had turned to great horned appendages. He dropped to all fours. His words had vanished into flaming breaths, and he paced before the throne with such anger that Tsion was glad Michael stood between him and this dragon.

His head grew horns and a crown appeared upon it, and suddenly his whole being turned fiery red. As Tsion watched in horror, the beast grew six more heads with crowns and a total of ten horns. Pacing and growing ever larger with each step, the beast shook itself in rage and threatened the throne and they that sat upon it.

And the voice from the throne said, "No."

With a great roar and stomping and shaking of its heads, the dragon postured threateningly and appeared to want to advance on the throne. Michael stepped that way, and the voice again said, "No."

Michael turned to Tsion. "Behold," he said, pointing behind Tsion.

Tsion turned to see the figure of a woman with clothes as bright as the sun. While Michael's brightness had nearly blinded him and Lucifer proved brighter still, the woman . . . the woman appeared as if clothed in the sun. It seemed she stood on the moon itself, and on her head was a wreath made of twelve stars.

Tsion was transfixed and felt a great kinship with the woman. He wanted to ask Michael who she was. Mary? Israel? The church? But he could not speak, could not turn. He was aware that the hideous seven-headed dragon was behind him but that Michael stood between him and that danger.

The woman was pregnant, her great sun-clothed belly causing her to turn and cry out in labor pains. She grimaced and her body convulsed in contractions, and as she held her abdomen as if about to give birth, the dragon leaped from his place before the throne, clearing Michael and Tsion and pouncing before the woman.

His great tail swept a third of the stars from the heavens, and they plummeted to the earth. And now he crouched before the woman who was ready to give birth, seven mouths open and salivating, tongues darting, ready to devour her child as soon as it was born.

She bore a male child who was caught up to God. The dragon watched in rage as the child was transported to the throne, and when he turned back to the woman, she had fled. He rose up to give chase, and Michael the archangel said, "Behold."

Tsion turned to watch him use both mighty hands to pull the golden sword from its sheath and swing it in a high arc over his head. Immediately he was joined by a heavenly host of warrior angels, who fell in behind him as the dragon's angels also mustered behind him.

Tsion had so many questions, but Michael had led the charge against the dragon. Perhaps Gabriel the announcer was close by. Tsion opened his mouth to ask, but when he said, "Who is the woman?" his words sounded plain to him and he felt enclosed. "Who is the woman?" he repeated, and his words woke him with a start.

He sat up and his blanket slid off. The TV still showed the slow moving line of mourners, bathed in the eerie palace courtyard spotlights. Tsion stood and peered into the playpen where Kenny slept, having not moved. He sat back down and stared unbelieving at the videodisc player clock. It read 12:59.

Movement in the cabin caught Buck's eye. In the darkness he saw Chaim unstrap himself and awkwardly kneel in the aisle, his elbows on the armrest. Buck touched T's arm and nodded back. T looked and glanced at Buck, who raised both fists and bowed his head. He turned sideways so he had one ear facing the cabin. The man who had been so endearing and so stubborn was finally on his knees.

"Oh, God," Chaim began, "I have never before prayed believing that I was actually talking to you. Now I know that you are there and that you want me, and I don't know what to say." He began to weep.

"Forgive me for coming to you only because I am afraid for my life. Only you know the truth about me, whether I am sincere. You know better than I. I know that I am a sinner and need your forgiveness for all my sins, even for murder, regardless that the victim was your archenemy. Thank you for taking the punishment for my sins. Forgive me and receive me into your kingdom. I want to give you all of myself for the rest of my days. Show me what to do. Amen."

Buck looked back to where Chaim remained kneeling, his head buried in his arms. "Cameron?" he called, his voice muffled.

"Yes, Chaim?"

"I prayed, but I'm still scared!"

"So am I!"

"Me too!" T said.

"You tested God?" Buck said.

"I did. I guess I won't know his decision until we crash and I wake up in heaven or hell."

"Oh, the Bible says we can know."

"It does?"

"It says his Spirit bears witness with our spirit that we are children of God. What does your spirit say?"

"My spirit says to land carefully."

Buck laughed in spite of himself. "Chaim, there is a way we can know in advance. Do you want to know?"

"With all my heart."

"T, turn the lights on back there."

David stood atop the observation tower again, watching the line. With a couple of hours to go before midnight, the air was cool enough to keep the crowd calm. The next day was expected to be over one hundred degrees, and he worried about health and tempers. The funeral was to begin in twelve hours, but David couldn't imagine the crowds having completely passed by the bier that soon.

From his perch he could see the final touches on the massive, black, hollow, iron and bronze image of the late potentate, made from a postmortem body cast. Guy Blod seemed about to burst, supervising the last welds and the winching of it into place. Guy would stand on a scaffold and do the final sanding and polishing himself, planning to have workmen roll the finished product near the bier sometime before dawn.

Fortunato and his lackeys were making the rounds, and Leon had a couple of folded sheets of paper in his hand and seemed to be taking copious notes. He and his entourage visited the statue-making operation, where Guy broke long enough to animatedly point out the features and accept accolades from the Supreme Commander.

The Fortunato juggernaut moved to the middle of the long line, where many had been waiting for hours. People bowed and knelt and kissed his hands. Often he lifted them and pointed up to the bier, and they stood nodding and gesturing.

Leon checked the various concession tents and stands, none of which would open until daybreak. When he got to the stand beneath where David stood, David's worst fears were realized. "Anyone seen Director Hassid?" Leon said.

While his people were shaking their heads, someone in the tent said, "He's upstairs, Commander."

"With whom?"

"Alone, I think."

"Gentlemen, wait for me, would you?"

He mounted the steps, and David felt the whole structure sway. David acted as if he was not expecting anyone and had not heard anyone come up.

"Director Hassid, I presume," Fortunato said.

David turned. "Commander."

"Want to join our little group, David? We're just greeting the people."

"No, thanks. Long day. I'm about to turn in."

"I understand," Leon said, pulling the pages from his pocket. "Have time to give me a little input?"

"Sure."

"I'm getting pressure from a few people

in Rome for a memorial service for Pontifex Maximus. Remember him?"

Leon had asked that seriously, as if David wouldn't remember the head of the one-world faith who had died within the week. "Of course," David said.

"Well, he seems to have faded from most people's memories, and I'm inclined to leave it that way."

"Not have the service, you mean?"

"You agree?" Fortunato said.

"I'm just asking."

"Well, I agree with you that we probably shouldn't have it."

That wasn't what David had said, of course, but there was no sense squabbling. Fortunato was likely eliciting the same forced ideas from everyone around him, and he would eventually find himself "acquiescing" to the counsel from his staff.

"I would like spiritual matters centralized here in New Babylon for good, and I believe there is a place for a personal expression of faith better than what that amalgam gave us."

"Everyone seemed to go for that all-faiths-into-one idea, Commander."

"Yes, but with mounting evidence that

Potentate Carpathia deserves sainthood, and the possibility that he himself was divine, I believe there's a place for worshiping and even praying to our fallen leader. What do you think?"

"I think you will prevail."

"Well, thank you for that. David, I have found you a most capable and loyal worker. I want you to know that you can name your role in my regime."

"Your regime?"

"Surely you don't see anyone else in line for Supreme Potentate."

David was tempted to tell him who the potentate would be very soon. "No, I don't suppose."

"I mean, if you do, tell me. I have people watching the three dissident kings closely, and I think Litwala has a lean and hungry look. You know where that's from, Hassid?"

"Shakespeare. *Julius Caesar.*"

"You *are* well read. What role would motivate you?"

"I'm happy where I am, sir."

"*Really?*"

"Yes."

"Well, how would you respond to a

healthy raise and a title change, say special assistant to the supreme potentate?"

David knew this would all be moot soon.
"I wouldn't oppose it," he said.

"You wouldn't oppose it!" Fortunato
laughed. "I like that! Look at this list of
people who want to say a few words at the
funeral tomorrow." He swore. "Self-serving
sons of the devil."

Takes one to know one, David thought.

"You want to say a few words?"

"No."

"Because I could squeeze you in."

"No, thank you."

"It'd be no problem, give you some visi-
bility."

"No."

"Going to get some rest, eh?"

"Yes, sir."

"And you'll be back when?"

"Daybreak, I imagine."

"Hmm."

"Problem, sir?"

"I was looking for someone from our
level to be here when the statue is put in
place."

"Blod's a minister."

"Yeah, but, you know."

David didn't know, but he nodded none-theless.

"Could you be there, David?"

"Whatever you say, sir."

"Attaboy."

Buck moved into the cabin as Chaim rose and turned to face him. He looked ex-hausted and was tearstained. Chaim now had his back to the armrest he had leaned on, and it caught him just above the knee. Buck put a hand on each of Chaim's shoulders, and the old man lurched back and plopped into the seat, his feet on Buck's knees.

"So, you saw it, did you?" Buck said.

"Yes!" Chaim said, rising. "And you can see mine?" He maneuvered until he was directly under a light, and he held a shock of white hair out of the way.

"I sure can, Chaim. You didn't believe us all this time, did you? That we could see each other's marks, I mean."

"Actually, I did believe you," Chaim said. "Not all of you would have lied to me. I was so jealous."

"No more."

"So God knew my heart."

"Apparently."

"That in itself is a miracle."

"Prepare for descent," T hollered.

"I can't say I'm any less scared," Chaim said.

"I'm scared too, friend, but a lot less than I would be if I didn't know my destination."

FOURTEEN

Leah was tired and bored, despite being fascinated by the change in Rayford and the relationship between him and his daughter. Even with the windows open and a chilly breeze coming through, the Land Rover was cramped and oppressive.

When her phone rang and it was Ming, she was alarmed but glad for the diversion.

"I am going to get to see my parents and my brother again," Ming said.

"That's great. How? Where?"

"At the funeral."

"You're going?"

"And so are they. I called to tell them I

had been assigned crowd control and they insisted on coming."

"Well, that's good, isn't it?"

"Leah, I am so worried about my parents. They do not know about either Chang or me being believers. They were *such* admirers of Carpathia that they are sick with grief. I want to tell them and persuade them, but it would take a miracle."

"It's always a miracle, Ming. We'll pray with you that it will happen."

"You don't know my father."

"I know, but God is bigger than any of that. How are you getting to New Babylon? I heard all flights were full."

"Military transport. I don't know how my family found seats, except that my father has a lot of influence with the GC. His business contributes more than 20 percent of its profits to New Babylon. They are expecting another million people there tomorrow. I'm telling you, Leah, even prisoners here are mourning Carpathia."

"When you're there, look up David Hassid and Annie Christopher."

"Believers?"

"Of course. Keep up the front. Pretend to argue with them. They'll notice your mark and play along to protect you. Introduce your brother. I'll tip them off that your parents don't know. Hey, any more news on Hattie or on Cameron Williams's family?"

A pause.

"You can tell me, Ming."

"Well, it's sort of good news and bad news."

"Shoot."

"The Williamses' home burned and two bodies were discovered, identified as Cameron Williams's father and brother."

"And?"

"This is unconfirmed, Leah, but there is some evidence that they may have become believers."

"That will be so helpful if Buck could know that for sure."

"I'll see what I can find out without being too obvious, but someone said the murders and the torching had to wait because they were at a church-type meeting."

"Does that mean the GC knows where the church meets?"

"Likely. They know more than most believers want to think."

"We've got to warn that church."

*　*　*

Buck listened to T talk on the radio to the tower at Kozani. "Very low on fuel. I may make one test pass, but I'd better go for it."

"On the downside, Super Juliet, we have no foam and no prospects to get any soon. You might want to jettison remaining fuel before the final attempt."

"Roger that."

"You have friends in high places, Juliet."

"Repeat?"

"You have new equipment coming."

"I'm not following you, tower."

"Man named Albie. Know him?"

"Heard of him. Friend of a friend."

"That's what he said. He's delivering a plane for you, assuming yours is going to need some rehab."

"Roger. What's he bringing?"

"No idea."

"How's he going to get back?"

"I believe he's planning to do the fix on yours and take it in trade."

"He'd better be bringing something pretty nice."

"Just hope yours is worth trading after you scrape our runway."

"Roger."

Buck looked at T. "Do you believe that? Rayford had to set that up."

"Wonder when Albie's expected."

Buck shook his head. "He's got a lot longer flight than we do, and who knows where he's getting the craft?"

"I can't wait to see it."

"I can't wait to see if we survive."

"I believe we will," T said. "We'll take a look at the situation, jettison, and slide her in there nice and smooth."

"I love the confidence in your voice."

"Must be my acting background."

"Don't say that."

"Truth is, Buck, I need both of you strapped in in the very back seats. I'll call out altitude readings. By fifty feet, you should be braced and tucked, but you can get into that position anytime after you hear one hundred feet. Got it?"

Buck nodded.

"We're close. Get Chaim ready."

Buck stood and was moving into the cabin when T said, "Oh, no!"

"What?"

The interior lights went dark. Battery-operated emergency lights eerily illuminated the control board.

"What's happening?" Chaim called out. "Someone talk to me."

"Let's just say we won't have to jettison fuel," T said. "Get strapped in now, back seats, and don't talk to me till we're on the ground."

"I'm ready for heaven!" Chaim said. "But tonight I prefer asphalt to gold, if you don't mind."

"Shut up, Doctor," T said, and he called the tower on batteries. "Mayday, Kozani tower, this is the Super J, and we're out of fuel, repeat, out of fuel. On battery backup, landing lights may not be fully operational."

"Roger, Juliet," came the response, as Buck settled in across the aisle from Chaim. "Landing gear retracted?"

"Roger," T said. "Wheels up. Stand by."

"Repeat? Did we get a wheels-up confirm?"

"Negative."

"Due to power out, or do you think wheels are not up?"

"Didn't feel anything."

"Keep in mind as you come in. You have us in sight?"

"Affirmative."

"All runway lights on."

"Thank you. Landing lights on."

"Roger. Repeat wheels-up procedure."

"Roger."

"Successful?"

"Negative."

"We'll try to see when you come in. It will affect your drag and what you want to do."

"Roger."

"Altitude?"

"A thousand and falling . . . nine hundred . . . eight . . ."

"Dropping too fast, Juliet! You must clear south fence."

"Affirmative. Working on it. Seven . . . six . . . five-fifty."

"Must slow descent, Juliet."

"Worried about airworthiness."

"Roger, but fence must be top priority."

"Roger. Four . . . three . . . two . . ."

Tsion stood and stretched and checked on Kenny. He felt as if he'd been out for hours, yet he was as weary as when he nodded off. While he was determined not to miss anything in New Babylon, he knew he needed sleep. He sat back down and settled in, hoping, praying he would again be transported to the very portals of heaven. He didn't know what to call what had happened to him or how to assess it, but it had been the privilege of a lifetime. He was left with so many questions and so much more to come. But before he slept he again felt compelled to pray for his brothers and sisters on the front lines.

David headed for his quarters, phoning Guy on the way. "I'd like to see the positioning of the statue when you're ready."

"Now?"

"I say, when you're ready. The regular schedule will be fine."

"You're asking permission?"

"I'm just saying I'd like to watch. There a problem with that?"

"I don't need my hand held."

"Believe me, Guy, I don't want to hold your hand."

"Protocol demands that you not refer to me by my first name."

"Sorry, Blood."

"It's Blod, and my last name isn't appropriate either!"

"Oh, I don't think it's that bad."

"Ooh! My title is Minister!"

"Sorry, Reverend Minister. But your supreme commander and mine wants a liaison from administration present when you move naked boy into position."

"How rude and tacky."

"That's sort of what I thought, but I'm surprised you agree."

"David!"

"Ah, Director Hassid to you, Minister Blood. Anyway, he chose me, so don't leave home without me."

"David! *I* am a minister, therefore *I* qualify as a liaison from administration. You just stay in bed until you can be civil."

"Sorry, Minnie, but I have a direct order. If you want to contest it, you may take it up with him."

"Just wait till he hears what you called the potentate."

"Oh, if you tell him that, please clarify that I was referring to your statue. And you might add that you yourself admitted it was— what did you say?—rude and tacky."

"Five A.M., Hayseed, and we're not waiting for you."

"Oh, good. I'd hate to miss that. Have a nice day."

*   *   *

Buck knew he should have his head buried, as Chaim did, but he was too curious. He leaned out into the aisle where he could see through the cockpit. The plane was too steeply nose down, and clearly T was going to try one last maneuver to somehow clear the south fence, which preceded about a hundred yards of grass and then the runway. It struck Buck that most of the tire marks on the runway were at least a quarter mile from the edge of the pavement and only a couple of others showed nearer, none of them really close to the grass. He would not bet T could get the Super J over the fence, let alone into the grass, forget the runway proper.

"Your landing gear is down, Juliet! Repeat, down! Full wheel on right, partial assemblage on left! Lift and good luck!"

"We don't do luck!" Buck shouted, as the fence disappeared from view. "God, do your thing through T!"

"Roger!" T shouted as he yanked on the stick; the plane bucked ever so slightly, clearing the fence, then swept tail first onto the grass.

The impact slammed Buck so deep into his seat that he felt it in every fiber of his being. Chaim had let out a terrific grunt on impact, and it seemed his face was near his shoes. Buck wished he'd been in the same position, because he felt soft tissue give way from his tailbone to his neck, and he was sure both shoulders had nearly been torn from their sockets. He felt it in his feet, ankles, and knees, and the plane was still nose up as the rear tore through the sod.

That meant at least one more impact was to come, but Buck couldn't imagine they would feel it in the back, at least not the way they felt the first one.

The angle and speed T had brought the plane in on somehow carried the craft all the way to the runway on its tail. When the tail hit the edge of the runway, the nose slammed down in a shower of sparks so fast that the front half of the fuselage tore away from the back and the two huge pieces of airplane went sliding and scraping, spinning in opposite directions.

Buck was aware of sky and pavement and lights and hangars and sparks and noise and dizziness, until the G forces were too much and he felt himself losing consciousness. "Lord," he said as blissful darkness invaded his brain, "I can recover from this. Leave me here awhile. Chloe, I love you. Kenny . . ."

Exhausted as he was, David could not sleep. He lay in his quarters, wondering why he got such joy out of tormenting Guy Blod. He couldn't shake from his memory Rayford's story of having tormented Hattie Durham's friend Bo, and how Bo had eventually committed suicide. Sure, Guy was a case, and David enjoyed beating him in a battle of wits and sarcasm. But was he laying groundwork for ever having a positive influence on the man? Guy's becoming a believer seemed remote, but who would have guessed David himself would have ever come to faith? A young Israeli techie with street smarts, he had been a skeptical agnostic his whole life. Could he start over with Guy, or would the man laugh in his face? Regardless, he had to do the right thing.

David tapped out a love message for Annie, telling her that while he agreed they should not even think about children until after the Glorious Appearing, he still wanted to marry her. Her response would

determine his next move in the relationship.

He took one last look at messages and
E-mail and thought he had an idea where
every Trib Force member was. All absent
and accounted for, he decided. By now
Buck and Chaim ought to be in Greece.
He wondered what Chaim was doing for
identification.

With a brief prayer for Tsion, who he
hoped would get back to his daily Internet
studies and commentaries soon, David fell
into bed. He asked forgiveness for how he
had treated Guy Blod and asked God to
give him special compassion for the man.
Of course it would not be safe for him to
declare himself a believer to a GC insider
yet, but he didn't want to shut the door to
opportunities once he and Annie had escaped.

Buck's eyes flew open, and he feared he
might be going into shock. The night air hit
him like a polar blast, though he knew it
was not that cold. He could not even see
his breath. He sat in the jagged back half
of the Super J, staring straight down the
runway to the front half, which faced him

about half a mile away. He had to get out, get to T, make sure he was OK. T had saved their lives. What a masterful job of flying the lifeless bird!

Chaim! Buck looked to his left to find the old man still curled upon himself, bent all the way forward, the back of his head pressed against the seat in front of him. How could he have not broken his neck? Did Buck dare move him?

"Chaim! Chaim, are you all right?"

Rosenzweig did not move. Buck gently touched Chaim's back and noticed that his own hand quivered like the last leaf on a maple tree. He clasped his hands together to control himself, but his whole body shuddered. Was anything broken, punctured, severed? It didn't appear so, but he would be sore for days. And he must not allow himself to slip into shock.

Worried about Chaim, Buck unstrapped himself and reached for his right wrist, which was by Chaim's foot, his hands tightly wrapped around the ankles. He could not loosen Chaim's grip, so he forced his fingers between Chaim's leg and wrist. Not only did he have a pulse, but it was strong and dangerously fast.

Buck heard footsteps and shouting as three emergency workers appeared, demanding to know if there were any survivors. "I need a blanket," he said. "Freezing. And he needs someone who knows what they're doing to get him out of here and check for neck injuries."

"Blood," one of the men said.

"Where?" Buck said.

"The man's shoes. Look."

Blood dripped from Chaim's face to his shoes.

"Sir!" they called to him. "Sir!" Turning to Buck, one said, "What is his name?"

"Just call him Doctor. He'll hear you."

Someone tossed Buck a blanket, and he saw more workers sprinting down the runway to the other half of the plane. He tried to stand. Everything hurt. His head throbbed. He was dizzy. He pulled the blanket around himself, feeling every muscle and bone, and staggered out the front of the wreckage to solid ground. He stood there, swaying, assuring everyone he was all right. He had to get to T. There was nothing he could do for Chaim. If the worst he had was a racing pulse and facial lacerations, he should be all right. It was too late to tell him not to use his own name.

Buck started toward the other end of the runway, but he moved so slowly and shook so much that he wondered if he could make it. The ground beckoned and almost took him several times. But though he knew he had to look like a drunk, he kept forcing one foot in front of the other. An emergency medical technician ran toward him from the cockpit half and another came from the tail end. As they got close to Buck, he thought they were going to carry him the rest of the way. He would not have resisted.

But they ignored him and shouted to each other. The one from behind him told the other, "Old guy back there looks like the Israeli who died in a house fire last night."

"He gets that a lot," Buck said, realizing that neither heard him.

"How's the pilot?" the first EMT said, but Buck didn't hear the response.

"What'd he say?" he called after the man, who was now running for the cockpit.

"He didn't!"

Buck hadn't seen the man shake his

head in response either, but maybe he hadn't been watching carefully enough. At long last he arrived at the front end of the plane. No one was working on T. That could be good or bad. He heard someone call for a body bag.

That couldn't be. If he and Chaim had survived the jolt, surely T had. He was in better shape than either passenger. One of the workers tried to block Buck's way into the plane, but Buck gave him a look and a weak shove, and the man knew there would be no dissuading him. "Please don't touch the body," the man said.

"It's not a body," Buck slurred. They had for sure misread this one, hurriedly misdiagnosed whatever the problem was. "It's a friend, our pilot."

The cockpit portion had come to rest directly under a huge runway lamp, which filled the wreckage with light. Buck saw no blood, no bones, no twisted limbs. He stepped behind T, who was sitting straight up, still strapped in. His left hand lay limp on his lap, his right hung open-palmed in the space between the seats. T's head hung forward, chin on his chest.

"T," Buck said, a hand on his shoulder, "how we doin', pal?"

T felt warm, thick, and muscly. Buck put a finger to the right pressure point in the neck. Nothing. Buck felt the blanket slide from his shoulders. He slumped painfully into the seat across from T and grabbed the lifeless hand in both of his. "Oh, T," he said. "Oh, T."

The rational part of his brain told him there would be more of this. More friends and fellow believers would die. They would reunite within three and a half years. But though he didn't know T the way Rayford had, this one still hurt. Here was a quiet, steady man who had risked his life and freedom more than once for the Tribulation Force. And now he had made the ultimate sacrifice.

"We need to remove the body and the wreckage, sir. I'm sorry. This is an active runway."

Buck stood and bent over T, taking his head in his arms. "I'll see you at the Eastern Gate," he whispered.

Buck dragged his blanket out of the plane but could walk no farther. He tried to sit on the edge of the runway but couldn't catch himself and rolled on his back. A stiff breeze chilled the back of his neck, and he didn't have the energy to protest when he felt a hand in his pocket. "Anyone meeting you here, Mr. Staub?"

"Yeah."

"Who?"

"Miklos."

"Lukas Miklos, the lignite guy?"

"Yeah."

"He's in the terminal. Can you make it?"

"No."

"We'll get a gurney out here."

Buck watched as T's body was lifted out in a bag. "Take care of the old guy back there," Buck managed, pointing the other way.

"We've got the old man," someone said. "Bloody nose and a jittery heart, but he'll make it."

And Buck was out again.

The skies began to darken in Chicago at around seven, but Rayford decided to wait until eight to venture out. He wanted the skies black and no one even looking their direction. The city had been abandoned, condemned, and cordoned off for months, and it wouldn't have surprised him to know that not even a leftover drunk walked those streets. Radiation or not, decaying bodies littered many streets. It might be a safer place to hide out, but it was not going to be a fun place to live.

He pulled slowly from under the L platform with his lights off, hoping to kick up as little dust as possible. There would be no shooting straight into the Loop on the Dan Ryan. Nothing was as it once was.

Between separate bombing raids and the great earthquake, some reconstruction had been attempted, but these were meant to be shortcuts, two-lane roads that cut straight through the city. But only a few were even half finished, so the most direct route anywhere was as straight a line as you could point—over, under, around, and through the natural and man-made obstacles in the best four-wheel-drive vehicle you could find.

Rayford guessed he had between fifteen and twenty miles to drive, his lights off most of the way, traveling at around ten miles an hour. "I hope this is all David says it is," he said.

"Me too," Chloe said. "For my sake. Of

course, I watched his little cybertour of the place. If it's half what it looks like, it's going to be as close to ideal as we can find."

Leah was asleep.

David showed up at the statue construction site a few minutes after five in the morning, Carpathia Time. Guy started in with something sarcastic about how now they could finish their work. David held up both hands. "Sorry if I held you up. Minister Blod, a word, please?"

Guy seemed so shocked that David had addressed him with proper protocol in front of his staff that he dropped what he was doing and joined him several feet away. David thrust out his hand, and Guy, clearly suspicious, shook it tentatively. "I want to apologize for speaking inappropriately to you, sir. I trust you'll find me helpful and not a hindrance to your work from here on."

"What?"

"I said I want to apologize—"

"I heard you, Hayseed. I'm waiting for the punch line."

"That's all I had to say, sir."

"I'm waiting for the other shoe to drop!" Guy said in a singsong tone.

"That's all, sir. Will you forgive me?"

"I'm sorry?"

"I said, that's all, sir—"

"I heard you; I'm trying to digest this. The supreme commander put you up to this, didn't he? Well, I didn't squeal on you. C'mon, who made you do this?"

David would have loved to have said "God" and blown Guy's mind. "No outside influence, Minister Blod. No ulterior motives. Just want to start over on the right foot."

"Well, count me in, mister!"

"Is that an acceptance of my apology?"

"It's whatever you want it to be, soldier!"

"Thanks. No sense holding up the work any longer."

"I should say not. We're ready to roll in five."

FIFTEEN

Buck struggled to open his eyes. He had never felt so beat-up.

The dawn sun peeked through the blinds in a small infirmary, he wasn't sure where. He had awakened to the quiet praying of three men who sat holding hands. One he recognized as Lukas Miklos. The others were a tall, dark-haired man about his own age and an older, smaller, Middle East-erner.

"How are you feeling, my friend?" Lukas said, approaching.

"I've been better, Laslos, but you're a sight. Where are we, and how is Chaim?"

Lukas stepped closer and whispered. "Chaim will be all right, but we had to come up with an alias for him. His nose was severely damaged and his jaw broken. So he has not spoken, and medical personnel are not suspicious, only curious. He is being operated on right now. Our document forger pulled off the impossible, so . . ."

"And our pilot is gone, right? I wasn't hallucinating."

"That is correct. Praise God he was a believer. His papers identified him as Tyrola Mark Delanty. Was this an alias, or—?"

"Didn't need an alias. He ran a small airport near us and was able to evade suspicious eyes."

Laslos nodded. "The GC will not allow bodies to be transported internationally. Let our church handle the burial."

Buck rolled his shoulders and rotated his head. Pain shot through his neck. "What's your guy going to do about Chaim's picture?"

Lukas looked over his shoulder. "Look what we planted after surgery." He showed Buck an ID with the photograph nearly scraped off, a bit of white hair peeking through the top. "Doesn't that look like it went through the crash? We tried to persuade officials to postpone surgery until the swelling reduced, but they're short staffed here, like everywhere. Meanwhile, he's Tobias Rogoff, a retired librarian from Gaza on his way to North America on a charter flight, the same one you're on."

"Does he know this?"

"We told him a few hours ago. Our story is that the charter insurance company has contracted with Albie Air to guarantee the completion of the trip as soon as you two are airworthy."

"I'm airworthy now," Buck said, looking over Laslos's shoulder toward the little Middle Easterner. "You must be Albie."

"I am, sir," he said with a thick accent and a slight bow. "Your father-in-law and your friend Mr. McCullum and I go way back. Also Abdullah Smith."

"How well I know. I did not expect to see your mark. Is my father-in-law aware?"

Albie shook his head. "This was very recent, within the week. I tried to contact Rayford, but I found him impossible to connect with. Of course, now I know why."

"And how did you come to faith, sir?"

"Nothing dramatic, I'm afraid. I have always been religious, but Rayford and Mac and Abdullah all urged me to at least consider the writings of Dr. Ben-Judah. Finally I did. You know what reached me? His assessment of the difference between religion and Christianity."

"I know it well," Buck said, "if you're referring to his contention that religion is man's attempt to reach God, while Jesus is God's attempt to reach man."

"The very argument," Albie said. "I spent a couple of days surfing the archives of Dr. Ben-Judah's Web site, saw all his explanations of the prophesied plagues and judgments, then studied the prophecies about the coming Christ. How anyone with a functioning mind could read that and not—"

"Forgive me, Albie," Laslos said, "but we must keep moving. We should tell you, Buck, that Dr. Rosenzweig's eyes danced at the prospect of a new identity. We don't know how long it will be before he can speak, but it's clear he can't wait to playact as someone else."

Buck slid off the side of the bed. "Are we near the airport?"

Laslos shook his head. "We're north of Kozani. Albie has flown the new craft to Ptolemaïs, and when you and, ah, Tobias are healthy, you'll leave from there. Meanwhile, as soon as we can get you out of here, you'll stay with us at the same safe house where we harbored Rayford."

"We have not met," Buck said, reaching past Laslos's hand to shake hands with the tall, willowy one.

"I'm sorry," Laslos said. "Pastor Demeter."

The pastor said, "Mr. Williams, I answered your phone awhile ago and talked to your wife. She and your father-in-law are checking out a new safe house, and she was very relieved to hear that you and Chaim are alive. Naturally, they are distraught over Mr. Delanty, particularly Rayford. Mrs. Williams wants to talk with you as soon as you are able."

"I want to get home soon," Buck said. "Albie, I'll bet you weren't planning on flying that far, were you?"

"I have nothing to return to Al Basrah

for, Mr. Williams. Could you use another craft and another pilot?"

"Oh, I think the Trib Force might find room for the best black-market contact in the world."

Demetrius handed Buck his phone. As Buck dialed, Laslos explained that so far they had not seemed to arouse suspicion on the parts of the local GC. "They believe Demetrius works for me and that you are an American come to study the business."

Chloe didn't like the plan. "Get out of there, Buck," she told him. "We've found *the* perfect safe house. Even my curmudgeon father hopes so. Chaim is smart, but this clandestine stuff is not his game. Let us get you two healthy here."

"You may be right, Chlo'," he said. "What time is it there? I've got to call my dad."

She paused. "Buck, it's after eight in the evening and earlier out west, but that was one of the reasons I wanted to talk with you."

He read it in her voice.

"Dad?"

"Yes."

"And—"

"Your brother too, Buck. I'm so sorry."

"How?"

"GC."

"Looking for us?"

"That's what we understand."

"But they didn't know where we are! That's why I never told them!"

"I know, sweetheart. There may be some good news too."

"What?"

"Our source tells us that the first attempt to get information out of them had to be postponed. They were at church."

"Chloe, don't."

"It's true, Buck. Leah found a believer at Buffer who has access to these schemes, and she says that's from a reliable source."

"Why wouldn't Dad have told me?"

"Maybe the timing wasn't right."

"I wish I could know for sure."

"Leah is trying to reach the church so they know what happened and can be on guard. She'll ask for the truth about your dad and brother."

Rayford had had to stop driving when news came of T's death. He walked a couple of blocks in the darkness, and when Chloe asked if she could walk with him, he thanked her but added, "I need a few minutes, hon."

Chicago was, naturally, a mess. Buildings in piles, rotting carcasses, vehicles crashed or burned. It seemed an appropriate ambience for Rayford's sojourn.

The hardest thing about living during this period, he decided, was the roller coaster of emotions. He would never get used to the shock of loss and the necessity to telescope mourning into minute slivers so it could be dealt with and yet one could get on with the business at hand.

In the past, with each death of someone close to him, Rayford had rehearsed the ever-growing list in his mind. He didn't do that anymore. He wondered if a person had a limit, some finite reservoir of grief that would eventually peter out and leave him with no tears, no regret, no melancholy. He stopped at what was once a corner and leaned over, hands on his knees. His grief supply was still stocked, and the pain of the loss gushed from him.

Hard as it was, Rayford had to condense the bereavement caused by yet another aching amputation into a few brief hours. He was not allowed to dwell on it, to jot his memories, to console a widow, to break the news to a congregation. There would be no wake, no funeral, not even a memorial service, at the rate they were going. T's church was likely to have one, of course, but there was no way Rayford dared attend. Who knew who might be watching, lying in wait?

Not enough of his comrades in the Tribulation Force really knew T. There would be little reminiscing. He was gone. They would see him in heaven. Now what was next on the crisis docket? It was unfair, unnatural. How was a person supposed to function this way and stay sane?

Rayford was grateful for his own return to what Dr. Ben-Judah liked to call the "first love of Christ," that wonderful season when the plan of salvation and the truth of grace are fresh and new. He was thankful for the counsel of Demetrius Demeter and the refreshing rest and new sense of resolve he enjoyed.

And now this. The thrill ride. He'd had enough ups for twenty-four hours, apparently. He had been due for some downs.

As usual when in a stretch like this, Rayford tried cataloging what he still had to be thankful for. Without fail, every blessing in his life had a name attached: Chloe, Kenny, Buck, Tsion, Leah, her new friend he hadn't yet met, the two Zekes, Chaim, David and Annie, Mac, Abdullah, Laslos and his wife, Demetrius, Albie. Rayford wondered why Albie had been so eager to help in Greece and what it was he was so eager to tell him, but only in person.

Rayford had to fight the knowledge that while his list might expand, it also had to suffer attrition. He had already lost so many, including two wives. He would not allow himself to think about losing more relatives.

When he returned to the Rover, Leah reported that she had reached the leader of the house church Buck's father and brother had attended. "I told him I'd love it if he could talk directly to Buck and he said he'd be happy to, but I didn't feel right about giving out Buck's number."

"That was wise," Rayford said. "Let Buck decide that. His phone is secure, but this pastor's is likely bugged if they just had a GC cleansing. Try Buck and give him the pastor's number. Let him work out the contact."

A few minutes later Rayford parked near Strong's and they cased the place, only to find it secure. The three of them sat on the sidewalk with their backs to the cold brick, and Rayford pulled out his phone.

Something about the New Babylon predawn David never liked. Maybe Israel was lusher. Both were desert areas, but the hour before daybreak in Israel had always invigorated him, made him look forward to the promise of the day. The dry, windless heat of New Babylon mornings, beautiful as the sunrises could be, David found suffocating.

Watching Guy Blod put the finishing touches on the huge image of Nicolae Carpathia did little to cheer David. Not a hundred feet away, hundreds of thousands of grieving pilgrims from all over the world moved in slow silence, waiting hours for their few seconds before the sarcophagus. It was sad enough that these blind, lost, misled minions clearly worried about their future due to the loss of their beloved leader. But here behind great curtains, Guy and his assistants rhapsodized over the finished product.

"Care to look close?" Guy asked David as he glided down on a motorized scaffold.

Not really, David wanted to say, but how would he explain passing on such a so-called privilege? He shrugged, which Guy interpreted as affirmative, and the sculptor sang out instructions.

"There's only room for one on the scaffold, and you have to run the controls yourself. Be careful! The first time I did it I nearly knocked over one of my own creations!"

Guy showed David the controls, which consisted primarily of a joystick and speed selector. He was tempted to point the thing at the statue's head, shoot up, and knock it over. As David tentatively and jerkily practiced maneuvering the scaffold before rising, Guy hollered his cautions. "Careful of the smoke! The fire is lit under the knees, and the face has the only exhaust."

"Why didn't you wait until it was in place to start the fire?"

"We don't want to distract the crowds. This sort of art is a duet between sculptor and viewer, and my goal is that they participate in the illusion that the statue is alive."

"Twenty-four feet high and made of metal?"

"Trust me, this works. People will love it. But it would spoil everything if they saw us dumping in the stuff for the fire."

"What are you using for fuel?" David asked.

"A form of shale," Guy said. "For kindling, onionskin paper."

"Where'd that come from?"

"Every tribe and nation!" Guy said, and his people laughed. "Seriously, we have an unlimited supply of holy books from all over the world, the last contribution of the late Pontifex Maximus. He shipped from Rome all the holy texts that had been confiscated and donated from the various religions and sects when the one-world faith was established."

David was repulsed, now certain he didn't want the closer look, but he was stuck. "Note the handiwork on the way up!" Guy said. What was there to see but polished black iron? "You can touch, but be careful! It's delicately balanced!"

Nearly two and a half stories up, David could hardly hear Guy anymore. Smoke wafted out the eyes, nostrils, and mouth of the quadruple-size image of Carpathia. It was uncanny. Though from that close the illusion was lost that the eyes were real, the features, having been made from the actual cast of the body, were perfect replicas.

David was high enough to see past the statue to the horizon, where the sun's pinks were just beginning to wash the sky. Suddenly he flinched and backpedaled, hitting the safety bar just above his waist. The whole scaffold shuddered, and he feared it might topple.

"Hey!" one of Guy's assistants hollered.

"What's going on up there?" Guy yelled. "You all right?"

David waved. He didn't want to admit what he'd heard, what had made him jump. He steadied himself and listened. A low rumble, echoing as if from the belly of the image. Muffled and sonorous, it was clearly Carpathia's timbre. What was it saying, and how had they gotten it to do that? A chip? A disc player? A tape?

He felt the vibration again, heard the hum, cocked his head to listen. "I shall shed the blood of saints and prophets."

David whipped the control so the scaffold lurched down about five feet and stopped, swaying again. "How did you do that?" he called down.

"Do what?"

"Get a recording in there!"

Silence.

"Well, how did you? Where's the hardware, and what does the phrase mean?"

Guy was still staring up at him, obviously holding out.

"Guy!"

"What?"

"What didn't you hear? Do I have to repeat everything?"

"What didn't I hear? I didn't hear anything but you, David. What the devil are you talking about?"

David began his slow descent. "The thing talks. How did you do it? Tape loop? Disc? What? And won't the heat or smoke destroy it?"

Guy rolled his eyes at his people. He whispered, "What are you, serious?"

"You know blamed well I'm serious, Guy."

"So we're back to first names, are we?"

"Can we not get hung up on that right now, Minister-Director-Poten-take-your-choice Blod? The thing speaks. I heard it twice, and I'm not crazy."

"If you're not crazy, you're mistaken."

"Don't tell me I didn't hear what I heard!"

"Then you're hearing things, Director Hassid. This thing hasn't been out of my sight since the shell was delivered. This isn't a theme park. I don't want giant talking action figures. OK? Are we all right now? May I have them start moving my big boy into position?"

David nodded and stepped back to let a monstrous forklift move in behind the statue. His phone chirped, and as soon as he answered he heard a tone indicating another call. "This is Director Hassid, hold please," but as he punched in the other call heard, "Dav—!" and recognized Fortunato's voice.

"This is Director Hassid, hold please," he said again, switching back to Fortunato. "Sorry, Commander. I'm watching the moving of the statue, and—"

"I'm sure that'll succeed without you, David. I'd appreciate not being put on hold in the future." David knew he should apologize again to keep up appearances, but he was dwelling on how important his getting up before 5:00 A.M. was to Fortunato last night and how incidental it was now.

"We've got a situation here," Leon continued. "I need you in the conference room on eighteen as soon as possible."

"Anything I need to bring or be thinking about?"

"No. Well, yes. Captain McCullum's schedule."

"Oh, he's—"

"Tell me when you get here, David. Quickly, please."

David switched to his other call. "That busy that early, huh, kid?" Rayford said.

"Sorry. What's up?" David walked backward as he talked, watching the statue emerge from the preparation room and become visible to the crowds. The murmuring grew louder as people nudged each other and pointed. The statue leaned back against the forks of the truck, and not until it came into the beams of the spotlights did it become apparent to all that it was, as Guy had so delicately put it, *au naturel.*

Oohs and *aahs* rose from the crowd; then they began applauding and soon cheering.

"What in the world is going on there?" Rayford said.

David told him. "I think they've waited so long to see the body that they would worship trading cards if we passed them out." Rayford told David what had happened in Greece. "I'm so sorry, Captain Steele. I only talked to Mr. Delanty a few times by phone, but I know you two were close."

"This is a hard one, David. They don't get any easier. Sometimes I feel like an albatross. The people who get close to me are soon gone."

David told him he was on his way to a mysterious meeting, and they debriefed each other again on what had happened at the Gala. "No matter what they say, sir, it's clear the shooting was accidental and that the bullet totally missed Carpathia."

"That doesn't make me any less of a scapegoat, but—"

"Oh, Captain, wait a second . . ."

"I hear the crowd. What happened?"

"Oh, man, it almost toppled over! They set down the statue, and it rocked forward! People were diving out of the way. The forklift guy moved up to sort of catch it on its way back so it wouldn't fall that way, and that just made it rock forward again! I don't know how it didn't go over. It's settled now, and they're nudging it straight. Oh, man!" He told Rayford of the built-in furnace but said nothing about what he'd heard.

"That jostling must have stoked the fire, because the smoke is really pouring out now. You know they're burning Bibles, among other holy books, in there?"

"No!"

"Sir, I'm heading inside now, and I never asked what you called about."

"I'm at the new safe house, David."

"Yeah? How is it?"

"It looks fabulous, but we have one problem. It must lock automatically in emergencies. We can't get in. Can you unlock it from there?"

David was near the elevator. "I can't talk here, sir, so let me just say yes, I'll get to that as soon as this meeting is over. I wish I could say when that will be."

Tsion took a call from Chloe, informing him it was likely they would be back very late. "Any evidence of GC nosing around?"

"None," he said, but he did not add that

he had been 93 million miles from Mount Prospect for at least two minutes.

She spoke briefly to Kenny, who kept wanting to pull the phone from his mouth and "see Mama." Finally he said, "Lub-you-too-see-ya-lader-bye-bye."

"Tsion, I appreciate this more than you know," Chloe said.

"He's easy," he said. "And you know I love him."

She told Tsion what to feed Kenny and to put him to bed at nine. Much as he had enjoyed the baby, that was good news. Kenny often slept through the night.

David had not given himself time to worry what the big meeting was about. He just hoped he would not be in there alone with Fortunato. David was the last to arrive. A dozen directors and above were there, including television personnel, most yawning and rubbing their eyes.

"Let's get started, people," Leon began. "We have a crisis. No one is leaving New Babylon. Despite the decimated population in the last three and a half years, hotels are jammed and people are even agreeing to double up, two whole families in each room. Others are sleeping in the street, under lean-tos. The airport is crowded with big jets. They bring in capacity loads for the viewing, but they're canceling most outbound flights for lack of interest. You know what's happening, don't you?"

"The viewing is not meeting their felt needs," a woman said. David recognized her as Hilda Schnell, head of Global Community Cable News Network.

"I'm glad it was you who answered, Hilda," Leon said. "We need your help."

"What can *I* do? I'm staying for the funeral too."

"We were not prepared for this size crowd," Leon said. "This will be twice as large as the Jerusalem Gala."

Hilda said, "I still don't understand how GC CNN can help. Even at the Gala we merely—"

"Bear with me," Leon said. "As you know, we already pushed back the funeral and burial to accommodate the crowds. We assumed that a million or so people would still be waiting to view the body by the time we were ready for the ceremony. With more than three million here already, another estimated million on their way, and virtually no one leaving, we have to re-group. Where are the big screens we used in Jerusalem and do we have more?"

Someone from Event Programming said they were in storage in New Babylon and that there would be enough—supplemented by smaller monitors—to handle the larger crowd. "But," he added, "that will require a lot of man-hours and, of course, a layout scheme. The way the courtyard is cordoned off now will certainly not handle a crowd that size, especially if the ones who have already passed by the bier stay for the funeral, and I can't imagine why they're still in the city if that is not their plan."

"My point exactly," Leon said. "I already have engineers on the new schematic. And let me be clear: laborers are starting to re-arrange barricades, chairs, crowd control ropes, and so forth. All this work will go on with no interruption of the viewing process. If the line has to be moved, that should be able to be done in an orderly fashion without stopping the procession.

"My question for you, Ms. Schnell, is whether your equipment can feed that many monitors. Some people, naturally, will be hundreds of yards from the podium."

"We don't worry about that, Commander," Ms. Schnell said. "We concern ourselves with providing the best visual and audio coverage of the event for television and leave it to your event organizers to make it work for their purposes."

Leon stared at her, expressionless. "What I am suggesting, madam, is that you *do* worry about it. We have singers, dancers, speakers, and the like to make this ceremony appropriate, not only to the occasion and the size of the live crowd, but also to the stature of the one we honor."

"Yes, sir."

"Yes, ma'am?"

"Just tell us what you want, sir."

"Thank you."

"Thank you for the privilege."

Now Fortunato was smiling. "That the big screens from Jerusalem are already here, Director Hassid, eliminates my need for one of your pilots to go get them. If we could make use of your entire hangar crew, cargo staff, pilots and all, in crowd control, I would appreciate it. Viv Ivins will be coordinating that, so let her know how many are available and who they are.

"The new times for the ceremony and burial are noon and 2:00 P.M. today respectively. Some dignitaries' speeches may be shortened, but those times are firm and may be announced effective immediately. Ms. Schnell, I'm assuming this event supersedes all other programming so that the entire globe may participate, including those who reach the airport in time to watch on television but too late to be here in person."

She nodded.

David fidgeted, knowing Rayford, Chloe, and Leah were waiting to get into the Strong Building. He wasn't certain he could remotely unlock a door, but he'd rather have been studying that than sitting through a logistics meeting. Fortunato soon left the details in the hands of his engineers, and David hurried out.

On the way to his office, he saw the laborers already at work refashioning the massive courtyard into a vista that would accommodate the expected flood of humanity. According to the snatches of news reports he caught on the monitors lining the hallways of the palace complex, Leon was right. People of every ethnic background were interviewed at the airport, in line, and on the streets. Nearly every person expressed a desire to attend the funeral, even if they had already passed by the body.

"This was the greatest man who ever lived," a Turkish man said through an interpreter. "The world will never see another like him. It is the worst tragedy we will ever face, and we can only hope that his successor will be able to carry on the ideals he put forth."

"Do you believe Nicolae Carpathia was divine in any sense?" the reporter said.

"In every sense!" the man said. "I believe it's possible that he was the Messiah the Jews longed for all these centuries. And he was murdered in their own nation, just as the Scriptures prophesied."

As David settled in behind his computer in the privacy of his office, he left on the TV monitor hanging from the ceiling in the corner. GC CNN had followed that interview with a live feed from Israel, where thousands were listening to enthusiastic preachers, running forward, falling on their knees, and then shouting of their new allegiance to Jesus the Messiah.

The Jerusalem correspondent had with her a religious expert, who attempted to explain. "In the vacuum created by the deaths of both the head of the One World Faith and the supreme potentate of the Global Community, whom many considered every bit as much a religious as a political figure, spiritually hungry people are rushing to fill the gap. Longing for leadership and bereft of the one man who seemed to fit the bill, they now find attractive this fairly recent craze of ascribing to the historical figure of Jesus the Christ the qualifications of the Messiah Israel has awaited so long.

"This phenomenon existed in small pockets of conservative fundamentalist Christian sects but was fueled shortly after the vanishings by Dr. Tsion Ben-Judah, an Israeli biblical scholar. He had been commissioned by the State of Israel to clarify the prerequisites of the prophesied Messiah for the modern Jew.

"Dr. Ben-Judah created an uproar, particularly among Jews, when at the end of the live, globally televised airing of his views he announced that Jesus the Christ was the only person in history to fulfill all the Messianic prophesies, and that the vanishings were evidence that he had already come."

David was impressed that the "expert," while clearly not agreeing with what was going on, had an accurate handle on the issue. Having studied under Tsion on the Net for so long, David knew that this further outbreak of evangelism in Israel would also spawn many more false christs and second-rate antichrists. Dr. Ben-Judah had often cited Matthew 24:21-24 in urging his followers—now referred to as Judah-ites—to beware:

> For then there will be great tribulation, such as has not been since the beginning of the world until this time, no, nor ever shall be. And unless those days were shortened, no flesh would be saved; but for the elect's sake those days will be shortened.
> Then if anyone says to you, "Look, here is the Christ" or "There!" do not believe it. For false christs and false prophets will rise and show great signs and

wonders to deceive, if possible, even the elect.

By now David was deep into the labyrinthine inner workings of the Strong Building. While whirring through the many security pass gates using code breakers of his own design, he had a phone tucked between his cheek and shoulder.

"Captain Steele," he said, "if I can do this, I'm going to get you in through one of the parking garage's inner doors. The gates will be down, but you can walk around those and get to the elevators."

"We were that far," Rayford said. "The glass doors leading to the elevators are the ones we need opened. We could break the glass, but we're afraid that would set off an alarm."

"Who'd hear it?"

"I know, but usually those kinds of alarms are attached to all sorts of interrelated devices. Like at the airport, you force your way through the wrong door, and certain systems automatically shut down."

"Bingo," David said.

"Excuse me?"

"You're in."

"We're not even on that side of the building."

"Well, get there," David said. "I can't wait to hear what you find. Listen, good news: the designers of this building did two very nice things, as if they knew we were coming. First, the electrical panel room and the telephone room, both of which are traditionally on the top floor or even above in some spire, are located on the first floor, one up from where you'll enter. Second, I think I have detected why the structure is so sound below where the bomb damage is. The blueprints show what's called a 'closure for stack effect' every fifteen floors or so. It happens that there is just such a closure one floor beneath where the bomb damage occurred. This closure acts as a new roof for the building. I'm not certain yet, but you may be able to land a helicopter there, if you can deal with the complications of a three-sided opening above that."

"Helicopter?" Rayford said. "We're in the garage, by the way."

"I can see you."

"You can?"

"See the monitor up in the corner to your right?"

The three waved at David and he almost waved back, forgetting this was not a two-way visual feed.

"Yep. I see you. The door directly in front of you should be unlocked. And yes, I said helicopter before."

"Where am I going to get one of those?"

"I don't know," David said. "Know anybody in purchasing anywhere?"

"We also need to start thinking about a new air base, closer to here. Different anyway. We have no friends at Palwaukee anymore."

"How was Kankakee?"

"Might work. How about we have Albie set up there as a small private transport company, maybe serving Laslos, who's still considered legit by the GC? Then we can come and go as we please out of there with no questions asked. And we can chopper our way up here when we need to."

"I like the way you think, Captain Steele."

"I like the options you provide, David."

"I'll try to keep track of you floor by floor

with the various monitors," David said. "But I may have to leave you abruptly too. You know where I am."

Leah and Chloe appeared to be working well together. Though David could hear only Rayford, he could see the women checking out sight angles from various windows.

"Leah wants to talk with you, David. Here she is."

"You're looking at blueprints?"

"On-line," he said, "yeah."

"Am I seeing this right? Are we not visible from the street, at least where we are now?"

"Affirmative."

"And what if we turn on lights?"

"That I wouldn't do."

"What if we spray painted the windows black?"

SIXTEEN

By ten o'clock Saturday night in Illinois, Tsion had survived two messy operations: feeding and changing Kenny. The boy was now sound asleep in his crib in the other room, and Tsion had turned the sound off on the television. He merely glanced at it occasionally, tired of the endless repetition.

How many times had he seen Rayford's photograph and history and the grave conclusion on the part of Global Community Security and Intelligence forces that he was the lone assassin, the lone gunman? Rayford was also constantly referred to as a committed Judah-ite. Tsion knew, because he knew the Tribulation Force, that Rayford Steele had ceased to exist. He would neither make himself obvious to the public nor leave a trail in his own name. Tsion prayed that would preserve Rayford for as long as possible.

Tsion pored over his Bible texts and commentaries, trying to make sense of the vivid dream. He pleaded with God for another of the same, but short of that, he wanted to understand the one he'd had. Scholars were divided on who the sun-clothed woman was, the one who wore a garland of stars and used the moon as her footstool.

Clearly she was symbolic, as no woman was that large or had a child in space. Some believed she represented woman-kind as mentioned in Genesis when God told Satan that the woman would produce a child whose heel Satan might bruise, but who would crush his head. That was a prophecy of the Christ child, and of course that woman turned out to be Mary. Yet further details of this symbolic woman indicated that she might symbolize Israel. The Christ came from Israel, and Satan pursued and persecuted God's chosen people even to the present day.

As Tsion studied the biblical texts about Lucifer and his being cast out from heaven, he became convinced that when he had seen the dragon sweep a third of the stars from the skies and they fell to earth, he was witness to eternity past. The Scripture often referred to angels, righteous or fallen, as stars, so he believed this was a picture of when Lucifer was first cast down due to his sin of pride.

Yet Tsion also knew that Satan, even up to the halfway point of the Tribulation—where Tsion believed history stood right then—had been granted access to the throne of God. He was the accuser of believers, yet when he pursued the woman and her child to devour them, a great battle was to be waged in heaven and he would be cast out for good.

Tsion was not aware he had fallen asleep again. All he knew was that the trip from the underground safe house into the chilly night air took less getting used to this time. He didn't worry about temporal things. He could see Kenny sleeping in his crib and himself dozing on the couch as clearly as he could see the oceans and continents of the beautiful blue planet. How peaceful it looked from up here, compared to what he knew was happening down there.

When he arrived at the appointed place, the woman had left her footstool. The sun-garment was gone with her, of course, as was the garland of stars. Yet brightness enveloped Tsion again, and he was eager to ask questions before this all faded and he awoke. Though Tsion knew it was a dream, he also knew it was of God, and he rested on the promise of old men dreaming dreams.

Tsion turned to the brightness, marveling again at the size and majesty of the angel. "Michael," he began, "is the woman Mary or—"

"Michael is engaged in battle, as you will soon see. I am Gabriel, the announcer."

"Oh! Forgive me, Prince Gabriel. Can you tell me, who is the woman? Is it Mary, or is it Israel?"

"Yes and yes."

"That was not as helpful as I had hoped."

"When you ponder it, you will find it so."

"And the twelve stars on her head. Do they represent the tribes of Israel?"

"Or . . . ?" Gabriel prodded.

"Or the . . . the apostles?"

"Yes and yes."

"Somehow I knew you were going to— so these things mean whatever we want or need them to mean?"

"No. They mean what they mean."

"Uh-huh."

"Son of earth, did you see what the male child bore in his hand?

"I'm sorry, I did not."

"A rod of iron, with which he shall rule the nations."

"So clearly he is Jesus . . ."

"The Christ, the Messiah, Son of the living God."

Tsion felt unworthy even to hear the description. He felt as if he were in the very presence of God.

"Prince Gabriel, to where has the woman fled?"

"Into the wilderness where God has prepared a place for her, where she will be safe for three and a half years."

"Does this mean God has prepared a place in the wilderness for his chosen people, where they too will be safe during the Great Tribulation?"

"You have said it."

"And what of the dragon?"

"He is enraged."

"And Michael?"

Gabriel gestured behind Tsion. "Behold."

Tsion turned to see a great battle raging. Michael and his angels wielded great double-edged swords against fiery darts from the dragon and his evil angels. The ugly hordes advanced again and again against Michael's mighty forces, but they could not prevail. As his comrades retreated behind him, the dragon fled to the throne. But it was as if a colossal invisible door had been slammed in his face. He fell back and tried to advance again to the place he had enjoyed before the throne. But from the throne came an insistent, "No. There is no longer a place here for you. Be gone!"

The dragon turned, his anger nearly consuming him. With his seven heads grimacing and gnashing their teeth, he gathered his own around him, and they all tumbled toward the earth. And Gabriel announced in a loud voice, "So the great dragon was

cast out, that serpent of old, called the Devil and Satan, who deceives the whole
world; he was cast to the earth, and his
angels were cast out with him." And now
louder still, with great joy: "Now salvation,
and strength, and the kingdom of our God,
and the power of his Christ have come, for
the accuser of our brethren, who accused
them before our God day and night, has
been cast down. And they overcame him
by the blood of the Lamb and by the word
of their testimony, and they did not love
their lives to the death. Therefore rejoice,
O heavens, and you who dwell in them!
Woe to the inhabitants of the earth and the
sea! For the devil has come down to you,
having great wrath, because he knows that
he has a short time."

"What happens now?" Tsion said.

Gabriel looked at him and folded his
arms. "The dragon will persecute the
woman who gave birth to the child, but
God will protect her. In his wrath the
dragon will make war with the rest of her
offspring, those who keep the command-
ments of God and have the testimony of
Jesus the Christ."

Michael stood next to Gabriel now, his

great sword sheathed, his warriors dispersed. Tsion could not speak. He opened his mouth to form words of gratitude, but he was mute. And he awoke. It was still ten o'clock.

By nine in the morning Carpathia Time, New Babylon was a sea of people. Opportunists had set up shop on every road that led to the palace courtyard. Sellers of chairs, sunblock, umbrellas, bottled water, food, and souvenirs preyed on the pilgrims. Some merchants were run off by GC Peacekeepers, only to set up again a quarter mile away.

It was clear the forecasted one hundred degrees would be surpassed before noon. A canopy was erected behind the bier to protect both it and the armed guards from the relentless sun. Still, mourners and officials dropped right and left and were ferried to medical tents, where they were hydrated and fanned and sometimes doused with water.

David returned to his perch above one of the med tents, though it had been moved more than two hundred yards from the courtyard to make room for the crowds.

Barriers, ropes, and makeshift fences forced people to snake back and forth in an agonizingly slow path to the bier. Street entertainers, jugglers, clowns, strippers, and vendors tried to keep people occupied. Here and there scuffles broke out, quickly quelled by the Peacekeepers.

Laborers continued to swarm, finalizing the reconstruction that would allow hundreds of thousands more in the courtyard. The huge screens were in place and operating, as were countless monitors surrounding the palace. When the ceremony was about to begin at noon, the line would be stopped and millions would fan out from the speaker's platform next to the coffin to more than a mile away.

From his spot David heard bands practicing, choirs rehearsing, dance troupes going through their paces. With binoculars he saw Annie manning her station nearly a half mile away. His phone chirped. It was a Peacekeeper at the airport.

"Director Hassid, I have a family here from China looking for their daughter, a GC employee named Ming Toy."

"Yes?"

"They say she told them to contact you

or Cargo Chief Christopher if they could not find their daughter. She's come from Buffer in Brussels."

"Do they know where she is positioned here? It's all numbered, you know."

The guard covered the phone and asked them. "No," he said. "They said they thought their daughter was trying to get assigned near Ms. Christopher."

"Ms. Christopher is stationed at marker 53."

"Thank you, sir."

David kept his field glasses trained on Annie and saw when the red-uniformed Asian approached and they embraced. They engaged in what appeared an animated conversation, and Annie grabbed her phone. David's erupted again. "Hi, babe," he said. "Ming's parents and brother are on their way from the airport and will look for her at your station. Did she get assigned—"

"David!" Annie whispered fiercely. "North American GC has identified the safe house!"

"What?!"

"Ming overheard it. She couldn't let me

know before because they gathered everyone's phones for security."

"Call Tsion! I'll call Steele."

Rayford believed the new safe house
might be the greatest gift God had bestowed on the Trib Force since the arrival
of Tsion Ben-Judah. Several floors had
been left virtually unblemished, and all the
systems worked. There were more bath-
rooms than the occupants could ever use,
and every service imaginable. It wasn't a
home, of course, so beds would have to
be brought in or fashioned. But the place
could hold hundreds, maybe more. He
didn't know how reasonable it was to think
a whole lot of people could hide out there
undetected, but he dreamed of inviting
every dispossessed believer he knew:
Leah's friend from Brussels, maybe her
brother from China, Albie, maybe the Mikloses one day, all the insiders from New
Babylon. A guy could dream.

He and Leah and Chloe were headed
back toward Mount Prospect just after midnight, Central Standard Time, when David
called with the news. "Annie's calling

Tsion," David said. "He's got to get out of there."

"There are certain things we have to have," Rayford said. "And Tsion doesn't have wheels."

"Captain, he's got to get out of there now."

"We have to go get him, David. Any way you can tell where we might run into GC?"

"Not in time to help you. You might have to take some risks."

"We'll also try to get Tsion on the phone. Who knows where the GC is or when they might strike? Our underground is a pretty good cover."

Tsion thanked Annie and rushed to shut off the power, trying to keep from hyperventilating. He felt his way in the dark and filled two pillowcases with necessities. The TV would stay. He gathered up essential medicines, a few reference works, and all the laptops, baby stuff, a handful of clothes, whatever he could fit into the bulging slipcases. He left enough room at the tops to tie them together and left them at the bottom of the stairs. There was only one way out of the shelter, and that was the way he had come in. Even if he were to throw a blanket over Kenny and lug him and the stuff out into the garage, that would be the second place the GC would look.

His best hope, he knew, was to hear the GC come in upstairs, pray that they would be stopped by the spoiled food in the phony freezer, find no one, and move on. Then he would be ready to flee as soon as the others arrived.

Chloe called, nearly hysterical. "Tsion," she said, "if the GC gets to the cellar, you have to promise me—"

"I'll protect the baby with my life."

"You have to promise me, Tsion, please! Under my mattress is a syringe with a po-tassium chloride solution. It'll work quick, but you have to inject it directly into his buttocks. You can do it right through the diaper. It doesn't have to be perfect; it just has to be decisive and sure."

"Chloe! Get hold of yourself! I'm not go-ing to harm Kenny!"

"Tsion," she cried, "please! Don't ever let them have my baby!"

"I won't. But I'll not—"

"Please!"

"No! Now let me do my work! I have to

watch and listen. For now, Kenny is down and out. God is with us."

"Tsion!"

"Good-bye, Chloe."

Tsion went to the edge of the underground with the thinnest barrier to the outside and stood listening for engines. Or footsteps. Doors. Windows. So far, nothing. He hated being trapped. He was tempted to lug Kenny and the stuff to the garage, then make a break for it if the GC broke into the house. It was foolishness, he knew. He'd get nowhere on foot. His more-than-lifelike dream had put him on a first-name basis with the archangels of God, yet there he stood, cowering in a corner. He guessed Rayford was, at best, nearly an hour away. And if he happened to arrive when the GC was already there, Rayford would have to disappear.

Tsion prayed the GC had decided to take its time, to come the next day or the next week.

Until he sat in a cramped jet for a transatlantic flight, Buck didn't realize how extensive were his injuries. He felt twenty years older, wincing and sometimes yelping when he moved.

A couple of hours after Albie had taken off in a refurbished Jordanian fighter, the type with which Abdullah was most familiar, Buck had gotten word from Leah about the pastor who wanted to speak with him. He told her to give the man his number but to be sure he called from a public phone. The resulting conversation was one bright spot in a harrowing weekend.

"Your brother was the instigator," the pastor told him. "He confronted your father about his stubborn insistence that he was a believer and always had been. Your brother visited our house church by himself the first two or three times, and to hear your father tell it, he finally came just to avoid being alone. Mr. Williams, it took a long time for your father to get the picture."

"It would."

"Your brother less so. It was as if he were ready. But he knew better than to push your father. One of the biggest obstacles was that he knew one day he would have to admit that you were right and he was wrong."

Buck fought tears. "That's Pop all right. But why—"

". . . didn't your brother call? Two reasons. First, he wanted your dad to be the one to share the news. Two, he was scared to death they were going to somehow give you away. He knew well your position and how dangerous it was, or I should say is."

"Only calling from a bugged phone would have caused a problem."

"But he didn't know that. I just want you to know, sir, that your dad and your brother became true believers, and I'm sure they're with God right now. They were so proud of you. And you can tell Dr. Ben-Judah that he has at least one church out here that could lose its pastor and never skip a beat. We all love him."

Buck assured him he would tell Tsion.

They were an hour from Palwaukee when Buck got the call from Chloe about the safe house. While Chaim lay across the backseat, humming in agony over his various ailments, Albie seemed to grow more and more agitated as he realized what was going on.

"How was the safe house compromised?" he said. "Did Miss Durham finally give you up?"

"We don't know, Albie. All we know for sure is that Dr. Ben-Judah and our baby are there without transportation, and we have no idea how far away the GC is or whether Rayford can get there in time."

"And you have a new safe house, some-where to go if you can get them out of there."

"Yes."

"Grab my bag from behind my seat."

Buck pulled it up, deciding it weighed more than Albie. "What have you got in this thing?"

Albie was all business. "Open, please."

The top layer consisted of Albie's under-wear.

"Dig, please. Find side arm and holster."

Buck dug past what looked like a GC uniform. "Is this what I think it is?"

Albie nodded with a pleased look. "See cap. Check rank."

Buck whistled. "Deputy commander? Where did you get this?"

"No questions, no obligations."

"C'mon, did you used to work for the GC?"

"Better not to know."

"But did you?"

"No, but no more questions."

"Just where did you—"

"I have my sources. Sources are my life. Call Rayford. Tell him to meet us at Palwaukee."

"He shouldn't get to the safe house?"

"We need a vehicle. We need it as bad as Rayford needs it."

"How so?"

"Watch and learn. At Palwaukee, where can I change into the uniform?"

"You're going to—?"

"You don't ask. You only answer."

"There's a spot," Buck said. "I can show you."

"Anywhere we can leave Tobias Rogoff?"

"I wouldn't, now that we don't really know anyone there."

"OK. Find my papers. Dig deeper. Between the fake bottom of bag and the real bottom."

Buck found Albie's straight ID, then, right where he said, a worn leather pouch.

"Open, please. How many of us will be in the vehicle, six?"

Buck thought and confirmed that.

"And Mr. Rogoff needs a whole seat to self."

"Maybe not."

"Hope not. Too crowded. Find the papers to go with the clothes."

Buck leafed through until he found documents proving Albie's high-level role with the GC Peacekeeping Force. The picture, in snappy uniform, was of Albie but over a different name.

"Marcus Elbaz?" Buck said.

"Deputy Commander Elbaz to you, citizen," Albie said with such conviction that for a moment Buck thought he was truly upset. Buck saluted and Albie matched him. "Call Steele now."

Rayford was heartsick that Chloe was so determined to kill Kenny rather than see him fall into the hands of the enemy. And yet as a father, he could identify with her passion. It terrified him that she had thought it through to the point where she had an injection prepared.

Rayford had found a way back to a short stretch of unobstructed open road without making it obvious he had emerged from a

restricted area. Now he had to find shortcuts and pick his way around debris and
craters while careful not to violate any traffic laws. When he was free of other traffic
he would make up for lost time and get to
the safe house at the highest speed he
could muster, his and his passengers'
heads banging the roof of the Land Rover
or not.

Buck's call was puzzling, and Rayford
demanded to talk with Albie.

"What's the deal, friend? What're you up
to?"

"Do you trust me, Captain Steele?"

"With my life, and more than once."

"So trust me now. You get to Palwaukee
and be waiting for us. Then be prepared to
get me to the safe house fast as you can.
I'll explain roles as we go. If we're lucky,
we beat the GC and we get the rabbi and
the baby out. If we engage, everything depends on me."

Tsion prayed as he waited, but God did
not grant the request to calm his fears.
He'd had close calls in his day, but waiting
for the enemy was the worst. He tiptoed
around, watching, listening. Then he found

the TV and bent to turn it on. He would only watch. But it would not come on. *Of course!* He smacked himself in the head. He had turned off the main power.

David hated this more than all the rest that came with working undercover in the enemy camp: knowing all that was happening half a world away, yet being powerless to do anything but warn and open the occasional skyscraper door.

There was nothing more he or Annie or Ming could do from New Babylon. The players were in their places and the dangers real. All they could do was wait to hear how it turned out.

Ming's parents and brother were reunited with her at marker 53, and David was struck by the formalities. As he watched through binoculars, Ming and Chang embraced enthusiastically and emotionally. Ming kissed her mother lightly on the cheek, and she and her father shook hands. Then came more animated conversation and soon Annie was on the phone again.

"Mr. Wong is insulted that you are not here to greet him."

"Well, I can hardly do anything about th—"

"David, just come. Can you?"

SEVENTEEN

"I trust Albie," Rayford said, "but I don't like this."

"What do you think he's up to?" Chloe said.

"I don't know. He's a pretty shrewd guy. The problem is that we have only one vehicle."

"Thanks for reminding me," Chloe said.

"I just wish he'd make arrangements for another car at Palwaukee. I don't like leaving Tsion and Kenny like this."

Leah, strapped in in the backseat, pressed her hands against the ceiling to keep herself from bouncing too high. "How much farther, Daddy?" she said.

Chloe made a face, but Rayford said, "At least one of us is keeping a sense of humor."

"David," Buck said on the phone, "Albie wants to talk with you. What's happening there? I hear the crowd."

"Let's just say I've pulled rank and appropriated an administrative golf cart. I'm on my way to mollify a public relations problem. At least I get to see Annie. Where are you guys?"

"Not sure. I'll let you talk to the pilot."

Buck handed the phone to Albie and listened as he peered out the window.

"David, my friend, good to talk with you again. I'm going to enjoy working with you. . . . We're within forty minutes of Palwaukee. If I represent myself as GC, will they ask for a security code? . . . They will? Is there one I can use?" He covered the phone. "Buck, write this down . . . OK, go ahead . . . zero-nine-two-three-four-nine. Got it. . . . So, anything that starts with zero-nine will be OK in the future and will go back through you for clearance. Good . . .

helicopter? Yes, we sure could! You can do that? . . . GC? Perfect! . . . I'll tell the tower it will be delivered when? . . . OK! I know we will meet one day soon."

David was struck by the variety in the crowds that lined the route to the courtyard. People of every ethnic background slowly moved toward the palace—young and old, wealthy and poor, colorfully dressed. Many appeared shell-shocked, as if they truly didn't know what they would do without Nicolae J. Carpathia to lead them through such a tumultuous time.

David called Mac. "Where are you, Captain?"

"Sector 94. Fun work."

"People must love that uniform."

"Yeah, they want to know if I know the supreme commander personally."

"And I'm sure you tell them how thrilled you are that you do."

"What do you want, David?"

"I need you to make a couple of calls for me. Get hold of the tower at Palwaukee and—you got a pencil?—refer to security code zero-nine-two-three-four-nine. Tell 'em they'll be hearing from one of our people who needs to hangar an Egyptian fighter there. Someone will be picking him up along with two passengers, and they must not be detained for clearances and paperwork. We will handle all that from New Babylon. Then call our base in Rantoul."

"Illinois?"

"Right. Tell them we need a chopper in Brookfield, Wisconsin, but all they have to do is get it as far as Palwaukee and we'll take it from there. Tell Palwaukee Tower that too. Can you do that?"

"Gee, I don't know, David. I'm better in the cockpit than on the phone. What's shakin' where you are?"

"Tell ya later. Get on those calls and we'll talk."

David arrived at sector 53, where Annie was keeping the peace and keeping people moving. She answered questions about the times of the ceremony and the burial and also told people how far it was to water, shade, medicine, and the like. In public, of course, she had to be formal with David.

"Welcome, Director Hassid. I would like you to meet our very special guests from

China. This is Mr. and Mrs. Wong, their daughter Ming Toy, who works with us in Belgium, and their son, Chang."

David bowed and shook hands all around. Mr. Wong was plainly unhappy. "What language you speak?" he said.

"Primarily English," David said. "Also Hebrew."

"No good," Mr. Wong said. "No Asian language?"

"I'm sorry, no."

"You know German? I know German. English not good."

"No German. I apologize."

"We talk?"

"I'd be honored, sir."

"You forgive bad English?"

"Certainly. Perhaps your daughter can translate."

"No! You understand."

"I'll try."

"You insult no meet me at airport. I tell you through daughter we come."

"I did get that word secondhand, sir, but I was too busy here. I apologize and ask your forgiveness."

"VIP! I VIP because of business. Give

lots money to Global Community. Very big patriot. Global patriot."

"You are well known here, sir, and your daughter is highly regarded. Please accept my apologies on behalf of the entire GC management team for our inability to welcome you in the manner you deserve."

"Son work for you someday. Not old enough yet. Only seventeen."

David glanced at Chang and noticed the mark of the believer on his forehead. "I will look forward to having him as a colleague when he's eighteen, sir. More than you can know."

"Whole family so sorry for Nicolae. Great man. Great man."

"I'll pass along your sentiments to the supreme commander."

"I meet supreme commander!"

"Have you?"

"No! I want meet!"

"I'm sorry, but we have been asked not to arrange any more personal meetings for him this week. You understand. Too many requests."

"Special seat! You arrange special seat?"

"Oh, I don't know. That would be diff—"

Mr. Wong shook his head as his wife took his arm as if to calm him. "No meet at airport. No meet supreme commander. Way back in line. You get us up front?"

"I'll see what I can do."

"No! You get special seat for funeral. We want in courtyard."

"I'll see what I can do."

"You see now. Tell us now. Take us now."

David sighed and got on the phone. "Yes, Margaret, do we have anymore VIP seating at all? . . . I know . . . I know . . . three."

"No! Daughter sit with us too. And you! Five."

"Five, Margaret . . . I know. I'm in a bit of a bind here. I'll owe you . . . just inside the court? That sounds fine, but I'm expected with administrative personnel in the—"

"We sit with you! You can do! Four join you in good seat."

"I'm having trouble appeasing him, Margaret. . . . It's not your problem, no. . . . Yes, it's mine. What's the best you can do? . . . He did? Well, there you go. We can kill two birds, as they say. I owe you. . . . I know. Thanks, Margaret."

David turned back to them. "It seems the sculptor wrongly arranged for his assistants to sit with him in the management section, and the supreme commander's office is going to reverse that."

"I no understand. We sit there?"

"Yes. The sculptor is going to be 'honored' by standing next to the statue and having his assistants with him."

"We sit with you or not?"

"Yes, you sit with me."

"Good! Daughter too?"

"Yes."

"Good! Her new friend here too?" he pressed, pointing at Annie.

"Ah, no. I wish."

"I really can't, Mr. Wong," Annie said. "I must stay here during the ceremony."

"OK, us then."

In the wee hours of Sunday morning, Rayford barreled in to Palwaukee Airport in a cloud of dust. The place was deserted except for a light in the tower. The only lit runway was one that accommodated jets. Rayford laid his head on the steering wheel. "I just pray we're doing the right thing," he said. "To have been so close to the safe house and not check on Tsion and Kenny . . ."

Leah leaned forward. "And yet if the GC nose around there and *don't* discover the underground, we might give our people away by showing up."

"I know," he said, "but I just—"

"No!" Chloe said. "Dad's right. We need to take our chances and get there and get them out. You know what the GC are doing to Judah-ite sympathizers. They killed everybody in Chaim's house and burned it. They killed Buck's dad and brother and burned their place. What happens if they don't find Tsion and Kenny but burn the place anyway, because it's obvious we'd been living there? How would they get out? Tsion would come running right up into a burning house."

"Chloe," Rayford said, "I feel like we should play out Albie's scheme here, whatever it is."

"He can't know our situation."

"Buck has filled him in. And he's right that it makes no sense for some of us to go to the safe house while others wait here for a ride. This way, if it's obvious the GC haven't been there yet, we need to get what we can and get out of there. That'll make eight of us, including the baby, so we won't have room for much else."

"Surely Tsion will think to bring the computers and necessities."

Rayford nodded.

"I'd better call him one more time," Chloe said. "He may not think to bring the notebooks with the co-op stuff."

"You don't have that on your computer?" Leah said.

Chloe gave her a look. "I always keep hard-copy backups."

"But you've got it on disks too, right?"

Chloe sighed and ignored her. And phoned Tsion.

David let the Wong family pile into the two-seat golf cart, first pointing Ming Toy to the front seat next to him and Dad, Mom, and Chang to the back bench. But Mr. Wong wouldn't budge, muttered something about "seat of honor," and Ming joined her mother and brother in the back. Mr. Wong sat straight, chest out, with a solemnly proud look as David carefully steered the cart through the throng toward the palace courtyard.

"They are not seating dignitaries until 11: 30," David said. "They'll begin with the ten regional potentates and their entourages, then headquarter management personnel and their guests."

"They seat you right away," Mr. Wong said confidently. "And we with you."

"They'll follow protocol."

"I talk to Supreme Commander Leon Fortunato. He make sure we seat right away."

"He's greeting dignitaries and getting set for the processional now, Mr. Wong. Let's just get to the staging area, and I'm sure they'll accommodate us in due time."

"I want sit now, good view, ready for program." He turned and grabbed his son's knee. "This spectacular, ay? You work here someday, make proud, serve Global Community. Honor memory of Carpathia."

Chang did not respond.

"I know you want to, Son. You not know how say it. Be patriot like me. Duty. Honor. Service."

David pulled up to a corral area where lesser dignitaries were already being led to a line that would eventually fill the VIP area. Manning the gate was Ahmal, a man from David's department.

"We'll take care of the cart," Ahmal said. "You and your guests wait under the canopy by section G."

"Thanks, Ahmal."

"You no introduce! You rude host!"

"My apologies," David said. He introduced the family, emphasizing Mr. Wong's support of the GC.

"An honor, sir," Ahmal said, raising a brow at David.

"We sit now."

"No, sir," Ahmal said. "You're being asked to wait in line at section—"

"Big supporter of Carpathia, Fortunato, GC no wait in line. No one sitting in seats. We sit there now."

"Oh, sir, I'm sorry. There'll be a processional. Very nice. Music. You all file in."

"No! Sit now!"

"Father," Ming said, "it will be better, nicer, to come in all at the same time."

Mrs. Wong reached for her husband's arm, but he wrenched away. "I go sit! You no want sit now, you stay! Where seat?"

Ahmal looked to David, who shook his head.

"Mr. Ahmal! Check sheet! Where I sit?"

"Well, you're going to be in D-three, sir, but no one—"

"I sit," he said, pushing past, daring someone to stop him.

"He's only going to embarrass himself," David said. "Let him go."

Mr. Wong caused a stir in the crowd when he moved up the steps to the permanent amphitheater seating and began looking for his chair. Even people at the viewing platform were distracted and looked to see who was being seated already. Assuming he was someone important, some applauded, causing others to do the same. Soon everyone was aware that an Asian was in the VIP section, and they shaded their eyes to see if they recognized him.

"Must be the Asian States potentate," someone near David said.

Mr. Wong acknowledged the crowd with a nod and a bow.

"He old fool," Mrs. Wong said, and her son and daughter erupted into laughter. "We wait with Mr. Director Hassid."

"I'm afraid I'll have to join you later," David said. "Will you be all right?"

Mrs. Wong looked lost, but Ming took her hand and assured David they would be fine.

David went behind the stage to check progress on the technical aspects. Everything seemed to be in place, though there was a water shortage. The temperature was already 106 and climbing. GC personnel wore damp rags under their caps. Singers, dancers, and instrumentalists moved into place. Banks of monitors kept TV technicians aware of what was happening.

David went up steps that led to the bier from the back, passing armed guards every few feet. He slipped in behind the canopy that kept the coffin and the guards out of the sun, which was directly overhead now. As he squinted out at the courtyard and beyond, the pavement emitted shimmering waves of heat, and the line moved more and more slowly. David saw many looking at their watches and deduced that they were trying to worm their way into up-front positions for the funeral ceremony.

Once mourners were unwillingly urged past the bier, they would not be hurried away. They slowed, lingered, hoping to be stalled for the start of the festivities like some massive game of musical chairs.

David peered past the armed guards to the glass coffin, wondering how it would hold up in this heat. The vacuum seal looked secure and was checked every hour on the hour by the technician. Would the heat soften the box? Build up steam like a pressure cooker? David looked for signs that the heat affected the makeup, wax, or putty Dr. Eikenberry had used. How embarrassing if the real body was cooling in the morgue when the phony one reached its melting point and turned into a pool before the world.

"Stop the line, please!" came the directive from a bullhorn down and behind David's right. Two guards hurried that way and stepped in front of a Dutch couple who had observed the occasion by appearing in native costume. They looked as if they regretted it already, red-faced, sweating, and panting. They seemed pleased, however, at being left first in line some one hundred feet before the stairs. As they waited and the crowd behind them slowly came to a standstill of realization as well, the several dozen mourners ahead of them continued.

When they had passed and started down the stairs on the other side, a wave of silence invaded the entire area. Everyone looked to the courtyard with expectancy, the only movement the last of the mourners, trying to clear the exit stairs. They did not want to leave, but the program would not start until they did.

The stragglers finally reached the bottom and many sat directly on the pavement. They found it so hot that they began taking off garments to sit on.

With everyone in place and still, the silence of four million plus was eerie. David slipped back down the steps behind the platform and saw that the staging area was full, everyone in place from Fortunato to his ministers and all ten regional potentates with their entourages. After that, high-ranking GC personnel filled the line all the way out of the courtyard.

From David's left, someone with a clipboard and headset signaled the director of the orchestra. With men in tuxedos and tails and women in full-length black dresses, the one hundred members of the orchestra mounted the back steps and made their way out onto the platform at stage left. Sweat poured from their faces, and great dark stains spread under their arms and down their backs. Once seated, they brought instruments into position and waited for their cue.

"Ladies and gentlemen," came the announcement over the massive public-address system, echoing in the courtyard, resounding for nearly a mile, and followed by instant translation into three other major languages. "Global Community Supreme Commander Leon Fortunato and the administration of the one-world government would like to express sincere thanks and appreciation for your presence at the memorial service for former Supreme Potentate Nicolae J. Carpathia. Please honor the occasion by removing head coverings during the performance by the Global Community International Orchestra of the anthem, "Hail, Carpathia, Loving, Divine, and Strong.""

As the orchestra played the dirge, weeping broke out among the crowd until great sobs filled the courtyard. The Global Community vocal band filed in, singing praises to Nicolae. Eventually a troupe of dancers, who seemed to move in slow motion and show remarkable balance, emoted with the music and the mournful groaning of the audience. As they performed, the VIPs filed in to subdued but sustained applause.

David finally made his way to the seat next to Mr. Wong, who gazed beatifically at the stage, tears streaming, both hands clutching his heart. David shaded his eyes and wondered if he himself was prepared to sit in this kind of heat for two hours. They were stage left with a clear view of the podium and coffin, about thirty feet away.

When the music finally ended, orchestra, singers, and dancers moved out and Fortunato and the ten potentates, grim-faced, moved into position one row up and behind the bier. One more joined the three armed guards who had stood behind it, and they moved two to each end of the casket.

The great screens and monitors showed a montage of Carpathia's life, beginning with his fifth birthday party in Romania, hugging his parents at high school graduation while holding some sort of trophy in each hand, being presented an award in college, winning an election in Romania, taking office as president there, speaking at the United Nations three and a half years before, and presiding over various major functions after that. The music that accompanied the visuals was poignant and triumphant, and people began to clap and cheer.

They reached fever pitch when Nicolae was shown announcing the new name of the one-world government, cutting the ribbon on the majestic palace, and welcoming people to the Gala just the week before in Jerusalem. Now fighter jets screamed in from the east and rumbled low over the event as the montage showed Carpathia mocking and challenging the two witnesses at the Wailing Wall. The crowd shouted and screamed with glee as he shot them dead. Of course, the show did not include their resurrections, which had been denounced as a myth.

The crowd fell silent as the jets swept out of earshot and the music again turned melancholy. The screens showed Carpathia back at the Gala, beginning with a long shot that showed much of the devastation from the earthquake. As the camera zoomed in on Nicolae, it changed to slow motion as he responded to the welcome of the crowd, introduced Chaim Rosenzweig, and joked with the potentates. Gasps and moans greeted the super-slow-motion replay of his turning away from a white puff of smoke in the crowd, tumbling over Dr. Rosenzweig, and lying there as the crowds fled.

The montage showed Nicolae being loaded onto a helicopter, GC logo emblazoned on the side, and here artistic license came into play. The screens showed the chopper lifting off from the stage, banking left between scaffolds and past great banks of lights, and almost disappearing into the darkness. The aircraft seemed to fly higher and higher until it pushed past the clouds and into the vastness of space.

Higher and higher it went, to the delight of the largest live crowd ever assembled, until the helicopter itself seemed to fade. Now all they saw on the big screens were space and a large image taking shape. The fighter jets returned, but no one watched. They just listened and watched as the screen morphed into the image of a man wide as the heavens. Standing in midair among the planets in dramatic dark suit, white shirt, and power tie, feet spread, arms folded across his chest, teeth gleaming, eyes flashing and confident, was Nicolae Carpathia, gazing lovingly down on the faithful.

The image froze under Nicolae's benevolent gaze, and the roar from the crowd was deafening. All stood and wildly cheered and clapped and whistled. David had to stand to avoid being conspicuous, and while he clasped his hands in front of him he glanced at Ming and Chang, who stood stone-faced, Chang with a tear rolling. David realized that no one was watching anyone else anyway, so complete was the devotion to Carpathia.

The symbolism could not be lost on anyone. He may have been murdered. He may be dead. But Nicolae Carpathia is alive in our hearts, and he is divine, and he is in heaven watching over us.

When finally the image disappeared and the music faded, Leon Fortunato stood at the lectern, his emotion-gripped face filling the screen. As Leon spread his notes before him, David noticed he was wearing a resplendent dark suit, white shirt, and power tie. It didn't work as well for poor Leon, but he apparently assumed his succession to the throne of the world, and he was giving the look all he had.

"I want to know if it was Hattie who gave us away," Chloe said as the Egyptian jet came into view.

"We can't know that," Rayford said, "unless she tells us. We can't contact her, remember? It's a one-way street right now."

Once the jet touched down, the light in the tower went off and a fat, older man came chugging down the stairs and out the door. Here was a guy with a job to do, and he was going to do it. "You're here to pick up GC personnel, am I right?" he hollered.

"Affirmative," Rayford said.

"Your number match mine? Zero-nine-two-three-four-nine?"

"Absolutely," Rayford said.

"Stay put, please. The airport is officially closed, and I must get the jet hangared and these people accommodated with dispatch."

He hurried off to the edge of the runway and went through a series of gyrations with his clipboard that would have been more effective with a flashlight as he tried to guide Albie toward the hangars.

This amused Rayford, who figured Albie had hangared as many small craft as anyone alive, and he watched as the jet steered a course straight at the tower man. He ran off the runway as the craft whined past and finished his signals with a flourish as if Albie had done precisely what he asked.

As the man ran to be sure the plane got into the hangar, Chloe shot past him. Rayford headed that way too as Leah waited by the car. It didn't take Rayford long to overtake the man, who clearly hadn't run around like this in ages.

The door of the plane, which was parked next to the Gulfstream, popped open, and Albie was the first one off. Rayford couldn't believe it. Albie had a presence, a strut. He looked a foot taller. Carrying his big leather bag, he pointed at the man and said, "You in charge here?"

"Yes, I—"

"Zero-nine-two-three-four-nine, GC, Deputy Commander Marcus Elbaz, requesting service as arranged."

"Yes, sir, Mr., er, Captain, Commander Deputy Commander, sir."

Albie said, "These people are with me. Let them help with my passengers. Refuel the plane overnight, check?"

"Oh, yes, check, sir."

"Now where can I change clothes?"

As the man pointed to a dark office at the end of the hangar, Chloe met Buck coming off the plane. "Careful, babe, careful," he said, as she wrapped her arms around him.

"Let's go, Buck," she said. "We've got to get to Kenny."

"Aliases," he whispered. "Help with Dr. Rogoff. He's had surgery."

Rayford climbed aboard to help with Chaim, who grinned stupidly at everyone and kept pointing to his forehead. "Welcome to the family, Doctor," Rayford said, and Chaim's grin turned to a grimace as he put weight on sore limbs and was helped off the plane.

Rayford noticed that everyone was on edge with the tower man around, but that was quickly taken care of when Albie emerged in uniform. Amazing.

"We're all set then, are we, sir?" Albie said.

"All set. I'll secure the door. We're not expecting any more air traffic tonight. I stay on the grounds, so I'll personally be responsible for the security of your aircraft."

"Both of them. The Gulfstream is ours too."

"Oh, I was unaware of that. No problem."

"Thanks on behalf of the Global Community. Now we have to go."

Leah had driven the Land Rover across the runway and into the hangar. She stayed behind the wheel while Rayford got in behind her and pulled Chaim in from the other side as Albie pushed. Chaim was plainly in agony as he slid across the seat, but once in and supported on both sides, he laid his head back.

Chloe sat next to Leah in the front with Buck on her right. As Leah backed up to pull out of the hangar, Chloe put her arm around her. "Thanks for bringing the car over. And forgive me."

"It's all right, Chloe," Leah said. "Just tell me you didn't get the potassium chloride idea from any of my texts."

"I did, but right now I'm glad I know Tsion would never hurt Kenny."

Leah sped back the way she had come and headed for the exit. Rayford turned to see the tower man securing the hangar door, and as they reached the road, the runway lights went out.

"OK," Albie said, "we need to get a few things out of the way first. Madam driver?"

"Leah, sir."

"Yes, ma'am, could you turn on the overhead light back here?"

Leah fumbled for it, and Buck reached to flip the switch. Albie took off his uniform cap and turned toward Rayford. "With little time to talk, just look, Captain." Rayford stared and blinked. The mark. "Don't say anything right now," Albie said. "There's too much to do. You can turn the light off. All right, next order of business. Captain Steele, will you surrender command to me, just for tonight?"

"You have a plan?"

"Of course."

"Carry on."

"How far are we from the safe house?"

"Less than half an hour."

"All right. Here's the plan."

EIGHTEEN

David was struck by the fact that Leon, for all his sanctimony, seemed genuinely moved. No doubt he revered Carpathia and was more than the typical sycophant. Clearly he was jockeying for position as new supreme potentate, but here also was a man who grieved the loss of his friend and mentor and champion. And while he did not have the polish, the panache, the charisma of his predecessor, Leon knew how to milk the moment.

"If you'll all be seated, please," he began, his voice so thick with emotion that thousands seemed to involuntarily cover their mouths to contain their own crying. David, his own uniform heavy with sweat, lifted one foot to cross his legs and felt the stickiness on the ground. The heat had made his rubber soles tacky.

Fortunato made a show of collecting himself and smoothing his notes with meaty hands. "Nicolae Jetty Carpathia," he began in just above a whisper, "excuse me." He wiped a hand across his mouth. "I can do this. I will do this, with your patience. Nicolae Carpathia was born thirty-six years ago, the only child of two only children, in a tiny hospital in the town of Roman, Romania, in the eastern foothills of the Moldavian Carpathian Mountains, a little more than two hundred kilometers north and slightly east of Bucharest."

Fortunato paused again to clear his throat. "The young Nicolae was a precocious and extremely bright child with avid interests in athletics and academics, primarily languages, history, and science. Before the age of twelve he won his first election as president of the Young Humanists. He was a stellar high school student, a celebrated debater and speaker, and valedictorian, repeating that honor at university.

"Mr. Carpathia excelled as an entrepreneur and began public service early, becoming a member of Romania's Lower Parliament before age twenty-five. His devotion to pacifism brought both criticism and praise and became the hallmark of his life's work.

"Mr. Carpathia once told me that he believed the zenith of his career, even after being swept in as president of Romania as a young man at the behest of his predecessor, was his invitation to address the United Nations some three and a half years ago.

"Honored beyond expression, the young head of state worked hard on his presentation, outlining the history of the UN, employing every one of its languages, and memorizing his speech in its entirety. Little did he know that just prior to his appearance at the General Assembly, the earth would suffer its greatest calamity, the tragedy we all know now as the day of the vanishings.

"Stripped of our children and babies—" Fortunato paused again—"and countless friends and relatives and neighbors, the world family grieved as one. We were not aware then of the truth that only a man such as Nicolae Carpathia could bring to light: that the phenomenon that brought such bereavement was preventable, one rooted in our war technology. All we knew when the Romanian president stepped to the podium at the United Nations was that we were terrified to the point of immobility. Despairing of the future, regretting the past, we prayed in our own ways to our own gods for someone to take us by the hand and lead us through the minefields of our own making and into the blessedness of hope.

"How could we have known that our prayers would be answered by one who would prove his own divinity over and over as he humbly, selflessly served, giving of himself even to the point of death to show us the way to healing?"

The crowd could not contain itself and burst into applause. Several times Leon held up a hand, but they would not be silenced. Applause turned to cheering, and then they rose, sector by sector, until again everyone was standing, clapping, cheering, mourning their slain leader.

David was nauseated.

"Give me the rough layout of the safe house," Albie said, "where it stands, what's around it, any other buildings, roads in and out."

"I don't know if you have anything similar in your country, Albie," Rayford said. "But picture a subdivision, a housing development maybe thirty years old that has been tossed into a blender. The roads were ripped up and twisted out of the ground, and so many of the homes and businesses in that area were demolished that after rescue efforts, the area was abandoned. Best we can determine, no one lives within three miles of the place. We took over half of a badly damaged duplex, two homes in one. We expanded a cellar to make an underground hiding place, which we didn't need—at least that we knew of—until now. We rigged our own makeshift well and solar power plant, and took various routes to the place that made it look as if we could have been headed anywhere."

"What else is on the property?"

"About fifty paces from the back door is a barnlike garage that originally served both halves of the duplex. We hid our vehicles in there. We are now down to one, and this is it, so the garage is empty."

"And the other half of the residence?"

"Empty."

"Other dwellings in the area?"

"Pretty much piles of rubble that have never been hauled away."

"What hides you?"

"Besides that no one comes to that area except by mistake, there are mature trees and lots of open fields beyond our place."

"And the usual route from the airstrip takes you into the area from what direction?"

"We use various routes to keep from attracting attention, almost always travel by night, but usually find ourselves coming in from the south."

"Miss Leah," Albie said, "if you find an inconspicuous place to stop, please do." Away from paved roads already, Leah pulled into a shallow gully between two small groves of trees. "Thank you. Now, Captain Steele, your best guess of how the

GC would approach the house, if they wanted to surprise."

Rayford searched for a scrap of paper and drew an aerial view of the place. "They'd come through the trees at the north," he said. "Buck, what do you think?"

Buck studied the schematic, then showed it to Chloe and Leah. They all nodded.

"All right, Leah," Albie said. "Come in from the south as usual. As far away from the safe house as you can, drive without lights. Stop about half a kilometer away, ideally where you can see the safe house but someone there would not likely see you."

"Half a kilometer?" Leah said.

"About three-tenths of a mile," Chloe said. "There's a little rise about that far away, isn't there, Dad? Just past where we turn to head toward Des Plaines?"

"Yeah, and we notice it because the rest of the whole area is so flat."

"Let's get there quickly," Albie said. "Lights off as soon as you're confident."

As Fortunato held forth, alternately bringing the masses to their feet and making them weep, David surreptitiously pulled his binoculars from a side pocket. Leaning forward, elbows on knees, he trained the glasses on the great crowds seated just past the courtyard. He found the placard that read Sector 53 and carefully panned, looking for Annie. At first he didn't see her but was then intrigued to see a pair of binoculars pointed his direction. Despite hands and glasses covering her face, he could tell it was Annie.

They stared at each other through the lenses, then tentatively waved with just their fingers. David, with his hand still on the binoculars, held up one finger, then four, then three. She mirrored the message, their code for the number of letters in each word: *I love you.*

"I shall have some closing remarks as well," Leon said, winding down. "But I want to give your representatives from every global region the opportunity to express their thoughts before interment in the palace mausoleum. We've requested these be kept brief due to the weather, but we also want these potentates to speak from their hearts. First, from the United Russian States, Dr. Viktor . . ."

* * *

"Captain Steele," Albie said, "call Tsion and tell him who I am so I may speak to him without his suspicion."

Tsion answered on the first tone. "Tsion, it's me. We're within a half mile of you. Are you OK?"

"So far. Kenny is asleep. I'm packed and ready to go and feeling claustrophobic. I want out of this place."

"Tsion, I'm giving the phone to my dear friend and new believer, Albie. You've heard me mention him before."

"Yes! And he is one of us now?"

"Thanks to your teaching, which we can discuss later. He is using the name Marcus Elbaz and posing as a Global Community Peacekeeping deputy commander."

Tsion sat on the steps in the darkness, phone to his ear, the two tied-together packed pillowcases at his feet. All he had to do was grab them in one hand and the baby in the other, and he could be up through the freezer and out the door in seconds. But for now, he had no transportation and no idea whether the GC was waiting to ambush him.

He had heard so much about Rayford's black-market friend, he could hardly believe he was about to speak with him.

"Dr. Ben-Judah?"

"This is Tsion, yes. Albie?"

"Sir, I want to get right to business, but I must tell you, I owe you my soul."

"Thank you, sir. It appears I may soon owe you my life."

"Let's hope so. Tell me, have you heard anyone, anything, that might tell you the GC are nearby?"

"To tell you the truth, I nearly phoned Rayford about half an hour ago. It may have been paranoia, but I heard vehicles."

"Close?"

"Not very, but they were north of here. What frightened me was that they were intermittent."

"Meaning?"

"Starting, stopping, moving. I didn't know what to make of it."

"You don't usually hear any cars or trucks?"

"Right."

"And you've heard nothing since about thirty minutes ago?"

"About that."

"All right, listen carefully. Do you recognize the sound of the Land Rover? I mean, could you confidently distinguish it from, say, a GC Jeep?"

"I believe I could."

"Would you hear it plainly if it came between the house and the garage?"

"Certainly."

"And you can hear garage sounds? Doors opening and closing?"

"Yes, but these aren't typical American garage doors. They are manual and they swing like barn doors."

"All right. Thank you. If in the next fifteen minutes you hear what sounds like the Land Rover, it will be us. Any other noises or sounds, please let us know immediately."

Each potentate was greeted by music from his region and wild demonstrations from his people. Some had their people largely together; others saw them spread throughout the crowd. Most of the speakers echoed the sentiments of the potentate of the United Russian States, who listed Carpathia among not only the greatest heads of state and military leaders the world had ever known, but also among the most revered religious leaders and even deities of various faiths and sects.

The Asian leader, the second potentate to speak, said, "I know I speak for every citizen of my great region when I say that my reverence for His Excellency, the supreme potentate, has only increased in his death. I worshiped his leadership, his vision, his policies. And now I worship the man himself. May his fame and legend and glory only grow, now that he is again in heaven from whence he came!"

The potentate of the United Indian States intoned that "while we once believed that a good man comes back at a higher level, and thus that a bright star like Nicolae Carpathia would be guaranteed the role of a Brahman, he himself taught us—with his brilliant vision for a one-world faith—that even such traditional religious views have lost their currency. Even those who have come to believe that when you are dead, you are dead, and there is nothing more, have to admit—and I say this directly to Nicolae Carpathia—you will live for as long as we live. For you will always be alive in our hearts and in our memories."

Though the throng responded enthusiastically, David was intrigued that Fortunato seemed to feel the need to clarify, or at least modify, the effect of that speech. Before introducing the potentate from the United African States, Enoch Litwala, Fortunato took the floor briefly.

"Thank you for those sentiments, Potentate Kononowa. I appreciated the reference to the one-world church, which shall reappear here in New Babylon as an even better expression of a pure, united religion. Ironic, isn't it, that of the two sects most resistant to the ideas of a unified faith, one saw our great leader fall in its own homeland, and the other was responsible for his assassination.

"I do not blame the Israelis, as they are a valued part of the United Carpathian States. They cannot be held responsible for the climate engendered by their stubborn Orthodox Jews, most of whom have resisted to this day the inclusive invitation of the one-world faith. And then the Judahites! Espousing such exclusivistic, closeminded doctrines as there being but a single path to God! Should we be surprised that the very assassin of our beloved potentate is a leading member of that cult?"

With that pronouncement and the attendant applause, the great black statue to Leon's left began to smoke profusely, the wisp of black vapor becoming billowing clouds. Leon seemed to take this in stride, quipping, "Even Nicolae the Great has to agree with that.

"But seriously, before our African potentate comes, let me reiterate. Any cult, sect, religion, or individual who professes a single avenue to God or heaven or bliss in the afterlife is the greatest danger to the global community. Such a view engenders divisiveness, hatred, bigotry, condescension, and pride. I say to you with the confidence of one who sat in the presence of greatness every day for the last several years, there are many ways to ensure eternal bliss, if anything is eternal. It is not by walling yourself and your comrades off in a corner claiming you have the inside track to God. It is by being a good and kind human being and helping others.

"Nicolae Carpathia would have been the

last person in the world to espouse a one-way religion, and look how he is revered. We will worship him and his memory for as long as we are alive. And that, my friends, will keep him and his ideals alive."

David wondered if the crowd would ever get as sick of itself as he was of the predictable clapping and cheering.

Enoch Litwala cast a pall on the proceedings when his inappropriately brief and lukewarm tribute fell flat. All he said was, "As potentate of the great United African States, it falls to me to express the sentiments of my people. Please accept our sincere condolences to the leadership of the Global Community and to those of you who loved the deceased. The United African States opposes violence and deplores this senseless act by a misguided individual, ignorantly believing what has been spoon-fed him and millions of others who refuse to think for themselves."

With that, Litwala sat, catching even Leon off guard. Two other tributes were lukewarm, which David thought made it obvious who were the loyal and the disloyal among the potentates.

* * *

Albie leaned forward and whispered to Rayford, "Come with me. Leah, watch for my signal. If I wave, proceed slowly, lights off. If I call again, stand by for instructions, but be prepared to come fast, lights on, and be sure to stop short of Rayford and me."

"I'm coming with you," Chloe said. "Our baby is in there."

"Just as well," Albie said without hesitation. "Three is better anyway."

They crept from the Rover toward the safe house. Rayford saw Chloe's look in the low light, one of fierce determination that was more than just that of a protective mother. If they were going to engage the enemy, she plainly wanted in on it.

Rayford was aware of the cool air, the sound of his steps in the sparse underbrush, and his own breathing. He felt great melancholy about the safe house as they approached. It had become his base, his home, despite all the places he had been. It had housed his family, his friends, his mentor. And he knew if he had the opportunity to step inside it once again, it would likely be for the last time.

*   *   *

When the last potentate had spoken, the crowd grew restless. From all over the courtyard and beyond, people stood en masse, ready to once again begin the processional past the bier. But Fortunato was not finished.

"If you'll bear with me a few more minutes," he said, "I have additional remarks I believe you will find inspirational. It should be clear to even the most casual observer that this is more than a funeral for a great leader, that the man who lies before you transcends human existence. Yes, yes, you may applaud. Who could argue such sentiments? I am pleased to report that the image you see to my left, your right, though larger than life, is an exact replica of Nicolae Carpathia, worthy of your reverence, yea, worthy of your worship.

"Should you feel inclined to bow to the image after paying your respects, feel free. Bow, pray, sing, gesture—do whatever you wish to express your heart. And believe. Believe, people, that Nicolae Carpathia is indeed here in spirit and accepts your praise and worship. Many of you know that this so-called man, whom I know to be divine, personally raised me from the dead.

"And now, as your new leader in the absence of the one we all wish were still here, allow me to be forthright. I am no director, but let me ask the main television camera to move in on my face. Those close enough can look into my eyes. Those remote may look into my eyes on the screen."

David knew what happened to people who allowed themselves to be caught in Fortunato's gaze. He looked left, past the Wongs, who appeared enraptured, and reached to touch Chang and motion with his head to Ming. When they looked at him he shook his head imperceptibly and was grateful they both seemed to understand. They averted their gaze from Fortunato's.

"Today," Fortunato intoned, "I am instituting a new, improved global faith that shall have as its object of worship this image, which represents the very spirit of Nicolae Carpathia. Listen carefully, my people. When I said a moment ago that you may worship this image and Nicolae himself if you felt so inclined, I was merely being polite. Silence, please. With global citizenship comes responsibility, and that responsibility entails subordination to those in authority over you."

There was such deathly silence that David doubted if anyone so much as moved.

"As your new ruler, it is only fair of me to tell you that there is no option as it pertains to worshiping the image and spirit of Nicolae Carpathia. He is not only part of our new religion, but he is also its centerpiece. Indeed, he has become and forever shall *be* our religion. Now, before you break your reverie and bow before the image, let me impress upon your mind the consequences of disobeying such an edict."

Suddenly, from the statue itself—with its great expanses of black smoke now nearly blotting out the sun—came a thundering pronouncement: "I am the lord your god who sits high above the heavens!" People, including Guy Blod and his assistants, shrieked and fell prostrate, peeking at the image. "I am the god above all other gods. There is none like me. Worship or beware!"

Fortunato suddenly spoke softly, fatherly. "Fear not," he said. "Lift your eyes to the heavens." The massive dark clouds dissipated, and the image appeared serene once more. "Nicolae Carpathia loves you and has only your best in mind. Charged with the responsibility of ensuring compliance with the worship of your god, I have also been imbued with power. Please stand."

The masses stood as one, appearing terrified, eyes glued to Leon or to his image on the screens. He gestured grandly behind him, past the glass coffin and the guards, past the ten potentates, three of whom glared stonily. "Let us assume that there may be those here who choose, for one reason or another, to refuse to worship Carpathia. Perhaps they are independent spirits. Perhaps they are rebellious Jews. Perhaps they are secret Judah-ites who still believe 'their man' is the only way to God. Regardless of their justification, they shall surely die."

The crowd recoiled and many gasped.

"Marvel not that I say unto you that some shall surely die. If Carpathia is not god and I am not his chosen one, then I shall be proved wrong. If Carpathia is not *the* only way and *the* only life, then what I say is not *the* only truth and none should fear.

"It is also only fair that I offer proof of my role, in addition to what you have already seen and heard from Nicolae Carpathia's own image. I call on the power of my most high god to prove that he rules from heaven by burning to death with his pure, extinguishing fire those who would oppose me, those who would deny his deity, those who would subvert and plot and scheme to take my rightful place as his spokesman!"

He paused dramatically. Then, "I pray he does this even as I speak!"

Leon turned to face the ten potentates and pointed at the three who opposed him. Great beams of fire burst from the cloud-less skies and incinerated the three where they sat. The other seven leaped from their seats to avoid the heat and flames, and even the guards backpedaled.

The crowd shrieked and wailed, but no one moved. No one ran. Every soul seemed paralyzed with fear. And the fire that left the three smoldering in tiny piles of ash disappeared as quickly as it had come.

Fortunato spoke again: "Faithful patriots

of the Global Community from the three regions formerly led by men of lying tongues, take heart. Their replacements have already been selected in meetings I have enjoyed with the spirit of Nicolae Carpathia himself. The Global Community shall prevail. We shall reach our goal of utopian living, harmony, love, and tolerance—tolerance of all but those who refuse to worship the image of the man we esteem and glorify today!"

It was clear Fortunato expected applause, but the gathered were so stunned, so filled with terror that they merely stared. "You may express yourselves," Leon said with a smile. Still no one moved. His eyes narrowed. "You may express your agreement," he said, and tentative clapping began.

"You need not fear your lord god," he said, as the applause continued. "What you have witnessed here shall never befall you if you love Nicolae with the love that brought you here to honor his memory. Now before the interment, once everyone has had a chance to pay last respects, I invite you to come and worship. Come and worship. Worship your god, your dead yet living king."

Rayford followed Albie's signal and fanned left while Chloe was sent right. The three, about thirty paces apart, advanced upon the safe house from two hundred yards away. They watched for signs of GC. Had they been there? Were they yet there? Were they coming?

Suddenly Albie dropped into the grass and signaled Rayford and Chloe to do the same. He had taken a call. Then he signaled them to join him.

"Tsion hears the engine noises again," he whispered. "Coming from the north, only steady this time, as if advancing." He spoke as he dialed Leah. "We're going to beat them to the safe house on foot, so be ready to run, and if we encounter GC, stay a step or two behind me. Leah? Give us about ninety seconds, then come fast with lights on. Just be careful not to overtake us. When we stop, you stop as close to the garage as you can. Stay in the vehicle with the lights on and don't worry if you see GC Jeeps coming the other way."

Albie slapped the phone shut, unholstered his side arm, bounced to his feet, and said, "Let's go."

As Rayford loped along in the darkness, wondering how many minutes he might have left on earth, he was impressed that Chloe had no trouble keeping pace. He also wondered at the strange difference in Albie. He'd always been resourceful, but was there something else about him now, besides his new profession of faith?

Rayford wondered, why had he not assured himself of the integrity of Albie's mark? Could he be sure of anything he saw under the dim interior light of the Rover, a wounded old man between him and Albie?

NINETEEN

Mr. Wong dropped to his knees next to David, weeping and crying out in his native tongue. His wife sat rocking, fists clenched, eyes closed, appearing more stunned than convinced.

Ming and Chang sat with hands covering their eyes, appearing to pray. To anyone else, it might appear they were praying to the new god of the world, but David knew.

He found it surreal that as Fortunato backed away from the lectern and joined the seven remaining potentates, they seemed to ignore the piles of ashes. They solemnly shook hands with their new leader, appearing to congratulate him on his speech and his display of power.

The security chief instructed his people to remove the barricade from in front of the single-file line. The couple in Dutch garb first refused to move toward the bier, but those behind them began to jostle and push, urging them on. The couple smiled with embarrassment, each clearly wanting the other to go first. They finally locked arms and shuffled along with mincing steps, seeming to want to see Carpathia's body but afraid of not only the gigantic speaking and smoke-belching statue, but also the seats behind the bier, three of which contained only ashes.

Fortunato and the remaining seven stood in front of the row of seats, just far enough behind the coffin to stay out of the guards' way and so that mourners would not be tempted to shake their hands or speak with them. It appeared to David that it suddenly came to Leon why people were shy about approaching. He turned first to one side and then the other and asked the potentates to move away from him.

Then he stepped back and, with a flourish, swept the ashes from each of the three seats, brushing and tidying them with his big hands. This stopped the processional and made anyone close by stare in amazement. With a satisfied look, Leon turned back to face the bier and motioned that the seven should rejoin him. As they did he clapped and rubbed his hands together, and the residue fell away. He and the potentates enjoyed a chuckle.

Three sets of headlights appeared on the horizon, maybe a half mile beyond the safe house. Rayford had feared this day, when the GC would swoop down upon them. He worried he would be gone or sleeping or unaware. How bizarre to be here and see it happening.

Albie and Chloe had picked up the pace and sprinted now. Rayford tried but found himself suddenly awkward and feeling his age again. "Closer to me now, Captain Steele," Albie called out, then hollered the same to Chloe.

Rayford and Chloe closed ranks, now ten or twelve feet on either side of Albie and about four feet back. Behind them the roaring Land Rover came bouncing over the terrain, projecting eerie shadows on the safe house.

It seemed to Rayford that the three vehicles advancing from the other way had slowed and separated. He and Albie and Chloe stopped between the old garage and the house, and Leah skidded the Land Rover to Chloe's right, next to the garage. "Hold," Albie said quietly. "Hold and maintain positions."

"We're vulnerable, Albie," Rayford said.

"Deputy Commander Elbaz, Mr. Berry," Albie said. "And you have ceded command to me, have you not?"

"Temporarily," Rayford said ruefully. If Albie was legit, he could take it as a joke. If Rayford had stupidly fallen for something and had sacrificed the Tribulation Force to a lapse in judgment, he was saying he would wrest back command and not go down without a fight.

The headlights before them now spread out, the vehicle to Rayford's left heading farther that way, angling toward them and stopping about seventy-five yards away. The one in the middle advanced closer, maybe fifty yards away. And the one to the right mirrored the one on the left.

"Hold," Albie said again. "Hold."

"We're targets here," Rayford said.

"Hold."

"I don't feel good about this," Chloe said.

"Hold. Trust me."

Rayford held his breath. *I wish I could. Lord, tell me I did the right thing.*

Rayford started when he heard someone jump out of the center vehicle, equipment jangling as he hit the ground, and move toward the house. While he could still see all three sets of headlights, Rayford lost behind the house the silhouette of the soldier hurrying their way.

"Hold."

"I'm holding, Alb—Deputy Commander, while they have an armed man on the other side of the house. What if he torches the place? What if the others join him? They have clear shots at us, while they're protected by trees and the house."

"Silence, Mr. Berry," Albie said. "We are outmanned twelve to three."

Rayford felt a deep foreboding. *How would he know that?*

"And unless one of you is packing," Albie added, "we are out-armed twelve to one."

"So, what," Chloe said, "we're surrendering? I'll die first."

"You might if you don't let me handle this."

Rayford had gone from suspicion to fear and now to full-blown dread. He had walked his charges into the biggest trap imaginable. Wasn't it Albie himself who had once counseled to never trust anyone? They could be dead or in prison within half an hour.

"Global Community squadron leader!" Albie shouted, his voice deep and clear and louder than Rayford had ever heard it. "Show and identify yourself! I am GC Deputy Commander Marcus Elbaz, and that is an order!"

David guessed the temperature at 110 degrees. He couldn't remember being out at midday in New Babylon when it was this hot. He removed his uniform cap and wiped a sleeve across his brow. He was dripping. There was no wind. Just the relentless sun, the body heat of four million people, and the acrid smoke from the imposing statue.

The image began to move as if an earth

tremor made it sway and bounce, but nothing else was affected. All eyes turned toward it in terror and word spread quickly throughout the courtyard that something was happening. For a long minute the thing seemed to vibrate in place. Then it rocked, and the smoke began to billow once more.

The image soon glowed red hot, and the smoke poured out so fast that it again formed clouds that darkened the sky. The temperature dropped immediately, but going from daylight to dusk so quickly made many fall to their faces.

The image roared, "Fear not and flee not! Flee not or you shall surely die!"

The blackness covered the sky in the immediate area, but when David sneaked a glance at the horizon, it remained light. At the edges, all the way around as he turned, lightning burst from the low-riding smoke and struck the ground. Seconds later the thunderclaps rolled in, shaking the area.

"Flee not!" the image shouted again. "Defy me at your peril!"

Leon stood with his arms folded, gazing at the statue as the seven potentates dropped to all fours, wide-eyed. The armed guards fell to their knees.

People at the far edges of the crowd turned and ran, only to be struck by lightning as the rest of the throng watched in horror. "You would defy *me?*" the statue roared. "Be silent! Be still! Fear not! Flee not! And behold!"

People froze in place, staring. The smoke stopped rising, yet the sky remained dark. It formed itself into roiling, growing black clouds mixed with deep reds and purples.

David, secure in his faith and believing he knew what was going on, still found himself shaking, shuddering, heart ablaze.

"Gaze not upon me," the statue said, now with no smoke coming from its face. As it cooled it faded from orange to red and back to black. It no longer moved. "Gaze upon your lord god."

It was as if the statue had shrunk, David thought, but it had merely become still, silent, and cold. People slowly rose, and all eyes turned upon the glass coffin where Carpathia, unmolested, remained reposed. Millions stood in the quickly cooled desert, the sky pitch, horrifying clouds churning.

The people folded their arms against the sudden chill. Shoulders hunched, they stared at Carpathia's lifeless body.

"I have eleven Peacekeepers with weapons trained on you, sir!" came the reply from the far corner of the safe house. "I'll need to see some identification!"

"Fair enough!" Albie called back. "But be prepared with your own, as I am your superior officer!"

"I suggest we meet on your side of the house with weapons holstered!"

"Agreed!" Albie said, making a show of returning his side arm to its strapped sheath on his belt.

"And your aides?"

"Same as yours, sir," Albie said. "Weapons trained on you."

The squadron leader stepped out from behind the house with his weapon secured, arms away from his body, hands empty. Albie stepped toward him with purpose. "Excellent approach, sir. I'm reaching for my papers now."

"As am I."

The squadron leader pulled a flashlight from behind his belt and they compared documents. "Sorry for the confusion, Deputy Commander," the young man said. "Do I know you?"

"You should, Datillo. I likely taught you. Where did you train?"

"BASALT, sir. Baltimore Area Squadron Leadership Training."

"I only guest lectured there. I was at Chesapeake."

"Yes, sir."

"Squadron Leader Datillo, may I ask what you're doing here?"

Datillo pulled order papers from his pocket. "We were led to believe this was headquarters of a Judah-ite faction, maybe even *the* central safe house. Our orders were to lay siege to it, apprehend any occupants, determine the whereabouts and identities of any others, and destroy the facility."

"Torch it?"

"Affirmative, sir."

Suddenly Albie moved closer to the young squadron leader. "Datillo, where did these orders come from?"

"I assumed New Babylon, sir."

"You assumed. Did you check them with the regional director?"

"No, sir, I—"

"Datillo, do you know what time it is?"

"Sir?"

"Do we not both speak English, Datillo? It's not my mother tongue, but it's yours. Is my accent too thick for you, son?"

"No, sir."

"Do you know what time it is?"

"After 0400 hours, sir. Requesting permission to check my watch."

"Granted."

"It's 0430, sir."

"It's 0430, Datillo. Does that mean anything to you?"

"Mean anything, sir?"

"Listen to me, Squadron Leader. I'm going to tell you this outside the listening range of your subordinates, though you don't deserve it. I'm going to resist the temptation to inform North American States Midwest Regional Director Crawford that you did not check orders through him before proceeding. And I'm even going to give you a pass on your *unbelievable* lack of awareness of the time zone differences between North America and the Carpathian States. I ask you again, Squadron

Leader Datillo, what is the significance of 0430 hours?"

"I beg your pardon, Deputy Commander, and I appreciate your lenience on the other matters—particularly not embarrassing me in the presence of my subordinates. But, sir, I am drawing a complete blank on the time issue."

"Honestly," Albie said, "I don't know where they get you kids or what you're doing during basic training. Did you or did you not sit in any of my guest lectures at BASALT?"

"I honestly don't recall, sir."

"Then you didn't, because you wouldn't have forgotten. And you would know what time it is in New Babylon when it's 0430 in your part of the world."

"Well, if you mean do I know the time difference, yes sir, I do."

"You do."

"Yes, sir."

"I'm listening."

"At this time of the year, there's a nine-hour time difference."

"Very good, Datillo. What time does that make it in New Babylon right now?"

"Uh, let's see, they're later than we are, so it's, ah, 1330 hours."

"Do I have to walk you through this, son?"

"I'm sorry, sir. I'm afraid so."

"What is today, Squadron Leader?"

"Saturday, sir."

"You lose. Try again. It's after midnight, officer."

"Oh, yeah, it's Sunday morning already."

"Which makes it what in New Babylon?"

"Sunday afternoon."

"It's Sunday afternoon in New Babylon, Datillo. Ring any bells?"

Datillo's shoulders slumped. "It's the funeral, isn't it, sir?"

"Ding-ding-ding-ding! Datillo hits the jackpot! You're aware of the moratorium on combat-related activity anywhere in the world during the funeral, are you not?"

"Yes, sir."

"And every GC directive requires CPR, correct?"

"Concrete Peacekeeping Reasoning, yes, sir."

"And the CPR behind this directive?"

"Um, that no untoward publicity crowd out the funeral as the top news story."

"There you go. Now, Datillo, I can tell you're an earnest young man. You and your people are going to evacuate this area. You may return at 1000 hours and torch this place, if I leave it standing. My people and I were onto this location long before you were, and we have already apprehended the occupants and evacuated the building. I have a crew here to comb the residence for evidence, and we should be finished by dawn. Do not return until 1000, and if you see smoke on the horizon before that, you'll have no need to come then either. Have I made myself clear?"

"Yes, sir. Any way my people and I can assist, sir?"

"Only by following orders and leaving now. And I'll make a deal with you, son. You don't tell your superiors of the serious mistakes you made this morning, and I won't either."

"I appreciate that, sir."

"I know you do. Now move out."

Datillo saluted and trotted back to the middle Jeep. It popped a U-turn, as did the other two before falling in line behind it. And they raced off in the darkness.

*   *   *

The sky was so black that the lights of the palace courtyard came on automatically. The TV lights were trained on the coffin, and David was sure every eye but his was too. He searched and searched sector 53 for Annie, praying she would stand strong. He couldn't locate her.

David turned back. Heat waves shimmered off the statue in the comparatively chilly air. The potentates appeared paralyzed. Even Fortunato had paled and wasn't moving, his gaze on the casket. A rim of light along the horizon looked like the rim of hair on a bald man. Clouds of ebony and other deep shades, produced by smoke from the statue, hung ominously over the immense gathering. People stood stock-still, riveted. Brilliant lights bathed the platform.

David's eyes were drawn to the body. What was that? Almost imperceptible movement? Or had it been his imagination? He had imagined a corpse's chest rising and falling at a funeral before. But until now, Carpathia's body hadn't given even the illusion of life.

Carpathia's left index finger lifted an inch off his wrist for an instant, then fell again.

A few people gasped, but David assumed most had not seen it. Then it rose and fell twice. Next it lifted half an inch, uncurling as if pointing.

One of the potentates apparently saw that and recoiled, trying to back away but falling over a chair. As he scrambled to his feet and tried to exit, lightning struck ten feet from him and knocked him back to where he had been. He stood shakily and brushed himself off, reluctantly looking at Carpathia again.

Now the index finger twitched, and all the potentates stiffened. The guards went into assault position, as if prepared to shoot a dead body. Carpathia's hands separated and rested at his sides. Those close enough began to weep, their faces contorted in terror. It seemed they wanted to escape but could not move.

Those ahead of David edged closer, careful to keep someone between them and the bier. Those in front held their ground or tried to step back, but no one behind them would have that.

Now it was clear that Carpathia's chest did rise and fall. Many fell to their knees, hiding their eyes, crying out.

Nicolae's eyes popped open. David stared, then tore his gaze away to see even Leon and the kings trembling.

The corpse's lips separated, and Nicolae lifted his head until it pressed against the Plexiglas lid. Everyone within a hundred yards of the coffin, including Fortunato, collapsed, covering their faces but, David noticed, most peeking through intertwined fingers.

As if stretching, Carpathia tilted his head back, grimaced, and lifted his knees until they too met the lid of the casket. He straightened his left leg until his heel met the large rubber stopper and forced it free with a loud *thwock!* The plug flew out and knocked the cap off one of the prostrate guards. He dropped his weapon and rubbed his head as the projectile bounced and rolled and finally stopped under a chair.

With the vacuum seal broken, Carpathia slowly brought his hands to his chest, palms up, heels of his hands resting on the underside of the lid. Moans and gasps and shrieks came from the crowd for as far as David could see and hear. Everyone was on the ground now, either peering at the screens or trying to see the platform.

Carpathia lifted his knees again, ripping the massive stainless steel bolts free of the glass. Then he pushed mightily until the top end shattered loose. The lid, more than eighty pounds of Plexiglas, flew away from the coffin, bolts flying, and smashed into the lectern, knocking it over and taking the microphone with it.

Carpathia catapulted himself to a standing position in the narrow end of his own coffin. He turned triumphantly to face the crowd, and David noticed makeup, putty, surgical staples, and stitches in the box where Nicolae's head had lain.

Standing there before now deathly silence, Nicolae looked as if he had just stepped out of his closet where a valet had helped him into a crisp suit. Shoes gleaming, laces taut, socks smooth, suit unwrinkled, tie hanging just so, he stood broad-shouldered, fresh-faced, shaven, hair in place, no pallor. Fortunato and the seven were on their knees, hiding their faces, sobbing aloud.

Nicolae raised his hands to shoulder height and said loudly enough for everyone to hear, without aid of a microphone, "Peace. Be still." With that the clouds ascended and vanished, and the sun reappeared in all its brilliance and heat. People squinted and covered their eyes.

"Peace be unto you," he said. "My peace I give you. Please stand." He paused while everyone rose, eyes still locked on him, bodies rigid with fear. "Let not your hearts be troubled. Believe in me."

Murmuring began. David heard people marveling that he was not using a microphone, but neither was he raising his voice. And yet everyone could hear.

It was as if Carpathia read their minds. "You marvel that I speak directly to your hearts without amplification, yet you saw me raise myself from the dead. Who but the most high god has power over death? Who but god controls the earth and sky?"

Hands still raised, he spoke gently. "Do you still tremble? Are you still sore afraid? Fear not, for I bring you good tidings of great joy. It is I who loves you who stands before you today, wounded unto death but now living . . . for you. For you.

"You need never fear me, for you are my friends. Only my enemies need fear.

Why are you fearful, O you of little faith? Come to me, and you will find rest for your souls."

David nearly fainted from nausea. To hear the words of Jesus from this evil man, whom Dr. Ben-Judah taught was now indwelt, Satan incarnate, was almost more than he could take.

"Only he who is not with me is against me," Carpathia continued. "Anyone who speaks a word against me, it will not be forgiven him. But as for you, the faithful, be of good cheer. It is I; do not be afraid."

David searched for Annie again, knowing that no one around him was even aware he was not paying attention to Carpathia. How he wished he could see her, know she was all right, communicate to her that she was not alone, that other believers were here.

"I want to greet you," Carpathia said. "Come to me, touch me, talk to me, worship me. All authority has been given to me in heaven and on earth. I will be with you always, even to the end."

The line that had frozen in place still did not move. Carpathia turned to Fortunato and nodded, gesturing to the guards. "Urge my own to come to me." Slowly the guards rose and began to nudge the people toward the stairs again. "And as you come," Carpathia continued, "let me speak to you about my enemies. . . ."

Tsion had sat praying as vehicles approached the safe house from two directions. "Is this the end, Lord?" he said. "I so long to come to you. But if it is not the due time for my beloved brothers and sisters and me to give our lives for you, give us all strength and wisdom."

The vehicles stopped, and he heard shouting. Tsion moved to the corner of the cellar where he could hear. A Middle Eastern GC commander was calling out a squadron commander. Tsion tried to slow and regulate his breathing so he could hear every word. Was that Albie, the one he had just spoken to, pretending to be GC? Or *was* he GC? He was so convincing, so knowledgeable. How could a man know so much about systems and procedures without being on the inside? Or perhaps he once was and had turned. Tsion could only hope.

Whatever he was, Albie had driven off

the squadron commander and his men, and Tsion knew his friends would now come for him. His first order of business? He turned the power back on and fired up the TV. His phone rang.

"Dr. Ben-Judah," Albie said, "are you down there and all right?"

"I am fine and watching the funeral on TV. Come down and see."

"Do you want to come and let us in?"

"Break in! I don't want to miss this, and we're not staying anyway, are we?"

Albie chuckled and the back door was kicked in. Footsteps. The freezer door opened, the rack pulled aside, footsteps on the stairs. Albie entered, followed by Chloe, who raced to pull Kenny from his crib and smother him with kisses. Then Rayford, looking grave even as he embraced Tsion.

"The others are coming," Rayford said.

"Yes, yes, and praise God," Tsion said. "But watch this. A great storm has invaded the palace courtyard, and I am convinced the hour is near."

Buck limped gingerly down the stairs and found Chloe and Kenny. Leah followed, carefully aiding Chaim. Bandaged, mute, and fragile, still he forced a grin when he saw Tsion, and the countrymen embraced. "I praise the Lord for you, my brother," Tsion said. "Now sit and watch."

"We want to get this done before dawn, people," Albie said. "I don't think our young friend will return until ten, but we'd better not test him."

"Are we really going to torch this place once we've got what we want?" Rayford said.

Tsion tried to shush them, but both ignored him. He turned up the TV. "This seems pretty risky," Buck said, emerging from the bedroom with Chloe and Kenny, "partying down here with GC in the area."

"I believe the indwelling is about to occur," Tsion announced.

"Put a videodisc in, Tsion!" Rayford said. "We've got work to do and fast."

"I am confident Albie's ruse was successful," Tsion said. "At least I hope so."

Rayford approached him. "Doctor," he said, "I'm back and I'm in charge, and I need to pull rank, despite my respect for you. Record that and let's get packing."

Tsion read such confidence and also concern in Rayford that he immediately popped in a disc. "Chaim, you can't work in your condition. Monitor this for me until we have to go." He hurried upstairs.

"Bring only what you can carry on your lap," Rayford announced. "Tying stuff atop the car would attract too much attention."

As Tsion busied himself, he worried about Rayford. It was natural for them all to be relieved and yet worried they were not out of the woods yet. Rayford was plainly agitated about something. After Tsion gave his room one last cursory glance for any indispensables, he saw Rayford pull Albie into Buck and Chloe's empty first-floor bedroom.

"You all know me as a forgiving potentate," Carpathia said, as the masses began to queue up once more to file past him. This time they would have the weird experience of touching and chatting with a man who had been dead nearly three days and who still stood in the remains of his own coffin.

"Ironically," he continued, "the person or persons responsible for my demise may no longer be pursued for murder. Attempted murder of a government official is still an international felony, of course. The guilty know who they are, but as for me, I hereby pardon any and all. No official action is to be taken by the government of the Global Community. What steps fellow citizens may take to ensure that such an act never takes place again, I do not know and will not interfere with.

"However, individual would-be assassins aside, there are opponents to the Global Community and to my leadership. Hear me, my people: I need not and will not tolerate opposition. You need not fear because you came here to commemorate my life on the occasion of my death, and you remain to worship me as your divine leader. But to those who believe it is possible to rebel against my authority and survive, beware. I shall soon institute a program of loyalty confirmation that will prove once and for all who is with us and who is against us, and woe to the haughty insurrectionist. He will find no place to hide.

"Now, loyal subjects, come and worship."

TWENTY

Rayford pulled Albie into Buck and Chloe's bedroom by his elbow. As he was shutting the door he saw Chaim staggering toward Tsion, gesturing, grunting through his bandages and wired jaw, trying to get Tsion to follow.

Rayford's phone rang. "Stay put," Rayford told Albie. Then, into the phone, "Steele here."

"Rayford, it's Hattie!" She was near hysterics.

"Where are you?" he said.

"The less you know the better, but get your people out of the safe house."

"Why?"

"They're onto you. Don't ask me how I know. And Carpathia has come back from the dead. Did you see?"

"No."

"It's all true, isn't it, Rayford?"

"Of course it is, and you knew that almost as soon as most of us did. I didn't think doubt was why you were holding out."

"It wasn't, totally. But I was still holding out hope that it couldn't all be just the way Dr. Ben-Judah said."

"What're you going to do about it, Hattie? You know how we all feel about it and about you."

"Nothing right now, Rayford. I just wanted to warn you."

"Thanks, but now *I'm* warning *you.* Don't wait any longer."

"I have to go, Rayford."

"Dr. Rosenzweig has made his decision."

"I've really got to—what? He has? He was supposed to be dead. Is he there? May I talk with him?"

"I'll have him call you when he's able."

"I don't want my phone ringing at the wrong time."

"Then call us back tomorrow, Hattie, hear? We'll all be praying you do the right thing."

David did not know where Viv Ivins had been sitting. Surely she had been in the VIP section, but he did not notice her until she appeared at Carpathia's side. Fortunato was to her right, so as people swept past they encountered first Leon, then Viv, and finally Carpathia. It was as if this setup was designed to put people at ease. They need not fear a recently dead man who wanted to touch and be touched.

Leon gently pushed them to Viv, who said something soothing and guided them quickly past Carpathia. He seemed to be looking each one in the eye and cooing something as he grasped his or her hand with both of his. No one was allowed to pause, and all seemed overcome as they floated away. Many swooned and some passed out. David did some quick figuring. If Nicolae gave, say, three million people five or six seconds apiece, it would take more than 200 twenty-four-hour days. Surely those who waited more than a few hours would give up.

*   *   *

"Can this wait, Captain Steele?" Albie said.

Rayford blocked his path. "Why, Albie?"

"Don't *you* want to see what's happening on the news?"

"I'll watch the replay."

"So, you want to see it too."

"Of course," Rayford said. "But I'm starting to wonder if we want to see it for the same reason."

"What are you saying?"

"What is your real name?"

"You know my name, Rayford."

"May I check your mark?"

Albie squinted at him. "In my culture, that is a terrible insult. Especially after everything we have been through."

"Your culture never had the mark before. What's the insult?"

"To not be personally trusted."

"You yourself advised me to trust no one."

"That's a principle, my friend. You think I would fake and lie to you about something I know to be so real to you?"

"I don't know."

"Then you had better check my mark. You could not insult me further."

"Take it as a compliment, Albie. If you're for real, you were so convincing as a GC commander that you made me wonder."

"I must have."

"You did. How did you know we were outmanned twelve to three?"

"I do my homework. It's part of the job. How do you think I outlived the average black marketer by two times? I'm careful. I don't just find a uniform and affect an identity without learning the nuances."

"How did you know three Jeeps carried four Peacekeepers each?"

"That is GC protocol. Night patrols are called squadrons and have a leader, three vehicles, and eleven subordinates. By day they travel in pairs."

"Uh-huh. And BASALT?"

"Never heard of it. I was glad he explained."

"Guest lecturing?"

"Made it up."

"Chesapeake?"

"Guessing. Hoping. I had read something about a GC training facility there. I'm glad I was so convincing, Rayford, because our lives depended on it. It's what I do."

"Midwest Regional what-did-you-call-him, Director—"

"Director Crawford, right."

"And you know him from . . . ?"

"A directory I thought it would behoove me to familiarize myself with."

"You've never met him?"

"How would I?"

"You're still a closet hater of Carpathia?"

"Out of the closet soon, I hope. I don't enjoy long-term playacting. Satisfied?"

"How did you know about the funeral moratorium and, what did you call it? CPR?"

"I read."

"You read."

"You should know that about me."

"I think I need to know a lot more about you."

Now Albie was mad. "I won't pretend not to be deeply offended," he said, ripping off his uniform cap and slamming it to the floor. Rayford was suddenly aware that they alone remained on the main floor and he heard no footsteps above. Everyone must have been huddled around the television in the underground shelter.

Albie unstrapped his gun and drew it,

Rayford retreating until the back of his head hit the bedroom door. Albie turned the weapon around so he was holding the barrel. He thrust it at Rayford. "Here," he said. "Shoot me if I am a liar."

Rayford hesitated.

"Go on, take it!"

"I'm not going to shoot you, Albie."

"Even if I'm a phony? Even if I've turned on you, lied to you? Compromised you? Even if I was GC after all? Let me tell you, Captain Steele, if that *were* true about me and I were *you,* I would shoot me without remorse." He stood offering the weapon. "But I will say this. If I *were* GC, this is where and when I would shoot you too. And I would kill every one of your comrades as they rushed from the underground. Then I would secure the place and let Squadron Commander Datillo burn the evidence to the ground. What will it be, Captain Steele? This is a limited offer. Hadn't you better check me to see if you signed the death warrants of all your friends? Or will you risk their lives to keep from insulting me further?"

Rayford would not reach for the gun, so Albie tossed it on the bed. Rayford wished he had taken it, not sure whether he could beat Albie to it now if he had to. Albie took a step closer, making Rayford flinch, but Albie merely stuck his forehead in Rayford's face.

"Touch it, rub it, wash it, put petrol on it. Do whatever you have to do to convince yourself. I already know who I am. If I'm phony, shoot me. If I'm real, assume I have turned command back over to you. Either way, you could not have offended me more."

"I don't mean to offend you, Albie. But I must—"

"Just get on with it! If you are to be the leader, take command!"

David scanned the far reaches of the crowd where carts zigzagged with bull-horns, advising the people that the GC re-gretted to inform them that "only those already inside the courtyard will be able to greet His Excellency personally. Thanks for understanding, and do feel free to remain for final remarks in an hour or so."

David searched and searched for Annie, finally telling the Wong family he had to go.

Mr. Wong, his face ravaged by tears and exhaustion, said, "No! You get us into receiving line."

"I'm sorry," David said. "They've closed the line."

"But we in courtyard! VIP seat! You make happen."

"No," David said, leaning close. "You're the VIP. You make it happen."

As the older man sputtered, David squeezed Mom's shoulder and embraced both Ming and Chang, whispering in their ears, "*Jesus* is risen."

Both responded under their breath, "He is risen indeed."

"Forgive me, Albie," Rayford said. "Please don't be insulted."

"You have already insulted me, my friend, so you might as well put your mind at ease."

"I'm trying to put *your* mind at ease, Albie."

"That will require more of an apology than you have the time or energy or, I may say, insight to give. Now check the mark, and let's get out of here."

Rayford reached for Albie, who seemed

to stiffen. A loud rap on the door made them both jump. Tsion poked his head in. "My apologies, gentlemen, but Carpathia has resurrected! You must come see!"

Rayford retrieved the gun.

"Keep it," Albie said, as they headed downstairs.

"But that would insult you even more."

"I told you, I cannot be more deeply insulted."

Rayford reached back awkwardly, holding the gun out to Albie.

Albie shook his head, grabbed the gun, and slammed it into its holster. As he snapped the strap he said, "The only thing more offensive than not being trusted by an old friend is your simpering style of leadership. Rayford, you and those you are responsible for are entering the most dangerous phase of your existence. Don't blow it with indecision and poor judgment."

Buck held the sleeping baby while Chloe finished packing. He heard Rayford and Albie descending and wondered why they were empty-handed after having been upstairs for so long. Maybe they had already carried stuff to the car.

"Did you see this, Dad?" he said, nodding toward the TV where GC CNN played and replayed the most dramatic moments from New Babylon.

"Better not refer to me informally in front of the rest of the Force," Rayford whispered, as he stared at the TV.

Buck cocked his head. "Whatever you say, Captain Steele."

He limped to where Chloe had gathered their essentials, traded the baby for a bundle, and slowly made his way out to the Land Rover. The coolness of the predawn refreshed him, though he caught himself sniffing the air and listening. The last thing he wanted, after the bizarre story of Albie's ruse, was to hear those GC Jeeps returning. What if the squadron leader was braver than Albie gave him credit for and he risked embarrassment and even reprimand to check out the story? He'd be back with more help, and they could all be imprisoned or killed and the place destroyed.

Buck worried about some of his injuries. He had pain in both legs that felt sharper than soft tissue damage, so he worried about broken bones. He was certain he'd also cracked a rib or two and couldn't imagine that Chaim hadn't as well. They shared whiplash trauma, even though their heads had first been driven forward.

Buck caught a glimpse of himself in the cracked outside rearview mirror of the Rover as he stepped away from the vehicle. Was it possible he was only thirty-three? He felt even worse than he looked, and he looked fifty. A fabric burn on his forehead he hadn't even noticed in the hospital had formed a large, ugly scab that was tender to the touch. That had to have come from the first impact and the forcing of his head into the back of the seat in front of him. Deep lacerations from dropping into a woody bush at the Jerusalem Airport what seemed eons ago had healed as high-ridged scars with crimson centers that covered his chin, cheeks, and forehead.

Worse, his eyes had that world-weary look, a deep fatigue that combined survival desperation, love and concern for his wife and child, and the sheer exhaustion of living as a fugitive and enduring searing personal losses. He took a deep breath that brought stinging pain to his ribs. He wondered where he might next sleep, but he didn't wonder if he would sleep well.

Buck would have returned inside to help, but in his condition he was more help staying put. The others began to straggle out under heavy bundles, except for Tsion who had just two full pillowcases tied together over one shoulder and was supporting Chaim on his other arm.

Albie, the last out, was on the phone. Rayford arranged the seating. He put Chloe, Kenny, Leah, Tsion, and Chaim in the backseat, where they were barely able to close the doors. Buck would ride shotgun in the front with Albie in the middle and Rayford driving. First, however, Rayford and Albie stood between the garage and the house—Albie still on the phone—and Rayford beckoned Buck with a nod.

"The chopper is at Palwaukee," Albie reported. "And the shuttle pilots are on their way back to Rantoul in the trail plane. You want my advice, Captain?"

"You bet."

"I say we go directly to the airstrip and put the wounded and as much of the luggage in the chopper as we can. Then you can fly the chopper to the new safe house, and someone else can drive."

"And you?"

"I should take the fighter to Kankakee. You can pick me up there later in the chopper, and I can fly the Gulfstream into Kankakee."

"How about torching this place?" Rayford said.

"You have materials?"

"Kerosene and gasoline in the garage. Some flares."

"That would do it. Have you left anything incriminating inside?"

"Not that I can think of. You, Buck?"

Buck shook his head. "I'd light 'er up."

"That's me too," Rayford said. "Just in case. Leave 'em nothing to find."

Albie looked at his watch. "I think we're pressing our luck. Let the GC waste time digging through it, and then *they* can cook it. We need to be gone from here as soon as we can."

"You're the expert," Rayford said. "You want a vote, Buck?"

"I'm with you, D—ah, Captain."

At Palwaukee Albie stayed in character and informed the in-residence tower man that the procurement of the chopper and the fuel for the fighter and Gulfstream should all be kept under the same GC order number. Greasy haired and short on sleep, the big man seemed as thrilled as he had been hours before to be doing his duty to the GC and particularly to the deputy commander.

"Did you see the news, sir?" the man said. "The wonderful, wonderful news?"

"Did I ever," Albie said. "Thanks for your kindness. Now we must be off."

"My pleasure, Deputy Commander, sir! A pleasure indeed. If you ever need anything else, don't hes—"

Buck was left to nod to the man. Albie was off to the freshly refueled jet, and Rayford to the chopper.

David searched and searched for Annie, unable to raise her on the phone and not willing to holler for her over the mid-afternoon crowds. Finally he rushed back to his office, flipped on the TV so he could catch Carpathia's final remarks, and got on his computer to be sure the new safe house was accessible.

He called Rayford, who filled him in on

everything since they had last spoken. "I *can* trust Albie, can't I, David?"

"Albie? He was your find, wasn't he? We've been working fairly closely lately. I think he's the best, and you and Mac always said he was. Anyway, he's one of us now, right?"

"Right."

"If you doubt him, check his mark."

"Apparently you don't insult Middle Eastern men that way."

"Hey! Captain! You're talking to one."

"Would someone checking your mark insult you?"

"Well, I suppose if you did, after knowing me so long. I mean, I don't think you ever have."

"If I can't trust you, David, who can I trust?"

"I'd say the same about Albie, but you're the one who needs to feel right about it. We're getting in pretty deep with him, looks like."

"I've decided to take the risk."

"That's good enough for me. Let me know when you get to the Strong Building. You going to try to put down inside the tower?"

"Not with this load. I'll keep the chopper as inconspicuous as I can so it won't be seen from the air."

"The most you'd have to worry about would be satellite shots, because no planes are flying low enough to shoot anything meaningful. But if you get unloaded and can determine before daybreak that the chopper can be housed way up inside there, you'd better do it."

"Roger."

"I'm unlocking everything in the place for you. I'd get in, get settled, and stay quiet and out of sight."

"We need some black spray paint."

"Can do. Where should I ship it?"

"Kankakee, I guess."

"You got it. Rayford? How is Tsion?"

"Chaim and Buck are the banged-up ones."

"But they're going to be all right, right?"

"Looks like it."

"Tsion is the one I worry about. We need him on-line and doing what he does best."

Rayford guessed he was halfway to the safe house. "I hear that, David. I just hope we can transmit out of the new place like we could out of the old."

"Should be able to. When the day comes for Mac and Smitty and Annie and me to get out of here, we'll come and set up the greatest communications center you can imagine. Hey, you've got your laptop, right?"

"I had left it in Mount Prospect. I'll get back on-line in Chicago."

"Good, because I sent you a list I found, made by a woman named Viv Ivins, Carpathia's oldest confidante. It shows the ten kingdoms with their new names, but it also has a number assigned to each one. There has to be some significance, but I can't decipher it, at least not yet."

"You haven't put one of your fancy computer programs on it by now?"

"Soon, but I don't care what it takes or who figures it out. I just want to know what it means and whether there's any advantage to our knowing it."

"We'll take a shot at it. For now it's going to be great to be back together, all in one place, getting caught up with each other, getting acquainted better with the newcomers, and reestablishing some order."

"I'll know when you get in. I've got my cameras on."

With his computer set, David wanted to return his attention to finding Annie. There were a thousand reasons she might be hard to locate, but he'd rather not consider any of them. He stood and stretched, noticing that the TV picture had changed. The network had switched from a wide shot of the receiving trilogy of Leon, Viv, and Nick and now moved in on Nicolae.

He had stepped down a few rows and looked directly into the camera. In spite of himself, David could see why the man was so riveting. Besides the rugged, European handsomeness, he really sold the care and compassion. David knew he was insidious, but his smarminess didn't show.

The announcer said, "Ladies and gentlemen of the Global Community, your Supreme Potentate, His Excellency Nicolae Carpathia."

Nicolae took one step closer to the camera, forcing it to refocus. He looked directly into the lens.

"My dear subjects," he began. "We have, together, endured quite a week, have we not? I was deeply touched by the millions who made the effort to come to New Babylon for what turned out to be, gratefully, not my funeral. The outpouring of emotion was no less encouraging to me.

"As you know and as I have said, there remain small pockets of resistance to our cause of peace and harmony. There are even those who have made a career of saying the most hurtful, blasphemous, and false statements about me, using terms for me that no person would ever want to be called.

"I believe you will agree that I proved today who I am and who I am not. You will do well to follow your heads and your hearts and continue to follow me. You know what you saw, and your eyes do not lie. I am also eager to welcome into the one-world fold any former devotees of the radical fringe who have become convinced that I am not the enemy. On the contrary, I may be the very object of the devotion of their own religion, and I pray they will not close their minds to that possibility.

"In closing let me speak directly to the

opposition. I have always, without rancor or acrimony, allowed divergent views.

There are those among you, however, who have referred overtly to me personally as the Antichrist and this period of history as the Tribulation. You may take the following as my personal pledge:

"If you insist on continuing with your subversive attacks on my character and on the world harmony I have worked so hard to engender, the word *tribulation* will not begin to describe what is in store for you. If the last three and a half years are your idea of tribulation, wait until you endure the Great Tribulation."

EPILOGUE

"Woe to the inhabitants of the earth and the sea! For the devil has come down to you, having great wrath, because he knows that he has a short time."
    Revelation 12:12

ABOUT THE AUTHORS

Jerry B. Jenkins (www.jerryjenkins.com) is the writer of the Left Behind series. He is author of more than one hundred books, of which six have reached the *New York Times* best-seller list. Former vice president for publishing for the Moody Bible Institute of Chicago, he also served many years as editor of *Moody* magazine and is now Moody's writer-at-large.

His writing has appeared in publications as varied as *Reader's Digest, Parade,* in-flight magazines, and many Christian periodicals. He has written books in four genres: biography, marriage and family, fiction for children, and fiction for adults.

Jenkins's biographies include books with Hank Aaron, Bill Gaither, Luis Palau, Walter Payton, Orel Hershiser, Nolan Ryan, Brett Butler, and Billy Graham, among many others.

Six of his apocalyptic novels—*Left Behind, Tribulation Force, Nicolae, Soul Harvest, Apollyon,* and *Assassins*—have appeared on the Christian Booksellers Association's best-selling fiction list and the *Publishers Weekly* religion best-seller list. *Left Behind* was nominated for Book of the Year by the Evangelical Christian Publishers Association in 1997, 1998, and 1999.

As a marriage and family author and speaker, Jenkins has been a frequent guest on Dr. James Dobson's *Focus on the Family* radio program.

Jerry is also the writer of the nationally syndicated sports story comic strip *Gil Thorp,* distributed to newspapers across the United States by Tribune Media Services.

Jerry and his wife, Dianna, live in Colorado.

Limited speaking engagement information is available through speaking@jerryjenkins.com.

Dr. Tim LaHaye (www.timlahaye.com), who conceived the idea of fictionalizing an account of the Rapture and the Tribulation, is a noted author, minister, and nationally recognized speaker on Bible prophecy. He is the founder of both Tim LaHaye Ministries and The Pre-Trib Research Center. Presently Dr. LaHaye speaks at many of the major Bible prophecy conferences in the U.S. and Canada, where his nine current prophecy books are very popular.

Dr. LaHaye holds a doctor of ministry degree from Western Theological Seminary and a doctor of literature degree from Liberty University. For twenty-five years he pastored one of the nation's outstanding churches in San Diego, which grew to three locations. It was during that time that he founded two accredited Christian high schools, a Christian school system of ten schools, and Christian Heritage College.

Dr. LaHaye has written over forty books, with over 22 million copies in print in thirty-three languages. He has written books on a wide variety of subjects, such as family life, temperaments, and Bible prophecy. His current fiction works, written with Jerry B. Jenkins—*Left Behind, Tribulation Force, Nicolae, Soul Harvest, Apollyon,* and *Assassins*—have all reached number one on the Christian best-seller charts. Other works by Dr. LaHaye are *Spirit-Controlled Temperament; How to Be Happy Though Married; Revelation Unveiled; Understanding the Last Days; Rapture under Attack; Are We Living in the End Times?* and the youth fiction series Left Behind: The Kids.

He is the father of four grown children and grandfather of nine. Snow skiing, waterskiing, motorcycling, golfing, vacationing with family, and jogging are among his leisure activities.